Sicilian Channel

By

James Marinero

Also by James Marinero

Fiction:

Gate of Tears

Non Fiction:

Susan's Brother

A *Wavecrest* Story

Published by Ezeebooks UK
Ezeebooks UK, 3 Murray Street, Llanelli
Carmarthenshire, SA15 1AQ, UK.
www.ezeebooks.co.uk

Sicilian Channel

First Edition 2016

Copyright © James Marinero, 2016

ISBN-13: 978-0-9568426-4-0

The moral right of the author has been asserted.

All rights reserved
Without limiting the rights under copyright reserved above, no part of this publication may be reproduced, stored in or introduced into a retrieval system, or transmitted, in any form or by any means including electronic, telepathic, mechanical, photocopying, scanning, recording or otherwise, without the prior written permission of both the copyright owner and the above publisher of this book.

With the exception of certain historical figures, events, scientific papers and news items for which references have been provided, all persons, organisations and events in this novel are fictitious, and any resemblance to actual persons, organisations or events is purely coincidental.

Printed on paper which accords with
UK: Forest Stewardship Council™ (FSC®) Mixed Credit.
FSC® C084699

Contents

No Peace for the Wicked ....
Nicos Loukatos 1
Cornered in Crete 2
Maudlin Maruška 3
Deb Deb 4
Regrouping 4
Passage to Piraeus 5
The Sicilians 5
Maruška Moves On 6
Death on High 7
Another Family Grieves 7
Planning Problems 8
Piraeus Preparations 8
Fiskardo 9
Buried with Byron 10
Holed up in Cephalonia 11
Changes Aboard 12
Maruška Aims for Malta 14
Tantalum 14
Nicos in Nidri 15
The Queen Katherine 15
Escape to the Maghreb 17
Maruška in Malta 17
Well Off Course 18
Finding Maruška 21
Sitrep 22
Cape Bon Onwards 23
Tobin in Tape 24
Breakfast with Bryan 24
The Search for Maruška 24
Key Problems 25
Evening Heat 26
Change in China 27

Taking Tobin 280
At the Villa 290
London 306
Epilogue 310
References & Further Reading 317
Author's Notes 319

James Marinero

ACRONYMS

ANDREW	Slang term for the British Royal Navy
DRS	Département du Renseignement et de la Sécurité or Department of Intelligence and Security – the Algerian Secret Police
DIA	US Defence Intelligence Agency. It is not a part of the Department of Homeland Security
ELINT	Intelligence information gathered using electronic sources
GIA	The Armed Islamic Group (GIA, from French: Groupe Islamique Armé) – one of the Algerian Islamist Groups which fought the Algerian Government in the Algerian Civil War
HMG	Her/His Majesty's Government (UK)
HUMINT	Intelligence information gathered from human sources
IOT	Internet of Things – the connection of our cars, domestic devices and other equipment to the internet
MIA	The Armed Islamic Movement – one of the Algerian Islamist Groups which fought the Algerian Government in the Algerian Civil War
TOR	The Onion Ring (a network of web servers for anonymising internet users and locations)

Prologue

The blade slipped in easily as she knew it would. A serrated ceramic edge with a keen point backed by several kilos of pressure at the perfect spot broke through the initial resistance of thin cloth and skin. It sliced effortlessly through muscle and fat – too much for a man of his apparent fitness. It met the muscle of the heart on the left hand side towards the rear and penetrated cleanly.

She felt the warm blood – more in her imagination than reality as she was wearing gloves. Her imagination was vivid but there was no doubting that this furiously struggling body was oozing its life force over her.

Later, she would replay the sequence in her mind as she derived more physical pleasure. She would find no technical error in the execution, no tactical mis-step.

The approach from the rear was standard. He was wearing a protective vest – it would be the best of vests for sure, made from the latest aramid fibre with metal foam inserts. It would be stab proof, bullet proof - .50 calibre excepted, or .44 magnum at close range when the percussive shock would be enough to kill. It was proof even against grenades and shrapnel. There was a collar to protect the critical areas around the neck, and other refinements. Still, it had to be wearable by a man with arms, legs and a head.

The hand over the mouth was standard. The MPG machine pistol was on a sling over his shoulder, and when she clamped her hand over his mouth, the MPG swung free as a he instinctively raised both hands to free his airway. His penis continued its stream, more hurried, missing the urinal, and spraying the wall. He had wriggled, tried the reverse head butt and foot stomp, the forward bend and flip. She'd met them before, expected them and countered them.

With her left hand she had located the tip of her blade in his left armpit, where the vest could not protect him, and pushed against its 'T' handle. The length of a bayonet – 8" give or take – but narrower, it was enough to do the job. Though it measured up in most respects, this was no bayonet. It would never be mated with a rifle or other long weapon, never feel the supersonic crack of a projectile passing over it.

She moved the handle gently back and forth as she pushed, lest the precision of her aim be imperfect, almost feeling the individual muscle fibres part. Delicate, tactile, even surgical but undoubtedly fatal and certainly sexual. Penetration.

He struggled furiously, tried to push her back against the wall, but she let his weight have its way and twisted her body at the last moment, and he swung against the wall. The grunt he made was a mixture of sounds, more a gurgling expulsion of an emulsion of blood and air as the hilt of the killing weapon was pushed deeper. Struggle was of no avail, the damage had been done. Three or four seconds, no more – and as he sighed his last sigh and his body relaxed and crumpled, she felt a warm glow suffuse her, started in her loins. Such personal killings usually had this effect on her.

She withdrew the knife, having to twist his left arm to free her hand and the weapon. Another death, another notch on her bedpost. This one was business, not pleasure in the purest sense but on these occasions there was an overlap. There was pleasure to be derived from a job well done, brief though it was.

That this way of killing could be said to be her unique 'MO' was not possible. Those who matched patterns and studied MOs in the nether world of assassination and terrorism knew that at least two people used this method, because one was left handed and one right handed. Or so the computers told them, and that suggested two individuals at most. Or maybe just one very clever operator. There were no training courses teaching this method. It was unique.

One agency, operating out of Fort Bragg, did take note, and eventually added the technique to its own training courses.

*

Sicilian Channel

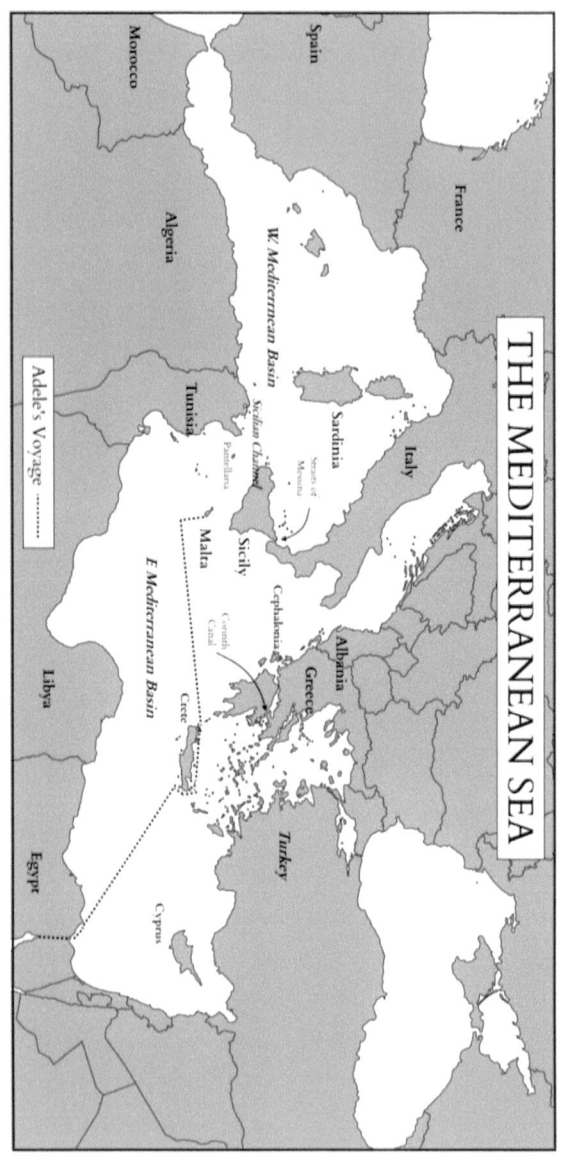

No Peace for the Wicked

Maruška received the text forwarded from her iPad. She ignored it, but knew that eventually she would be forced to answer. Then the next arrived, and then the next again, over a space of a few days. Finally, a couple of weeks after the first text, following the regular sharp pains near her spine – in fact, close to her C6 vertebra - she took the Metro to the Simplon stop. Since her return from the Middle East several months previously she hadn't been to the Rue Simplon apartment. Her eventual escape from Djibouti via Ethiopia couldn't have been achieved without the help of her controller, Wan Chuntao, via the Chinese Embassy in Djibouti. The escape from the police there had been easy enough – they just didn't appreciate that a woman could better them hand-to-hand and with weapons. It was a cultural and misogynistic problem for them that led to laxity on their part and opportunity for her.

Over just the few months she had been away from Paris, the Simplon area had become rougher, with more junkies and prostitutes in evidence – it was almost as if the area had lost faith in itself and was losing its self-esteem. You could always tell the quality of an area by the cars parked in the streets, and Rue Simplon was beginning to look like a scrapyard, albeit enhanced with some stylish graffiti (well, it was Paris, after all). Her 'safe' apartment hadn't been broken into, fortunately, though there was little worth stealing (at least anything that could be found without a thoroughly professional search). She did think, though, that maybe now was the time to relocate her Paris safe house – she knew for certain that Wan Chuntao knew its location, Michael Mannesmann certainly did, and the French were surely hunting her. Mannesmann was unfinished business which she would have to attend to soon. She smiled to herself, thinking of that pleasure to come.

Under the floorboard, her latest Chinese smartphone, passports, euro and dollar reserves, pistol and ready-to-run bag were dusty, but just as she had left them. As a matter of habit, she checked the gun, then took out the phone and called Chuntao.

"Chuntao, you called?"

"At last. I hope you are recovered. I have details of your next assignment for you. But first, how are you after your reconstruction?"

Two weeks and forty thousand dollars lighter, her left ear was now looking almost perfect after another reconstruction in Geneva, though reconstruction wasn't perhaps quite the right word. It had been replaced. Or at least, the new ear replaced a gap.

The Vacanti ear as it was known, was a simple ear-shaped cartilage structure with her cultured skin cells covering it. It looked good, and with her changed hairstyle she had felt comfortable with it. But it had failed to take properly, and the new ear was much better. It had been 3D printed using the ITOP system, placing her own cultured cells on a bio-degradable gel 'scaffolding. It was a mirror image of her right ear, based on a cast.

Baldwin's near-miss shot in Golfe Bleu, Djibouti, had hit a window frame and the splinters had shredded her ear. There was still a score to settle with Baldwin for that, a big score. Not only had she lost her ear, he had captured her – that was the first time she had been in custody. Now her DNA was on file, together with her retina scan and heartbeat profile. That was a big setback, but not an impossibility to fix – with the right connections retina scans and heartbeat profiles could be altered.

"I am fine, but I'm not taking another assignment. I am retiring."

"There is no urgency for the assignment, within reason, but I don't think that retiring is a good idea. You have been a very great help to the Chinese people, and you know we Chinese are good at waiting. Are you feeling any pain?"

"Pain? No, I'm fine."

"How is your back, between your shoulder blades?"

"My back is fine, no problems" she lied. "Why are you asking?"

Just a reminder, Maruška thought. I don't need them.

"I thought you might have been feeling some pain there."

Maruška felt a searing stab of pain between her shoulder blades and as her legs weakened and trembled, she leaned against the wall and closed her eyes whilst the pain cleared. Some pain she enjoyed as part of her private life, but this was not the sort of pain she enjoyed, and it was not private.

"Just remember Maruška, we are not far away, ever. I will call again soon to talk about the new assignment. Au revoir."

Wan Chuntao knew that that the pain was caused by a nanochip which had been implanted near Maruška's spine. A Chinese surgeon had inserted it during a training visit by Maruška to an island in southwest China, near Hong Kong, several years previously. The trigger to the pain from the implant was on Chuntao's Agent Management screen on her tablet computer, eight thousand miles away in Beijing. Wan Chuntao played Pavlov, and Maruška Pavkovic was the French poodle.

*

"Incoming, Go Go Go" he shouted and Saunders reacted.

The truck lurched over a bump and the first bullet passed through the windscreen and smashed into Saunders's left forearm. Saunders floored the accelerator just as Pavkovic fired smoothly and carefully again. The second bullet caught the front left pillar of the windscreen as he was punching out the windscreen glass and drawing his pistol, trying to keep the 4x4 on the track. The third shot came through the side window and into the headrest next to Saunders's ear. Pavkovic was leaning out of the window and firing again, but the truck was lurching and her shot hit the doorpost. He got a shot off through the open windscreen as another shot came through the rear side window and the next hit the rear tire. His next shot caught the window frame next to her head and he saw her head snap back as the truck got past the end wall of the hotel and neither had a line of fire.

"Stop stop stop" Steve shouted at Saunders, whose right arm was still spraying blood over the centre console. "There – my truck is there – let's go. I'm driving." He grabbed the bags and ran across to his truck, followed by Saunders, who was limping, with blood spurting over his trouser from his wound. He scrabbled for his keys and within seconds they accelerated away from the rear of the kitchen. They hit the security barrier at fifty miles an hour and woke up the gateman with a start.

Saunders was putting pressure on his wound as Steve accelerated on to the main road, heading for Tadjoura, less than two miles away. Glancing across, he could see that Saunders was looking pale – he'd probably lost a pint of blood already. Pulling off the road, he tore the arm off Saunders's shirt, tied a tourniquet above the elbow, and got going again, all within less than two minutes. As he pulled back onto the road, a police 4x4, lights flashing, passed them, undoubtedly heading for the Hotel du Golfe Bleu. The last rays of the sun were fading away into the brief tropical twilight as they approached Tadjoura dock.

"We've got a choice, Da'ud, we either drive round to Camp Lemonier in this, or nick a boat. If we could find a RIB then we'd do it in fifteen minutes –*if* we could find a RIB, and then start it. It's nearly dark, and I'd feel safer at sea, but we'd have a problem at the other end – we can't take a taxi with you like that. Marie – Pavkovic – will probably know what we're driving, though she may be out of action – I think my shot caught her. We're going to drive, OK?

"That seems to be the best option" grunted Saunders "but we'll need to adjust this, on my arm, the..the… tourniquet." Steve could see him grimacing as he spoke – the adrenaline was wearing off and shock was setting in.

Steve woke with a start, lying in a pool of sweat on the vinyl berth-cushion. He rolled off the berth and at the galley splashed cold water over his head and face. Adèle's motion was regular and comfortable as she sailed northwest with the easterly breeze on the starboard quarter. He checked the clock and groaned - just ninety minutes sleep, of the lowest quality.

The dreams had disturbed his voyage on Adèle all the way up the Red Sea and through the Suez Canal. Now in the Mediterranean *en route* for Crete, the dreams were at last becoming less frequent, but no less vivid. It was fortunate that the life of a solo sailor could accommodate the broken sleep pattern.

Straightforward action had never been a problem – he'd seen enough of that and learned to live with the dreams and the sweaty awakenings. He knew that they would eventually fade away. This dream was not the worst, but he raged against the fact that Maruška Pavkovic could invade his most private times.

The worst dream was about Tom Brown. He'd barely known him, but despite a stupid cover name – if that's what it was - respect had developed quickly. Brown had disappeared in Djibouti, and it was Steve's sleeping mind's ability to dream up a wide range of death scenes that was most disturbing. He didn't even know for sure that Brown was dead. Steve shivered in the Mediterranean late morning heat as he boiled water for coffee and prepared to note the midday position in the ship's log.

"If only Dad could see me now". He said it aloud – there was no one to hear him and he often talked aloud, using Adèle, the boat herself, as a sounding board. Strangely, she always seemed to have answers.

"I know, he'd laugh."

He thought again of his father, who had been a fisherman. Steve had been born and brought up as an only child in Portsmouth where the family home had been a council flat near Fratton, a mile or so from the docks. Social housing they called it, but Steve's socialization had been tough.

His father made a living at fishing, just, but when the catch was poor then he would come home after a skinful at The Bridge – a pub on East Street hard by the Camber - and give Steve's mother a beating. When the catch was good Mike, his father, would celebrate with a skinful, then come home and give his mother a beating. Steve started fighting at school on a regular basis (and out of school too for that matter) and this was coming to the attention of the educational psychologists.

By the time he was thirteen, Steve had started stepping in-between his parents during their nightly battles and getting a hiding for his trouble, but as he matured and grew he started giving almost as good as he got, and his father became more wary. Nevertheless his parents had split up by the time he was sixteen. Steve still saw his father occasionally – his father had taught him beach fishing at six years of age, and by the time he was ten years old he was helping out regularly on the trawler at weekends. By that time his relationships with his father was pretty good, as he knew that his mother was safe; his father had shacked up with another woman down in Southsea, but Steve knew nothing else about that side of his father's life.

He was far from a star pupil in school at the Priory Comprehensive, but he'd stabilised since his parents had split up, and was able enough, though not academic. The fighting was in the past – he'd won his reputation. He still missed a day from school occasionally and took his gear down to the beach at Southsea to do some fishing. He watched the ships – tankers, warships, cruise liners and more – entering and leaving the Solent, and his horizons widened as he matured.

Then he'd started thinking about joining the forces. Pompei – Portsmouth – was a naval city and had been since even before Henry VIII. The Royal Navy appealed, but after a discussion at the recruiting office in the city he wondered if there would be enough action. Yes there was travel, yes there was the sea, but he was unsure. He'd talked to his father about it, but his father was keen for him to go into partnership with him on the trawler. Then one evening over a beer in The Bridge, after a good day with the nets, his father suggested he think about the Royal Marines.

"Steve, get it out of your system", he said, "do a few years, sow your wild oats, and come back to the trawler. We'll buy a new boat when you return and you can take over."

He had been non-committal, but by the end of the week Steve had taken the first step and committed to the entrance assessment. A visit to the Royal Marines museum across the road from the beach at Southsea had cemented his resolve. Physical sports had never really been his thing, and he had to work himself hard to get up to the fitness levels required to pass his entrance and aptitude testing. Running on the shingle beach in Southsea for an hour twice day worked his stamina up, and he joined a Portsmouth boxing club to gain access to the gym and a trainer, though the weekend work on the trawler had built him a half decent upper body.

He passed his entrance with flying colours, and then worked his way through the batch of tests and trials and completed the 32 week training course as an outstanding candidate. He passed all the timed physical tests at better than the standard required of an officer candidate, which itself was significantly higher than that of a trooper.

Sicilian Channel

A year later, when he returned from a winter survival exercise in Norway, Steve heard that his father had been lost. Then, within a year, his mother was dead.

*

Nicos Loukatos

Nicos had been born up in Nidri, on Levkas, in 1965. What remained of his family had moved there from Cephalonia after the Second World War.

The war had decimated the males of the family, and Nicos's father, Andrei, was the only male in the immediate family to survive. He had hidden in a cave for six months, high in the mountains behind the town. Andrei climbed up the goatherd's trail into the mountains in the autumn of 1944 with ten toes and ten fingers. When he next came down the trail there were only seven toes after losing three toes to frostbite in the bitter winter snows. He had amputated the toes himself. Two brothers and his father were taken by the German Alpine Brigade and executed.

The anniversary of the Cephalonia massacre of the Italian Acqui Brigade and many islanders is still remembered in May each year, with a formal ceremony in many towns across the Ionian Islands.

The islanders were proud of their traditions and proud of their resistance to the Third Reich.

They were also proud of their island status and shunned a permanent bridge to the mainland, because that would mean that politically they were no longer an island. Loss of island status would also mean a loss of regional grant aid. So, the swing bridge across the 'Levkas Canal' continued to swing whenever a yacht or fishing boat required passage, and does so to this day.

Nidri lies some seven miles south of Levkada town at the entrance to the captivating and almost completely enclosed bay of Ormos Vlikho, across the narrow channel from Tranquil Bay on the island of Levkas. It is focused these days on tourism and yacht charter, but still has its dramas with microbursts of extreme wind into the cauldron of the bay in hot summers. These short storms kill yachtsmen and locals alike, in minutes.

Nidri is also the town which supplied many of the farm and estate workers to Aristotle Onassis's private island of Skorpios, ferried out daily less than two miles to the south east. 'Nick the Greek's' Taverna was the watering hole of many of the Onassis visitors and there were legendary tales of excess to be heard there.

After the war, Andrei Loukatos found work repairing fishing boats, and then bought a fishing boat of his own. He married an island girl, Ariana, and Nicos was born a year later. There would be another brother, and a sister, too, over the next few years.

Fishing was both a pastime and a cover. Smuggling was the game – brandy and cigarettes - but when Nico was in his late teens Greece joined the European Union and the taxes on human vices levelled out and cargoes changed. The war in Boznia-Herzogovina opened up the weapons smuggling business. Andrei specialised in the Libyan connection, when Gaddafi was keen to incite any problems he could for the West which was desperately trying to find a solution to another of the age-old religious wars that regularly beset the Mediterranean lands.

Nicos was just reaching twenty years of age when that war in Bosnia-Herzegovina started. He'd been steeped in the smuggling tradition by his father, and together they bought a larger, faster trawler with more capacity and the ability to work in rougher seas. Albania was just up the coast – thirty or forty miles - and people smuggling became more profitable than tobacco and alcohol, though generally, Albanians were dirt poor and so transport rates were low. Serbians too were on the move, though that was more dangerous as they had to run their trawler further up the Adriatic Sea. Rates for trafficking Serbs were much better.

Guns on the way up the coast, and people on the way back. Fish too, occasionally, to keep up appearances.

One day, as he left Nidri on another trip, Nicos reflected on his years of smuggling - as always glancing up at the cemetery on the hillside overlooking the town where his father and mother were buried. They had been killed late one night two years earlier in a car accident. Returning from a wedding party a few miles up the coast at Kariotes, their car had hit a goat and gone over the cliff into the sea. He crossed himself and shook his head.

Smuggling was a dirty business, but a man had to make a living, feed his family and do the best he could for them. It was in his blood. Moral ambiguities were all around him.

In Libya, Muammar Gaddafi would do whatever he could to dig a hole under western society. He'd blown the Boeing 747 'Maid of the Skies' out of the sky over Lockerbie in Scotland with a bomb placed in her hold in Malta. He had armed the IRA, sent weapons into Bosnia. Yet, when he was physically beaten before his death, he accused his attackers of non-Islamic behaviour.

With his reacceptance into world political circles, and the infamous 'hug' by the British Prime Minister, Tony Blair, in 2008, Gaddafi had become much more discreet in his subversion. More insidious methods were necessary.

Drugs became the new cargo for the Loukatos family business. Landed on the Greek coastline, the cargo was trucked with olives and walnuts through Macedonia and into Serbia, where a Serbian gang took it for onward distribution throughout Europe. Nico had met and got to know Srecko Vidovic. That very unpleasant individual ran an outfit called the SNP which translated from Serbian as 'Seven Legged Spider'. They were a nasty bunch – the worst in fact - but business was business and they had always paid well. Vidovic had been transforming his group of paramilitaries into a more traditional model of organised crime in readiness for the anticipated end of this particular

Balkan war. Modern business was all about continuous change – whichever side of the law it was.

Then, Andjela Karanovic had taken over the SNP after Nicos had smuggled Vidovic down the Adriatic and into Malta. That had been a risky trip. Vidovic had been on the run from the UN and numerous international law enforcement agencies. The last he'd seen of Vidovic was on the TV. It seems he'd been captured in South America and was being tried in The Hague for war crimes.

Andjela had disappeared a couple of years later. The word was that she had been murdered near Beograd. Nicos wouldn't lose any sleep over that one, she was evil and the thought of her made him shiver and shake his head. Vidovic had been a saint compared to her.

Business with the SNP continued, though it was not quite so well organised after both Vidovic and Andjela had gone. There had been a problem with one payment during the early days after the woman's disappearance, but that had been sorted after some heated words. The Loukatos family was known to be honourable and reliable in its dealings – even criminal ones - and that counted for a lot in the smuggling business.

Then came the Tunisian revolution, followed by the Libyan civil war and a wavetrain of unrest and revolution across the Middle East. In the early days of the Libyan war, the drugs shipments had stopped, but change was opportunity and business boomed for Nicos, carrying human cargo from North Africa and into the European Union. Genuine refugees came across on chartered ferries into Malta, or on fishing boats to the Italian islands. But after the war, the European borders were closed tightly again – at least that was the intention. The Italian islands of Lampedusa and Pantellaria were carefully patrolled by the Italian Navy and those of Malta by the Malta Defence Force, and there were regular interceptions. Many got through but there were many deaths too. Thousands of emigrants had attempted the passage and died.

The Greek coastline remained relatively porous to human cargoes, and Nicos knew the south and west coasts like the back of his hand. The big movement of people from Syria through Turkey and across to Lesbos was out of Nicos's area. In Greece, the police state mentality that the colonels had established during Junta between 1967 and 1974 still persisted. Nicos though, was not concerned about the papers that the illegals carried – once he landed them they were on their own. They were given dire warnings about what would happen should they disclose any details of their trip from Africa.

These refugees had money and they were not interested in getting stuck in a Greek transit camp for administrative processing. They had initiative and a will to succeed.

He knew maybe thirty or forty places between Kalamata in the south and Igoumenitsa near the Albanian border, where he could land his human cargo discreetly. He avoided the Ionian Islands because the only way his passengers could move on would be by ferry or plane, and that would raise too many questions, some of which would inevitably lead back to him and cost money to fix.

Picking up the cargo was difficult too. He couldn't run into Libya or Tunisia – he left that to his contacts on the other side, and the transfer of cargo was usually made off Libya in the Gulf of Sirte. This at least was much the same as he and his father had done for many years whatever cargoes they had handled. He didn't make the run regularly, just a couple of times a month, when the weather was right. His price was now $10,000 US per head – age unimportant, no discounts for children. Eight to a maximum of twelve passengers at a time. The money was good. Sixty percent for him, with the rest split between Andrei junior (his brother) and Georgiou, his crew.

Nicos's retirement villa near Nidri, on Levkas was taking shape nicely, and another year would see it finished.

Unfortunately, brother Andrei was not the brightest, having had the umbilical cord round his neck at birth, so retiring early and passing the business on to Andrei was not an option. His sister had done well in school and landed a job in a bank. She was now working in New York, and had married into the Greek community there. She wouldn't want to run a smuggling business.

So, he'd keep on working once his villa was finished, then when he saved enough to pay for the weddings of his daughters, and married them off, he would retire. Perhaps his sons in law would turn out to be enterprising individuals – but there were few of those left in Nidri. The marriage prospects for his daughters were not wonderful, despite their better than average looks. That would be a good few years away yet, and he didn't relish the interval.

The risks were increasing all the time, patrols were heavier, and he would have to start taking the fishing more seriously, and that was something he didn't really want to do. He'd already given up the drugs – that had petered out a few years after Andjela's disappearance. He guessed that the Serbs were now bringing them in by truck through Northern Iraq, Turkey and Bulgaria. He was glad to be out of it.

Though he was not a racialist, he refused to take people who were very dark skinned with facial features not of Arabs, but typical of the Tuaregs of the Central African republics. They stood out like sore thumbs in rural Greece and led to too many questions. He had turned away several, refusing to take them aboard late at night when transfers were made, often in rough seas and little moonlight. Gaddafi had used a lot of Tuareg mercenaries and when Libya was in turmoil many of these unemployed soldiers tried to get into Europe rather than return to impoverished homelands. Nicos's Libyan business partner had finally learned not to include such people in the cargo.

He had got through the bad business in 2014/15 when volume shipments of human misery had been put on autopilot for Italy and Greece. Sticking to his business model of low volume, high quality hand-delivered refugees, he had been able to ride out the EU's panic reaction to the mass drownings in the Libya-Malta sea area.

For appearances sake, he still went out fishing regularly though he didn't take it seriously. His catches cleared enough money to run the boat and keep the tax officials at bay. He hadn't been stopped at sea yet, but took no chances. Who would be keen to climb into a hold of smelling fish to search for contraband? It was a thin disguise though – fish had to be sorted and iced quickly in the warm climate – and he couldn't bury his human cargoes under tons of fish and ice.

*

Cornered in Crete

Steve sat in the taverna 'O Passos' on the harbour side at Siteia, in eastern Crete, with a bottle of local Rethymnian Blonde beer. He could see his yacht, Adèle, from the table, moored stern-to along the south mole of the harbour – he'd been lucky to find a space even though it was early in the season. Built of steel, designed by the Frenchman André Mauric in the 1970s, she had been his home for over ten years, and was due a serious refit, which he had aimed to do at Malta or Gibraltar. 36 feet long, with a displacement of 12 tons, she was his pride and joy.

Through thick and thin, across the Atlantic (twice), the Pacific, the East Indies and the Indian Ocean, Adèle had been his steady companion when all the other women in his life had cut and run. And it hadn't been just the sea they'd had to contend with – she had saved his life on more than one occasion. There had been brushes with Al Qaeda in the Malacca Strait and piracy off the Horn of Africa. Steady and uncomplaining like the best of women, and cheaper to keep – though only just. She had her blemishes too – just like any woman, hidden well with makeup, or invisible to the casual acquaintance and known only to her lovers.

His fisherman father had equipped him well for the life he now lived – home life hadn't been easy in Portsmouth but his father had taught him all the essential skills of maintaining a boat, even down to overhauling the engine and welding a hull. Sailmaking was a skill he'd had to teach himself from book and other sailors – his father fell short there and in other more personal areas.

"If your engine stops when you're off St Catherine's, with a spring ebb and a sou'wester blowing hard against it all the way from the Azores, then you need to be able to sort it yourself. The lifeboat may have another shout – maybe a weekend yachtsman with a young family." He could hear his father's words then. "When the chips are down, you've only got yourself."

Independence was deeply ingrained. He preferred to do all the maintenance himself, but fewer and fewer boatyards were these days prepared to let owners do their own work, and he half expected to have to go down to one of the Moroccan harbours to find a suitable and agreeably cheap boatyard. That, though, was some weeks away yet in the plan, and in the meantime his cash reserves were dwindling and he would have to find temporary work.

His independence and ability to work and survive alone had led him along a career path through the Royal Marines and beyond into even more dangerous company and assignments. He'd found a family there, every man (and the occasional woman) interdependent but individually tough.

In the past year a suicidal mission into a Chinese naval base in the Yemen, followed by an underwater demolition job which had lined him up for the chop as a mercenary for the Chinese left him with a bitter taste in his mouth and an even stronger distrust of authority and governments. The promised generous payment for that 'work' in Aden and the Red Sea had not come through, and in reality he didn't expect to see it. He'd been told that his missions had not been 'properly authorised' and could not be paid for, and he'd lost all contact with whoever it was had assigned him. One dead for sure, one wounded not to be seen again, and a US pal who apparently didn't exist. Bastards.

He swore audibly as he held his coffee, causing a stir with a couple of tourists on the next table as his mind bitterly wandered back to Djibouti and all the shit with that Maruška woman.

"Sorry, mosquito bites", he said as he rubbed his arm, and tried to smile at them. They were German anyway he guessed, and didn't understand – at least not all of it, but some words are universal.

After that job in Aden, his planned trip up the Red Sea had been long and boring, taking almost four weeks to cover the thirteen hundred or so miles from Djibouti through to Alexandria and the Mediterranean. He had been glad to get away, finally, after recovering from the mission set up by a British traitor.

Although he loved the Yemen and Djibouti, he had seen enough of the Gate of Tears to last him a lifetime. The name had certainly been propitious. After the Red Sea and the changeable weather of spring, the Suez Canal had been, as usual, a black hole for cash in the form of *baksheesh*. After two days rapid replenishment in Alexandria, he had set off north-westwards on the three hundred mile leg to Crete.

The plan had been to catch the last of the winter southerlies, and sail straight through to Malta, where he would clear Adèle into the EU. His dismal cash situation had put his plan into flux, and the delays in his schedule due to the fracas in Djibouti and the poor sailing conditions in the Red Sea had compounded and meant that he would have to delay the maintenance haul out of Adèle by six months.

Calling in Crete or Greece hadn't been in his plan – he'd never visited the country. All he'd heard about it, and the riots following the financial bailouts of the EU and the refugee crisis, gave him no appetite for a visit. However, his later than planned departure from Alexandria had meant that the last of the winter/spring southerly winds had almost expired, and although it was too early then – thank goodness – for the full Meltemi winds, he had a day of light and variable wind and three days of moderate north-westerlies, which really didn't suit. In fact, they sucked.

The planned destination of Malta had at first been trimmed back to the entry port of Kali Limenes in southern Crete, where he could clear in to the EU. Then, as he approached the Cretan south coast late one afternoon, the northwest winds had strengthened and the dangerously violent gusts from the mountains, which the pilot books warned about, became all too frequent and unmanageable. He hadn't had a Greek Waters Pilot book with him, and had been working from the US NOAA pilotage file which he had on his tablet PC, written more for big ships than for yachtsmen. Its general navigational information was very useful, and had made him cautious about the south coast of Crete. The bald words had intrigued him and he became curious about Crete itself – an insular island and a tough, independent people.

His approach to the forbidding island had been difficult. The violent gusts had intensified as he approached and made Kali Limenes an unrealistic prospect that day. So, he and Adèle turned tail and broad-reached east-about the end of Crete overnight, past the ancient city port of Irepetra (which was dangerous to enter at night) and after a stressful and sleepless night's sailing, he had moored stern-to as dawn broke in Siteia.

After a few hours of sleep his breakfast was interrupted by a policeman. He gathered his ships papers and started the bureaucratic clearing-in procedure in the Taverna with a beer. The procedure was complicated in Greece where, according to what he'd just read online in a cruisers' forum, the regulations were often subject to local interpretation. He hated officialdom with a vengeance but there was little he could do about it and he'd learned that it was best to take a good book along when visiting the various offices, and to be patient.

He had to report to several authorities in a specific order - immigration, health, customs and the port police. Then, using a reference number provided by the police, he had to pay a small tax at the tax office and obtain an invoice. The invoice enabled the port police to provide him with a DEKPA – a transit log, to be stamped (theoretically) at every port he visited. As it was Adèle's first visit to Greece, she was subject to another, albeit small, entry tax.

After digesting this cumbersome routine, he decided to have another beer, and then it was lunchtime before he got to the immigration office. It was closed. Later that afternoon, after his siesta during the quiet time, or *mesimeri* as he didn't know the Greeks called it, the customs clearance went surprisingly smoothly and by early evening he also had health clearance and he was able to haul down Adèle's yellow quarantine flag. He then went in search of an ATM and a good taverna. It was downhill from there.

*

After the blow-out in the taverna and his first experience of Greek (specifically Cretan) food which he had thoroughly enjoyed, he woke up the next morning with a sore head and only vague memories of the previous evening. This was a typically sailorly scenario for a seaman after a hard passage – indeed a passage of any kind. He still had his wallet with cash inside, and as far as he could remember he hadn't picked up a girl. There were no bruises on his face, so he must have avoided any punch-ups. His buttocks though were aching. What was that about?

Fuel was on his mind. Fuel for him, fuel for Adèle. He walked into the first tavern he reached, 'O Passos' and ordered strong coffee. The bartender laughed and chattered to the waitress – Steve was clearly the subject. There was obviously a story from the night before which Steve could not remember, but he heard the word 'Zorba' mentioned several times. He planned to pick up diesel fuel in cans and got directions to the fuel station. This was his exercise for the day, carrying a hundred litres of diesel in twenty litre cans a quarter of a mile around the dock from the fuel berth. He could have moved Adèle to the fuel berth, but it was his practice to do things the physically challenging way and thereby keep himself fit, or at least as fit as was practicable when he was in harbour. The next day he would resume his shoreside running regime.

After refuelling the main tank and topping up the cans to carry a hundred litres lashed on deck, he took his notepad to the Taverna and checked his email. There was no blood family to catch up on - the Royal Marines had been his only family for many years, and most of his closest mates were dead or struggling with civilian life and alcohol.

There was one obscure email from Rick – Richard Borthwick – or Dickwick as he was inevitably known.

He read the email twice:

"Baldy,
Heard that you were heading from Egypt into the Med. Short notice I know, but there's some work come up for my outfit – only two or three weeks, but the pay is $1k/day, Eastern Med, all exes paid. Baby-sitting a superyacht owner. I'm putting a crew together. Let me know ASAP, latest by the end of May. The job starts mid-June in Piraeus.
Rick
Scutum Est
Security – the Best
www.scutumest.com"

Steve stopped a moment to wonder what the date was. He'd filled in the immigration and customs forms, filled in the ship's log, but that was one good hangover away. Then he saw it on the wallscreen where the Greek news was running. 27th May. Where the hell was Piraeus? What was *Scutum Est*? He read it again. No, it really was *scutum est*, not scumtest.

He looked up the website – it was a simple site, just a placeholder:

Scutum Est
Personal Security – Discreet, comprehensive, worldwide.
Email us at enquiries@scutumest.com with a contact number, and we will call you.

So, either Dickwick was broke, or he was so successful that he didn't need to do any marketing. The website certainly didn't seem bothered whether you wanted to use them or not.

Googletranslate told Steve that *Scutum Est* was Latin, and meant "Is a shield" – or at least as far as he could make out that's what it meant.

Clever, but that was Rick – the hidden side. Rick was a bluff Yorkshireman, hard as nails, fists like hammers, and a face like a brick that had been broken into pieces and re-assembled badly. Just on six feet tall, and wiry. He had been raised in the Dales, carrying sheep in thigh high snow when only a teenager with God knows what muscle – he didn't seem to have any in his whipcord build. But what a man to have next to you in bar when the locals turned nasty and even the MPs thought twice about getting involved. And in worse places too.

Steve knew that Rick had been to Oxford or some fancy college, on his merit, not his father's farming money (or at least, those were the rumours). Straight into a commission in the RM. No wimps made officer in the Royal Marines – the officers' physical entry standards were set higher than those of the troopers. Steve knew that – and he had himself exceeded the officer standards in his induction.

Steve's father had been a fisherman – fishing and farming. Living off what nature provided, he and Dick shared a bond. Not a million miles apart, but Steve' father was dead, drowned off the Nab Tower when his trawler, the Jenny 'C' went down one wild night. No college for Steve. Mother dead from cancer shortly after. He pulled himself back to reality.

So, what could he work out from the mail? Personal security, a team of six. That would mean two people around the clock, three shifts. Not a family then, just an individual to protect. Just enough time, maybe to get to Piraeus, but did he really want it? He certainly wanted two weeks at a thousand dollars a day. He knew that he could trust Dickwick with his life, but six people for two weeks – there must be some heavy threat anticipated before laying out that sort of money? He decided it would keep a few hours, at least until after lunch.

The barkeeper came over to his table, smiling.

"Steve, OK?" the proprietor laughed. Steve looked bemused.

"You forget – I am Cristos! Last night you make good fun. You try to dance. Ha! Very funny!"

Steve smiled back, squirming on his aching buttocks and ordered some meatballs and beer.

The beer was brought over by a very attractive dark girl – twenty-something years old, he thought, with a wide generous mouth and obsidian eyes, a figure to die for. He'd heard of Greek Sirens. Was she one? There was no ring on her wedding finger – maybe she hadn't trapped a man yet. That was hard to believe.

She was laughing.

"Steve, OK?" she laughed. Steve was dumbfounded.

"You forget – I am Helena!" She had a wounded look on her face.

"Last night you make good fun. You try to dance for me. Fall over. Ha! Very funny. Cristos – he my father."

She laughed again as she pointed at Cristos behind the bar. She shook her head with a flourish and her dark hair – long and thick, with a tendency towards undulation, like her body – swung freely. Now it was not only Steve's buttocks that were uncomfortable.

Shit, he couldn't remember a thing about the night before, he realised. Still, Cristos had laughed, so he'd obviously behaved himself with Helena. As she continued her work Steve continued to watch her, trying not to be obvious. She wasn't heavy breasted but he could imagine that she would tend that way after children. He didn't get the impression that she was yet a mother. Her hips though – as best he could judge given her long skirt – were wide and promised easy childbirth. As she cleared the crockery from the next table, he judged her rear as almost perfect for his taste – not too flat and not tending towards the overloaded cheeks that some men preferred. He shook his head and smiled, wondering why he was thinking about such things, just as she turned towards him.

The hands which had delivered his coffee were square and practical, without the taper and long fingers that one might associate with an artist. They were well cared for, though not manicured, and wore only a clear varnish. Her smile was ready, easy and freely bestowed – even on the Germans – from a face which enjoyed the sun, but without promising a leathered middle age.

"What were you smiling at?"

"Nothing really, erm…just a happy memory."

She could see his discomfort and a reddening around the lighter, less burnished skin of his throat.

"Tell me about it."

"Maybe some other time."

Her eyes glittered. "I will look forward to it."

Waving a small plate of pastries under his nose she asked "You like *kritis*?"

His face creasing into a smile Steve opened his palm and Helena laid the plate before him.

She turned away and Steve watched her as she headed back to the counter, light on her feet and well-balanced. Again he shook his head and smiled to himself.

Cristos pursed his lips and caught Steve's eye. Steve couldn't read the expression.

What sailor would not be smitten after a long haul up the Red Sea and the challenges of the Suez Canal and Egyptian bureaucracy? Laptop porn was no substitute for the scent and touch, the warmth and laughter of a real woman.

*

Coffee led to a beer and then lunch. He enjoyed the meatballs – the lamb was good – and the beer was even better, but by the time he was wiping the sauce off his plate with the bread, he'd decided to find out more about the job Dickwick had on offer.

With another Rethymnian Blonde beer, he fired off a reply to Dickwick, swearing as he dropped breadcrumbs in his keyboard.

After lunch he headed back aboard and caught up on some sleep, then bought some fish on the quay for supper. He planned an early night, and after cleaning the fish he went back to 'O Passos' for a beer and to check his email. There was a reply from Dickwick and a phone number.

Another beer arrived in the delightful hands of Helena, and Steve had difficulty concentrating – her eyes were drawing him into hidden depths. The Siren was calling him again. He snapped back to reality.

"Helena, please, help me, where is Piraeus?"

She smiled and he forgot time and place again, even his question.

"Atheni. Piraeus is the harbour at Atheni."

"Ah, you mean Athens?"

"Yes, Atheni. Three hundred kilometres. Ferry from Iraklion. One day. Or plane."

"Thank you."

"*Efharistó.*"

Steve looked puzzlingly at Helena.

"Thank you – *efharistó*. Your first word in Greek" she added with a smile.

"Ah. Farsto", Steve stumbled and Helena laughed again.

"*Eh-far-is-tó*" she enunciated slowly, as if teaching a 3 year old child, marking each syllable with a wave of her index finger.

Steve got it at the fourth attempt. At least it might have been the fourth attempt. He wasn't counting – he could get to enjoy Greek language lessons. Though he spoke French and Arabic very fluently he didn't think he'd ever forget his first lesson in Greek.

In a dream again he left a generous tip and headed back to Adèle to cook his fish. He smiled as the grouper went into the olive oil. Group 'er. I'd love to, he thought. How long had it been since he'd last had a woman? He couldn't remember. He had come close to it, though, with that psychopath in Djibouti. Close to a few things, too close.

*

After supper, he set up his laptop with a wifi amplifier and could just pick up a signal from 'O Passos' across the harbour. He fired up SkypeWorld and called the number that Dickwick had sent him.

"Hi Rick."

"Baldy, how are things? Where are you?"

"On my boat in Crete. Signal's bad, so no video on this call."

"I don't do video calls anyway. Security. Crete you said? That's handy then. Just a hop from Piraeus."

"Where are you?"

"In Blighty, London actually, tying up loose ends. Got to drop in at the farm up north to, to sort out some problems. Just got in from a job in Canada. Trying to sort out a crew for the next one now – hence my email to you."

"Got your own outfit now then have you?"

"Yes, had enough working for other bozos – thought I could do it better myself. You up for this jaunt then?"

"Could be, what's it about?"

"Just two or three weeks close personal security for a billionaire on his yacht in the Greek Islands. As far as I know now, it's from Piraeus west to Argostoli and then maybe Corfu. When the job's done we'll be leaving the yacht at one of the islands. Probably Corfu. Plan could change though. You alright for three weeks?"

"Fine, though any longer and I'd be pushed – I need to get moving with Adèle."

"Got yourself a woman have you? French by the sound of it, pushing you around. Tasty?"

"That's my boat, Dickwick! She carries me!" Steve laughed in reply.

"Oh, sorry. Sounds like a better arrangement anyway!" They laughed together, good friends catching up, friends who had come close to death together.

"About the job. Six of us, you say. It must be some yacht."

"Yes, over 200 feet long. I can't mention any names."

"Sure, I understand."

"How does it sound then?"

"So far so good. A grand a day US you said, two weeks in advance?"

"Yes, that's right, plus exes, cash if you want it that way."

"That would suit me great."

"You can handle boats?"

"I'm a Royal Marine just like you were – you're not Dickwick for nothing are you? I live on a boat. I've been more than halfway round the world on this one, my dad had a trawler."

There was a laugh at the other end of the line. 'Gotcha!"

"You bastard, winding me up like that."

"Couldn't resist it!"

"What about tools?"

"Don't bring any. I'm going to sort that out. The Greeks are a bit easier about these things than the Brits. Revolutions and hunting are in their blood. We shouldn't need them anyway, but you know, be prepared and all that. You still fit?"

"Pretty good, I've done some work recently – dives, knives, guns, runs."

"Great, and are you still the same size?"

"Size what?" Steve laughed.

Rick's Yorkshire voice came through strongly over Skype. "Stop jossing, you're not with a lass now! We'll be wearing uniform. Not military, just smart casual, all in the same gear. I'll sort it out. I'll go with what I can remember."

"OK, just the same, no extra pounds. Regular all over."

"Just the ticket. Ok then, be in Piraeus on 15th. We'll do some orientation, get to know the ship and check out the security set-up."

"How will I find you?"

"Don't worry, we'll find you. Don't put any details in emails. See you Baldy – the 15th, remember."

"And you, Rick. Thanks for the work."

"No sweat."

After the call, he poured himself a generous brandy in celebration of funds to come, and to make it easier for the Siren Helena to draw him into sleep. He checked the pilot book and started to plan a week or so seeing Crete, maybe on a motor bike.

He would then secure Adèle and take the ferry to Piraeus. Planes were OK, but this was a chance to see some of the islands – the Cyclades at least - in passing and see what people raved about. Then, an early arrival in Piraeus and maybe a trip to see some of Athens for a couple of days. Take the chances as they came. He'd start checking the ferries the next day, if he could sleep at all.

The brandy didn't work. He was going to have find a woman in the next couple of weeks if he was going to sleep properly again. He wasn't sure about Helena's charms though, he wouldn't want to tangle with Cristos – he'd have to start visiting other bars. Tourists might be a better option. He'd need a haircut first though.

Maybe Cristos knew someone who could keep an eye on Adèle whilst he was away? Steve made a mental note to ask him, or maybe he'd ask Helena first – any chance to learn more Greek from her would be more than welcome. After a long passage, when he had been sleeping in spells of maybe fifteen or twenty minutes every few hours, his body became attuned to the broken sleep pattern. Then, when back in harbour the body took a few days to re-adjust. Thoughts of Helena didn't help the re-adjustment, but sleep did come eventually.

*

Maudlin Maruška

China watchers, or Sino-political commentators as some called them, had cautioned the West about Chinese intentions, global political ambitions and territorial expansionism.

The Chinese themselves saw it in more simple terms. They wanted to retain control of their population both in size and in politics. To do this they had to satisfy its needs for consumer goods, food and a rising standard of living. Policies were in place to control its population growth, and the one child policy had worked for a time – if only to raise awareness. Then the policy had been dropped as health standards improved and infant mortality fell.

Industrial strength and people who were not hungry necessitated secure commodity and food supplies – China itself could never be completely self-sufficient. This led naturally to much higher levels of international trade and a need to protect its trade routes – as other countries had done for centuries.

It was building a blue-water naval capability, had acquired and built aircraft carriers and nuclear submarines. It even had a space program and manned spacecraft. With a largely captive population and a huge manufacturing base which the United States (and other countries) had foolishly exported there, it was poised to be the pre-eminent superpower of the late 21st Century.

There were sceptics aplenty, but a number of events conjoined to create serious concern in Washington, London, Paris and Moscow.

One notable item was the crisis developing in late 2015 over the seemingly oil-rich Spratly Islands in the South China Sea – claimed by China, but also by Vietnam, Brunei, the Philippines, Malaysia and Taiwan. China had reclaimed land on one of the atolls and had built an airport and harbour. In December 2015 the US carried out a flyby of the island using two B52 bombers after earlier sending the USS Lassen into the area.

Then in January 2016, China announced the building of a second aircraft carrier at Dalian shipyard. The first – the Liaoning – had been bought second-hand from Russia as a technology exercise. Now it was clear that China's blue-water naval ambitions were very real and very global.

On a less obvious but equally sinister level, the Chinese intelligence networks, both human and electronic, are vast, highly capable and effective. They continue to exercise themselves in cyberwarfare, diplomatic and industrial espionage against other countries. The agency known as 'Guoanbu' has over 100,000 agents worldwide operating not only out of embassies and consulates, but out of Chinese takeaway restaurants, bazaars and larger businesses. They were hooked into universities and anti-government groups, business networks – virtually every type of social, political and economic organisation worldwide. They also had their black teams, operating against the more serious dissenters.

The electronic intelligence strategy of the Guoanbu is known as the 'Golden Shield' and permeates even as low as 'chips' – integrated circuits – for computers. The West had been buying them by the million, but in 2012 Australia banned the use of certain chips made in China. These particular chips are used in computer network controllers and have specific design features which render them a risk to security. One might say that the Chinese were embedding a 'listening capability' in the chips – they could replicate and redirect specific network traffic – i.e. email and chat messages.

Chinese research had also been at the forefront of 'subdermal medical devices" using miniscule chips to monitor the human body, control muscles and eves use acupuncture stimulus points to control pain. These devices also had insidious uses. The idea of a 'programmable army' was of interest to many governments and the concept of a 'programmable population' was emerging from the nightmares of science fiction.

*

An idea, which she didn't like, had begun to form in the periphery of Maruška's consciousness, as she began to associate the attacks of pain with communications from Chuntao. Pain she enjoyed – giving it to others, and occasionally, in appropriate circumstances, experiencing it herself – though she rarely trusted anyone to dole it out to her, as her requirements were very specific and personally very constraining. A month later, following a series of nagging texts and another attack of intense pain between her shoulders (which doctors had been unable to detect the source of), she went to Rue Simplon and called Ewan Chuntao, her Chinese controller.

"Maruška, I hope you are well. I will keep it brief. Your next assignment is the chairman of a mining conglomerate called TRI – his name is Charles Tobin. There is certain information that we require from him before you terminate him. You are to make sure that he understands that his death comes with the compliments of the People's Republic of China.

"I'm not doing anything until you stop these fucking attacks of pain in my back!"

"You will not be bothered with these attacks as long as you answer my communications promptly. Remember, we are never far away."

"You bitch!" Maruška's frustration exploded – she knew that Chuntao could out-think, out-fight and out-drink her – it had been proven - and she felt trapped.

"That is a mis-statement of the facts. We require a software decryption key from him. I will provide you with more details when he is in your captivity."

"Chuntao, it is very difficult to travel now. My retinal scan is held by international agencies – certainly Homeland Security in the US and Interpol have it."

"I have it too, right here in front of me. It is easily rectified. You can come over to Hong Kong and we will have your retinal pattern adjusted with laser treatment. Your eyesight will be unaffected, but the scan will offer a less than fifty percent match to the database."

"No thank you, I've had enough of Chinese medicine. No-one can find that implant you put in my back. No-one believes that there is anything there."

"Yet you still get the pain."

"Yes."

"So, you see, Chinese medicine is the best. Maruška, there is another way. We can arrange to have all the existing records replaced in those agencies, even the backups."

"I'll think about it. I don't trust you."

"Always a healthy attitude - that is why you are so good, so valuable to us."

"Keep your flattery Chuntao, I don't need it."

The call ended, and Maruška left the apartment in a fury, completely contrary to her normal emotionless approach to her work. Emotion was alien to her, and it made her feel distinctly uncomfortable. She, and her life, were changing.

After more than ten years working for the Chinese what had she achieved? She had made plenty of money for sure, and had some fun following the path she had chosen for herself. Compared to Carlos, the Jackal, she measured herself as far superior and much more successful; but she was not notorious, except amongst those who, now, evidently knew, and of course, the Chinese, but what was that worth? The next assignment could be her last, and not by choice. She was surely being hunted.

The French, she knew, were desperate to get her after she had, during a rare public performance, taken out a squad of their marines in Djibouti. She had been lucky, very lucky, but the assignment had good and stimulating memories, too. She'd lost Hans and Petr in Djibouti with Hans killing Petr – that was an unprofessional accident - and she was instrumental in Hans's death. Shit happens. And now, here she was, back in Paris, hiding amongst the French and passing (rather well) as an attractive French lady of uncertain age and uncertain sexual attitude.

Her return to France had been difficult, having to avoid the retinal scans, but she'd finally come in via a small boat from Tunisia to Malta and then a series of ferries through Sicily, Sardinia and Corsica. Now approaching forty years of age, her reactions were slowing and her motivation – well, what was that? Even with multiple identities, travelling was much more difficult given advances in technology, heartbeat patterns and retinal scans. The days of instantaneous DNA scans at airports could surely not be far away. She realised that she was losing confidence and drive, and had started to play with the idea of retiring.

She had plenty of money, but no family. Maybe she should look for a woman she could settle with, buy a villa on Cap d'Agde, learn to paint, keep cats and grow old gracefully? Bardot? She just couldn't see it and winced at the thought.

At least she had some personal business to attend to, with Mannesmann to meet and Baldwin to beat. Then, maybe, one big public job to put her name in the history books before retirement.

New retinal patterns would mean new passports and identities. She still had a half dozen spare personas and documentation, but was losing enthusiasm for acquiring new ones. Age again, she thought. I'm losing motivation.

Short term, it looked like she'd have to take her chances with the database hacks. Longer term, maybe there was a clinic in Geneva who could fix her eyes – retiring meant that she would have to hide from the Chinese too – it was doubtful that they would let her retire with her secrets. For them there would only be one sort of retirement.

That same afternoon after her rage had subsided, she found another apartment a couple of blocks away from Rue Simplon but still in the Serbian quarter. She rented it in the name of Andjela Vidovic. Within a couple of days she had transferred what little there was from the previous 'safe' house. It was risky, but she had visited the original apartment only twice, after careful observation and in heavy disguise. Now the move was complete.

At her 'French' apartment on the Rue Llomand in the Latin Quarter, she resumed her Paris life as Mlle. Broussard with regular visits to the Piscine Pontoise and her martial arts club, and occasional late-light forays, as Senka, to her one of her favourite lesbian or S&M clubs.

*

Deb Deb

Algeria 1955

The six year-old boy awoke to the sound of shouting and his mother's wailing. He could hear the rough wooden door being smashed down and then heard shouts in French. He recognised the language as that of legionnaires, but he understood little. There was commotion and the sound of breaking furniture. He heard men on the flat roof above him. Then the door to the room in which he slept was thrown open and two legionnaires burst in, with torches.

'Il n'est pas ici' one said as they turned his bed over and scattered his possessions, trampling the rug and dragging him out into the family room where a legionnaire had broken a paraffin lamp over the wrecked table with a rug thrown on it. The trooper took out an old brass cigarette lighter which reflected the flame as he set the fire in the dark living room.

His mother was outside, wailing as the soldiers removed her clothes, exposing her shame. There was no sign of anyone else beyond the legionnaires. The village remained silent as the flames took hold and the boy heard the dry wood of the poor furniture crackling wickedly. The air pockets expanded and burst the cellulose fibres, feeding the eager fire and sending sparks up through the fallen roof.

The boy was tied to a camel and closed his eyes as his mother was violated, but he could not close his ears.

The fire was now roaring but would soon run out of fuel and die. Spitting and groaning the roof timbers were surrendering their load and falling inward. There was another crack, louder than the noise of the fire, and a legionnaire fell to the ground.

'Merde' uttered one of the troopers. The squad did not panic, they fell to the ground almost as one man, rolling, seeking cover and trying to locate the source of the shot.

They were exceptionally well drilled and their MAS-49 rifle shots cracked systematically at vague, shifting targets in the light of the burning house. Capitaine Moitessier shouted to the sergeant. Cease fire was ordered. A further order was given quietly and one of the legionnaires broke cover to run to the next building, across the stony track which ran between the homes. Their injured comrade – not a true compatriot as the squad comprised many nationalities – was groaning as the medic hauled him into the shadows cast by the waning moon. In his pain he had fallen back on his native tongue, though none of his squad understood the Gaelic prayers. It was well after midnight as they watched and waited silently and patiently. The bait offered by the trooper crossing the open ground to the next building was without effect, no further shot was taken at them, no fire was drawn.

For weeks they had been trying to locate this one man. Tonight they had information that the young boy's father knew the identity of the 'spectre' as he was known. One shot, one death – and so it had been for three months in this area. One or two legionnaires were picked off every week. Morale was falling.

A few minutes later, Moitessier was told that the injured trooper was gut-shot and bleeding heavily, with little chance of recovery. He walked across and shot the man through the temple. Life was hard out here and those of the squad who still thought that there was a god – or were just regularly superstitious – crossed themselves. Every one of them would have made the same choice in the circumstances even though there was hardly a choice to be made.

They loaded their dead comrade onto a camel and after a quick headcount set off for their base.

*

Ghudamis is a town in Libya near the conjunction of the Libyan, Tunisian and Algerian borders. Today the N53 route which heads south for Tassili N'Ajjer National Park, a World Heritage site, becomes the N1 onwards to Tamanrasset. This is classical French Foreign Legion country. To the south lies the Aïr Country of Fort Zinderneuf where Algeria meets Niger and Mali - the setting for the novel Beau Geste.

The people of this region are Tuareg – an ancient nomadic tribe who inhabit central Africa and pay little heed to borders. They are classified as a Berber tribe and their DNA extends across much of North Africa. Tough and warlike, many were hired by Muammar Gaddafi to form his elite 'presidential guard' in Libya.

Just south of Ghudamis lies the village of Deb Deb.

The night that Le Capitaine Moitessier and his platoon visited Deb Deb is not forgotten there, even more than seventy years later.

Under the burned out house, the air in the soft rock tunnel had warmed up, but was still tolerable as the young boy's father shimmied his way through. He could hear nothing, and when he emerged from a home further down the track the squad had already left the village.

The officer had decided that losing one man was enough – there would be no search of the village this night. The men would take it out on the woman. As for the boy, they had lost him. In the confusion, although tied to the camel, he had urged it out of the village at a trot. Too late. The shots were aimless - he had escaped and the spent bullets fell uselessly into the sand.

Two hours later, the boy met his father a mile away from the still-cooling embers of what had been their home. The man spoke in Arabic and there was no reaction. He tried French and the camel dropped onto its knees. The boy remained silent as the father cut the boy's bindings. Then he mounted the camel and made his son comfortable on his lap. With gentle urging in the man's limited French, the camel set off.

They did not speak of the boy's mother as they located their water reserve hidden in a nearby cave. They quietly loaded the goatskins and headed south towards Tassili N'Ajjer. Abdel Zhair was proud of his son and grieved silently for his wife – he had no illusions that she would be dead by the time the sun was above the horizon. Although they did not know it, the wife and mother was already dead and had given nothing away before she died. She knew about the tunnel but little about his activities. Knowing even that was too much and did not save her.

*

In the early 1950s, Algeria was in revolt, as was the French Foreign Legion. The plan to cede Algeria to its Nationalist party – the front for the terrorists or freedom fighters, depending on one's perspective – had caused military rebellion in France. The OAS (Organisation de l'Armée Secrete) featured in the headlines daily.

Many French soldiers had been born and raised in Algeria and were of mixed – even pure – Arabic parentage. They considered themselves thoroughly French. Generally, the idea that France should give up a part of itself to terrorists was anathema and the OAS had been born. It was less than secret, founded and run by disaffected French Army Officers and able to mobilise many men as well as strong opinions in France and Algeria. France had just disengaged from Vietnam after the disaster at Dien Bien Phu in 1954, effectively ending French colonialism.

As with some other European countries, colonialism had left a bitter aftertaste and even today the Algerian Arabic ghettoes in France are places of hopelessness and raise xenophobic and racist feelings in some French people.

Sicilian Channel

In Algeria itself, a whole generation grew up with a legacy that stimulated many to associate themselves with groups such as Al Qaeda and to try to establish Sharia Law.

*

Regrouping

Charles Tobin was a gold entrepreneur who had established the genetic technology for extracting gold from seawater in industrial quantities. He had manipulated the world gold markets in a complex futures and options scam. This adventure had made him enemies in the highest reaches of the Chinese government and China had seriously damaged the business in a combined air/sea operation in the Red Sea. Certainly, he strongly suspected that the UK, US and South African governments had been involved in the events though the truth of the matter, even to insiders, was impossible to establish. Few people, if any, could see the full picture.

Following the abortive trip to Djibouti after his *Universal Harvester* production platform in the Red Sea had been sabotaged and his supertanker *Universal Trader* had been sunk by ageing Yemeni MIG fighter-bombers, Tobin had gone back to his roots in Australia to regroup and re-plan, but also to get as far away as physically possible from three specific investors in his gold extraction project.

Two of the investors were based in Italy, and one in the U.S. Tobin was in no doubt that until he had a clear and convincing plan prepared, he should steer well clear of them. He was, though, under no illusions. If they really did want to terminate him, then it would be nigh on impossible to stop them unless he acted first. He believed that it was unlikely that they would terminate him without at least an initial attempt at recovering their funds (which he had told them were secure). In the interim, he had managed to provide dividend payments from his cash reserves, though these had now dwindled seriously. His much publicised difficulties – he had, after all, in a moment of blind rage publicised them himself on the BBC – had caused his investors some concern, but he had managed to smooth that over - at least for the time being.

Sicilian Channel

His commodities trading business, run by Richard Thompson, was making good money – the rise in the price of gold following the attack on his gold production platform had been welcome for all the wrong reasons and the value of his reserves and that of Tobin Resources International had been significant before the losses started.

The repair of the *Universal Harvester* platform's plumbing to the sea bottom manifold would have been straightforward, but the political ramifications had been huge – a major confrontation between NATO and China at the 'Gate of Tears' in the Red Sea – and a new location for the *Harvester*, where it would not cause an international incident, was one of his priorities. The UK Government had rescinded his extraction licence, a joint venture with the Chinese was out of the question, *pro tem*, and the *Universal Harvester* was currently sitting idle in Yanbu, a Saudi port on the Red Sea.

He had another production platform – the *Universal Miner* - in India, almost ready for deployment. Two platforms, no location and a massive cash outflow. The reserves of gold-laden *Theovulum Aureus* in seawater tanks at the refinery in Wales were being refined and fed out slowly to the bullion market, but this was small beer in comparison to his overall cash problem and he expected to have to announce that his smokescreen gold mining operation at the old Roman goldmines at Dolaucothi in Wales, would be closed down.

The smokescreen was no longer necessary now that his genetic gold refining technology had been publicised, but the fact that it had been a smokescreen was something that very few people knew, and it would have to remain that way. The government grants which he had secured to build an 80 mile pipeline across an environmentally sensitive area of Wales, using some subterfuge and a lot of blackmail (a government minister, no less) would be subject to legal action for recovery by the Exchequer. He would have to manage that, though the sums involved were relatively paltry.

As he sat on the veranda of the estate he owned, overlooking the Swan River in Perth, he reviewed these facts as he had done every morning for six weeks, hoping for a new insight.

He had spent many of his formative years in Perth before the family had returned to Bendigo in Victoria. One of his companies still owned a huge mining operation a few hundred miles inland, near Kalgoorlie. Here in Perth he had learned to sail and had learned to make love. Somehow, for someone who was the epitome of alpha males, being in Perth had an effect which gave him a different perspective on the world, a perspective that usually gave him new ideas.

His priorities were clear in his mind, although they came up on the screen of his tablet every time he logged in, just to reinforce his determination:
- stay alive by buying time from his key investors
- find locations for the gold production platforms
- finalise the development of the *theovulum tantalus* bacterium and start production.

He knew that the second priority would solve itself soon. As to the first, he expected the Saudis to be unable to resist a deal and his Red Sea production to resume. Everyone knew how much the Arabs loved gold. There was practically unlimited gold in the sea, and he had spent more than a hundred million dollars developing the genetic technology and systems to extract it economically in commercial quantities. Once the political dust had settled a bit more the Saudis would bite, though in all probability he would have to give them a cut so large that his other investors would react. Nevertheless, that was manageable.

He planned to tackle the first priority head-on. He'd have to meet up with his private investors and break the news about the cash flow and the projected fall in returns. Sooner was better, though. He called Richard Thompson, head of his investment vehicle, Livengood Futures, in London. Thompson had been a Government minister until Tobin had persuaded him that there was a better future for him with Livengood Futures than being part of a major government sex scandal.

"Richard, come to a meeting on the *Adventurer* in three weeks' time. Pencil in seven days, we'll make a short holiday of it as well. You'll be meeting me in Argostoli on Cephalonia, in the Ionian. We'll be moving on to Sicily for the meeting with my investors."

"Bloody hell Charles, I can't possibly take that much time out. The markets are jittery at the moment and I need to be on the spot. Beside which, Sicily is going into the lions' den isn't it? Three days maybe."

"It's seven days, just do it. We need to prepare for the meeting. I'll arrange some entertainment as well. Don't worry about Sicily, that's my problem."

Thompson squirmed, as Tobin knew he would, though he couldn't see it as the video link was off. Although Tobin had engineered Thompson's denouement as a Cabinet Minister in the British Government, he had made Thompson extremely wealthy in his own right under Tobin's patronage when they had manipulated the world gold market in what had become known as the 'Gate of Tears' gold coup. Previously Thompson had been 'just wealthy' with a lesser fortune built on financial trading software. That funding had enabled him to go into politics. His political star had risen quickly until Tobin had threatened to eclipse it with blackmail.

Tobin's three private investors were very hard-nosed men from a family of Sicilian origins. They had several hundred million laundered dollars invested with him. Thompson would not be looking forward to a meeting with these carnivorous shadow investors.

"Very well Charles, I'll make the arrangements. Is there anything I need to bring?"

"How good are you with a handgun, Richard?" Tobin joked.

"It's not funny Charles, this is serious."

"Chill Dicky boy, chill. It will be fine. Plan to be in Argostoli on 20th. I'll be arriving there a couple of days before. Flights are easy – international airport. Sorry I can't spare the Gulfstream."

Tobin cut the call and pondered. Thompson did have a point. Maybe going to Sicily was a step too far.

He sighed and finished his whisky, then called Bill Johnson, skipper of *Auric Adventurer*, Tobin's motor yacht. She was the second of his yachts to carry that name, and had been built by Cantieri Liguri of Riva Trigosa in northern Italy. When built she had been amongst the largest private yachts in the world, at 70 metres length overall, sumptuously appointed to accommodate 22 guests, with a range of 4,000 miles. Now she was just a toy compared to Mallya's Indian Empress at 95 metres and Abramovich's Eclipse at 163 metres and 13,000 tons. And now Sheikh Kalifa's Azzam, at 180 metres overall. Tobin sighed. He still had a long way to go.

Still, whatever the scale of boy's toys, *Auric Adventurer* was nevertheless Tobin's pride and joy, and much cheaper than the America's Cup yacht racing campaign he'd gotten embroiled in a few years ago. That had cost him dearly, both financially and in the hit to his personal prestige.

The phone was answered on the third ring.

"Bill, Tobin here."

"What can I do for you today, Sir?"

"How long will it take you to move *Adventurer* from Piraeus into the Ionian?"

"She's ready to go, and we can clear out tomorrow morning. It's just a couple of hundred miles - two days max, depending on where you want us - west through the Corinth Canal."

"I was thinking about Argostoli on Cephalonia, Bill."

"Fine, 2 days then."

Sicilian Channel

"Good, I'll be arriving about the 18th, so be there by then, with a couple of days in hand."

"Yes, Sir, we'll be there."

"One more thing. We'll need to beef up security. Richard Thompson will be joining us plus I'll be having some special guests and their companions aboard. Mike Robinson will deal with it. Six extra crew, I think. No amateurs. We'll be going on to Sicily."

Bill Johnson was used to tight security aboard – he'd been with Tobin for many years – though he did not know why Sicily could be a particular problem – Tobin had problems wherever he went. There was no more demanding a boss than Tobin and he'd had prime ministers and presidents aboard his ships over the years. This, though, felt different. There was something about Tobin's voice, a lack of the usual enthusiasm.

"I plan to spend ten days or so in the Ionian Islands – you know, Corfu, Cephalonia and Skorpios. Richard and I will have personal company – the same group of people as last June. We'll be looking for some night life and some private bays. And the girls will want to go shopping, so sort out an itinerary."

Tobin cut the call. He'd call the girls later. Their diaries were always clear, for which he paid them very well.

*

Passage to Piraeus

Steve changed his plans about the trip to Piraeus, and decided to catch the ferry from Siteia to Iraklion, and then to Athens. Although the ferry called in Milos in the Cyclades islands, he didn't break his journey there.

The trip over to Piraeus had been crowded with tourists, even though it was early in the season, and he was keen to get on with the job and put the dollars in the bank.

He took a cab from the ferry terminal in Piraeus, out to Flisvos marina, where Dick's latest email had told him to join the yacht but when he saw it he realised it was clearly a small ship.

"Rick, great to see you."

"You too, Baldy."

They hugged in a way that only men who have been close to death can do, having absolute trust and knowing that being alive is all that matters with no concern about what others might think.

Rick had been waiting at the bottom of the boarding steps when Steve got out of the cab.

Auric Adventurer. That had come as a shock when he looked the vessel up on Google. There was not a lot of information – rich owners were careful about their security – but enough to tell him that she was owned by Tobin Resources International.

"I'll show you your cabin, and then we'll get to know the others. You'll be bunking up with Henri – no last names, you know the drill." Steve's bunk was in a two berth crew cabin up forward on the starboard side. Rick explained that Henri was an ex-Legionnaire, off the ship at that moment.

"So what have you been up to Baldy?"

"Just come up through the Red Sea, to Crete. Got involved in a scrape down in Djibouti. In fact, it was a bit of a shock when I found out about this ship. Tobin's the guy who caused the fracas that nearly did me in. HMG stitched me up big time too. The boys in the Andrew were great though."

"You ok with this guy then?"

"Yes, nothing personal, just a surprise that's all. Small world. You know how it is with the super-rich, ha! What about you?"

"Just finished a big job in Canada, covering a meeting of software billionaires stitching up some new technology deal – who does what, who gets what in the world markets. Strictly not kosher. Those guys – and one woman – have so much power. I've said too much already. Fucking egos as big as planets, can't stand them."

"Sounds like our current employer then?"

"Too right. It pays well, though. Ours not to question why and all that crap. Anyway, let's get on with the program."

*

It was good to see Rick again, and get to know the others – they seemed a capable bunch. They met the crew too, though the girl could be an unwelcome distraction – men still naturally had a first instinct to protect women, which could get in the way of efficiency.

The first day had been spent on ship orientation, following an introduction by Mike Robinson. They looked at the plans, walked the bridge, cabins, galley, engine rooms, the ship's launches and boys toys garage at the stern. Top to bottom – if required they might have to find their way around in dark and dangerous circumstances. Evening runs were out – the ghastly Athenian smog – the *nefos* – had been bad in the evening, during a period of light offshore winds, and was more damaging to their health than the running was good for it. The smog wasn't too bad in the morning though, and the run round the dock area was interesting. They had use of the ship's gym until the guests came aboard in a couple of days' time. It was air-conditioned and a welcome relief.

At the end of the second day the team was up on the foredeck where they were allowed to relax – the stern was for guests only. Rick was briefing them, with Mike Robinson sitting in.

"These are your last beers, guys for quite some time. As from 08.00 tomorrow we are officially on duty.

We'll cover some final security details now. Mike will issue the daily passwords at 08:00 every morning, to us and the crew. We will not use 'duress' code words - the positive approach works best for me. Passwords as ID on the radio, no names. Using your name means there is a problem or duress.

"We are leaving the dock at 10:00 tomorrow and have a passage booked through the Corinth Canal in the afternoon. We'll not be changing watches in line with the crew – they do 4 on 4 off around the clock. We'll be doing 6 on and 6 off, rolling. That way we get to know all the crew and don't have a 'weak' window when both ship and security teams are changing watches at the same time – though it will happen, but only occasionally.

As you know, we're only four and there should have been six of us, but I don't think we're any less secure for that.

On ship, they do two 'dog watches' every afternoon – each is half a full watch. It rotates the watch pattern. We'll do the same. Mike will be floating. Baldy here will head team Bravo with Henri, and I'll head team Alpha with Aldo. I'll hand over to Mike now, who will run you through the ship's security systems – area access, CCTV, alarms, fire control, evacuation, damage control, panic button, abandon ship. We will also cover anti-piracy measures including the secure citadel for the owner plus the owner's escape minisub. The regular safety briefing PLUS. Sounds heavy I know, but we're not on terra firma now and we need to know this stuff to protect our Principal, who we're calling 'Mr T'.

Mike here has a useful background which he doesn't talk about, but he thinks like us and he's almost" - smiling at Mike as he said it – "up to our standards. I report to Mike."

Mike took over and ran them through a comprehensive list – a lot longer than Rick had intimated. He gave each one of them a coded access tag to hang around their necks, and a discreet self-contained comms headset with bone conduction microphone and no wire down the neck.

After almost an hour of intense briefing, he handed back to Rick.

"One thing to add – I can't remember whether Mike mentioned it or not, but your security tags give you complete access to all areas of the ship, except the owner's suite and office. Mike has an access tag for that suite, as does the captain, Bill Johnson, but those are dual key tags. There will be important people aboard, so don't go nosing around without very good reasons. Any doubts, call me first. One more thing. Read the fucking emergency manual!" They laughed but the message was serious, and they knew it.

'Important people?' thought Steve – 'they shit shag and shave just like everyone else, more or less'.

"Any questions?"

"Yes Rick, what about weapons?" asked Henri, the French member of the team.

"We will have what we need, within reason. Mike will cover that when we're under way tomorrow."

"Yes, Rick, I'd like to know why we've been employed" said Aldo, the apparently US member of the team. He was stocky and balding with what Steve thought was probably Italian or Greek extraction - must be Italian with a name like Aldo.

"I'll answer that, Rick" said Mike Robinson, rather quickly, "it's no secret – there are some business meetings coming up on the ship, and Mr T wants extra security and extra privacy. His guests are very high powered, and some may have their own security as well. He wants the best, so we're using *Scutum Est*. I assume that Rick has hired you, Aldo, because you are the best."

"Yeh sure I am, we are" grinned Aldo affably, "but are there any specific threats, Mr Robinson - it might help us prepare" Aldo persisted.

"None that I've been told about. If there were, I'd share them with Rick, obviously, who I am sure would brief you as he thought appropriate. Mr T's business interests have been well publicised in the press. He's probably pissed off some people along the way, but no more than your average billionaire."

"Yeh, I guess. Ok, thanks Mr Robinson."

Then Rick rounded off. "Fine, if there are no more questions, then, enjoy your evening guys. We need clear heads for the morning, so get an early night. Alpha team takes first watch 08:00."

The meeting broke up, and the guys stood chatting at the rail. Sally, the stewardess brought their final beers out as they stood watching the eclectic mix of yachties, wealthy Greeks and passers-by promenading on the quay.

Steve was talking to Henri and glanced at a couple passing by, apparently intent on one another, but not holding hands. She was wearing a sunhat and sunglasses (didn't everyone?), he a baseball cap, peak down and sunglasses too. Not too smartly dressed, practical, is how Steve would have described it. There seemed to be a strange distance between them, an awkwardness not typical of close friends or lovers. They stopped about twenty yards away to take some photographs of each other, with the ship as a backdrop. Henri's words brought Steve back to the present and away from the camera, but with a nagging feeling – there was something about the man, or was it the woman? Maybe the way she walked, her confidence. Yet, she was physically close but somehow appeared aloof, posed almost.

"I'm getting paranoid" he thought as he turned to answer Henri's question, and drained the last of his beer. Still, he was now working as a security consultant. He was paid to be paranoid. It was a healthy attitude and kept people alive.

Henri headed down the companionway to their cabin, as Steve was talking to Aldo.

"Hey Steve, I guess that our team seems a bit heavyweight for business meetings, know what I mean?" Aldo was still puzzled.

"Yes, I see where you're coming from, but Rick is a straight guy – we go way, way back, and I've trusted him with my life. He hasn't let on to me about anything unusual on this job."

"Well, I sure hope that he's fully in the picture. I reckon Robinson's keeping something back."

"His type always do, but let's not get too hung up on this, just do our jobs, watch out for each other and the Principal, and we'll pick up our pay and go on our way, to where ever. No need to be paranoid, OK?" Steve said with the finality in his voice not quite sounding sincere.

*

"Well, Steve, what did you think of Athens?" Henri said, as they stood on the lower aft deck at the crew entrance and the *Adventurer* slipped away from the dockside.

"Once is enough."

"Yes, people say that the Athenians are a different race to the rest of the Greeks, who think they are thieves and cheats. The French say the same about Parisians. I should know - I am a Parisian."

That morning during their run together, Henri had told Steve a little about himself – his upbringing in Clichy-sous-Bois, his problems with the police, and of then joining the Foreign Legion. Steve knew that Henri was probably not his real name, just his declared identity. In the Legion he had lost his police record and his birth name, and adopted a new identity, in common with every other Legionnaire before 2010. Now he was Henri Laporte.

"But I am not, now, a thief and a cheat."

Steve laughed with Henri knowing well that Henri could probably add killer to the list of Parisian traits. They were cooling down now, jogging gently along the quay towards the *Adventurer* when Henri suggested a coffee at the café.

"Good idea."

Steve glanced ahead. It was just after 7 a.m. and the early tourists were out including a couple on the quay, at the café, taking photographs.

"Actually Henri, I think I'll pass on that coffee. I need to take a shower before my watch starts."

"*D'accord*. I'll see you on watch."

Steve was sure it was the same odd couple he'd noticed taking photographs the evening before.

*

"Rick, it's probably nothing, but you never know. I saw a couple taking pictures last night on the quay."

"So? Holidaymakers?"

"Maybe, but they were on the quay again this morning. Looked like the same couple. The ship was a backdrop on each occasion."

"Ok, Steve, probably nothing as you say, but I'll mention it to Mike - make sure that we take a look later before he wipes the video. Well spotted. I'll speak to the others too, see if they noticed anything."

*

The Sicilians

The brothers, Giuseppe and Giorgio Tumino, had met Tobin in the days when he was developing his Alaskan mining business and had started operations in Nevada, recovering minute traces of gold from miners' spoil heaps.

Serendipity? Perhaps. Tobin had seen it that way at the time, back in 2004. Tobin's operations in Alaska and Canada had been expanding strongly and his businesses were worth over six hundred million dollars, his patented recovery processes, including, by then, a strain of bacteria for bio-oxidation during gold extraction, were being licensed to other mining conglomerates.

That year he bought a major stake in a gold mining operation in Nevada in the United States. Gold mining was a major industry in the state, and Nevada is still, even today, one of the largest sources of gold in the world. Another major industry in the state was gambling, and Tobin liked poker.

Though Tobin had built his business by his own wit, outrageous commercial gambles and technical innovation, the brothers were being prepared to inherit from their father. Unlike some other Capos, their father had not retired to grow grapes, as befitted the stereotype, he had retired to fish. He was one of the few in his line of business who had seen his retirement plan mature.

Their father's story had been yet another example of shining American enterprise and hard work, building a business from scratch in Las Vegas, a business which was eventually to include San Francisco and Los Angeles, with outposts in Hawaii.

Angelo had started on the streets, selling product in the alleys. A local businessman had taken a shine to him and given him the opportunity to demonstrate his ability. Of course, connections were important and his Sicilian lineage was certainly a great help - essential in fact - in joining the business.

He made his bones when he was 18 using a throwdown Saturday Night Special and following through, atypically, with a knife. Ears were not a typical Mafia trophy but he thought that he would be remembered if he took a pair to his sponsor. He liked to do things a bit differently, adding his own flourish to his craftsmanship, marking himself out as someone different. Working hard, he extended his franchise, and took on distribution as the 1960's dawned and flower power came to the West Coast. By then, he was a number three, level ranking with three others, but had started causing problems for his patron with the competition. The other West Coast families did not like his ambition and his Capo was warned.

One warm Wednesday evening he was called to a meeting with the Capo.

Angelo knew it could go two ways – sleeping with the fish, or acceptance but curtailment. He had made his plans carefully. It was rare, if not unique, for a third-ranker to make a move for power in a family structure, but he did. The move was politically masterful, and ingeniously executed. He not only decapitated his sponsor family, he took the shoulders off as well. His flourish was clear, and the other Families could see that he had the touch for the business. They clans wanted a quiet life and he would need to be watched very carefully. Police attention was not welcomed and so internecine war was avoided.

The basic businesses of drugs, protection/extortion, construction and prostitution produced massive cash flows which had to be re-invested. There was plenty of business for everyone, provided they played by the rules. Donations to politicians' campaign funds, payoffs to the police, and minimal preferably no, headlines, in the press.

These were the days before there was any significant legislation and machinery to control money laundering. But even then, the more farsighted Families were moving strongly towards legitimate businesses as an outlet. Having the money sitting in a bank in the Cayman Islands was not its most profitable legitimate use. Some individuals even dreamed of leaving the illegal side behind. Angelo was one of these smarter entrepreneurs, although his innate nature was still that of a serious criminal.

*

In 1960, Angelo's wife, Carmela, gave birth to twin boys. They were identical, and three minutes apart. She died thirty minutes later despite the best medical care that money (and ultimately the surgeon's life) could buy.

Angelo named the boys Giuseppe and Giorgio. Though Giorgio was the younger, he would grow to be the stronger and the three minute age difference would always be contentious between them. Angelo moulded them as he had been moulded, but without the necessity for them to make their bones - directly.

Many times he had told them:

"Don't keep a dog and bark yourself."

With college business degrees they were well equipped for the economic growth that followed the end of the war in Vietnam, but had been bred with ruthless business brains and a stop-at-nothing attitude. They had direct experience of what their father would do to succeed in legitimate business using illegitimate means.

*

Charles Tobin was a high-roller when it came to poker. He usually came out ahead, as he had done in school in Geelong in Australia and as he'd done when winning the wages off his workmates up in the goldmines of Jualin and Red Bear in Alaska. He'd fought and won at poker and brawls in the rough bars of the mining towns in that cold State. He was even mean enough to win the wages back off some of his employees when he'd set up Tobin Mineral Resources Inc., in Alaska. He soon realised that converting his workforce into slaves was not a sensible way forward, and wasn't a politically sensible way to fund business growth. Poker was important to him and his early winnings had, way back in Alaska, contributed to his business start-up fund.

When he met the Tumino family, the poker was for fun and for high stakes. Texas Hold'em had been the game, and he took the pot of 200,000 dollars at their casino.

Casino security had checked him out after the long night at the table, and told him that he was no longer welcome. He had complained, and they had looked at his background in more detail, and referred it upstairs. Upstairs had referred it to the capo in the estate on the La Madre overlooking the city.

Big winners were good for business, and the kudos of having a well-known gold baron playing there was not lost on Giuseppe Tumino. Giuseppe was astute, and was running the casino that year as the brothers worked their way round their father's organisation, ready for succession.

As he looked down on the glittering strip just before sunrise that morning, he called for the car, and told the casino manager to invite Charles Tobin up to the Owner's Suite and offer him champagne – the best – and make sure he had Rachel to keep him company.

*

"Mr Tobin? I'm Giuseppe Tumino, I run this casino. It is a family business and we like to make sure our customers enjoy themselves and come back for more. Are you comfortable? Has my manager Sam looked after you?"

Giuseppe smiled as he crossed the room firing questions, hand extended, smooth as a gliding shark smelling the blood of prey.

"Thank you, yes, except that your manager has stopped me from enjoying my poker here."

Giuseppe gestured and they settled into leather settees opposite one another. The interior decoration was, in Tobin's eyes, garish. Even the girl was overdone. Sure, it was breakfast time, and maybe she hadn't had a hard night, but when she opened her mouth the sound was not pleasant to the ear, and the content was no better. At least she kept her mouth shut when Giuseppe was in the room.

"Yes, well, we too are in business. At least with poker you are winning off the other players and not the casino. After all, you have the two hundred grand pot. The problem is that if someone as skilled as you wins too regularly, then the other players will go elsewhere to play. Perhaps there is some way we can resolve this?"

"I hope so, although the other players seemed to enjoy the fact that I was winning."

"The Strip is all about gold Mr Tobin, one way or another. I hear you have gold interests in Alaska."

"Yes and in Canada too. You have good sources."

"I pay for the best. We need to be sure that our high rollers are credit-worthy."

Tobin's eyes didn't blink as he looked over Giuseppe's shoulder at the gross piece of kitsch passing for art on the wall and thought about Rachel, the empty caricature (or some man's dream) of womanhood who had been on offer for him. Giuseppe was surrounded by kitsch. No class at all, he thought. Still, he had funds.

"Indeed," Tobin responded as his eyes returned to meet Giuseppe's."

"Will you join me for breakfast?"

"Your offer is very gracious Mr Tumino, but I have to refuse this morning. Thank you, but I have to get back to my hotel and change. I have some meetings arranged this morning." If Giuseppe's breakfasts were as good as his best art and his best women then he'd rather eat with his miners…

"Ah, well, maybe some other time. How long are you in town?"

"Two, maybe three days."

"Well please, be my guest and play poker with us while you are here. We have a special game room for our most valued customers – Sam will introduce you. I will put the Presidential Suite at your disposal. And of course, Rachel."

"Perhaps on my next visit although I doubt I am a good customer. I come here and win."

"We need big winners, Mr Tobin, whatever the game. Losers like to dream. Poker for us is like a stock exchange, win or lose we take a rake. Sam, give Mr Tobin your card. Mr Tobin – Charles, if I can call you that – next time you are visiting Vegas, call Sam and he will see you have everything you need. He will let me know, and then maybe we can have dinner together and talk about gold. Gold for you, and gold for me, I hope."

"I'll be sure to have one of my secretaries call your manager next time I plan on visiting…."

Giuseppe put on a smile.

"…and yes, perhaps we can have dinner if there is space in my diary." Tobin stood up.

"Arrivederci, Charles."

"Until next time, Giuseppe."

"And call me Beppe."

"Very well. Arrivederci Beppe."

And so a business relationship was formed, one that was to prove very useful to both Tobin and to the twin brothers Tumino and their father. Neither side was under any illusions about the other and although Tobin played poker many times in the Tuminos' casino, he never left as a loser.

*

Maruška Moves On

Her research was typically thorough and she uncovered an apparent linkage between her mission in Djibouti (when she'd come up against Baldwin) and Tobin's gold production platform. It seemed to her that there were too many coincidences and although she was intelligent and analytical, she put a lot of trust in her instincts and intuition. Could Tobin lead to Baldwin? Unlikely, she thought - her supposition had to be that Baldwin had been tied in with the UK government, but he did have that boat – Adèle, wasn't that the name? Maybe she could track that?

First though, she wanted to meet Michael Mannesmann again - he had been her first male lover when they met in Serbia and she was barely out of her teens, already with a string of sectarian murders to her name and a reputation revered by the men in SNP (the Seven Legged Spider) – the paramilitary group to which she belonged. Mannesmann's background was ex-East German special forces and it was he, when they had last met in Paris several years before, who had introduced her to the Chinese and arranged the explosives training course in Libya.

Two days after she sent the encrypted email to the black hole in Geneva using the TOR network, she read the post by 'MSNP' on the arachnophobics.com forum. Previously they had agreed never to meet again, in the interests of professional safety – more from her side than his – but he had now agreed to a meeting to 'discuss their phobia'. Same place. same time, as 'their last first meeting', and on her birthday. She remembered that meeting as being outside the Hennes and Mauritz department store on the Rue Neuve in Brussels precisely at 11:20 a.m. on her June birthday. For each of her passports, she had different birthdays. The June birthday was for her 'real' French identity – Mdlle Broussard - but how in hell did he know that birthdate? She would enjoy finding out…

*

Wan Chuntao came through with the information she had requested. The Chinese intelligence services were obviously efficient – but if they employed agents as effective as their assassins, such as Maruška, then the best was only to be expected.

She decrypted and scanned Chuntao's report: Charles Tobin was in Perth, but his motor yacht *Auric Adventurer* was in Piraeus, Athens, and expected to move through the Corinth Canal to the Ionian Sea and meet him in Argostoli on 16th June, just a few weeks away. The skipper of the yacht had been recruiting a security team, and it was expected that Tobin would be entertaining three investors aboard.

Wan Chuntao was unable to provide names – somehow Tobin had bypassed the usual communications to make the arrangements. Maybe the Chinese were not so efficient after all…

Getting the required information out of Tobin might require a few hours – say three maximum - and she would have to deal with the crew. Maruška tried to find plans of the motor yacht on the web, but they were unavailable. Chuntao would have to sort that out

She analysed the options to identify the best place to capture him. There were only three: on his plane – take-off or landing, between the airport and the yacht or when he was on the yacht.

After a few days' deliberation, she discarded the plane option, and didn't want to wait for a later opportunity, she wanted to get on with it. The mission was information first, then termination at her leisure. Hitting the car would mean that she would have to kidnap him in public. Not ideal. The yacht seemed to offer the best option. The crew could be coerced to move her to somewhere secluded, and then she could work on Tobin.

Sicilian Channel

She would definitely need help to hijack Tobin's yacht. One possibility was to get hired as a stewardess aboard the Adventurer, but she knew nothing about the job, and working undercover near a target was not her style – it would be too hard to avoid tracks and traces. In and out. That was her way.

While reviewing the options, she'd checked the geography and realised that it was not all that far from her original home in Serbia, just a few hundred miles up the Adriatic. She felt no emotion about her past. That was her strength. Neither did she feel any concern about discovery; her tracks had been covered well, though the international law agencies now had a whiff of a scent with DNA from Djibouti.

She booked a flight to Athens, using a package holiday in the Canaries as a cover. When she got there, she would change identity and take a charter flight from Las Palmas to Berlin and then a Lufthansa flight to Athens. Time was tight. As long as she stayed within the European Union she could travel on ID cards and retinal scans could be avoided.

Subconsciously she had long realised that retirement was not an option. Now it was a conscious realisation. She was taking more risks. She would never end up imprisoned as Carlos the Jackal had been. Did she have a death wish? No. But death was inevitable. Just a matter of timing and method, planned or unexpected, quick or slow.

Her realisation about increased risk taking was very sobering, and that night she went out clubbing, as Senka, her BDSM alter ego.

A cat had nine lives it was said. She knew hers were running out.

*

The middle aged Parisian was new to the club scene. So far, all his contacts had been via websites and internet chatrooms, leading occasionally to meetings and to evenings – and some afternoons – of pleasure. That night he had it made with a very sexy, black-haired, leather-clad woman as they went back to his apartment. He loved the black bob cut and the razored neck, the shapely arse held tight under the leather. As the elevator climbed the eight floors, he looked forward to a long night of pain and maybe passion, thought about the handcuffs in the box under his bed, nipple clamps, a gag, other toys for insertion, for giving pain and for receiving it. He'd be happy either way, or preferably with a bit of both.

Maybe she was a simple girl and clothes pegs would do. He looked forward to finding out as he conjured with the possibilities whilst they groped each other. Then she used her fingers to rub herself and then brushed them across his lips - albeit only the smell and taste of leather.

He was right, it was long night. And there was pain, pain aplenty.

The apartment block's concierge found him three days later when neighbours complained about an unpleasant smell. There were copious amounts of female DNA identified at the scene by the Parisian scene-of-crime team, but database matches were zero. Zero, that is, until they were found to match a woman's body discovered a week later in a copse in a park.

*

Maruška's preparations continued. She downloaded a 'Learn Greek' app to her iPad and grasped the basics. Her facility with languages had developed when she was talking her way through IFOR checkpoints in Serbia as a teenager, and she enjoyed the challenge of a new language and alphabet.

*

"Hello Michael, it's been a long time."

"Hi, Andjela." He looked startled.

Maruška glared at him from under a soft red velvet trilby, from behind dark glasses.

"My name is Marie, you forget so easily. Use the wrong name once more and I will kill you. There is no such person as Andjela."

She smiled unconvincingly as she said it, and he relented.

"Ah, yes, you are correct of course. Just my little joke, yes?" His English was heavily accented, with that overtone of excessive formality so typical of the Germans, but perhaps with just a trace of something – a hesitation.

"And mine too, how could I possibly kill you?"

"Marie, I know that you would without a moment's hesitation."

"I'm sure that the reverse is true too, Michael."

They embraced briefly, *fait le bise*, kissing each other's cheeks. There was much history, stretching back to Serbia. She owed him a lot, she knew. He had been her introduction to the Chinese. He had also been her introduction to sex with men.

It was the last week in May. She had taken the train into Brussels and met Michael Mannesmann outside the Hennes and Mauritz department store on the Rue Neuve. Again. Their last meeting there had been many years before, though they had met briefly, in Paris, a few months later.

They had both aged and changed. He was now approaching fifty years of age, and given their line of work, he had done well to survive.

A few other things had changed too. Their meeting place was under a CCTV camera.

At first he hadn't recognised her, hadn't noticed her, hadn't even seen her approach. He was annoyed that she should get the drop on him. She knew it. He knew that she knew. She smiled to herself at the thought.

"Shall we get some coffee and a pastry then, a little too early for lunch I think?"

"Jahwohl."

When they were settled at a discreet table away from CCTV – it was just too late for the regular coffee crowd, and too early for lunch, so privacy was easier and the conversation quickly focused.

"I have an assignment and I need your help Michael."

"You know that we can't work together, we should not even be meeting."

"I don't give a fuck what others think. I need your help."

"Why me?"

"Because I don't have the time to put a team together and build the level of trust and understanding necessary for the operation. You I know well, perhaps too well."

"That was a long time ago, perhaps too long."

"Some things are never forgotten."

"Maybe, like the forest outside Pristina."

She scowled at him. "Never say that again."

"You do want my help?"

"Yes."

"Well then, if we are to be bedfellows, you had better get used to my bad habits." He smiled as he said it, but there was no warmth. He knew he would have to tread carefully with her. Success and a long life in their business relied on a sixth sense – if you had it well-developed, you stayed alive longer than most. He was still rankling over her unseen approach a few minutes before. "How much time do you have?"

"Two weeks."

"That's very tight. How far advanced is your planning?"

"Just starting. We will hijack a motor yacht and her crew, and her owner. No ransom, just information and termination."

"*Scheisse*, Marie, that's complex, hijacking and abduction - very risky. How many in the team?"

"Just you and me."

"*Gott in himmel, ungläublich!*"
"There is no God in the sky, and it is believable."
"What do you know about motor yachts?"
"I can drive one, a small rubber one."
"Is there any good news?"
"Yes, sunshine."
"Where?"
"First I need your agreement."
"First I need to know where. Travel is not easy these days. Identities are expensive to build, and take time. Besides, you have a public profile now, after Djibouti. That increases the risk."
"I don't know what you mean."
"*Scheisse*! Do not give me fucking bullshit Marie. If you want my help then you had better be straight with me. Your adventure in Djibouti is well known. The French want you, desperately. As do others. Anyone who is with you is at risk."
"Don't worry about my risks, I have taken care of them. You have people chasing you too."
"Yes, but not so publicly."
"Greece."
"Greece? Well maybe that's not so bad – we can travel overland. They have no history of me there, either."
"I wouldn't be here if I thought it was too risky. I will book my own travel."
And so the arrangements were made.
Back at his hotel, Mannesmann checked his iPhone - a coded text from Chuntao. Call her. At least she'd spared him the pain this time. He had tried for many years to get the Chinese off his back but they always tracked him down. He knew it was better to respond promptly and avoid pain, but first he reached for the antacid pills.
Chuntao would want to know if Maruška was on the hook.

On the train back to Paris, Maruška reflected that this assignment could work out well – two birds with one stone.

Sicilian Channel

Death on High

It was a hot June afternoon in the Strait of Messina. Many Italians and Sicilians were at their *riposo* – the southern Italian version of the *siesta* - as were the swordfish. These magnificent fish migrate south through the Strait in spring, and then back north in June. In the heat of the afternoon sun they laze on the surface of the sea. *Spada* – swordfish – is a popular dish in Sicily and most of the catch is consumed locally.

Fishing for swordfish in the Strait was more akin to a scene from Moby Dick then to the large scale commercial fishing off the north east USA. In the North Atlantic, fishing lines of up to 20 miles in length with thousands of baited hooks were towed across the edge of the Gulf Stream. At the edge of the Stream, the sea temperature changed sharply, food accumulated and the marine food chain focused its efforts, with the swordfish at the pinnacle.

In the Strait of Messina however, the swordfish lazed on the surface, and were harpooned for their idleness. Brutal perhaps, but a bit more personal than being on the end of 20 miles of line. The boats used to catch them are no longer rowed by four oarsmen with a lookout on a 12 foot mast and a harpoonist in the bow. Modern Messina swordfish boats are at the extreme of development and optimised to catch these fish.

They are powerful and fast vessels, typically sixty feet long, with an additional bowsprit as long again, for the harpoonist to stand on. The mast is an extending lattice tower, much like a TV transmission mast, up to eighty feet high. Bowsprit and mast are held up by a complex set of rigging.

At the start of the day's fishing, the *capitano* is hoisted up this mast using an electric winch, and there he sits in a chair steering the vessel and looking for swordfish, eighty feet above the deck. The harpoonist stands way out on the bowsprit. The arrangement allows the fishing boat to creep up on the dozing swordfish and spear it.

Angelo Tumino owned one of these boats and fished *spada* for pleasure. The *Carmela* was built for him nine years previously, when he retired to Syracuse from Las Vegas. His second wife, Giulietta, resented the name of the boat and the fact that Angelo had been unable to relegate the memory of his first wife to a less conspicuous location. He loved his boat and he loved Giulietta, but he kept them apart.

That particular afternoon, there was no breeze in the Strait as the 'Carmela' headed back to Syracuse. Her hold was empty, the swordfish had been lucky. One of his twin sons, Giorgio was visiting from Las Vegas, and father and son were out fishing together. Giuseppe was holding the reins back in Vegas.

Angelo Tumino spoke through the intercom to let his crew know that he was about to descend from the masthead, after which they could then retract the mast and bowsprit before entering harbour. He disengaged the remote engine and rudder controls, and Giorgio, down in the wheelhouse, took control of the *Carmela* while his father descended. Giorgio shook his head in amazement – his father was eighty three years old and still wanted to be atop that ridiculous steel tower. He did not understand fishing as a sport, but time with his father was important.

The winch started, and the chair jerked into motion, beginning its eighty foot descent.

The crew did not see the small cloud of red mist as the bullet went through Angelo's skull taking the side of his head with it on exit. By the time the blood mist, bone and brain splatter reached sea level it had almost dissipated, and the *Carmela* had moved forward a hundred yards or so, travelling at twelve knots. Some fragments of skull and other tissue reached the sea sooner, but these too had been left in the *Carmela's* wake. The spent bullet plopped into the sea fifty yards away on the port side, falling not through lack of energy, but lack of aerodynamic efficiency due to its distortion. Angelo Tumino was dead by the time his chair had moved an inch, and it was down and stopped when Tomaso, one of the crew readying the ship for harbour noticed the spreading red stain and the slumped body in the *capitano's* chair.

He shouted for Giorgio at the wheel, and all hell broke loose.

*

Giorgio called Giuseppe with the devastating news, and whilst arrangements for a grand family funeral in Siracusa were being made, the brothers and Alfonse, their consigliore worked to identify who was ultimately responsible for the decapitation of their family.

The bullet was never found, but markings and traces of nickel on the top of the lattice mast suggested to the police that there had been two, perhaps three shots, with the final shot clean and clear into Angelo's skull on the right hand side. The entry wound suggested a 7.62 mm calibre weapon but the exit wound looked like it had been a tank shell. The fact that the marksman was an expert shot of the highest order (or inordinately lucky) was self-evident. The crew had been eighty feet below, and although there had been one or two missed shots (and perhaps even more), no ricochet had been heard – the boat was, after all, driving hard for harbour at that time. Certainly, the *capitano* had no time to call the crew, so the two or three shots must have been very quickly cycled, again suggesting the very best of marksmen. The crew swore that there had been no other boats nearby, and the difficulty of the shot made it almost certain that it must have been made from the shore – good half mile away from the *Carmela*.

She had been heading south for Messina harbour when the fatal wound was inflicted and so the location of the executioner was impossible to determine, other than the fact that he (or she) was on Sicily and not the mainland side. There were very few marksmen who could have successfully made that shot at a target moving at twelve knots with a heat haze shimmer over the calm, mirror-flat sea. Undoubtedly though, someone had been capable.

Angelo Tumino had laid out a succession plan, with the traditional primogeniture dictating Giuseppe - by three minutes - as the new *capo*. Their family organisation, in the business sense, was compact and efficient, and their legitimate businesses professionally managed.

They could identify no obvious candidate for a strike-back, either within or without, but it was clear that they could not sit idly by and not respond, and Giuseppe was all for a hit as a matter of principle. Giorgio and Alfonso, their consigliore, urged patience and caution.

*

In fact, the shot that killed Angelo Tumino had come from a Knight M110 sniper rifle, the first semi-automatic sniper rifle to be practical.

Usually, the recoil of a powerful long gun such threw the gun out of aim and the time taken to eject the spent cartridge and load another using a bolt action (or automatic mechanism) was immaterial, as the marksman needed time to re-acquire the precise aim-point. The history of this particular weapon included a journey to Iraq from its factory in Titusville, Florida via Fort Bragg, and then a series of illegal shorter trips ending up in Sicily on Angelo Tumino's last day on earth.

With the recoil-elimination technology of the Knight rifle the marksman could squeeze the trigger repeatedly without having to reacquire the aim-point. A spread of five shots could be squeezed off in less than two seconds. The other advantage of this was that allowances – for example for cross wind – would be less likely to have changed in the time it took to make the kill. This made killing more efficient – longer range kill percentages went up. High short-range kill percentages could be achieved by lower quality marksmen, albeit at more risk, as more shots increased the likelihood of discovery.

Not all snipers who had learned with the Barret 50 or other traditional sniper rifles could make the change to the new technology. This sniper could and had made the change.

Efficient sniping was based on innate ability, good eyesight and bodily control – steady nerves, steady eyes and controlled breathing. Not all top marksmen could make the grade as a good sniper either. Sniping was also about stealth and concealment, working well as a two man team with a good spotter, the art of camouflage and above all, patience.

However, even those skilled marksmen who could not make the grade as a front line sniper, found roles, even after the Army. They did not need to work in two man teams and rarely needed to wear camouflage gear.

Such was the man who took the three shots that hot June afternoon from an apartment window in a sea front building just north of Siracusa. He loved the M110 as he loved a woman, even more. He cleaned her and oiled her, talking gently as her barrel cooled down. As he packed her in her case he stroked her one more time and spoke to her again.

"Andjela, I love you."

Within an hour of those shots he was on a hydrofoil ferry back to the mainland, drinking a beer and sending a coded text with a bank account number – a different one to that where his 50% down had been transferred in a series of smaller transactions a week before.

To account for the payments, a series of fictitious invoices had been prepared by his client, a Mr. Robins, and processed through one of a series of funds set up for such purposes. Money had been transferred using a series of bank accounts and several 'cut-out' cash transfers to a Cayman Islands account controlled ultimately by the German mercenary. Michael Mannesmann enjoyed occasional lucrative private assignments when not otherwise engaged on work for the Guoanbu.

Andjela was taking a different route using Fedex and would arrive in safe storage at a Vienna address the following day. She had a sister (a Barret 50) in Belgrade, outside the EU, and a twin sister in New York. They too had their exercise from time to time although they never met. Travelling was not easy these days.

*

"Jesus, Beppe, I still can't believe it. Papa, shot."

The brothers were on the terrace at their dead father's villa in Syracuse.

"This isn't the style of one of ours."

"Is there such a thing as a 'style of ours' anymore? It must be one of the other families."

"But why?"

"The reasons are always the same. Territory and product. Just business."

"I can't believe it, though I wouldn't trust one of those bastards with my donkey. Papa was retired, why not one of us, or both of us? That would make more sense."

"Maybe that is the sly trick, make us think it's outside the Families. Who else could it be? Should we start to look inside our own family? Consigliore?"

Alfonso hesitated, then shared his thoughts with them.

"It's been ten days now, and no one has moved, there have been no problems, not even with that black trash down in Watts. No moves on our territory at all. Giuseppe, you have been away from Vegas for what – eight days?" Giuseppe nodded. "Ok, if it's not in the Families, we should look at our legitimate investments, and find out if any are in trouble, maybe something we don't know about. That will take time because they are legitimate, and we don't watch them day-to-day, we just look at monthly reports. If there is a problem serious enough to lead to this dreadful sin against your mother…"

"Stepmother" interjected Giorgio.

"…stepmother and the family" corrected Alfonso "then the reason will be well hidden. I have asked our financial advisers in New York to start reviewing our investments."

"Yes", said Giorgio, "but what about those that are…you know…grey, shall we say? Papa's friends. Our friends."

"Yes, we will need to check those too. I am doing that personally. There are not many candidates."

*

Another Family Grieves

The funeral was orthodox and took place within 24 hours of his father's death, as was the custom. The lung cancer had taken him quickly – despite his hatred of the French there were some things that lingered. The French eventually had their revenge, unknowingly, and with the help of Gitanes which had been cheap and plentiful, feeding his 40-a-day habit which had started when he was in his teens.

His family had a proud history. In 1956 his father was a young boy and had escaped south into the Tassili N'Ajjer area on a camel with his grandfather. They had spent the winter there, man and son, at a concealed base where his father had become a young man. He had learned to fight, to shoot and had received a modicum of education. He had skirmished with the Foreign Legion and learned to stay cool in the heat of a firefight.

He was noted for his cunning and intelligence. Commanders marked him out for further education – the new Algeria would need sound and capable men to run the new, independent country.

Within the family (and other circles) his father was legendary and had become a formidable figure in the building and administration of the new, wealthy Algeria which was rich in oil and gas besides extensive fertile farmland.

Abu ben-Zhair was in many ways like his father and grandfather, but the need for more change in Algeria was driving him in his own way. He had enjoyed the privileged education as a child of a senior government official, including attending university in Moscow. In Algeria, the Islamists in the form of the GIA had been causing problems within major terrorist acts against tourists and the government alike. Eventually, a form of co-existence was established between the Government and the extremists. This continued through the so-called Arab Spring which had led to the liberalisation of Tunisia and Egypt, and major civil war in Syria.

Abu ben-Zhair was an opportunist and a practical revolutionary. For him, the Islamist accommodation with the Government was a betrayal. The Arab Spring was a surrender of Islamic control to Western consumerism, aided and abetted by the cheap technology that global businesses had shipped into those countries. The 'YouTube' revolutions some called it, but to him they were not revolutions, they were abject surrender.

Every morning when he shaved and examined himself critically in the mirror, he said to himself 'I will re-frame the picture of Islam and roll back revolutions'.

The year after Abu Ben-Zhair buried his father in Algiers, he conceived a plan.

The French had long since departed Algeria.

*

Planning Problems

Wan Chuntao's news was bad.

Maruška had arrived in Athens on a new passport, having travelled down on the Orient Express (or what, at least was called the Orient Express). Neither the train nor the service bore any resemblance to what had once been a grand and elite experience.

It was a special journey for Maruška – it had been almost twenty years since she had travelled on the train – in the other direction. She had left behind her real identity of Andjela Karanovic, assuming that of her lesbian lover Maruška Pavkovic, groomed for the purpose and then killed. She had also left behind her life with the SNP - *Sedam Nogu Pauk* – the Seven Legged Spider. The SNP was Srecko Vidovic's gang of Serbian paramilitaries, competing with Arkan's Tigers for the title of the most ruthless and extreme of the irregular Serbs. After the war in Bosnia-Herzegovina, Vidovic had morphed the SNP into a seven-legged organised crime outfit, which Andjela had been running for him after he had moved to South America to escape an international arrest warrant (and to open a new drug smuggling channel).

Since then, she knew her identity as Maruška was probably compromised, which had led to the complex matter of her retina scan.

En route, she had received the email telling her that Charles Tobin's skipper on the *Auric Adventurer* was taking on an additional four crew members – they were listed on the Crew Manifest which he had filed at Piraeus. Chuntao's colleagues at the Guoanbu had easily been able to hack the Greek Port Police database and the DEKPA transit log that yachts and ships travelling within Greek waters have to carry. It declared that the next port of call for *Auric Adventurer* would be Argostoli in Cephalonia, an island in the Ionian, with a provisional departure date of 18th.

Chuntao also sent her a set of plans, of *Auric Adventurer*, which her team had been able to hack from the CAD computer at the naval architects office in the shipyard Cantieri Liguri in Italy, where she had been built.

She'd had to request that the files of the plans be converted to a format she could read on her laptop – it was not like Chuntao's team to overlook this sort of detail – and that took another couple of days. She was frustrated by these complications, as she had no way of contacting Michael Mannesmann before their planned meet–up in Athens. Time was getting tight. The odds were not good and getting worse, and she wondered whether she would bother to tell Mannesmann given that his shelf-life was to be very limited anyway.

*

It took a few days for her to review the plans and decide on a set of options. Assault was the wrong word - this had to be a stealthy takeover. She'd also had to consider access to weapons and other equipment, inside Greece, and this had proved tricky. She had contacts in the Ionian Islands – a smuggler – Nicos, she thought his name was. They'd used him to ship weapons, and later, drugs, in from Libya when she was working with Vidovic in the SNP. In those days, she used her real name, Andjela, but she'd left that behind, in a dead body with no eyes and three amputated fingers, beaten, raped and overdosed on sodium pentothal in a Range Rover in Beograd. At least she thought her identity was clean, but according to Chuntao, the episode in Djibouti had compromised that. Blood from her ear had been taken from a window frame at a hotel in Golfe Bleu.

So, Nicos was not a practical solution, though she was sure he would have access to what she needed. The weapons shipments had occasionally been a crate or two short - "the sea was rough and they fell overboard during the transfer" he'd shrugged and said. As smugglers went, he'd been pretty straight – some shrinkage was to be expected. But when it came to the drugs the shipments had always been intact. Clearly he had not wanted any downstream involvement in distribution.

Although Maruška was not keen to do so, she would have to make use of Chuntao's resources. She prepared a list and sent a secure email using the Chinese version of the Onion Ring. Within the hour there was a reply from one of Chuntao's aliases, asking why the list was so extensive. "Backup" is the reply she sent, not having told Chuntao that she would have assistance. She usually hired her crews without providing any information to Chuntao, and sorted out her own supplies, taking time in country to set up a job. It was swings and roundabouts, but she preferred to arrange her own logistics – except of course when it came to documentation such as passports, although even that was a two-edged sword.

This occasion was different – she wanted to get on with the job and time was pressing. If she had to hit Tobin when he was in England or Australia, then safe travel for her would be much more difficult. Now was the best opportunity, in Greece.

The more she considered the facts, the more difficult the assignment appeared. Assassination was straightforward, but interrogation required time and patience, and an undisturbed environment. If the prisoner knew that time was short, then that could work against the interrogator – depending on, of course, how frightened the prisoner was – or she could make him.

Many of her other assignments for the Chinese had involved interrogation, but she'd always found the solution to access and time. In a couple of notable instances though, the targets had expired before the information was forthcoming – several of her targets had been middle aged businessmen not in the best of health. Percentage-wise, her record was good. She didn't want to lose another target prematurely, and struggled to improve the plan she was starting to sketch out in her mind.

She met Mannesmann in Athens on 16th. They stayed in separate hotels, and then moved down to Piraeus.

When she had arrived at her hotel in Athens she followed her usual security protocol including setting up her pinhead wifi webcam - it had saved her life more than once, and cost one person his life, painfully and slowly. She googled up a nearby business mail drop and sent the address to Chuntao. It was a pointless exercise really – she knew that her hotel and every move would be tracked by Chuntao, though she had no idea that she was tagged with a GPS locator in the nanochip buried near her spinal column. She strongly suspected, though, that the Chinese had implanted something in her body, probably when she did her 'induction' in China, all those years ago.

An hour after she had checked in to the hotel she received a secure text providing an address. Then the reception desk called and she received a small packet – a bubble wrap envelope. It contained two keys.

She checked the address on Google – it was on the edge of Athens in an industrial park at a secure storage business, relatively simple to get to in a hire car. She checked the other businesses on the estate under the Kelly business listing and then called a hire car company. After breakfast the next morning she headed out, walked two blocks and hailed a taxi, one of those Greek robbers on wheels. She wanted to retrieve the gear and re-store it elsewhere before Michael arrived later that day.

This taxi driver didn't look remotely like a Greek – Pakistani was more likely.

"You speak English?"
"A little, yes."
"Well, this isn't the way to the address I gave you."
"Yes, is, I know short cut."

"This is no shortcut" she replied as they stopped at a set of traffic lights. She leaned forward and put her hands around his flabby throat.

"Nobody cheats me, ok, you fucking Moslem fuck!" in her rage reverting to her native Serbian tongue.

She squeezed, he struggled, tried to grab her head behind his, tried to pull her hands off, scratch her eyes. She counted slowly, out loud. He struggled. His foot slipped off the clutch and VW jerked forward and bumped gently into the car ahead. She reached ten, and released him. He was just alive and conscious, and his heart was just good enough to take the shock. She'd killed plenty of men, had got used to the feel of a body approaching death, and knew when to stop. The counting calmed her. Her spoken Greek was still basic, but enough to tell him he was lucky. She threw a twenty Euro note on the seat, and got out of the cab, sunglasses on, hat pulled low, and walked briskly away as the driver ahead got out of his car, shouting and gesticulating and the piled up traffic hooted behind.

Killing him would have complicated matters, and she was annoyed that the situation had maddened her to the point of action. She rarely if ever lost control of herself. Not good for business, not good at all – she was definitely changing, taking more risks. What was happening to her?

After a coffee three blocks further down the road, she hailed another cab. Straight to the address – those were her instructions to the driver, but as they turned into the industrial estate she told him to stop, paid him off and walked the last few hundred yards, telling herself to be extra careful. She retrieved the two holdalls from the secure store – it had been prepaid – and headed out of the business park. They were heavy, and she struggled a bit, cursing. Two hundred yards down the road she turned left and saw the olive exporting company. She checked her watch – she was a few minutes late. In the visitors car park was a white Peugeot 707, as arranged. The rental company man was sitting in the front seat with the aircon on, talking on his mobile phone. She tapped the window. He nodded, clicked the boot open and continued talking on his phone whilst Maruška put her bags in the boot, trying not to get mad, again. They drove back to the hire car office where a pleasant Greek girl photocopied her German driving licence, checked her passport and she completed the paperwork. She paid cash.

As she left the office, she clicked the link on her iLive phone, and after a struggle with the Athens traffic and incorrect directions from the iMove navigator app, she found the other storage depot and stored the bags after taking out a couple GPS microtags and a Glock pistol, with 2 spare clips.

Next was Michael. He should have arrived that morning, though she didn't know his travel arrangements, and didn't need to, though she doubted he'd fly into Spáta airport. A text came through just as she got back to the hotel. The phone number included in the text with 'Call me at' was not a Greek phone number, though it looked like one. It was a set of coordinates and a time. She checked her pistol.

Where do two people arrange to meet discreetly in Athens? The Parthenon? The Acropolis? Lovers perhaps, but not terrorists. Popular tourist sites are usually well covered with cameras. This team met in Zappeio Park, in a copse, though they were not being watched either by eyes or cameras.

At the moment of their meeting, Chuntao's laptop monitor screen in Beijing flashed a discreet box in the lower right hand corner, advising her that two of her agents were at the same location. She clicked the popup, and smiled. They shouldn't be together, ever, hence the warning popup. But she knew they would be, sooner or later that week, it was in the plan.

Piraeus Preparations

"So, are we on track?"

"Yes, I've got the equipment, and the ship's plans. We need to talk about the approach. We'll go to Piraeus this evening and check her out at the dock, maybe get some pictures. She's at a place called Flisvos, in the marina there."

"Have you got any idea where or how we'll hit them, or is this just another job without a plan?"

"I never work without a plan, so there is no need for your sarcasm!" Mannesmann saw her taught jawline and rising anger.

"What is happening to you *liebling*? You get mad so easily these days."

"There is nothing wrong with me! Just shut up and listen! I will outline the plan when we are travelling, but we obviously can't do this job at the dock in Piraeus. The ship is leaving tomorrow for Argostoli in Cephalonia. So, check out of your hotel – we will not be coming back to Athens. I'll check ferry times for the trip to Argostoli. There's a railway to Patraikos and we can get a ferry from there to Cephalonia. I've downloaded all the maps."

"I think we are too much in the dark. Where's she headed, how much do we know about her route, where the fuck is Cephalonia?" Mannesmann was sounding very dubious and his stilted English amplified his doubt further.

"What we know for sure is that her next port of call is Argostoli. Cephalonia is an island near Corfu – maybe you have heard of that?

"Yes, I heard about it. A decadent capitalist island."

"Your don't do humour Michael, it doesn't work for Germans. Anyway, the ship has booked a transit for the Corinth canal, which goes from this side of Greece to the other, for tomorrow afternoon. The canal is less than eight kilometres long and saves a day or two going round the coast. We can't take her in the canal, but we take the train and then a ferry across to Argostoli. I have access to her movement plans, The Greeks are bureaucratic about foreign boats in their waters. Come on Michael, you know how it is when we set up an operation, usually information is not perfect, and we improve the plan as we go. We'll be able to take her at one of the islands, maybe at an anchorage. I know small boats."

"*Schatzi*, we know zero about attacking a small ship. Small boats are different."

"I'm not your *schatzi,* Michael" she said angrily, emphasising the German pronunciation of his name, as if clearing her throat of something filthy.

"Perhaps, but I just want to be sure of the details. It's my life and freedom too."

"Naturally. As I said, we'll discuss it in the car, not out here. You wouldn't be here if you had no confidence in me or thought that the plan was suicidal."

Of course, there was another reason that he was there, and before he checked out of his hotel he sent an update to Beijing.

*

As they drove to the marina at Flisvos, they discussed the options. They didn't know what the plan was for the ship in the Ionian, but Maruška suggested that she might be able to chat up one of the crew in Argostoli, maybe talk to the harbour staff. "I checked the ship on the marine traffic website and her transponder is on, but it might not stay that way if they are conscious of security – and we know that they have a security team aboard. We will have to tag her ourselves and trail her in a hire boat."

"You are serious for sure, no? Go to sea? Us? I can swim well, but that's it."

"Well, there are ways. I know people in the area." Maruška knew she was not sounding convincing, and didn't want to get involved with Nicos but maybe there were ways, if he was dispensable.

"I know someone who has a boat, a big boat which he used for running weapons and drugs from North Africa into Greece. He has a good record and is trustworthy."

"That sounds better. I have to say that this operation is not getting off to a good start. Everything is so rushed, it is not thought through in detail. You said you had a plan."

Fucking Germans she thought, though she knew he was right. The rush was all on her side. Why was she pushing so hard, taking risks? And why was he being so abrasive?

"Well, Michael, that's why you are here – two brains are better than one." He did not appear flattered. "I checked out some hotels on the web and put them in the navigator. I don't think there's a risk if we stay in the same hotel." He looked at her and raised his eyebrows. "No, definitely not", she said. "Turn the volume up and let's get directions through this fucking traffic."

"Ah, remember Pristina?" he said, *sotto voce*. She didn't hear him.

*

They checked into the hotel in Flisvos. It wasn't outstanding, but discreet was what they needed and discreet was what they got.

Maruška took the usual care about not leaving traces in her room and rigged her pinhead webcam.

Michael updated Chuntao, whose tagging database had been continuously flagging the co-incident locations of these two of her agents.

Then, an hour or so later, about 6.30, they met in the hotel lobby and wandered down to Flisvos Marina, pretending to be a holiday couple – though it looked more as if they had fallen out, as couples often do on holiday. The sun was setting and Maruška wanted to get some pictures of the ship before it was too dark.

They were impressed, and who wouldn't be, by $60 million worth of motor yacht? There was red carpet alongside her on the quay, 200 feet of it, with brass posts and red rope keeping the public at bay. It looked like film première night in Times Square. Her dark blue hull was gleaming, and there were five decks above the waterline, with an open bridge atop, behind which was a helipad, complete with a Bell Jet Ranger Mk9 helicopter. The bridge mast gantry bristled with antennae and satellite dishes, which Michael captured in one of their innocent holiday pictures. A crew member in uniform was sitting at a table at the top of the wide boarding steps, which had a stainless steel chain across the access opening in the deck rail.

The unconvincing couple posed for each other near the stern, taking in the docking platform and crew entrance below the aft deck, with its own *passarrelle* for access. Then they meandered along her length. Some crew – these were dressed differently to the others – were on the foredeck. She and Michael further along the dockside then stopped for some more photographs.

"She is beautiful" Michael said, as they ate moussaka in a taverna an hour later, with a bottle of retsina between them, looking across the road at Tobin's superyacht.

"Well, he will not own it for much longer. I wonder what his will says. He has no wife or children."

"Who were those men on the foredeck?"

"Probably the security team."

"*Jawohl*, they really did not look like guests. *Scheisse*, this is not good for the operation."

"Ok, ok. You are right. There has been much to arrange and prepare in a short time. What I know is that the normal crew is the captain, Bill Johnson, then a first and second officer, two engineers, 3 seamen, a chef, a steward and stewardess."

"Those men on the deck had the look about them – you know what I mean – military, capable."

"Yes, they could be a problem which we will have to solve. We'll look at the pictures back at the hotel. See what we're up against."

Just then her smartphone jingled and she looked at the screen. An urgent email from Chuntao. She didn't open it.

"A problem?"

"No, just a friend."

"Marie, you don't have friends. I don't have friends. It's too dangerous, and we are not social people anyway. It's not in our nature to get close to people."

"Yes, in theory, but you know how it is. Shall I say an acquaintance then – just like you?"

"As you wish." He was clearly uneasy.

*

Back at the hotel the news from Chuntao was not good. Some hacking had revealed that the additional crew were provided on contract from a respected, efficient and discreet security company called *Scutum Est* which usually employed ex-forces staff. There were believed to be four, possibly six extra staff aboard. They should be considered very able, and well-armed. There were no indications that the extra security was related to Maruška's operation. The internal security at *Scutum Est* was first-rate and had so far proved impenetrable to the Guoanbu. It would take more time.

"Shit, shit, shit" she said to herself. More risk. Should I abort? She checked all her tell-tales and her webcam – no intrusion, and she felt clean, unobserved and under the radar. No, the plan would go ahead. There would be plenty of opportunity to abort.

She called Mannesmann and they arranged to go over the travel arrangements and ships plans, and of course, the photographs. While she was waiting for him she connected to one of her private cloud websites where she stored encrypted contact and other information such as bank account details, passwords and so on. She moved the data from one site to another before each assignment, no longer relying on the technology she carried – it could be stolen, fall under a bus or just fail. Her data was spread about the cloud behind the Onion Ring and was as secure as anything could be, although the several government agencies had cracked it. She found Nicos's details and decoded them, then transferred the dockside pictures to her iPad.

There was a knock at the door which told her it was Mannesmann and she let him in.

They sat at the table and reviewed the data. The pictures gave them no clues as to the men on deck – they all seemed to be looking somewhere else and had hands to faces or beer glasses obscuring a direct image.

"They are careful, professional, not wanting to be in someone's holiday pictures" he said. "This may affect our plans. Do you have any information about them?" Chuntao was not sharing any operational intelligence with Mannesmann, as that could complicate or compromise what she had planned for him. All information went through Maruška.

"None" Maruška lied, "and yes they are careful. I will try to find out more." It sounded thin, and it was. "With careful timing and planning we can take them. You know how to do it, with your training."

"The Army was many years ago. Tactics have changed. I never trained to assault a ship. We need more people to do this."

"No, no others. We will do this alone." she said, with finality.

"Your plan will have to be very good if you want me to work with you on this."

"My plan is very good – I have gas, night vision gear on top of the usual equipment. We will have everything we need. Even suits to swim in. Stop worrying." She smiled at him, not feeling as confident as she looked, and changed the subject. "I need to contact someone I knew in Greece, the smuggler with the fishing trawler. He knew me before I left Serbia. He will be thinking the woman he knew from the SNP is dead. He needs some time to get used to the idea that I am still alive."

"Will he cooperate?"

"Yes, for sure. He may not want to, but he will."

"That's good. What about travel?"

"There are trains every 90 minutes to Patraikos. I think we will have breakfast in that café at the dock. It will give us another chance to see the ship. She is checked out to leave at 10 am. Then we can leave to pick up the equipment and go to the train station."

"We need to tag the ship."

"I have magnetic GPS tags."

"Putting them on the ship is the problem."

"Yes, Michael. That's why I have you with me. You have no plans for the rest of the evening?"

"Take these then, we'll use two to be sure. Don't forget to switch them on – the batteries don't last forever." They were each about the size of a 50 cent coin.

"And exactly what will you be doing while I'm fixing the tags and contacting this man Nicos?"

"I will be working to reduce the risks – checking maps of the islands, finding charts, looking at the layout of Argostoli, booking hotels, checking boat hire, ferry tickets, firming up the plan…"

"What plan? There's nothing solid that you have told me. This is not a plan. This is *scheisse.*"

"Flexibility, that is the key to this, keep on their tail and then hit them when the opportunity presents itself. Taking over his ship is a constant – only the location may change. It's not as if he could be in any hotel. The layout of the ship is fixed, wherever it is. That's what we focus on, that and access to the ship."

"Yes, I can see your point. You are right and you are also wrong. In the Stasi I was trained as a mountain and winter warfare specialist, nothing with boats, maybe that is what is making me think that this is not a workable plan."

"It's not like you to admit to any nervousness."

"I am not nervous, let us just say that it is caution. I want to stay alive."

"Don't we all?"

"I'm not sure – sometimes I think you have a death wish. So many risks!"

"This discussion is not taking us anywhere. Let's look at the ship's plans. Here is a copy for you" she said, handing him an inductive memory patch for his tablet computer.

"Well, there's our first problem", he said, "it says here 'Hull construction 20 mm aluminium below load waterline, 15 mm above load waterline, whatever that is. You have given me magnetic GPS tags. Aluminium is not magnetic. This is not good. I do not know ships but metals I do know. Schoolboy stuff."

"I don't want to hear about problems Michael, I want solutions. Haven't you used these before? Peel the plastic backing off and they have a glue pad."

"Ok, ok, I will find a way. I hope the glue works in water. Suppose they fall off? It all adds to the risk."

They spent another half an hour discussing the ship's layout, finding the best access points, and starting to commit the layout to memory.

"I am going now", he said, getting out of his chair just after 11 pm. "I have to put these tags somewhere on the ship. Just a minor detail." Late at night his sarcasm was lost on her – Germans were not the best at delivering it.

"OK I will see you in the lobby at 8 am, then. Goodnight Michael."

As she closed her hotel room door, Maruška wondered why he was sticking with it when it was looking more like a mission doomed to failure.

*

Mannesmann went back to his room and changed into black jeans and blue shirt, with a lightweight black blouson. With a squeeze of the plastic case he switched the first tag on – the micro LED blinked once only, it would not blink again and he knew it was active. Then the second one. That was one less detail to worry about later. He left the hotel with only the tags, a couple of hundred euros and no plan.

He strolled back to the dockside kafeneion and sat at a table outside in the warm night air, still heavy with fumes after the rush hour. Looking across at *Auric Adventurer,* he worked slowly through a heavy Greek coffee.

There were a couple of guys on the next table, and he picked up on the tail end of their conversation as they rose, throwing some Euros on the table. All he caught were the words:

..".thought it would be a joyride Bill, but all the extra security – what's it all about?"

Then the other man:

"Buggered if I know, Robinson's keeping it close to his chest, but what I do know is that…"

At that point, Mannesmann lost track as they headed across the quay to *Adventurer's* gangplank.

He sipped his coffee and wondered whether he would tell Marie. Maybe the extra security would do the job for him at the right time."

Next the tags, what was he to do?

*

Just after 8.00 am, Maruška and Michael were seated in the kafeneion with pastries and coffee. Some guys in shorts and T shirts came running up the quay and turned up the gangplank at the stern to the crews entrance.

Marie did a double-take, her eyes wide open, and Michael noticed. "What is it?"

"Nothing, just that they are fit and look professional. They must be two of the group we saw on deck yesterday. The other two are up there - one on the bridge and one on the foredeck."

Michael slowly glanced up and could see two men apparently talking to no-one. "Definitely security" he said, "they are using wifi communicators."

Maruška's didn't hear him, her brain was spinning. It was too much of a coincidence, and she dismissed the notion that it could have been her old enemy. She snapped back to reality.

"So, you got the tags aboard?" The question was rhetorical, she'd checked the location with her iPhone, as had he. Both tags were transmitting, and the iPhone App put their range at less than 100 metres, in the direction of the *Adventurer*. Maruška also knew that they had been activated at that location since just after one am.

"You checked them?" he said.

"Of course. How did you get them aboard?"

"One went onto the underside of the ship's dumpster which was on the quayside for emptying. And the other..."

There was a shouted order heard through the ship's tannoy and they looked up to see the *Adventurer's* hydraulic gangplanks being retracted and stowed, as her main engines started. The red carpet had disappeared. Michael could see two men on the flying bridge, and thought that they were probably those from the night before, though he couldn't see them distinctly.

"Security – one at the front and one at the back on the walk-around deck" Maruška said quietly, with distinctly non-nautical language.

"No sign of any others."

"Probably two on and two off duty then. Four in total as we thought last night."

"There were five in the pictures."

"Don't forget that the ship's crew includes a permanent security manager. Name of Robinson, that's my information."

"Yes, yes of course."

"That must be the ship's permanent security man, there, look, just coming out onto the deck. Dressed differently to the others, and not in white uniform like those two on the top giving orders."

The other two men – the runners whom they had seen returning fifteen minutes earlier, came out on to the aft deck.

The lines were now being cast off, and Maruška stood up to pose on the pavement at the cafe, with her back turned to the ship, as the crew organised the lines and the *Adventurer* slowly moved away from the dock.

"They are leaving early. Take some pictures, now, then we'll pick up our gear and catch our train."

*

Fiskardo

The Ionian Sea, off the west coast of Greece, is the source of many legends. The islands of Ithaca and Cephalonia are as close as brother and sister, with Levkas to the north and Zakynthos to the south – the islands are written about in Greek mythology; the scenery is wonderful, the summer weather benign. South of Levkas, the area is known as the Inland Sea - a popular cruising ground for charter yachts with families, and for billionaires and their political intimates.

It is here, where the high peaks and ridges, keepers of so many summer lightning displays, and so many winter snow cloaks, slope coarsely into the Inland Sea.

It is here that Aristotle Onassis bought his own island of Skorpios. This is the island where Jackie Onassis, the former first lady of the United States, spent much of her later life as Onassis's wife, alone in her simple beach cottage, swimming daily off the south beach where family charter boats now anchor for lunch after their own swimming in the crystal clear azure waters.

Perfect it may be for many people, but it was not Onassis's first choice. Before Skorpios, he had spent many years attempting to buy the town of Fiskardo at the northern end of Cephalonia, just a few miles west of Ithaca from where Odysseus is said to have set out on his Odyssey.

From Skorpios, Cephalonia lies about eighteen miles southwest, down through the stunning Stenon Meganisiou (Meganisi Channel). On the west side of the narrow passage, the goat farmed hills of Levkas rise to almost 1200 metres, with the much lower ink-blot shaped idyll of Meganisi with its olive groves, to the east.

*

Cephalonia is the largest of the Ionian islands, and is the highest, having a rugged backbone running from north to south, with Mount Nero, the highest in the Ionian, rising to over 1,600m.

The Ionian Islands have a close affinity with Italy, and during the Second World War they were an 'easy win' for Mussolini's Alpine Division. *'Il Duce'* was seeking to elevate his status in Hitler's eyes and a successful invasion seemed like a good idea. In Cephalonia, the Italians' control, with about ten thousand troops, was never total, and the eventual outcome was totally unexpected.

In 1943, Hitler sent in his own forces. There was a bloody confrontation as the Italians fought the Germans over the course of a week, and only three thousand Italian Alpine troops survived. For their defence of the Greeks, these survivors were lined up and shot, reportedly on Hitler's direct order. A few dozen survived, and it is said that one swum the channel from Cephalonia to Ithaca.

Today, the affinity with Italy is as strong as ever, and Ferries between Greece and Italy thread their way through the islands several times daily. The area has an affinity with Britain too, as an ex-governing power, and cricket is still played there.

The island is, as is the whole area, prone to earthquakes, with the last major earthquake in Levkas in 2015.

*

Onassis dispensed his largesse with the locals in the town of Fiskardo, and courted the politicians, but buying Fiskardo could not be achieved by him.

Despite all his power and wealth, the objections of the Greek Orthodox Church and some resistant landowners prevented him buying the town and making his base there. Not even earthquakes could change things in Fiskardo as it 'floats' on a base of clay which makes it relatively immune from earthquake shock waves.

Sicilian Channel

The town has a small harbour, facing east, rectangular in shape, looking across the channel Stenon Ithakis, towards Ithaca. The summer afternoon winds come up quickly and blow strongly down this channel past the haven. From the tavernas, a short walk past the ferry terminal and through the pinewoods leads to an old Venetian lighthouse and a Norman Church. The tide of invaders, religions and cultures has ebbed and flowed here through the centuries.

These days, Fiskardo is known as Chelsea on Sea.

In summer, it is packed with tourists and sailors of all nationalities.

In winter, it has population of about fifty, braving the cold north-easterly winds which blast across the Inland Sea from the high mainland.

In summer, tourists and their cars arrive by ferry in the congested harbour, met by the local police just in case any undesirables should deign to visit this jewel. The tide of charter boats ebbs and flows daily, anchoring stern-to at the quays after entertaining manoeuvres with cross anchor chains and gusty winds. Some just tie up to a handy rock. The crews eat and drink at the harbour-side tavernas, or at Nicholas's Taverna, on a hill overlooking the harbour from the north. The next morning, with sore heads, they untangle their anchors from their neighbours and depart for the next jewel, the next taverna in the tiara of jewels that is the Inland Sea.

In winter, no-one comes to Fiskardo, but snowstorms are regular visitors as the biting northeast wind sweeps down from the Russian steppes over the rugged mountains of Greece.

The town enjoys the reputation of being the only town on Cephalonia which was not flattened in the 1953 earthquake. Therefore, its architectural charm continues undisturbed, whereas the other towns such as Sami, Ay Euphemia and the capital Argostoli, are bland in their building, cheap in their architecture and impoverished in their personalities – some even built with wooden frames and tin sheet walls which are much cheaper to reconstruct after earthquakes.

To the south of Fiskardo is a bay where the water boats used to tie up in the days when fresh water was transported from the mainland, the days before reverse osmosis water purifiers, the days when life was much more basic. Between this dilapidated water pier and Fiskardo are some shallow bays, little more than indents. These inlets are overlooked by detached houses set in the trees – summer houses for the very rich and ordinary-rich. These baylets are where the visiting motor yachts of the very wealthy anchor briefly during their summer meanderings in this paradise.

They anchor because they are too big to enter the harbour at Fiskardo; they anchor briefly, because there is so much to see, and never enough time.

Once anchored their smartly uniformed crews launch their gleaming tenders and ferry their owners and guests into the trinket shops and tavernas at Fiskardo, a voyage of no more than a few hundred yards.

They depart the next afternoon after lunch – there is not much to see in Fiskardo and an hour or two is plenty of time to browse the expensive jewellers and overpriced gift and designer fashion boutiques. The wealthy continue their sightseeing itineraries through the Inland Sea.

The setting of Fiskardo, though, is memorable, though it is to the blasé perhaps just one more memorable setting in paradise and many more to be visited.

It was one such lazy afternoon, just as the northerly breeze down the channel was setting in strongly and the whitecaps were staring to tumble, that *Auric Adventurer* dropped anchor in 20 meters of water just off one of these bays. Charles Tobin was in town.

*

Sicilian Channel

Tobin's Gulfstream had flow him from Southampton into Argostoli, the international airport, two days before. Argostoli is at the southern end of the island, about twenty miles away from Fiskardo as the crow flies, flying high to cross the spine of the island which averages 1,000 metres high. By yacht, the distance was forty miles west-about, but that was not the prettiest route. The passage east about the island, up the Ithaca Channel, was more than sixty miles, but the scenery was stunning. The passage was best done in the morning, before the fresh afternoon winds set in between the islands. As is often the way with such people, Tobin missed most of it. He was on the phone, with Richard Thompson next to him at his desk in his private office, as they prepared for their meeting.

After picking up Richard Thompson from the airport, the *Adventurer's* First Officer, Sam Pritchard, had driven him back to the motor yacht which was occupying a berth at the ship terminal in Argostoli. No cruise vessels were expected for a few days, and there was no need to lie at anchor.

The day had not started smoothly. At 08.00 that morning, the *Adventurer's* master, Bill Johnson and Sam Pritchard had met as usual at the change of watch, to discuss the day's plan.

"I'm not a pimp, Bill. I'm supposed to be your First Officer, not Tobin's tit taximan."

"These girls – ladies - are old friends of Tobin's. You've met them before – last year in Antibes."

"How could I forget! Diana and Pippa – consummate professionals of the highest order – and cost, I'll bet. If I had his money I'd be changing them regularly."

"You're not him, you don't have his money and I'm beginning to doubt your intelligence!"

"I'm not employed to ferry his fuckbuddies about. Send one of the stewards."

"You are here to follow my orders, Sam. Anyway, the rental cars are not insured for the stewards."

"Fuck that - this is Greece. Anything goes out here in the sticks. Thompson is fine, but the birds wind me up."

"Pulling your plonker then are they?" Johnson couldn't resist the dig.

"Bugger it, Bill, it's just not on."

"Look, it's got to be done. Do it, that's my final word. Pick up Thompson, 10.05 arrival from Gatwick, bring him back, then go get the women from the 11.30 Paris arrival. We will be waiting to cast off as soon as you are aboard. The boss is itching to get going."

Pritchard acquiesced grudgingly, though Bill knew he shouldn't have had the little dig. Sam was uncomfortable with these women, but Bill hadn't yet figured out why.

It was a golden rule – in fact a contractual term - not to get involved with the guests, especially Tobin's. If Sam couldn't see that, then he'd never run his own ship. Involvement with the crew was a different matter. There were two girls aboard – a deckhand/stewardess and a stewardess. They were professionals both, young, smart and doing the job that enabled them to travel and be in the right places with the right people, even if only in reality they were servants. Sam could play with them whichever way he swung. The pay wasn't brilliant, but then the compensations were pretty good for the young and carefree. There were no entanglements yet as far as Bill knew, and the field there was open for Sam. Johnson knew he'd find out given time, but hoped he could forestall any potential trouble.

Next job that morning was a meeting with Tobin's ship security manager, Mike Robinson, to review the plan for the next few days. Nothing significant was expected for the new team to do – the main guests (that is, those for whom the security had been arranged) would be arriving after the weekend, at sea. The 'hard squad' had been smaller than planned – only four had shown. The other two were, apparently, 'unavoidably detained.' Bill had not enquired further, and Mike was not saying. Certainly, from what he'd seen of the four, they would be capable of taking on a small army. Provided, of course, that they had weapons. That subject was on the agenda for the meeting.

The extra security team had been picked up at Piraeus almost a week previously, and had familiarised themselves with the ship and the crew on the leisurely trip through the Corinth Canal and on through the Gulfs of Corinth and Patraikos. Boredom could have been an issue, but 'waiting' was an art that soldiers perfected and these guys clearly knew how to wait. Two of them were familiar with boats – one seemed to be very experienced - and the others could handle a RIB skilfully. Bill hadn't asked how or where they had learned their boatmanship. Their CV's were sketchy – they had all served in the forces – one French, two British and one US. Rick Borthwick, their leader (or was it manager?) didn't volunteer much information. They were fitness fanatics though, and had used the ship's gym when at sea as there were no guests aboard. Bill's only concern was that they would wear out the equipment – they really did go at it.

At Argostoli, they'd gone off each morning to 'run up hills' as Borthwick had described it. To Johnson, the 'hills' to the east of the harbour looked like mountains, tough even for goats. 'Keeps them out my hair' he thought.

Superficially, security was apparently fairly low-level on the *Adventurer,* though there was much more than met the eye. Important guests brought their own security, and Tobin occasionally had Reed aboard with him – the company head of security. Reed was a manager, not a hardman, more into IT security than head-butting. The previous head of security, Matt Hardacre, had been the other kind and had been sacked under a big cloud after the attack on one of his production platforms in the Red Sea - Tobin would not have his name mentioned.

The usual security issues - when Tobin was not aboard – had been about preventing theft and stopping rats – human or rodent - from getting aboard. The last year, though, since his production platform had been attacked, had seen a step change in the already security-obsessed Tobin. New secure comms equipment had been installed using high-bandwidth broadband satellite comms on private (and hugely expensive) satellites owned by NewsCorp; all the existing crew had been re-vetted by Reed (who also personally checked out all new crew, thoroughly, before Johnson could employ them). No casual crew were permitted, which was a real problem for the skipper, as crew illness and holidays could not easily be covered.

The anti-piracy plan had been reviewed and updated, and the crew trained. The ship was swept monthly for bugs and after any visitors, even tradesmen. All radios were checked (the handheld VHF radios were scrapped every three months and new ones bought in), computers dismantled, crushed and replaced quarterly. The crew were given smartphones and their personal phones were locked away with batteries removed. These responsibilities had added significantly to Johnson's workload, and he was still waiting for the salary raise that the obsessive Tobin had promised.

Finally, after complaints to Reed that he should be doing more to relieve the security workload, Johnson had a head to head with Tobin with the result that Mike Robinson had been employed. He reported to Reed, and of course, to Tobin. He was now in charge of ship security, and lived aboard. Smart and fit, with a naval background ('don't ask' Reed had said to Johnson) he was a positive addition. He doubled up as a second engineer ('degree in engineering at university old boy' he had once quipped to Johnson when asked about his skills). Much to Johnson's surprise he had once dismantled and repaired a fuel injector pump which the Chief engineer had given up on.

Over the previous winter, *Adventurer* had spent three weeks up on a slipway at Manoel Island Shipyard in Malta for maintenance. The crew took holiday, but Johnson's work did not stop, neither did Robinson's. Whilst there, a secure arms locker had been welded into the hull, and discreet 'panic buttons' wired in around the ship. Other concealed 'lockboxes' were fitted in strategic locations around the motor yacht.

The owner's mini-sub – a commonplace anti-piracy measure on megayachts – had been overhauled and re-certified, and the 'citadel' – the owner's panic room – had been re-worked and updated.

Stocking up the arms locker had been an interesting exercise, involving a rendezvous at sea. Johnson and Pritchard had been sent on a 'Security Course' which included familiarisation with a selection of pistols and shotguns. It seemed that Mike Robinson had no need of the course. Bill was not happy about having this training – if you knew how to use a gun, then you were more likely to do so, and once you raised a gun you increased your own chances of death significantly. Robinson thought it a waste of time 'I could have given you that course' he told Bill. However, in the modern world, with a prominent, even infamous, owner, this training was the norm. It went with the territory.

The issues about declaring weapons to authorities were significant, but in general customs officers knew that on *bone fide* vessels the security was adequate, and did not want to be bothered with the paperwork. In most countries it was illegal weapons that were the problem. The British authorisation for weapons on the ship extended only to tasars and pistols, although there were shotguns for the skeet-shooting pleasure of guests. That was the official authorisation. The reality was quite different.

Knowledge of, and access to the weapons store was restricted to Johnson, Pritchard and Robinson - and, of course, to Tobin.

Tobin was capable with pistols and rifles. His knowledge extended back to periods of his youth in Bendigo, Australia, shooting dingo and 'roos. When, after college, he had cut his family ties, left his gold-mining inheritance and gone to make his own fortune in Alaska, carrying a gun had been fairly normal, required even - if one was working out in the country and bears were about a man needed a gun to stay alive. And it had to be a man's gun to stop an Alaskan brown bear. So, Tobin took a close interest in these arrangements on *Auric Adventurer*.

*

Once the guests were aboard, the *Adventurer* cast off from the quay at Argostoli on time and turned out of the small bay first heading south, then south east passing the airport, to weather the rocks off Ag Pelagia Point. After another fifteen miles on that course they would pass outside Kakava Reef, off Mounta Point, the most southerly part of Cephalonia, and round the corner of the island at Kapros Point, coming on to a north-north-westerly heading for the magnificent final twenty five mile stretch up the Ithaca Channel to Fiskardo. Johnson had allowed three hours for trip to the anchorage at Fiskardo.

The wind was light south-westerly, and the air warm - over 30 centigrade - as they approached Mounta Point, overtaking a gentle westerly swell. The girls had unpacked and were in the lounger area on the foredeck, topping up their all-over tans; *Auric Adventurer* was loving the conditions, twenty five knots and just a gentle pitching. Johnson was on the bridge – he and Pritchard knew this area well, and had a bet on as to how long the girls would last after they rounded Mounta Point. They knew what was coming.

What had been a gentle breeze from ahead changed as they turned. The afternoon breeze was well set-in down the Ithaca Channel when they got to Kapros Point, and twenty knots of wind, added to the twenty five knot slipstream of *Adventurer* gave the ladies a rapid chilling - despite the windscreen - and they ran shrieking in through the forward companionway as the *Adventurer* thundered into the short, choppy sea and warm spray flew. Johnson put a waypoint on the chart plotter and measured. It was nearer to Pritchard's guess, and he handed Sam a €10 note in settlement of their bet.

"I told you they would never stay on the foredeck for the extra two miles" Sam said to Bill as he pocketed the note with a laugh.

"Don't get too cocky yet – I've got plenty of time to win it back!"

"Not today – we'll be anchoring off Fiskardo within the hour."

"Well, they're here for at least a week anyway, and the Boss might want them here longer."

*

Buried with Byron

Sally Burnside was an only child and had been brought up in Dorchester. From a young age she had sailed out of Weymouth with her parents on a variety of small family yachts, and she had qualified as a Yachtmaster whilst tasking a degree in English Literature at Exeter University. After graduating she headed off to the Ionian to work as a contract stewardess on luxury yachts whilst pondering a future career. Her first engagement was on the *Auric Adventurer*.

She was off duty on the evening that Tobin and his guests had gone ashore for dinner at the Cafe Nicholas overlooking Fiskardo harbour. They had been accompanied by Baldwin and Henri. Robinson had the night off and accompanied Bill Johnson in the RIB into Fiskardo for a some local beers, leaving Pritchard on watch with Sally and Terry, the seaman, aboard, along with Nicola, the other stewardess.

"Ok, they're down to minimum crew" said Maruška, lowering the binoculars. "The first officer is on the bridge, the others are below. Get the anchor up."

"This is madness."

"Be quiet Michael. We've been over the plan twenty times. We can take this ship easily. Our only major issue is the two remaining security men. They will be relaxed now that Tobin is ashore."

Maruška slipped the hired RIB into gear and without lights they headed out of the cove and looped around and across towards *Auric Adventurer,* approaching her from well astern. Near the stern Mannesmann slipped into the water and swam for the platform. Once aboard, he gave her the 'all clear' and she manoeuvred in to the platform. "We only go forward" said Maruška as her diver's knife sliced into the air tubes of the RIB. She stepped lithely onto the platform as the 250 horsepower engine on the rib dragged it quickly down through the shoal of fish gathered under the floodlight hull. "You are one mad bitch" whispered Mannesmann. Their adrenaline was coursing.

She grinned back "they have others here, and soon we shall have a ship. Come on, let's get started."

The crew quarters were up forward, but on a hot evening it was very possible that some would visit the foredeck for air and perhaps for a smoke, but Maruška's plan had factored in that possibility. Rear entry was her preference.

From the docking platform they made their way forward through the starboard 'boys toys' storage area. The intelligence provided by Wan Chuntao's team was that swipe cards and thumb prints were used to control internal access. Hacking had provided thumb print signatures of the skipper and first officer, who had ship-wide access. The plastic impressions prepared on a 3D printer in Piraeus worked faultlessly, and they gained access to the engine room. Forward of the engines and generators they located the air conditioning room. Using her smartphone, Maruška checked the ship's plans and nodded to Mannesmann. They identified the ventilation trunking to the crew quarters and he unscrewed an access panel. With a nod to each other they put on their gas masks and the gas canister was triggered in the ventilation duct which led to the forward part of the ship. Mannesmann reattached the panel as the blowers pushed the gas forward to the cabins of the crew. Then, they made their way to the promenade deck. With the owner and guests ashore, the chef was having a night off and the galley was clear. They checked the rest of the guest accommodation and headed towards the bridge.

Up on the bridge, Pritchard had stepped across to the washroom. As he stepped back in to the bridge he noticed the flashing red light as the VHF set on his belt vibrated gently. The computer knew that he couldn't be in two places at once.

Maruška rolled up her wet suit top to expose her chest and entered from the portside bridge wing whilst Mannesmann waited starboard-side. Pritchard turned at her whispered 'Psst', open mouthed at a woman in a gas mask with a very nice pair of breasts on display, then his mind clicked into gear and he dived for the panic button. He was too slow by half a second as Mannesmann stepped in behind him and the butt of the P228 pistol connected with his skull.

"The old tricks always work best" Mannesmann said as he wound the duct tape wound around Pritchard's limbs and over his mouth. "it's a long time since I've seen those. They've improved with age – what is it? Almost 20 years and not sagging yet?" He grinned wickedly. "Shut up you German pig" Maruška snapped back over her communicator. "You will certainly not see them again!"

They found the security camera monitor screens which confirmed that the deck area was clear. The security display showed them the onboard crew locations. Maruška located the video equipment and trashed it electronically with a magnetic pulse generator from her backpack. Wuntao would remotely locate and clean the Cloud backups.

They moved down the companionway through two decks to the crew quarters, checking each cabin in turn.

Dickwick and Aldo were unconscious, as were the others. Duct tape was liberally applied and cable ties were used to immobilise them. Sally Burnside's cabin was right for'ard and when Maruška opened the cabin door, Sally looked up in surprise and dropped her open copy of 'The Collected Works of Lord Byron' as the double tap from Maruška's silenced Chinese QSZ-92 pistol killed her before she could utter a sound.

"Looks like the gas didn't get this far" Mannesmann said as he looked in over Maruška's shoulder.

"No, it was difficult to know how much to use. We've accounted for them all I think. Eight ashore, ten here."

They went back to the bridge to wait. They expected Tobin to be ashore for at least a couple of hours, and that his security would alert the ship before their return.

Maruška walked over to the watch seat where Pritchard was now conscious and looking at them. With her knife she sliced open the front of his trousers.

"This ship is now under my command. The other crew are all dead. If you do anything to jeopardise my mission I will kill you. Nod if you understand."

Pritchard's eyes widened with fear and surprise and he nodded. Her knife glinted under the bridge lights.

He closed his eyes, shaking his head as she moved the knife towards his groin and cut into his thigh with the knife. In just the right spot there was lots of pain and little blood. He struggled and screamed under the gag.

"Are you using duress codes?"

Pritchard shook his head.

"Are you telling me the truth?"

He nodded wildly. She believed him. He was a sailor not a soldier.

Maruška gave the instructions, and sat down to wait. Pritchard's eyes watered at the pain and his seemingly dead colleagues.

*

Tobin was in full flow at the table in Nicolas's Taverna. "Some Greek food can be quite good, and even the wines can be palatable at times." He was being his usual condescending self to the proprietor, Nicolas – named after his father who had founded the restaurant.

"It is good to have you visit us Mr Tobin, I hope you will return again soon."

"You know me Nicolas, if I'm in the Ionian I always stop in. I can always rely on your fish."

"Of course, we have the best."

"It is almost perfect, but from here I cannot see my ship. Can you move the Taverna before my next visit?" This was a standing joke between them.

"Of course Mr Tobin. For you anything is possible!" he replied laughing.

"You said that last time."

"Well, local permission is difficult to obtain. Maybe I will have the headland removed, and then you could see your ship?"

"Good idea Nicolas! The captain keeps telling me that the water is too deep to anchor further out – that would be the simplest solution. Anyway, we are leaving now."

"Will you need a taxi?"

"No, I think we can manage the few hundred yards to the harbour."

"Have a good holiday Mr Tobin. Please come back soon."

"We will, Nicolas, though this holiday is mostly work as usual."

"I'll drink to that" said Thompson, raising his glass, as the ladies raised their eyes to the heavens and nodded.

"That's enough cheek from you lot" said Tobin, smiling. "Let's get back and have some fun."

Tobin nodded across to Nicola on another table.

"We're ready to go. We're walking to the launch. Sort the bill out, would you Nicola, and leave a generous tip. Tell Johnson I want to move tonight, up to Corfu, for breakfast."

"Understood Mr Tobin. I'll take care of it." Nicola spoke to Steve and Henri who were waiting at a table outside. Steve called Pritchard on his hand held VHF and nodded to Henri.

Tobin spoke to the women who smiled at one another – Fiskardo was a bit of a backwater and there was more life and better shopping in Corfu.

"I didn't take this job to be a fucking gopher" Steve whispered to Henri.

Sicilian Channel

Henri shrugged. "Sometimes such things are necessary. The money is good anyway." Steve shook his head in resignation.

*

At 10.30 p.m. they heard Steve call "Adventurer, Adventurer, Alpha One here" over the VHF radio.

Mannesmann unwound the duct tape from Pritchard's mouth and handed him the VHF handset as Maruška pressed her knife against Pritchard's groin.

"Steve, Pritchard here."

There was a slight pause as Steve recognised the specific radio protocol.

"We'll be returning in 30 minutes"

"Roger that, I'll page Bill and Mike, they'll be back straight away."

"It's OK, they already know – Mr T wants to leave immediately for Corfu – he's told the Skipper."

"OK Steve, I'll rouse the crew and prepare. Adventurer Out."

Steve looked at Henri and raised his eyebrows. Henri nodded, almost imperceptibly.

*

As they walked downhill from the Taverna to the dock, they could see the ship's RIB tied up at the rear docking platform, under the floodlights. Henri swore softly and called the ship on the radio. "Adventurer, Alpha two here."

There was no reply. Henri tried again.

"Adventurer, if you read me can you get one of the crew down to take our lines, ETA 15 minutes?"

Maruška pushed knife harder against Pritchard's throat.

"Henri, Sam here. Will do."

"Adventurer, thanks, we're standing by."

Steve took his handheld radio out and keyed the security channel. Neither Dickwick nor Robinson was responding.

"What's the problem?" said Tobin, irritated at the delay.

"Just a routine security check, Sir, probably nothing. We'll just take some precautions."

"Come off it Baldwin, they're probably getting a coffee, get us back, man."

"No, Mr Tobin. We do it my way as long as I am on your security watch. You and your guests stay here for now, in one of the bars in a dark corner, we will come back for you shortly. I'll call Nicola when we know it's clear."

Tobin could judge men and could hear the steely edge in Baldwin's voice.

"Very well, carry on, it's what we pay you for."

"OK Sir. It's probably a minor hiccup, but just in case, this is what we are going to do."

*

Guests visiting the *Auric Adventurer* by launch usually docked at the rear platform. Built of teak and stainless steel, it led to a grand flight of twenty teak steps, thirty feet wide, up to the 'promenade deck'. On this deck lay the gymnasium, the day salon and the main dining room, with four principal guest suites at the forward end.

At the level of the docking platform to each side of the stairway, there was 'garage', in which were kept jet skis, scuba gear, windsurfers, a sailing dinghy, diving chariots and all the 'boys toys' thought necessary for the perfect holiday. The starboard-side garage ordinarily housed the launch and the two RIBs lived port-side.

*

The launch came in slowly at an angle and stopped gently against the fenders edging the docking platform nearer the open starboard garage. Henri jumped off, turned and crouched, pushing the launch off with his feet in one movement as he rolled across the platform raising his gun. The launch moved slowly forward with Nicola crouched at the wheel.

Steve took the launch forward to a watertight door which usually used for deliveries of stores and access by harbour pilots.

He undogged the door locks with his remote and boarded *Adventurer*. His weapon was ready as he made his way carefully through three decks to the bridge. He saw Pritchard bound in the chair, his trousers open and his thigh bleeding slowly. He cut the duct tape off and Pritchard gasped "The stern. Two of them – man and woman. Armed, tough, killed the others." Pritchard started freeing his feet.

"How's the leg?"

"Painful, but not bleeding badly. I don't need a tourniquet."

"OK."

Maruška and Mannesmann waited inside the starboard garage, hidden behind the jet skis. The garage lights were out, but the docking platform was starkly illuminated by two floodlights. Maruška heard the quiet words "*Grosse scheisse*" from Mannesmann on the other side of the garage as they watched Henri jump aboard and roll as the launch moved away with someone at the wheel, and someone forward. The numbers didn't add up. Why had the launch moved away?

"OK Sam, stay here, give me 60 seconds and then hit the Emergency button. You know where it's fitted. We want the public version, not the silent alarm." Steve turned and moved like a ghost, pout of the bridge and into the innards of the ship.

He slid easily down the companionway rails heading for the engine room and the stern docking platform.

*

She stepped out, gun raised, moving cautiously and still in the dark interior of the garage. Mannesmann was obscured to the starboard side still behind a rack with two jet skis one above the other.

Edging towards the stern, crouching, anticipating, her senses were sharply tuned. Then a siren wailed and all the lights came on. She was startled, and Mannesmann cursed.

Exposed in the light, she moved for cover as Steve burst through the door behind them staying low to the starboard side so that he and Henri would not be in crossfire. Mannesmann turned, keeping cover and snap shot at Steve, three quick panning shots, none finding target. There were no ricochets, just crunches as the bullets embedded themselves or passed through the lightweight carbon fibre structures.

Then Steve was on his knees, his gun barking sharply in contrast to the suppressed spitting of his targets' weapons. He could just see one black clad figure turning and staggering backward, brightly illuminated and in seeming slow motion. There was a diver's balaclava over the head. He saw the body twist and fall off the platform into the sea. Henri continued firing as Steve turned towards Mannesmann.

He was rolling now, under a windsurfer rack as another round crunched into the gear rack above his head. He returned fire, one, two, three shots connecting with metal.

Mannesmann was crouched, and he felt wetness on his arm. Then the smell. Petrol. *Scheisse*. He broke cover and ran for the stern platform as Henri fired. The two shots were well aimed, but Mannesmann was moving low, quickly and took them in his side as his momentum carried him into the sea. Henri turned and fired after the body which was disappearing under the surface. Dead or alive? He wondered but was not going after them.

"Henri, cease fire for Christ's sake. Petrol leak."

Steve grabbed a fire extinguisher and doused the leaking jet ski's pool of petrol with a blanket of foam.

"We need to check the rest of the ship. Pritchard says there were only two and the crew are dead."

It had been close, but shouldn't have been. Pritchard had gotten the message across, but security had failed.

*

After the attack Steve had freed the crew and given the vessel the all clear - the crew had nothing more than headaches and there appeared to be no immediate after effects from the gas.

Meanwhile Henri had taken one of the RIBs and dropped their pistols into the Ithaca Channel, ½ mile out where the water was over 150 metres deep. Bill Johnson went ashore with Robinson to brief Tobin who took the car with his guests and headed for a hotel in Argostoli.

Borthwick and his team carefully cleaned themselves and sanitised their story, but there was nothing that could be done about Sally Burnside – it had to be a police matter. Finally, the police were summoned and the next day the vessel was escorted to Argostoli.

*

James Marinero

Holed up in Cephalonia

She brought her gun up and moved towards the stern as soon as the lights went on and the siren sounded; she had seen the man leap off the launch and roll to starboard and tried to track him with her pistol, her eyes still adjusting to sudden illumination. Once, twice her gun fired with a flat 'psst' and then as she turned she felt the bullet hit her, its momentum accentuating her turn and upsetting her balance. She pirouetted, lacking the elegance of a ballerina, tumbling over the docking platform into the water, hearing more bullets smacking into the water around her. Her backpack was pulling her down as she kicked hard away from the lights and moved around to the side of the ship. She struggled to get her head above surface to breathe, the effects of adrenalin masking the pain of her wound.

Further along the side of the ship her hands found a spray rail on the hull and she rested briefly. She could hear the alarm on the ship, but knew that most of the crew were still captive below. After a few minutes, she set off for the shore – it was about 100 metres, she thought. Swimming sidestroke, it took her the best part of an hour and she dumped her gear when she was well clear of the ship. Daylight would show that it was the best part of a quarter of a mile – what little evening wind there was had shifted, the cold air rolling down from the mountains as the katabatic breeze increased and the ship swung on her anchor, away from land.

Coming ashore at a small headland, she climbed over the rocks which were slick with algae, slipping and cursing as she tried to avoid injury in the dark. Under an overhang, she rested for an hour and then washed her wound in seawater. The bullet had gone in along the muscle of her upper left arm and there was no exit wound. The bone was undamaged as far as she could tell and no major blood vessels had been torn, otherwise she would be dead, she grimly realised

What of Michael?

*

Twenty four hours later Maruška was getting ready to move. It had taken most of what had been left of the night, but she had found a house which, unusually, was closed up for the summer. One of the door locks was old and intruder-friendly. Very carefully, she had cracked it using her diver's knife.

She expected police to come calling. Sure enough, at first light they appeared, and after a cursory external check which missed the damaged doorlock, they left – apparently satisfied. Violent crime wasn't common in Fiskardo.

The house was a substantial property, but somewhat neglected. It was set in some myrtle trees overlooking the Ithaca Channel, a few hundred yards back from where she had come ashore. She could not see whether The *Adventurer* was still at anchor.

There was no food in the house, but she found some bottled water and an old first aid kit. She'd managed to dig the bullet out and patch the wound. Self-sufficiency was a way of life on a Serbian farm when she had been a child and she silently thanked her parents for the little knowledge they had been able to give her. They were dead – killed by Muslims, but she had avenged their deaths many times over.

The day was hot – the power supply was off and she kept the windows closed. From an upstairs window she'd finally spotted the *Adventurer* still at anchor with police divers and launches alongside. As she was watching the search continue, she remembered with a start that man she'd glimpsed as she'd been turning, shot and falling. She swore, a foul torrent in her native Serbian, words learned from the men of Vidovic's SNP in the mountains during the Bosnian war, words which were misogynistic and violently sexual, spat out like a man. There was no doubt. It had been Baldwin she had seen on the ship in Piraeus, and he was here.

What had Baldwin been doing there? She would dearly have loved to have settled that score, but instead she had ended up with a wound and a failed mission. At least, a mission postponed.

'You haven't beaten me yet, you bastards" she shouted, her words echoing around the house.

*

As the evening came on, her plan firmed up. She left the house and checked the outhouses. In one she found a moped with some petrol in the tank - that was a start.

Next she would check her hotel in Sami, just ten miles down the island. Hopefully the police would not yet have eliminated all other possibilities. The transient summer population of the island would present huge problems for them to check and cross check.

In a perverse way that one bullet in her arm had saved her life. Her plan had been risky and one way or another Mannesmann wasn't going to see the end of the mission. Where was he? He wouldn't willingly talk if he was alive, she knew that – it would open a Pandora's box beyond his control. It was a loose end she needed to tie off. Even so, everyone talked at some point, and if they had any inkling about his background then it would surely go up the security hierarchy and they would try everything to open him up.

"Remember the forest in Pristina?" His taunting phrase came back to her. He would pay for that too.

Baldwin was another loose end. Yes it was personal, but not in the same way as Mannesmann. With Michael it had been sexual at first and revenge was rational, but with Baldwin it was...well she didn't really know what it was, except that he seemed to make her become irrational when she thought of him. Killing him would be a profound thrill for her, and she looked forward to it.

*

After checking out of her hotel in Sami she had bought a tent and set up at a campsite near Argostoli. The web was full of the story, though details were scarce. There were suggestions that it was linked to Middle East terrorism and the immigrant problem. Tobin's name and his links to Saudi gold were prominent. She learned that one man was under guard in the local hospital, and that police had no details of his identity. He had sustained wounds in the shooting on the ship.

Three days later she had located Mannesmann.

Time bought relaxation, and the two guards outside the room in the hospital were bored. Despite the air conditioning it was hot – they were wearing combat gear and flak jackets. Just going for a piss took ten minutes, and it took one man all the rest of his life.

She savoured the moment, remembering the feeling. His MPG hung by his side, his cock in his hand, sighing as his stream strengthened into the urinal. The ceramic knife was in her hand – her left hand despite the weakness in her wounded arm – and then the brief, predictable struggle was quickly over. The blade had slipped in easily as she knew it would. A serrated ceramic edge with a keen point backed by several of kilos of pressure at the perfect spot broke through the initial resistance of thin cloth and skin. It sliced effortlessly through muscle and fat – too much for a man of his apparent fitness. It met the muscle of the heart on the left hand side towards the rear and penetrated cleanly.

She felt the warm blood – more in her imagination than reality as she was wearing gloves. Her imagination was vivid but there was no doubting that this furiously struggling body was oozing its life force over her.

Later, she would replay the sequence in her mind as she derived more physical pleasure. She would find no technical error in the execution, no tactical mis-step.

The approach from the rear was standard. He was wearing a protective vest – it would be the best of vests for sure, made from the latest aramid fibre with metal foam patches. It would be stab proof, bullet proof - .50 calibre excepted, or .44 magnum at close range when the percussive shock would be enough to kill. It was proof even against grenades and shrapnel. There was a collar to protect the critical areas around the neck, and other refinements. Still, it had to be wearable by a man with arms, legs and a head, and that was the opportunity.

After a wait, the other guard had called on the radio, and had then come to check when there was no response. With both bodies in the toilet and the 'Out of Order' notice still on the door, she squirted superglue into the handle mechanism. It was quiet at this time of night, and she wore a white coat, a stethoscope and heavy black framed spectacles.

Maruška had slipped into the room, with the syringe ready. As the plunger had slid smoothly in and the air went into his bloodstream she looked at him and said 'Remember the forest in Pristina?"

He had been barely conscious, too weak to struggle or to see the pleasure in her eyes. Although there was little time to prepare, she had been meticulous and was pleased with the execution – both of the operation and of Mannesmann.

It had been very risky, but now Mannesmann was a closed chapter. High risks were becoming addictive. But then, Senka, her alter-ego, knew that.

*

Mannesmann's death had caused some perplexity in Beijing. Wan Chuntao knew that he was dead – his light had gone out on her control screen, and the technology was infallible. The human body which powered the nanochip had expired, of that there could be no doubt. Tracking had recorded the proximity of Maruška and Mannesmann shortly before his death, Maruška had merely said that he'd been shot in the attempt to kidnap Tobin, she'd enquired at the hospital, but had been told he had died.

Her report of the operation had been accurate as far as Chuntao could determine from other sources within the police and intelligence agencies, but she doubted the truth of her agent's story.

Maruška had been gently reminded with more pain that the Tobin operation was very much a live operation and that results were required.

Over the years Maruška had paid a lot of money for the best investigations – x-rays, CAT scans and blood analyses - but still the cause of her back pain could not be found and she fully realized that Wan Chuntao controlled the pain - and her. Tobin's death was necessary business, but Baldwin's would be all pleasure.

*

Changes Aboard

A week after the attack, Sally Burnside's distraught parents buried her, thinking it fitting that she should rest on the same Ionian island as Lord Byron. The novice stewardess was the only fatality amongst the crew.

*

"Skipper, I've decided to look for another ship. I've looked at it all ways, and think it's time for me to move on. You only got threatened and locked up but I came close to having my ticket punched. Murder – that's more than enough for me. Sally – just shot, that really got to me."

"She was a bright spark with a great future whatever she'd chosen to do. I didn't know that you were so keen on her."

"I didn't touch her – not even a kiss – but I had hopes."

"It's Ok, Sam, I understand, I'll put the word out. A few of the other crew are leaving too – it's hardly surprising.

We'll be stuck in Argostoli until the Greeks say we can go. The Embassy says it'll be a few weeks until the police close the investigation. Having illicit weapons on the ship has not gone down well at all – it's been very awkward, even though Henri and Steve were not caught in possession. Anyway, I'm staying on – I've been with Mr T for years and I'm not bailing out now, but you – well you've only just made First Officer. Still, security experience will look good on your log."

"Not sure I wanted that kind of experience, Bill! I'm still limping."

"It did get a bit exciting. The security guys are cut up too."

"Yes, Henri told me. Baldwin isn't saying anything at all. Their story was a bit thin."

"Well, the police divers found the RIB and one pistol under the ship. God knows where the others are.

"He doesn't talk about it and the fact that there's a missing body is causing problems too. The guy in hospital is a real mystery man, though the police don't give much away. Tobin is spending a fortune trying to keep the press out of it, but it's pretty hopeless. We still don't know what gas they used, but it appears to have been innocuous. Sally might still be alive if she hadn't turned off the aircon in her cabin."

"There have been some heavy military types about – even the police are deferring to them."

"I don't know what's up, but I'd guess they are anti-terrorist."

"Christ, what have we got into?"

"Well, you're shipping out so it's not your worry anymore. Mr. T seems to attract a pretty rum crowd. The security guys are really on edge. I doubt that we've seen the end of it. Robinson's head is on the block too."

"I don't know why – the security protocols worked well."

"Maybe, but Mr T is not a happy man."

"Would you be?"

"No, that's why I'm moving on."

*

The bullets extracted from Mannesmann did not match the pistol found on the sea bottom, but did match those found in Sally Burnside's body. Baldwin and Henri had been swabbed for gunshot residue, but eventually the police had to accept the story that the intruders had got shot in their own crossfire. They did know that at least two weapons had been used and no blood had been found on the docking platform. Henri and Steve had spent an uncomfortable 48 hours in police custody saying little. The investigating magistrate was not convinced, but in the absence of any evidence they could not be held.

It took 3 weeks before the police had allowed them to leave Cephalonia, and Steve was fretting. Still, he had been paid in advance.

Steve Baldwin signed off his contract and headed back to Crete. Henri and the rest of the team stayed on with Mike Robinson whilst Bill Johnson recruited a new first officer and other crew. *Auric Adventurer* remained stuck in Argostoli while the grindingly slow wheels of Greek island police procedure turned.

Tobin had installed himself in a villa in Argostoli, chafing at his inability to leave the island. He had ranted at Robinson about 'useless security' and a review was held. A new team was being put together and Borthwick's contract was being terminated. The story was being kept tightly controlled. The weapons issue was kept under wraps, although a Bahamian permit for the ship to carry 'unspecified firearms for defence against piracy' was held ready by Tobin's lawyers.

Sally Burnside's parents were still pushing the police hard and Tobin's lawyers had their work cut out (and a big bag of money) to stop them talking to the press. It proved futile.

*

After arriving back on Crete following the Fiskardo fiasco Steve kept himself busy, avoiding any thoughts of Maruška, and even doubting that it could have been her that night.

Deep inside, he knew he was not mistaken.

He gave himself a couple of weeks to check Adèle over and make sure she was seaworthy. He reviewed his charts and pilot books, restocked his food lockers, fuel and water and with a fresh easterly wind forecast for the next four or five days, he prepared to leave. His plan was unchanged - to head west, with maybe a stop in Malta or Tunisia, even Sardinia if the winds were kind.

One evening, a few days before he was due to leave, he received an email from Dickwick, asking him to meet up with an old friend who would be looking him up in Siteia. The message said little more and Baldwin groaned inwardly as he deleted it. Fifteen minutes later he was stepping ashore on his way to 'O Passos' for supper.

"Hi Steve. Don't mind if I call you that do you?"

The man's voice was behind him. He hadn't seen him approach, hadn't known he was there. Caught, flat footed. He was getting old.

"Dick Borthwick should have let you know to expect me."

"I've got nothing to say. The last guy who approached me like this was never found. Stay away from me."

"Oh, but he was found. Tom Brown's body – or at least his skeleton - was found by a shepherd in the mountains south of Djibouti city, a couple of months after he disappeared. There wasn't much left, but we believe that he was butchered and then shot. 'Victim was bound with rope' is what the coroner's report said."

Steve looked at the man with little emotion visible in his eyes.

"Yes, confirmed by DNA. So, you can accept my *bona fides*. You can call me Cassidy, Mark Cassidy."

"What is this Cassidy? Want to shaft me again do you? Where's the Sundance Kid then? Fuck you and your kind. You lot have screwed around enough with me."

"I understand, and I won't bother appealing to your loyalty to King and Country, *etcetera*! However, I will appeal to your more base instincts if you have any. Let's try revenge. How about that? Did you know that the bloodstain on the stern of Tobin's ship shows a DNA match with one Maruška Pavkovic?"

Steve's eyes could not hide his surprise and his body tensed.

"There was no bloodstain."

"Oh but there was – you and Henri missed it in your clean-up. Yes, she nearly killed you in Djibouti but you shot her ear off. Unfinished business. Why not finish it? HMG would be very happy for you to terminate her. The order has been signed."

"Nobody signs orders for wet jobs."

"That's where you're wrong, but no matter."

Steve said nothing.

"And Steve, they still haven't found the second body. And that story of 'crossfire' – them shooting each other? That was a load of bollocks. Don't talk to me about Butch Cassidy and the Sundance Kid – your story had more holes than a fishing net. If it wasn't for our lot, you'd still be in a Greek jail with your pal."

"Look, Pavkovic is in the past. I don't need revenge."

"We got you out, we need you to find her. Maybe you don't need revenge, but the world needs to be protected from her and her kind. Let me tell you about the man with her – the guy you shot on Tobin's yacht. He was ex East German special forces, out of sight for over twelve years, untracked. He was found dead in his hospital bed two days ago. Cause of death an air embolism. There is no doubt that it was deliberate. Injected. He had a 24 hour guard – Greek anti-terrorist squad no less - CCTV, the works. She killed one of the guards with a knife when he was taking a piss. Expert job – we haven't seen the technique before. Black Widow we're tagging her. Don't pretend to look surprised - we have a pretty good idea how it went down on Tobin's yacht, almost first hand. Dickwick is my mate too, and he has a lot tied up in Government contracts. He put two and two together – once he'd recovered from the gas.

Now we are – in conjunction with our esteemed European security colleagues - starting to backtrack the movements of the mystery patient, recently deceased. Some very dirty business is showing on his CV."

"Look Butch or whatever your name is today, don't you get the message? I'm not interested, I don't do revenge, and I'm done doing any more favours for HMG. They still owe me for the last one."

"OK, for now, but think about Tom Brown and others like him who die painful deaths to keep you free to sail your yacht pretty much where ever you like. Malta next is it? Have fun. Give 'Decency' a thought. Tom was good guy, one of the best. I worked with him too." He offered his hand and Steve took it, nodding.

Cassidy held his hand with an iron grip and looked him in the eye. The 'cover' – if that's what it was – of being a tourist with a camera and a bag of shopping would fool many people. But that's what it was, just a cover. Baldwin could see that despite the man's slight build there was core strength, both mental a physical. A good man to have with you in a tight spot.

"We need your help, Baldwin."

With that, he released Steve's hand, turned and walked away. Steve headed on for 'Os Passos'. Tom dead – that was little surprise. He'd hardly known him anyway, but he knew the type. Those guys played it both ways when they ran agents. But that bitch Maruška – on the *Adventurer?* That was hard to believe, what was she doing *there*?

It felt like a night for Greek brandy. He ordered at the bar and eased onto a stool. Something felt very odd – he didn't usually carry a wallet. No, it was a mobile phone in his pocket that was causing the bulge.

"Bastard. How the hell had he done that?"

*

After more brandy and some of Cristos's special of the day, he looked at the weather chart in the newspaper. It was all Greek to him, but the chart at least was understandable.

It looked as if the incessant north-westerlies that they had experienced for the last ten days would swing to the north and then the north east, promising a few days to help him get started on the leg west towards Malta. It was almost 550 miles to the west – four to five days with good winds.

To the south of his planned course lay Libya and the Gulf of Sirte, to the north lay Sicily. He would have a current against him, which would tend to push him to the south., so it was important to stay to the north and not get pushed down towards Libya – that would add time and distance to the passage, and make it hard work if the wind went to the northwest again. He didn't enjoy sailing to windward – 'uphill' as some called it. Although Adèle was perfectly capable, it would be tiring for a single hander. He'd been to Libya anyway, way back at the end of Gaddafi's rule, and had no desire to return - Libya was a political disaster area.

Ahead was the Sicilian Channel.

*

The Sicilian Channel separates Europe and Africa. It was one of the very first intercontinental channels that humanity navigated. Unlike the Straits of Gibraltar or the Bosporus (which also separate continents and cultures), one side is not visible from the other. In the early days of navigation – thousands of years before the Phoenicians - when men sailed and rowed small craft, crossing this channel was usually accidental, certainly not by design.

The Channel has seen thousands of years of trade, wars and deaths deliberate and weather inspired. It has transported civilizations and cultures and has enriched and diversified the human gene-pool.

At its narrowest it is 77 nautical miles wide, between Cap Bon (the Good Cape) at the north east corner of Tunisia, and Capo Feto (Baby's Head) at the south west corner of Sicily. It is fringed by reefs, and is shallow, with an average depth of less than 100 metres.

The Channel divides the Mediterranean Sea into two distinct areas – the deep western basin between Gibraltar and Tunisia – close to 3,000 metres deep in places, and the eastern basin which is even deeper, exceeding 4,000 metres at a point equidistant from Libya, Sicily and Greece.

Not only does it divide continents and cultures, it divides the climate, with distinct difference between the weather experienced in the western and eastern basins of the Mediterranean.

Whilst the weather between the East and West basins might have its differences, the rapidly shallowing depths in the Channel creates vicious short seas, particularly when the north easterly 'Gregale' (the Maltese name) has been blowing for a few days. It was the 'Gregale' which drove Saint Paul's ship ashore on Malta one wild and stormy night when he was travelling to Rome from the Holy Land. Likewise, the prevailing winter westerly winds, blowing a thousand miles from the Pillars of Hercules at Gibraltar, pile up a powerful, steep and merciless sea on the western reefs and through the Channel.

So, it is a gap between continents, but more than that it is a bridge – a sunken bridge. Although a sunken bridge composed mainly of limestone, there are stepping stones scattered across the Strait.

The geological formation of the strait was complex, and the Channel is littered not only with reefs, but islands. There are the so-called 'Italian Islands' (Pantellaria, Lampedusa, Linosa and Lampione) and Malta, Comino and Gozo, with other smaller islets. There is still change under way, as Italy and Sicily are quite active with regular earthquakes; of course Mount Etna in Sicily is erupting almost continuously and Pantellaria is volcanic in origin.

The complexity is a result of the interaction between the African and Eurasian continental (tectonic) plates and activity which pushed the limestone up to form what now appears to be a bridge.

Many of the western reefs in the Channel take the names of famous ships or of explorers who discovered them or were wrecked there: Biddlecombe, Hecate, Talbot, Graham, Terrible.

Man has used these island stepping stones for millennia to cross between the continents. Just as the Gate of Tears was a bridge for human civilization to spread eastward out of its birthplace in Ethiopia, so in a lesser way the stepping stones across the Sicilian Channel aided migration into southern Europe. Man continues to do so today. It is the setting for hundreds of deaths every year as refugees and economic migrants try to enter the soft underbelly of Europe and drown at sea.

In the 21st Century, the Channel is a conduit for much of the world's trade between the Middle East (via the Suez Canal) to Western Europe and North America. It saves five thousand sea miles and the often dangerous passage round the Cape of Good Hope. It also carries the huge Far East Trade to Europe.

Tunisia is, of course, part of the Barbary Coast (that part of North Africa known also as The Maghreb) and as trade developed across and through the Sicilian Channel, it was at the mercy of the Barbary Pirates. And there was not much mercy. Cargoes and ships were plundered, and crews killed or sold into slavery in North Africa. The Maghreb retains its sinister face even today.

The Sicilian Channel is not noted these days for piracy, though it does occasionally happen. Yachts and small craft are advised to keep well off the Algerian Coast, and any vessels approaching the Algerian coast are strictly controlled.

The Mediterranean has historically provided an abundance of fish to the peoples on its shores, and although the 20th Century saw overfishing and eventual action by governments to prevent the exhaustion of this vast resource, fishing still continues today. The fish are nourished by the complex flows of currents over the rugged, shallow bottom. The western and eastern Mediterranean basins exchange water through the Sicilian Channel. There are two layers of current in the channel, one flowing east and one flowing west. Fishermen from Algeria, Tunisia, Libya, Sicily and Malta congregate there to exploit the diverse wealth of marine life.

Despite the exploitation, the Sicilian Channel is still a rich source of food and fuel for many people - and the final resting place for countless others.

Helena came over.
"Can I get you anything else Steve?"
"Just you Helena, just you."
She laughed as he continued.
"I'm leaving in a few days. It may be tricky getting to the west – I think I'll stop at Souda before finally leaving Crete. I could do really do with some help. Do you know anyone who might be interested in sailing with me for a few days, just to Souda?"
"Steve – I thought you'd never ask!"
"What? You Helena? Don't joke with a lovesick man."
"I'm not joking, and you are not lovesick."
"You can't know what's in my heart."
"It's not your heart that's the problem." She laughed again and shook her head. Her long dark hair waved like a black curtain – she normally tied it back, but today it was unfettered.
"I can't believe it – you'll sail with me to Souda? What will your father say?"
"My father? He died three years ago."
"But Cristos – he is your father?"
"No, No."
She laughed, and beyond her Steve could see Cristos laughing – then raising a glass to him.

"What is this about?"

"We tell all the visitors that Cristos is my father, then they don't bother me because – well Cristos is so fearsome is he not?"

Shaking his head and smiling, Steve looked at her then across to Cristos.

"But you live here, in the Café."

"I never said that, and you never asked."

"But, but…"

Steve broke into laughter as Cristos brought a bottle of brandy across. He'd been had, good and proper.

"Tonight we drink Metaxa, together!"

*

The evening started badly – Steve was preoccupied with Cassidy's news about Tom - it had hit Steve hard.

Tom Brown – as he had introduced himself – had approached Steve in Djibouti, about a year previously. As Steve had later realised, Tom was recruiting him and had become Steve's handler leading to two missions – first into the Chinese naval base in the Yemen and then to sabotage Tobin's gold production platform in the Red Sea. The operations had been sabotaged by a Chinese mole in MI6 and duplicitous government action. Steve had been well and truly set up, dumped on from on high.

Then Tom had gone missing in Djibouti and now Steve knew that Serbian bitch Maruška Pavkovic had killed him. He hadn't known that she had tortured him to death.

She had almost killed Steve, too, in Golfe Bleu, though he'd taken off most of her left ear with a bullet. And she had also put a bullet in Tom's replacement - but he'd lived thanks to Steve. To think she'd been in the cabin in Adèle, nearly dead, and he'd saved her. He cursed and wished he'd strangled her there and then.

And then, in Fiskardo, they'd come face to face again. Either he or Henri had put at least one bullet in her. 'I'm damned if I'm going off on a hunt for her', he thought. 'Cassidy can go and swing.'

Then, after the second brandy, the evening started to improve and he got into the lively mood of the taverna – and the traditional last night ashore of a sailor.

*

It was 2 a.m. as Steve meandered back towards Adèle. He was replaying snippets of what Helena had told him about herself. The brandy had been of the best that Greece could muster, and he was still laughing – he had his blind spot where Helena was concerned. Some things he never saw. Helena had even kissed him goodnight, though she would not tell him where she lived. "Some mystery is good" she had said to him.

In the alley leading up the steps away from the harbour, the old drunk was snoring gently as Steve leaned over and gingerly slipped Cassidy's mobile phone into one of the greasy pockets of his filthy jacket. Diversion was better than straight obstruction.

*

Steve was up early despite his late night and hangover. He'd been awake in his bunk for a while thinking about Tom and what Cassidy had said. Eventually he managed to push the bad thoughts aside and started to think about Helena. Company for the sail west sounded good, Helena sounded better. He'd picked up that she had trained as an English teacher and was working at 'O Passos' was just a fill-in for the summer – she had a job coming up in Iraklion when school restarted after the break.

His head reminded him about the brandy – it might have been the best that Cristos had in the bar, but that didn't make the headache any less painful. It was high quality all right.

Just as he was on his second cup of coffee, he sat at the chart table to add another line to his long list of jobs.

There was a knocking.

"Steve, Steve are you there?"

He looked round in surprise – it was Helena's voice. He climbed out into the cockpit. She was on the quay fiddling with one of his lines.

"Helena! Come aboard, please. It's great to see you."

"First I will tie this line properly."

Steve gawped at her, speechless for the moment. There was only one way to tie a bowline and Helena was clearly correcting his.

"The free end must be on the inside, like this."

She held it up for him to inspect.

"OK, you are right – I knew I done it wrong in a hurry when I was tying up, but with the wind. How do you know the difference?"

"My father was a fisherman here in Siteia. He taught me well. I also learned to sail, crewing for a charter yacht company here for a couple of years."

He shook his head - this woman was full of surprises.

"And your mother – she is an angel, I guess?"

Her face became serious.

"My mother is dead – she died with my father."

"I'm so sorry."

"You were not to know." Her face brightened. "Now show me this boat – I want to be sure that she is safe for me to sail on!" With an exaggerated nod, she offered her hand and he helped her aboard. There isn't a lot to see in 36 feet of yacht, and not a lot of space to manoeuvre, but Steve enjoyed the proximity and the way they seemed to brush against one another, regularly.

She did not seem too bothered about the 'heads'. Toilets on boat are not the sweetest of suites. She turned to him and said 'I think it is better than the bucket that my father gave me to use!"

With that she kissed him. This kiss was not chaste, it was full on and unexpected by Steve. She grasped the back of his head as her tongue probed his mouth. She held it tightly as the kiss went on. She pushed herself against him and he tipped back against the chart table. With a flourish she suddenly withdrew.

"I like Adèle very much but your coffee will kill me! That is the last time I kiss you."

The disappointment was obvious on Steve's face.

She smiled. "The last time I kiss you after you have been drinking your dreadful coffee! Now I must go – we open at 11am and I have much to do. Cristos will be angry."

*

After Helena had left he poured himself a glass of water and went back to the chart table to check his departure 'to do' list. He opened the chart drawer to pull out the chart for Souda.

There in the chart drawer, in plain view, was a mobile phone, just like the one he'd left with the tramp the previous night. He cursed, and picked it up warily. Someone had been aboard either before he got back last night, or when he was asleep.

It didn't occur to him that there might be another explanation.

*

Steve had no expectations for the week ahead with Helena, though as always he had a plan. The plan covered the sailing aspects of trip and he'd gone over it with Helena the evening before they left - she'd brought her gear aboard in the early evening, then gone back to wait table at 'O Passos'. Steve had gone with her, eaten there and chatted with her whenever there was a gap in business. So she had a vague idea about his intentions – to get to Souda within the week, stopping overnight *en route* at a couple of anchorages, weather permitting.

Helena's contribution had been to suggest that Ayos Nicolas was worth a visit, and he'd pencilled in Rethymnon and the bay at Amfinallion as other possibilities. The coast was rocky and the bottom steep-to, so anchorages were relatively few and far between on the coast.

Ideally, he'd like to check Adèle's bottom and give it a scrub – he hadn't checked it in almost a year, back in Djibouti. He smiled – the statement usually brought a smile to landlubbers. He'd need to check her stern gland too. To do that he'd need a quiet bay – clear water was not a problem at this time of year – there were no silt-laden rivers in spate.

The personal possibilities for the trip were intriguing him, but he knew that a week was all it would be, with nothing after. It would take a lot to make him swallow the anchor and live ashore. She was young, with a career and probably the idea of a building a home and having children sometime in the next few years. The chance could be there for him, but he didn't really want to settle and have kids. Anyway, he had nothing to offer her.

He wandered around Siteia, searching for a gift for her. They had arranged to meet in 'O Passos' at 11am, then after an early lunch they'd head off, westward, on the first 20 miles to Ayos Nicolas.

He'd taken on enough provisions for a few weeks, and would top up with fresh produce at Souda. Fuel and water had been topped off and everything was ready. The gift was a problem – he had never been any good at buying things for his girlfriends – they were usually misjudged and often raised laughter. Finally, just before 11 a.m.he gave up, determined to find something at one of their stops – after all, he would know her better then. How much better, though? He wondered.

He saw her as welcome company for the week and hoped that there might be more, but he was a realist. Still, she'd invited herself hadn't she? That raised all sorts of questions.

Just then, as he approached 'O Passos', he remembered the phone in the chart table. He might as well make use of it? Five minutes later the purchase of the sim card was completed and he met Helena. He was looking forward to the week ahead, with only an idea of what the sailing might hold. As for the rest – well that was unknown territory.

*

When he arrived at the taverna, Helena was waiting. They had lunch together, served by a new waitress whom Helena introduced to Steve as Arianna. Steve had his last beer at 'O Passos' with lunch, after which Helena kissed Cristos on the cheek. Cristos in turn put his arms around Steve, said his goodbyes crushingly, then handed Steve a paper bag. "Zorba! A gift from me for your voyage!"

In the bag, Steve saw a bottle of Metaxa. He laughed. The memories of that alcohol-fuelled first night in 'O Passos' were still vague, but last night's were still vivid. No one would tell him the story, though Helena dropped hints occasionally, about 'his dancing'.

Hugging was not in his nature, but he handed Helena the brandy and caught Cristos unawares. They laughed and then, arm in arm with Helena, Steve walked out on to the quayside.

In his turn, he had kept the details vague about his trip to Piraeus and early return from Argostoli. That was an episode he wanted to bury. Unfortunately, the name Maruška was impossible for him to forget.

*

James Marinero

Maruška Aims for Malta

The automatic identification system that ships use, AIS, can be monitored by anyone with access to an internet connection. It has a limited line-of-sight range and ships cannot be tracked unless they are close to a shore station – or another ship (which is their main purpose). This range is typically 20-30 miles.

All ships over 300 tons have to use a transmitter, though there are exemptions – naval ships are typical - although merchant ships too can turn the system off if there are potential security issues (the so-called *stealth* mode).

Although AIS had been turned off for *Auric Adventurer* on security grounds, Wan Chuntao had used her team at the Guoanbu to hack the Greek databases which collated ship movements.

Johnson had 'cleared out' from Argostoli, citing Valetta in Malta as the *Adventurer's* next port of call. He had also been in touch with Grand Harbour Marina in Malta and booked a berth for 6 weeks and notified Malta authorities of a problem with the ship's AIS. The uneventful trip had taken less than 48 hours, but the *Adventurer* had been tracked by Maruška all the way by the signals from GPS tags.

With the ship's arrival information she started to plan an operation to deal finally with Tobin. She would need a larger team, of that there was no doubt. Taking risks was one thing, but suicidal missions was quite another – Fiskardo had been her fuck-up and she knew it. But at least it had resulted in revenge for the 'forest in Pristina'. She was purged of that, for sure.

Six hours later the next message from Chuntao came through on her iLive smartphone:

'Meeting Malta on 23rd July re five-a-side football match. More details to follow.'

That would give her the team. By the time she had read it twice, the message had disappeared.

*

Travel was an issue. Flying was risky, but since that terror incident in Malta ferries were also undergoing enhanced security checks. Argostoli-Patras-Brindisi would work for her, with taxis and trains to Catania in Sicily and then a ferry to Malta. It would take 4 days. Not enough. She needed to regroup, but getting back to one of her bases – either Paris or Geneva - would take too long. She felt a driving urgency to hit back quickly, as quickly as the planning would allow. She also needed to change her appearance and put some papers together.

It would need time, time she did not have. Three days maximum. She prepared to contact Nicos.

*

As Maruška was planning her next move on Tobin, ben-Zhair finally received the coded notification he had awaited, confirming that the funds had been deposited in his numbered account in Zurich. Using the Muslim *hawala* money transfer system he started to discreetly and slowly distribute the working capital in small amounts to other countries and currencies where it would be put to practical use.

*

James Marinero

Tantalum

The Tuminos had flown into Malta by helicopter from their father's home north of Siracusa. It wasn't their preference to meet Tobin on his motor yacht, but their family yacht was in Augusta for her annual refit, besides which they wanted to keep Tobin at a certain distance. From Luqa airport they had installed themselves in the Corinthia Grand Hotel in St George's Bay a few miles to the north east of the airport.

When in Las Vegas they lived in one of their hotels and thought themselves connoisseurs of the hotel business. They had a lot more to learn but lacked the sense to learn it. What the Corinthia offered did not suit their business model or their rather coarse tastes. Even though the Corinthia was a 5 Star 'resort hotel', it offered few of the more 'specialised' facilities that their own brand of sex and gambling resort hotels provided. It was altogether much more refined.

Auric Adventurer was moored off Portomaso, a mile or so to the south if their hotel – she was much too big to enter the marina there which was for mere millionaire footballers, assorted 'B' and 'C' list celebrities and their mass produced plastic powerboats.

On the Tuesday morning, the day after their arrival, a limousine delivered the Tumino brothers, their *consigliori* and minders to the quay at Portomaso where Tobin's launch collected them for the meeting. It was an airless, stifling July day in Malta with the humidity pressing down on them as the launch headed out to the anchorage, generating a relieving breeze if only for the few minutes voyage at 25 knots over a placid sea.

At noon, together with Alfonso, their consigliore, and two silent but seriously capable looking 'security' men, they stepped aboard the *Adventurer* to Tobin's greeting.

"Beppe, Giorgio, so good see you, but such unfortunate circumstances. I'm sorry I could not attend the funeral of your father. Come, let's get out of the sun and into some privacy."

"It's a pity that your yacht is not big enough for our helicopter to land on."

Score one to the Tuminos.

"Oh, but it is, it's just that my Bell Jet Ranger is awaiting a spare part – otherwise I would have had it collect you, but the deck is definitely too small for me to land my Gulfstream on" Tobin riposted.

They laughed, uneasily.

"You have a good sense of humour Charles." Beppe wiped his brow. "I hope that you have air conditioning – at the least the heat in Vegas is dry."

"Of course we have air conditioning, but the climate is just like Sicily isn't it - you must be used to it? Here let's sit around the boardroom table. The steward will bring us some refreshments. Would Krug suit you?"

"I prefer Cristal, but if Krug is all you have then that will be fine."

"I'm sure we have some Cristal. And you Giorgio?"

"The same as Beppe."

The steward nodded and moved away to get the drinks.

"Thank you Charles, for your message of condolence and the flowers at the funeral, though we were disappointed that you could not be there in person" said Beppe as Giorgio cut in "We trust that you do not have any more bad news for us."

"I have, shall we say, good news and bad news, but I am sure that the good outweighs the bad. But first, have you discovered yet who committed this terrible crime against your family?"

"No we have not. The Polizia and Carabinieri find it very amusing when someone such as our father meets such an unfortunate death. They say that lack resources" said Beppe as his brother cut in "But our resources are extensive, and we will find the murderer and see him eat his balls."

"Shut up, Giorgio." There was clearly tension between the twin brothers. Tobin thought that the unsavoury prospect of him having to eat his own balls was very unlikely to become reality. His strategy was starting to have an effect – cut off the head and the body wriggles uncontrollably.

"I understand that you too have some problems, Charles."

"Yes, that is why I have had to change my plans and not visit you in Sicily. We live in dangerous times."

"Do you have any idea who it was?"

"No idea at all. They were clearly professionals. One crew dead and nothing stolen. I can only assume it was a ransom attempt. I've had to find new crew at short notice, and at this time of the year in the Mediterranean it is difficult. I hope you will not be disappointed by my hospitality."

"Yes, finding reliable staff is always a problem." Giorgio's banal comment met with silence and a glare from his brother.

After the steward had opened champagne he closed the saloon securely and Tobin began his presentation. The Tuminos' security men stood on deck outside the door.

"First I will explain the good news, then deal with the current financial situation, which is not so good – but only temporarily so. Then finally, we can discuss the overall situation and the way that I propose we proceed to increase our returns."

"OK, but we don't have all day" said Giorgio.

"Charles, despite my brother, we have as long as it takes. This is important business."

Tobin thought that things were shaping up nicely, though it was very unusual to see such men disagree publicly – their father would surely have beaten them for displaying such fractured opinions outside the family.

"I won't waste our time. I'm going to tell you briefly about Tantalum. Tantalum is an interesting metal – it highly resistant to corrosion – even that of acids. Most people have never heard of it, but many people own some. They own it in their phones and other electronic devices such as smart watches and computers, where its electrical properties are used for small, high efficiency capacitors.

The prime source of tantalum is in Australia but it is found elsewhere including Africa, China and Brazil. It is deposited in several naturally occurring ores, and one form, *coltan*, has been responsible for war in the Congo, with, it is said, over 5 million deaths. Yet the Congo produces only 1% of the world's tantalum output.

Weight for weight it is not quite as valuable as gold or the best diamonds, though gold and diamonds have an aesthetic and cultural value which the metal tantalum does not possess. It is thought to make up 1 to 2 tons in every million of the earth's crust."

"So what, if you can't wear it or give it as a gift like gold or diamonds to a broad, I'm not interested."

"Shut up Giorgio, and listen" Beppe said angrily. Please continue, Charles, though with less science."

The consigliore, Alfonso, was reluctant to get involved between the two brothers, and sat quietly with a suitably serious face, watching Tobin and listening very carefully.

"It was discovered in 1802 by Anders Ekenberg, in Sweden. He named it after 'Tantalus' – a Greek god from whose name the verb 'tantalize' is derived. He was said to have been cursed to stand up to his knees in water, with fruit over his head, forever. If he bent to drink the water, its level fell, and if he tried to pick the fruit, it moved away from him. The name was used to recognise its peculiar chemical properties.

It is closely related to platinum, and also found with niobium - Niobe was Tantalus's daughter according to mythology."

"Ah" said Giorgio, "now platinum I understand like gold and diamonds. But all this myth... myth'logy stuff I don't do, not history."

"Then now is your chance to learn if you shut up and listen" retorted his brother.

Tobin was enjoying the brothers' sour fencing, and continued "Other of its uses include surgical applications – human tissue will bind with tantalum, and it is often used as a coating for replacement hip and knee joints, and for surgical instruments.

There is also a more sinister application, though it is not known whether it has been tested in practice. Nuclear bombs. 'Salting' a nuclear bomb – that is, coating the spherical core of plutonium with tantalum adds special properties, similar to that of 'salting' with the element cobalt."

"OK. Enough. Cut the lecture Charles. What use is this to us?" Beppe was now beginning to lose patience. "We don't plan to build nuclear bombs, do we Giorgio?"

"No, dynamite works fine for us."

"It is known as a strategic metal, and that makes it valuable – hence the war over it in the Congo, Beppe. And I can produce it for one tenth of the price of other methods, at a high purity." Tobin knew he had stretched a point on salted nuclear bombs, but did not expect the Tuminos to enquire further. A little bit of truth went a long way in a big lie.

*

During the years that Tobin's genetics team in West Wales had spent developing his gold extracting bacteria, *Theovulum Aureu*s, the analysis of the bottom water samples they had taken from the Red Sea showed useful quantities of Tantalum.

Tobin had always been a gold miner, brought up in a gold mining family in Australia, and a golden harvest from the sea bottom had been his focus. This led up to his coup in the gold markets which had been initially disguised by supposed manganese and molybdenum extraction, and it had been necessary to divert resources to remove mercury (and other contamination) as the *Theovulum Aureus* had mutated. He began to see possibilities other than of gold. Removal of mercury using a strain of *theovulum* had proved lucrative in its own right, though this was kept from the Tuminos.

When Tobin left Australia as a young man in 1992 to go and make his fortune in Alaska, he was disowned by his family. He was successful in building an international gold mining conglomerate, but always kept away from Australian mining, although that had been his heritage. His arrogance was such that any return to Australia would only be when he could buy out the family business, an ambition which he eventually achieved. After he had finally bought out his family's gold and minerals business in Australia, Tobin Minerals Pty. from his dotty aunt, Suzanne, she died and left him the proceeds.

Then when he was rationalising and reorganising the business after the takeover, he found that the portfolio of subsidiary minerals companies included a tantalum mining and pre-processing business. After a strategic review of the business, he could see that it was one which had potential. He hung on to it, and took the pain of the losses for several years, deliberately neglecting to re-invest. Then as the mobile phone and miniaturised electronics market started to grow, the value of the tantalum ore reserves started to grow too.

Later, when his production of gold from seawater was under way on his platform in the Red Sea, he had moved his team's research focus to tantalum. *Theovulum Tantalus,* as Tobin had named it, was close to readiness for production.

Unfortunately his gold coup had inadvertently precipitated the 'Gate of Tears' crisis and temporarily closed down his extraction operations.

He had not foreseen the extent to which the Chinese would be affected, just as they began to transform themselves into an outward looking global power. It had also caused him problems with his shadow financial backers – men whom it was not wise to disappoint – and two of whom sat before him now. The third, their father, had been buried in Sicily the previous month.

*

"So," said Tobin as he wound up, "I now have the bacteria to extract Tantalum from seawater, just as we have done with gold."

"But why not just stick to gold?" asked Beppe.

"Because Tantalum is less 'public' in its ability to invite criticism and all the problems that we had in the Red Sea with gold."

"You said it was in the earth's crust – that doesn't sound like seawater to me." This almost intelligent statement from Giorgio invited Tobin to respond "Over many millions of years, the earth's crust has been washed into the sea, and molten crust comes up through vents in the sea bed. That's why we extract gold in the Red Sea, and will extract Tantalum too.

It's not as valuable as gold, but it's 400 times more abundant and demand is growing phenomenally. The current price is $600 a kilo – roughly $600,000 a ton, whereas gold is almost 100 times that. But as we have seen, gold has difficult political issues surrounding it.

I'll come back to other reasons after lunch, but that is the first part of my good news. Now let me deal with the bad news – I would not want that to give you indigestion."

*

In fact, the opportunity for Tobin was quite different to the one he proposed to the Tuminos. Certainly, there were big profits to be made from high volume, low cost production but he had made a quick fortune in gold market futures in the 'Gate of Tears' coup. Now the prospect for the tantalum market was beckoning. He well knew that this was only a good but not brilliant deal as a long term prospect, but with an announcement about it he could be sure that some major mining companies would suffer big share price falls – and he would strike.

*

The brothers ordered the driver to take them straight to the airport.

"I don't trust that fucker. Bad news, he said – what does he take us for? 'A problem with the next dividend'. That wasn't bad news, that was a kick in the teeth for us. And he expects us to put more money in? Jesus, what does he take us for? Papa trusted him, he invested heavily in his project – and we had a good return. And now this!"

"Papa can't help us now - we have to make our own decisions?"

"What do you think Alfonso?"

"I think your father would have reduced the level of investment and demanded better terms. I've looked into Tobin's current situation and he is definitely under pressure. We can take advantage of that."

"Take over his operation you mean?"

"That's madness!"

"Shut up Giorgio and let him finish."

"It's a possibility, although I think it is too complex for us – we would have to be able to control him."

"How?"

"I'm still thinking about that."

"Well don't take too long – we don't pay you to stare into the sky."

"It would require careful planning. That cannot be done quickly."

"OK, ok. Could he have been behind Papa's murder?"

"Jesus, Beppe, do you think that's possible?"

"Sure it's possible – he's got the balls, but why would he do it? Alfonso, what do you think?"

"It could be him, but as Beppe said, what would be his motive?"

"The loan, obviously. Let's look at him a bit closer, and at his people."

"I'll see to it. But even after your father, the loan still exists."

"So, if he took out Papa, then he'd want to take out us?"

"Yes."

"We should have given him four weeks to repay the whole loan and leaned hard on him. No more fancy plans with tantalum or whatever it is."

"He got the message all right. It's just as well we got Franco and Transglobal involved in his security. Hacking the ship's network was a good idea of mine."

"Your idea? I thought of it first."

"No you didn't, it was me."

"Beppe, Giogio, the facts are that Franco has not found anything that points to Tobin taking out your father."

Twenty minutes later they were airborne and heading northeast towards Siracusa, still arguing.

Eighty miles away in Siracusa, the man scanned the helipad once more, then put down the binoculars and drank some water from a bottle. He stretched his limbs and then once again the pressed the 'Test' switch to check the circuit. The led flashed green.

He pushed an earpiece into his right ear and turned on the radio scanner. Two minutes later he sat up straight, fully focused.

"Casa Bianca, Casa Bianca, this is Airforce One, come in."

Sicilian Channel

He laughed quietly and checked the scanner. Marine band VHF, channel 8. It would have been legal if the helicopter was a boat. The Tuminos were stupid and vain with a house called 'Casa Bianca', and a call sign 'Air Force One'. Not their official call sign – the pilot would only use that on an air traffic band.

The radio squawked again.

"Casa Bianca, Airforce One. ETA 18:30. Landing lights please. Acknowledge.

He knew that there would be no reply from the house. It was approaching dusk and the landing lights were on to allay suspicion. He hoped they would assume that there was a radio problem. He didn't need them to land.

Twenty minutes more and he would be on his way and he could confirm to Franco Abadelli that the job had been successfully completed and his final payment would be transferred.

Likewise, Abadelli would receive his bonus from Tobin, paid through Tobin's London office as part of his salary package, entirely legitimately.

*

James Marinero

Nicos in Nidri

Nicos was in the bar in Nidri when the "Number withheld" text arrived. He spilled his beer as he read the message:
'Call me, let's talk about a January night off Fano. Urgent'.
There was no mistaking what the message referred to. Only two people alive knew what happened that night. One of them was his son, and all the others were dead – or so he had thought.
It had been a routine winter night run with a couple of Serbs, some crates of weaponry and a half ton of heroin. A Greek naval boat had picked them up on radar off the Island of Fano, north of Corfu at 02.00 hours, and a chase has started. They'd ducked into Albanian waters and the Greeks couldn't follow.
The event, although more than eight years previous, was indelibly imprinted in his memory. He shook at the thought.
One of the Serbs was a woman he later came to know as Andjela. She drew a pistol and called the shots, literally. He followed her orders without question. He was a hard man, but he recognised something much harder and almost alien, in her. She was not to be crossed.
The weather had not been bad, with a light wind and a slight swell from the north-west. Although the Greeks couldn't follow, they were spotted by the Albanians. An Albanian patrol boat came alongside with ease – it was about the same length as Nicos's trawler, but lighter and more manoeuvrable. The Albanian captain announced over the loud hailer that the trawler was in Albanian waters without permission and was being arrested. She came in close, they bumped gently together and lines were passed across.

Three heavily armed Albanian crewmen jumped aboard with weapons levelled, while others covered them from the patrol boat.

Nicos could not recall the precise details of what happened next, it was so fast and unexpected – even by the Albanians. He saw Andjela open fire killing the seamen on deck and then jump across onto the patrol boat. Nicos had ducked as a burst of fire had raked the trawler's deckhouse. The other Serb had been concealed up forward on the trawler and had taken out the patrol boat's foredeck gun crew, shot out the deck lights and jumped across to fire through the bridge window. Within two minutes all the Albanian seamen were dead and grenades had destroyed the bridge of the patrol boat. Other crew had been picked off as they emerged from below, but the Serb did not return.

Nicos was sent aboard to scuttle the patrol boat and within 30 minutes she had disappeared beneath the swell. They set course to merge into the shipping lanes heading north as Nico's brother Georgiou helped the surviving Serb to dump the three bodies overboard. The radar and showed that the Greek Patrol boat was over 20 miles away and heading south. There was no sign of any other vessel within 10 miles.

Andjela took the brandy bottle from his hands and raised it towards him in a toast "Welcome to the team. We will do plenty of business together."

As he sat in the bar in Nidri looking into his brandy chaser, he recalled how close he had come to death that night. They could not have got away with what they did if they had been stopped in Greek waters. That had locked him in - Andjela had kept him on the hook with money and threats, and he had done many trips for her since that January night. News of her death had come as a relief and as the wars in the Balkans had been resolved he had bought a new trawler and moved away from drugs and weapons into human trafficking for the Serbs, and later the Arabs.

Now Andjela was back and the nightmare was real again.

*

Nicos made the call. It was Andjela for sure. How could it be so? He had no idea, but knew she was capable of anything, even faking her own death. She was close by just a few miles to the south, on Cephalonia. She wanted to be taken to Malta, within 3 days. He had no choice in the matter even though he usually stayed well clear of Malta. He called the Bezzina Brothers ship repair yard in Marsa Creek in Malta, and arranged to be hauled into their dry dock for 'emergency underwater repairs'. Fortunately they had a space in one of their floating dry docks for a week. At least he'd get some painting done.

He called Georgiou to ready the trawler for sea and then headed home to collect his gear and tell his wife he would be away on business for a week.

*

The Queen Katherine

Mr and Mrs David Rowbotham, and their close friends Harry Naismith and his long term partner Julie-Anne Newey, had joined the Cunard cruise liner RMS '*Queen Katherine*' at the Western Docks in Southampton ten days previously, for her maiden voyage. Their long-planned cruise had been booked through the Daily Telegraph website one Sunday afternoon three months previously, after a long and boozy lunch. Stolidly middle-class, they were all members of a golf club near Solihull in the West Midlands. The men played in a foursome regularly every Sunday, and their wives played with each other mid-week.

David was a senior IT security manager in a local datacentre. Harry ran – or until recently, had run - a hygiene company, servicing soap dispensers and hand-dryers, changing toilet rolls and cleaning toilet pans. Not that he did that himself, of course. He employed 140 people to do that for him – officially. There were quite a few others too, although they didn't appear on the books. Or had employed them, until four months previously he had sold his company, lock, stock and toilet brushes to Signature Services, a large national company. What Signature really wanted was access to the lucrative contracts which Harry had sewn up with surrounding local town councils and other public bodies.

The cruise was a celebration of that business sale, of 18 years hard work. The children had been packed off to grandparents for a couple of weeks, and Harry and Julie-Anne had asked their best friends to go on the all-expenses paid cruise with them.

So, they had been picked up by stretched limousine and driven down to Southampton to join the Cunard *Queen Katherine*. Their neighbours had quietly thought that the limo was a rather undignified and flashy way to travel, but they were definitely not going on a coach.

Leaving Southampton's Western Docks at high water, one Tuesday evening in July, the *Queen Katherine* had taken 24 hours to their first stop in Lisbon. The trip had a rough start, turning southwest down the Channel at the Nab Tower into a freshening and unseasonal westerly gale with the first of the neap ebb tide. The Bay of Biscay had been unkind, but the seasickness had been transient and they were more or less back to normal by the time the *Queen Katherine* had turned northeast up the Tagus estuary and by Thursday morning they were in Portugal, moored alongside the outer wall hard by Alcantra Dock, next to the '25 April Bridge', overseen by the statue of '*Cristo Rei*'. Lisbon was vibrant with history, steaming and smelly, enchanting and exotic all at once.

Late the following afternoon, the ship cast off and set out southwest down the Tagus estuary into another stiffening and unseasonal summer gale, next stop Gibraltar. They were glad to move on from the continuous noise of the trains and trucks booming across the bridge over the River Tagus, though enchanted by their short stay on Lisbon. Portugal was not new to them – the men golfed on the Algarve every couple of years or so – but they had never visited the capital.

The trip down around the most westerly part of Europe via Cape St Vincent passed without incident and they turned southeast for the last 100 miles or so into the Mediterranean Sea, arriving in Gibraltar before breakfast. The itinerary rolled on, another day, another port. Barcelona, Marseilles, Genoa, Naples, Palermo. The final ports were to be Valetta in Malta, Palma in Majorca and then Vigo in Spain, before the last leg across the Bay of Biscay and back to the uncertain British summer weather.

*

The *Queen Katherine* had all the facilities most passengers could wish for – even a small pitch and putt course so that they could keep their hands and eyes in. The competition between the companies which built these pleasure behemoths was intense, and had been going on for well over a hundred years, since the first Transatlantic liners had been conceived. The naval architects and interior designers vied with each other to use the vast spaces and volumes to attract new generations of cruise passengers.

The RMS *Queen Katherine* had been built by Chantiers de L'Atlantique in St. Nazaire, France, the same yard as built her predecessor, the RMS *Queen Mary 2* launched in 2003.

She was a greyhound of the seas, a proper ocean liner, the largest of the type ever built. At a little over 85,000 tonnes displacement she was some 10,000 tonnes heavier than the *Queen Mary2*, and lighter than the heaviest cruise ships afloat, such as Royal Caribbean's MS *Allure of the Seas* at 100,000 tonnes.

Her design had created many challenges for her designers. Her height had to enable her to pass under the Verrazano Narrows bridge in New York if she was to offer the classical transatlantic service, but that constraint was the only major design compromise. She was too big to pass through the Panama Canal and as a result, she circumnavigated South America via Cape Horn to cross between the Atlantic and Pacific oceans, or took the longer route via Australia during her annual world cruise.

Of course, being built as a trans-oceanic liner required considerably higher speed capability and rough weather comfort than typical cruise ships such as *Allure of the Seas* offered.

Powered by the latest generation of integrated electric propulsion systems, her combination of gas turbines and diesel generators produced enough power to supply a small city. Her four 30 Megawatt propulsion pods gave her a capability of 36 knots at full power, and she was able to maintain a cruising speed of 27 knots in the roughest of ocean weather, as befitted a true ocean liner designed to provide a service between Southampton and New York, as well as premium round-the world cruises.

*

The foursome from the Midlands met two other small groups of like-minded English couples on their dream cruise and swapped stories, family histories, but stopped short – just – of swapping partners. By the time they had reached Naples, they were thoroughly acquainted with the ship and beginning to tire of 'another day another port', and passed on the trip ashore, taking a rest day.

At Palermo in Sicily there was a lot of dust in the air driven west on the easterly breeze from Mount Etna – the Goddess of Fire. She was always grumbling, occasionally raging, and as they left Palermo astern and settled down to dinner the sun was setting a deep red over their wake, the colour accentuated by the dust. They would not be going west-about Sicily and through the Sicilian Channel that night – they were told that the ship was heading east for the Straits of Messina.

There would be a full moon and the *Queen Katherine's* captain was forecasting a clear night and a display from Stromboli, sixty miles to the north and referred to as the oldest lighthouse in the Mediterranean.

The captain's bulletin also told them that he expected to turn south and pass down the Straits of Messina shortly after midnight. On the starboard side, they would pass Charybdis (the 'Sucker-Down) – the ancient whirlpool which devoured ships. Since the times of the Greeks and the Odyssey, geological activity as late as the 18th century had reshaped the seabed and taken the edge off Charybdis's hunger for ships. The whirlpool was in modern times only a danger to small boats at certain times of the small localised tide.

Sicilian Channel

On the port (mainland) side, they would pass Scylla, likewise a whirlpool (and in some ancient accounts a waterspout). The region was alive with history and mythology.

Most passengers who had any interest believed that the Mediterranean was free of tide, the pull of the full moon on a night such as that, combined with the difference in salinity (saltiness) of the Tyrrhenian Sea to the north, and the Ionian Sea to the south create a significant slope in the water through the Straits and currents of up to 4 knots; whirlpools, eddies (*bastardi*) and bores (*tagli*) would occur at different stages of the tide. No problem for the *Queen Katherine* or other engine-driven vessels whatever their size, but for the ancients, with only oars and sails it was a frightening prospect – these waters were creations of the gods and were used to express their displeasure of man.

Although that night was fine, the effects of the land masses of Sicily and the Italian mainland separated by only 1½ miles across the Strait, combined with the mass of Etna spewing millions of kilowatts of heat into the atmosphere to disturb the airflow and create a microclimate. Together with smoke and dust, big thermal gradients were created and severe gusts of wind were commonplace. To the north of the Strait towards Stromboli, the area is known as the Aeolian Triangle where Aeolius's legendary crew released contrary winds from a bag with disastrous consequences. Sailors today regard it with interest as an area where the winds are often fickle, sometimes violent and rarely predictable. These matters were of no concern to the officers of modern ships - they treated the gods with contempt.

Even today, people still believed in gods and were prepared to do their bidding, however dreadful.

*

The night turned out as the captain had predicted. Harry and Julie-Anne, with David and Rebecca, enjoyed Stromboli's eruption from one of the lounges, followed by a late-night brandy on the balcony of Harry's first class starboard-side outer cabin watching Etna's much weaker – almost non-existent - display, and they turned in just after 2 am. The *Queen Katherine* would be in Grand Harbour, Malta for breakfast. With two other couples, they had reserved in advance two of the horse-drawn carriages which plied the tourist trade in Valetta. After the carriage ride, they planned lunch ashore. The guide books mentioned that Malta had 365 churches – one for each day of the year – and although they were not religious people, Harry and his party intended to visit at least one. They had been recommended Del Borgo's in Birgu for lunch, and that was their plan.

*

Harry and Julie-Anne, David and Rebecca, together with over two thousand other passengers – most still asleep - passed out of the southerly end of the Straits of Messina and on past Mount Etna. They passed Catania, landing place of thousands of modern day refugees and embedded IC terrorists, pas Siracusa and the ancient city of Ortigia, and then round Cabo Passero into the area which Italian weather forecasters called the Canale di Sicilia – the Sicilian Channel. The *Queen Katherine* turned just west of south, for Malta, with less than sixty miles to Valetta, leaving Sicily astern and with the Sicilian Channel ahead.

Overnight, the Marie-Anne, a forty-ton stern trawler now flying the Italian flag, had also been heading for Valetta from the north after a long roundabout trip which involved a change of identity. Her current voyage originated in Libya and she expected to arrive in Malta, finally, at about 9 am.

The trawler's owners, Zammit Seafoods, a small fishing company based in Valetta, had reported her missing three weeks before when they had lost radio contact, and an intensive air and sea search had failed to locate her. When not fishing, she was usually berthed in the busy fishing port of Marsaxlokk on the south east tip of Malta, near the Freeport.

Most of Malta's imports came through the Freeport, which had been set up as a way of generating revenue for the island, with minimal taxes and duties attracting transhipment business. The biggest container vessels, having come through the Suez Canal, split some of their load here, for transport by small container ships to the hundreds of smaller ports around the Mediterranean margin.

The shallow bay of Marsaxlokk was still pretty, if viewed from some angles. Though the Freeport was just out of sight round past the commercial boatyard, in Birzebuggia, the vista past the busy fish and lace market was of the power station and de-salination plant.

That morning, Marsaxlokk was still mourning a trawler and her crew of local fishermen.

The gap on the quay where she usually moored was painfully obvious, and fishermen along the quay were still speculating about her loss. They could only put it down to a sudden catastrophic failure of the hull, maybe a collision with a submerged shipping container or her nets being caught on a submarine. There had been no distress signal, but some wreckage had been recovered by the fishermen – just the trawler's inflatable RIB and a few oil drums. The emergency beacon had not activated. They shrugged, crossed themselves, and said a quick prayer. Life went on. Fishing went on. It was a dangerous business.

That morning, however, the Marika Z was not headed back to Marsaxlokk, and her regular crew of six was no longer aboard - their bodies were at the bottom of the Mediterranean, in the Sicilian Channel.

Now renamed the Marie-Anne, she had been repainted, rather badly, but adequately for the purpose at hand. Many of the Marsaxlokk fishing boats were painted in the traditional Maltese livery of blue, red and yellow, often with an eye painted on each bow – a Phoenician tradition. As the Marika Z, she had been in the green colours of Zammit Seafoods, but as the Marie-Anne she was in painted white.

The planning had been meticulous. The new crew comprised three Pakistanis and one Algerian fanatic for whom the MIA had not been extreme enough. Her forward fish hold was stacked with her new cargo, but this was not fresh fish netted from the Sicilian Channel.

*

Most passengers were on deck for the entrance into Grand Harbour. On the starboard side, to the north, was St Elmo's fort, the last bastion to fall to the Turks during the great siege. The entrance to the harbour was sheltered from the worst effects of the occasionally violent northeast 'Gregale' wind by a breakwater. There was a narrow and shallow northern entrance, suitable for very small craft only.

Ships used the southern entrance which was wide and deep, but with some wartime wreckage still remaining on the bottom. Despite the wreckage, there was a good 50 feet of depth across most of the entrance. To the south, on the port side of the ship was Il Ponta Ta' Ricasoli, with its massive fort, one of the chain around Grand Harbour built by the Knights of St John, way back at the time of the Crusades when Malta was the main stronghold of Christianity against the soldiers of Islam.

Accompanied by a coastal patrol boat of the Malta Defence Force, the *Queen Katherine* glided past Kalkara Creek, then Dockyard Creek and finally French Creek with its ship repair yards on the southern side, all the time overlooked by the supposedly impregnable bastions of the city of Valetta to the north. The ship slowly made her stately way southwest-wards into the heart of the harbour, accompanied by fireworks. It was her first visit to Malta.

Sicilian Channel

Crowds were thronging the quays and the walls, vessels in the harbour were on stop as she glided majestically to her berth on Valletta waterfront below the district known as Floriana.

As the line handling launches took the lines ashore, two tugs from Malta Towing Company fussed to nudge the ship alongside the ancient dock wall under the massive natural ridge of limestone on which the City of Valetta was built. She was berthing 'starboard side-to', with her stern to the harbour entrance.

Tugs saluted her with water jets, harbour sightseeing and tourist boats had saluted her with their sirens and then got back to business. Commerce had to proceed, even on such an important day as this. Her crew prepared to disembark more than two thousand passengers as quickly as possible.

Two yachts were departing from Grand Harbour Marina in Dockyard Creek, heading perhaps for Greece or Sicily. Astern of the yachts was a brightly painter trawler, which turned south west making to pass the *Queen Katherine*, and head towards the end of Marsa Creek which was a bustle of small ships and trawlers, salvage craft and tugs, even an old submarine.

*

Malta guards the eastern entrance to the Sicilian Channel, and has been prized for millennia for its strategic position. Its people are an amalgam of Arabic, Norman, Germanic, Spanish, Italian and many other tribes and bloodlines, and speak a language which has elements of Arabic, French and Italian, with a unique alphabet.

One of the finest natural harbours in the world, Grand Harbour and Malta itself has been regularly attacked and invaded over the centuries. Valetta and the island itself had been defended to the death during the Great Siege of Malta when the Ottoman Empire attacked with its vast military resources.

Most recently it was defended almost to the death by the British and the Allies in the Second World War when it was a strategic base for ship repair and supply, and for intercepting Axis convoys crossing from Italy to North Africa.

The island had been saved ultimately by a last ditch attempt to get a supply convoy through the Sicilian Channel. The convoy had been attacked daily by German and Italian planes. This last-ditch convoy was decimated, but several ships got through with food, ammunition and essential supplies. The convoy included the oil tanker 'Ohio' which carried vital fuel supplies for the Spitfires and machinery which kept Malta's defences alive. The Ohio had been bombed several times, and on 15th August 1942, the mortally wounded tanker entered the Harbour, with a British warship strapped to each side of her, keeping her afloat.

The view from the 'Ohio' was ghastly (as was the view of the 'Ohio' herself, seen by the cheering onlookers). The 'Three Cities' across the harbour from Valletta – Cospicua, Senglea and Vittoriosa (Birgu) - had been reduced to piles of rubble by Italian and German bombs, the population was living in holes in the ground and had taken horrendous casualties.

The Three Cities had been constructed of limestone blocks cut from local quarries centuries before by the Crusaders. After the blitzing of the Second World War, the Cities were a jumble of ruined masonry, with barely recognisable streets. Grand Harbour and its creeks were littered with damaged and sunken ships.

Later, George VI, King of England, awarded the George Cross to the Island for its bravery.

Over the centuries the Maltese people had been regularly subjected to attack and merciless slaughter, and this day would write another chapter in that bloody history book.

*

Sicilian Channel

"Salaam Alaikum."
"Alaikum Salaam."

Abu ben-Zhair and Anwar Zaman exchanged greetings. Abu ben-Zhair walked up the gangplank and on to the stern of the motor cruiser in Grand Harbour Marina. The 'Meltemi' was flying the Maltese flag, and had been bought a month earlier since when Anwar had been preparing her for this voyage.

"Everything is ready?"

"Yes, *Insha'Allah*, we are ready to leave."

"Good, then let us not waste any time, we have only a few minutes." He checked his tablet pc, and could see the trawler on the marinetraffic.com display under her new identity of Marie-Anne.

Anwar had already warmed up the engines. Ben-Zhair was not a seaman, and followed Anwar's simple instructions about when to let go the bow lines to let them sink. They were moored stern-to, and it would not do for them to snag a line around a propeller at this crucial moment. As they turned in Dockyard creek, they could just see the stern of the Cunard liner *Queen Katherine* as she moved majestically towards her berth.

They headed slowly out of Dockyard Creek, where Nelson had provisioned on his way to fight the battle of the Nile. To starboard was the city of Vittoriosa, and on their port side was the town of Senglea, rising from the Creek and towering high above them. Valetta faced them ahead, a few hundred yards across Grand Harbour to the north. At the entrance to the Creek they passed the largest motor yachts in Grand Harbour Marina, where billionaires came to play with their toys.

There was a huge hi-tech sailing vessel – 'The Maltese Falcon' - occupying the most northerly berth. Just inside her, though she was longer, was a ship – it could be called nothing less – *'Auric Adventurer'*. Ben-Zhair shook his head in wonder – and hatred of Western capitalism - as Anwar turned to starboard heading for the entrance to Grand Harbour and the open sea. They passed the steps where only minutes before, Abu ben-Zhair had said a final few words of encouragement to his team as he stepped off the trawler Marie-Anne. Some of the crew had been hyped up with a glaze of religious fervour in their eyes, others were quiet and reflective. A couple of news drones buzzed overhead, recording the arrival of the *Queen Katherine*.

A historic harbour, indeed, he thought. And today, he, ben-Zhair would go down in history.

*

The hubbub in the harbour was immense as the Queen Katherine nudged into her berth. A fire tug was playing a jet of water into the air in welcome, sirens were hooting and there were fireworks crackling and banging around the harbour. Malta was proudly independent but still valued its historical linkage with Great Britain. Welcoming the new Cunard flagship on her first visit was certainly something to celebrate. Abu ben-Zhair noticed few of these details. He looked up at the bastions of Valetta where so many Muslims had died trying to defeat the infidel Crusaders five centuries before, where human heads had been used as cannonballs fired across the harbour. There was no limit to man's inhumanity when it came to war – *jihad*. Nothing had changed in five centuries.

He took out his smartphone and selected a phone number. He switched to 'edit number' and keyed in the final three digits to complete the number. His finger hovered over the 'dial' icon on the touchscreen as he watched the Marie-Anne make her way up the harbour, the distance between them increasing steadily. He asked Anwar to slow down and hold position, just inside Il Ponta Ta' Ricasoli, at the entrance to Grand Harbour.

As she was almost level with the *Queen Katherine*, approaching one of the tugs, the Marie-Anne appeared to accelerate and turn sharply to starboard. A police launch turned to intercept her.

Abu ben-Zhair was a half mile away, but felt the blast of heat as the Marie-Anne, driven at a full 14 knots, wedged into the gap under the stern of the *Queen Katherine*, hard against the stone jetty, and detonated the four tons of a generic Semtex explosive which had been obtained from Libya's fractured weapons stores. The demise of Gaddafi had opened Pandora's Box.

He smiled as through his sunglasses he saw the stern of the majestic cruise liner, all 120,000 tons of her, rise 10 feet into the air and tilt sharply to port as the blast wave reflected off the bottom of the harbour and quay wall and lifted the ship bodily. His smile turned to open-mouthed awe. He saw the blast of heat and stone, focused in the small gap between ship and quay, tear up the side of the liner where many of the passengers were lined up, taking photographs and enjoying the moment of arrival. The blast ripped open the side of the ship like a tin can, peppering the quay with glass and shrapnel. It drove debris up into the Floriana district, more than a hundred feet above the ship's berth and overlooking the quay.

The blast tore into the stern gear of the ship, ripping a vast hole, stretching up four decks and halfway down to the ship's keel, it pushed the ship out from the quay, rocking her and lifting her, generating a wall of water which rolled out into the harbour, and another one as the ship's stern dropped back into the hole and slammed into the bottom of the harbour, wrecking all the propulsion pods.

Though Abu ben-Zhair didn't know it, Harry, Julie-Anne and Rebecca were on Harry's balcony on the starboard side whilst David was refilling his beer glass. Their balcony railing and its glass panel was torn away, with many others, and with many other passengers, their already broken and lacerated bodies arced up into the air and then fell several decks down onto the stone quay, in pieces.

Less than a second after the detonation, the blast wave hit ben-Zhair, painfully. He screwed up his face with the pain in his ears. And it hit them again and again as the sound wave echoed around the stone walls of the harbours and creeks that made up this beautiful historic harbour, reverberating to the core of the island. Some later said that the shock wave had been felt through the ground at the churches in Mdina over five miles away.

In a split second, the harbour-side passenger terminal block had been flattened, killing staff and visitors by the score. The line of plush, black painted, brass trimmed carriages were destroyed entirely, together with their drivers and horses. The waiting line of white Mercedes taxis and coaches was reduced to burning junk.

The ship tottered, rocked and pitched. Ben-Zhair knew she wouldn't sink – the water at the quay was barely 60 feet deep, the ship's hull was divided into many watertight compartments, and she drew forty five feet. This he knew from the operational plan. No matter, she would rest on the bottom for some considerable time.

The blast wave moving southward under the stern threw a huge wall of water and debris out towards the centre of the harbour, catching the police launch and throwing it fifty feet into the air, rolling as if it were a child's bath toy, the crew falling out, broken and torn as the launch smashed down three seconds later onto the fort at Senglea Point flattening a group of camera-carrying tourists whose bodies had already been internally pulped by the blast wave.

Anwar stood open-mouthed on the flying bridge of the '*Meltemi*', but ben-Zhair was smiling.

Even at almost a mile away, debris was starting to rain down around them. The tug nearest the stern of the cruise liner had been capsized. All around the harbour there was chaos, as smoke from the fires on the ship, the tugs and the shattered buildings ashore was starting to rise in the already warm morning air.

"Let's go, Anwar. Allah be praised, the heroes have done his work. The infidels will never forget this day."

"*Allahu Akhbar*" he replied, and punched the air with his fist.

"*Allahu Akhbar*" responded ben-Zhair.

The twenty feet high train of waves raised by the explosion hit them and they lurched as '*Meltemi*' accelerated out of the Harbour.

'Perfect', thought Abu ben-Zhair. 'Perfect. This is just the start of our revenge for the Crusades.'

*

James Marinero

Escape to the Maghreb

The 'Meltemi', a Fairline 45, accelerated as it went out through the southern entrance to Grand Harbour, her twin 400 hp Caterpillar turbodiesels driving her easily up on to the plane on the flat sea. As it reached the top of its bow wave it levelled and accelerated further as Anwar adjusted the trim tabs.

Debris was still falling and the plume of smoke over Grand Harbour was spreading with the wind, carrying the smell of burning oil, plastics and flesh.

The patrol boats of the Malta Defence Force were based in Marsamxett Creek, over on the other side of Valetta, up towards Pieta and the Gozo ferry berth, right under the vertical northern bastions of Valetta itself The ugly, apparently ungainly patrol boats were aging now – they had been bought from Australia twenty years before, but they still posed a threat.

They would surely have been scrambled by now and would soon be coming through the narrow north entrance under St Elmo's Fort, where the old storm gates used to be – if they could squeeze under the footbridge. No matter, he was well on his way. Anwar knew the planned course, and turned to starboard to head down past Marsascala.

Naval activity had ramped up in the years since the immigrant crisis which started in 2014, but they did not anticipate being challenged.

Abu ben-Zhair smiled again. All the signs were that the attack had been a success. His presence up until the last few minutes had been only to encourage his team, to keep them steadfast and remind them of the glory of the act that they were performing, to say their prayers with them, and to remind them that their place in heaven was assured. So much for the rhetoric, he thought. It sounded good, but the real benefit was that his grip on the organisation would be stronger and he would be able to get rid of the dead wood.

Besides, a great leader had to be seen on the front line – or at least close by.

Ten minutes later they passed the entrance to the shallow bay of Marsascala and on down past the fish farms to pass the Freeport. Looking over the starboard quarter he could see the plume of black smoke, already several hundred feet into the air over Malta, drifting slowly west from the carnage at Grand Harbour. Success, so sweet. *'Allahu Akhbar'*.

It hadn't been necessary for him to use the mobile phone bomb trigger - the heroes had done as ordered and driven the Marie-Anne right in between the stern of the *Queen Katherine* and the quay wall, detonating their cargo. It was a sign of his skill at managing his team that they had not faltered. He looked at the mobile phone in his hand and threw it over the stern into Meltemi's wake.

In a couple of hours the videos of the martyrs would be published on Al Jazheera and would be going viral on the web, as millions of people clicked to watch it on their smartphones and head-up displays, and then share it with their friends, gawping at death and disaster filmed from the drones. Or, if they were true Muslims, he thought, they would be glorying in the strike against the hated city of the Crusaders.

This was the new age of terror.

Cruise ships were easy targets, as the Palestine Liberation Organisation had shown in 1985, but with a lack of strategy.

Four heavily armed Palestinian freedom fighters hijacked the *'Achille Lauro'* cruise liner off the coast of Alexandria, Egypt. 320 crewmembers and 80 passengers were taken hostage, but hundreds of other passengers had disembarked the cruise ship earlier that day to visit the Egyptian pyramids. If their demands for the release of Palestinian prisoners were not met, the freedom fighters threatened to blow up the ship and kill the 11 Americans on board. The hijacking of the ship was not what they had planned – they had been caught unawares with their weapons. What happened next had been creative and outrageous, perhaps, but to no avail. In the event they killed a disabled US Jew in a wheelchair and pushed his body overboard. This one act set the world against them and they had eventually been captured.

The whole episode had been financially and politically disastrous for the PLO. Even Assad of Syria had refused to help the hijackers.

The lessons were clear. Hijacking was an outmoded terrorist 'business model' and there was no point in trying to negotiate with the West. That was for fools.

Airliners contained relatively few people and security was difficult to penetrate. Cruise ships offered far larger concentrations of *infidels* – and cities even more.

His strategy was far superior – a series of escalating attacks of which the *Queen Katherine* was only the start. It was all a question of scale. Bin-Laden had shown the way, but with his, ben-Zhair's, strategy, deaths of the infidels would number in the tens of thousands – and then even the millions, *Insha'Allah.* IC would make demands in due course, demands the like of which had never been seen before. There would be no negotiation. The infidels would have no room for manoeuvre or trickery.

Ben-Zhair looked at the horizon and steadied himself as the 'Meltemi' hit a bigger wave. In less than an hour he would have cleared Maltese waters and the Italian Island of Pantellaria would be to the south of them. Then, they would continue on up through the western end of the Sicilian Channel, past Cape Bon in Tunisia, turn west by south outside Tunisian waters and then follow the coast for over a hundred miles. Then they would be in Algerian waters.

By then, the whole world would be in shock.

*

Sicilian Channel

To fanatical Muslims (or people who called themselves such), the Crusades represent a massive bloodstain on the history of their religion.

The most appalling acts of terror and genocide in history have been caused by religious bigotry, and it still continues. There are no good sides and bad sides. Genghis Khan, the Romans, even the British, French and Spanish killed millions of Native Americans, north and south, and treated Africans as savages and animals. The twentieth century had seen Stalin, Pol Pot and Hitler, though the latter had plumbed new depths of sickness. The list is endless and grows even today.

But for Muslims – or Islamists as the most extreme are now identified – the Crusades are still a painful collective memory in their consciousness.

Abu ben-Zhair reflected that the island of Malta is largely Catholic in its religious balance, but given its history there is a small Muslim community, and there are mosques to support their worship. Inter-religious tolerance and respect was the norm, at least on the surface. But Malta as a whole stands as an outpost of Christianity facing the Maghreb – the Muslim coast of North Africa. Facing the Maghreb, but backed by the power of Rome, only a few hundred miles away. More than that, Malta is a glaring modern day reminder of the Crusades, when millions fought for control of Jerusalem - a holy city for three religions - and the religious devotion of the populations of the Mediterranean countries, north and south, east and west.

It doesn't bother most people, but these thoughts ran through ben-Zhair's mind as the 'Meltemi' altered course to head west by north to pass the island of Pantellaria. As they turned, the engines started changing note regularly as the hull rode a small swell from the east.

He turned to the helmsman.

"Today, Anwar, we have struck a glorious blow for Allah – may He be praised - against the Infidels, the

Crusaders, and the British. It will go down in history next to the destruction of those towers of filthy American commerce on 9/11."

Anwar turned and smiled,

"*Allahu Akhbar*".

"*Allahu Akhbar*" acknowledged Abu ben-Zhair as he passed Anwar a bottle of fruit juice.

He didn't take any himself. His stomach could cope with mass murder, but a gentle swell was its limit at sea. He consoled himself with the thought that fasting was a religious commitment, and that religion was merely a convenient lever of power.

He smiled grimly. The crew had been heroes and fools at the same time, blowing themselves up for the promise of a few virgins in heaven. Useful fools.

'It is power that matters, power to do what I have done today, power to bend others to my will.'

He could talk the talk, and today he Abu ben-Zhair had walked the walk - but he was under no illusions about those above him in the chain of command. They too harboured no illusions, either about Islam or about power. Or about him. They would watch him and he would watch them - and then he would climb over them. He had come up through the GIA and fought in the Algerian Civil War. Then he had joined the Salafist party and become street legal. Success getting to the top of that organisation and playing a part in government was not enough. The government was soft, and he had retained his radical links as IS came to prominence in Syria and the Levant. In Algeria he was shaping the future and he would control ICIM – the Islamic Caliphate in the Maghreb.

*

Ben-Zhair planned to go ashore just to the east of Cape Rose in Algeria. There was a sandy beach there in the Golfe de Canier, about 20 miles to the east of Annaba (or Bone as the French had known it), a major port. The beach was no more than six miles from the Tunisian border, and they would stay well offshore until they had crossed into Algerian territorial waters – this area was heavily patrolled by both sides and there was a narrow 'corridor' into Annaba which vessels had to use.

"Anwar, your orders are to take us to Annaba."

"*Aiwa.* We have fuel for more than 500 miles – I have prepared as instructed."

"Good, we must be at Annaba early tomorrow morning, when the patrols are sleepy. Ensure we stay at least 50 kilometres miles off the Tunisian coast – I do not want to see any Tunisian patrol boats. Change that flag at the back to a Moroccan flag. We are now a Moroccan boat, and I am a wealthy Moroccan businessman returning from a visit to Sicily. Is that clear?"

"*Aiwa.* We have talked about this before, and I remember all the details. Everything is ready."

"Good, I will give you new papers when we get nearer to Annaba. Let me know when we are off Cape Bon. I am going to sleep now – it has been a long night, and a wonderful morning."

"It shall be. In five hours we will be off Cape Bon. I will call you then. Allahu Akhbar."

"Allahu Akhbar."

The real plan was different, thought Ben-Zhair, though Anwar did not need to know that. The real events would be different too, but even Ben-Zhair could not know that.

*

James Marinero

Maruška in Malta

Zabbar

The voyage to Malta had been uneventful, though Nicos was clearly unhappy to see 'Andjela' again – and to be in Malta. He had kept well clear since that trip when he had smuggled Vidovic in. Getting in to Malta, even after the attack in the *Queen Katherine* had not been a problem. Beforehand, Nicos had been very concerned about being stopped and searched, but in the event it had not been a problem. It was vessels that were leaving that were being challenged, together with any approaching the Freeport in the south. The ship's papers were in order, though Maruška remained hidden in the hold. They had come in through the chaos of Grand Harbour which was still suffering major disruption but now open at last, then docked in Bezzina's boatyard late in the afternoon. Maruška had slipped ashore in the night.

She finally managed to find a small guest house in Zabbar, nearby. The room was cheap and simple but all she needed. Almost all accommodation on the island was taken following the attack on the ship and prices had risen astronomically. Taxis were very busy, but Mrs Thake, the guest house owner, had wasted no time in telling her that her husband Louis and his car were available for hire if she required transport.

She called the numbers she had for her team – five had become two because of increased security on the ferries and at the airports – and arranged to meet them and get the plan in motion.

*

Del Borgo

"I hope you don't mind us interrupting – we couldn't help noticing that you had the sea bass."

Tobin glanced up.

"Ah so that's what it was – I thought it looked familiar. The menu didn't sound very appetising -'Spnott, Maltese style' but it was very good. I love to take chances – even with menus. Sorry, do I know you?" He peered up in the low light just as one of his bodyguards approached. Tobin waved him away.

"It's ok Luigi, I'm fine."

Tobin stood up and held out his hands. "My name is Tobin, call me Charles".

"My name is Marie and this is my friend Yasmine." Tobin was keen to kiss each of them on the cheeks. Their perfumes were expensive and different - and he could not identify them despite considering himself to be an expert. He spent a fortune on perfumes for Diana and Pippa and they were forever testing him with new ones. Marie and Yasmine wore no other make-up.

Marie was an attractive woman, fortyish with a dark complexion, black fair cut in a bob, and piercing blue eyes. She looked trim and fit, lithe even. Yasmin was darker, Arabic in appearance with black eyes and a similar height – maybe five feet six.

"I pride myself on recognising a lady's perfume, but you have both got me baffled. May I ask what brands you use?"

"You can ask, but we're not telling."

Marie winked at him and Yasmine replied "They are unique perfumes which we have made for us in Paris."

Marie continued "Each has an ingredient unique to each country which we have visited."

"Ah, a mystery! I love puzzles. Tell me some of the countries, and I will try to guess the ingredients."

"We would be here for a week – there are too many countries, too many ingredients."

"Fair enough, though I would like to try. Will you join me for a brandy?"

"Why not, as long as it's a quick one? We have an early flight tomorrow. Why do you friends not sit with you?"

"They're not friends, just associates, they work for me."

"Really, yet you eat alone?"

"Yes, my other colleague was ill and couldn't make it tonight. I have plenty to do anyway", gesturing to his tablet computer.

The brandy came and went and the chat continued. Tobin discovered that they had both lived in Tunis until the troubles had led them to Paris. They were coy about their work, describing themselves only as entertainers, a double act. Yasmine was very reserved and her French accented English was not good. He did most of the talking, bragging about his yacht and his private jet, saying that he had been in the gold business but was now looking for new investments.

He showed them some pictures of the *Adventurer* - that usually clinched the deal with women. His thinking was being influenced by alcohol and hormones and he was starting to imagine the two of them on his circular bed in the *Adventurer*.

"So, what really brings you to Malta?"

"We're just simple tourists!"

"I hardly think so. You two are not typical tourists."

"Well, we're really looking to open a club – a special club. We like the dungeon atmosphere here in Del Borgo, although it's only a restaurant."

"I thought you must have had some dark secret. Why don't you both come back to my yacht for another brandy and tell me more, in private."

"We'd love to, but we really have to catch an early plane."

"Can't I persuade you? My car can take you back to your hotel."

"No, really, thank you."

"Maybe another time then? Although I get to Paris quite often, I am sure you can show me places I have never been before. Maybe I could come and see you perform?"

"Why not? I will give you my number, you can always reach Yasmine through me."

They touched phones and swapped details.

Tobin called for the bill and led the way out of the restaurant. "I'm going this way down to the harbour – come on, let's have one more."

"No really, thank you."

He kissed Marie on the cheeks, but Yasmine had already started walking up the slight hill and turned down a steep alley.

"Ok – I look forward to seeing you in Paris. Have a safe journey."

"You too, *au revoir,* Charles. I think we will see you again very soon."

Tobin and his guards strolled to the corner and turned downhill towards the *Adventurer*.

His brain heard the spitting sound but before his consciousness could register the fact a hand clamped over his mouth and a sweet, sickly vapour flowed up his nose and into his lungs. The blood from the guards briefly sprayed on to his legs as they dropped, dead from head shots. Strong arms stopped him falling and then half-carried, half-dragged him around the corner and down towards the dock.

Any casual observer would have thought that the tall man had had too much to drink and was being carried home by his friends.

Yasmine had started the engine and held the boat against the quay while Marie and Mansur Abdul-Hadi loaded Tobin's inert frame aboard. Running without lights, they headed out from Grand Harbour Marina and around Senglea Point. Marie wrapped duct tape around Tobin's mouth and hands. The north side of the harbour was lit by floodlights as salvage barges worked non-stop on the hulk of the *Queen Katherine*. They motored slowly along past the grain terminal and then followed the dog leg round past Dock 7 and towards the Cassar shipyard. Nicos's trawler sat darkly in one of the floating dry-docks on their port side. They motored on past an oil drilling rig which was in for overhaul, on past the hulk of a patrol boat and the old submarine and turned into the area which had been taken over by North African refugees. It was now nearly 1 a.m. and there was nobody in sight, although a faint light shone from a security hut.

They hauled Tobin up and into the back of a van.

"Mansur, you know what to do. Dump the RIB in a dock and head back here."

Less than a minute later the van passed through the tall wooden doors of the old warehouse at Marsa, and Tobin was hauled deep into the old building. A space had been cleared amongst high stack of cardboard boxes which had been covered with plastic sheeting.

He was roughly taped to an old wooden chair. Two massive tusks attached to a huge papier-mâché wyvern - the remains of a carnival float - overhung the cardboard boxes on one side, Marie nodded to the monstrous apparition. "That should give him something to think about when he comes around. Yasmine, I will be gone for no more than half an hour. Give him water only then tape his mouth again. Mansur should be back before then."

"Did it all go to plan?"
"Yes, Chuntao, we have him safe. What is it you want me to get from him?"
"I want a key."
"A key?"
"Yes, a cryptographic key. He may not know he has it."

"This is stupid. You send me a bunch of African monkeys to work with – they are less than useless – and now you want me to find out if Tobin knows something that he may not know he has."

"It is probably a word or phrase. I leave it to your skills to find out. You have not failed to extract information – at least this far. Once he tells you, tell me. No-one else is to be present at the interrogation, do you understand?

"Yes"

"Good, get that key."

"How will he know if he has it?"

"Confirm that he sent an email – yes, an email – from a Starbucks in St. Mary Street, Southampton, England on Saturday the sixteenth of November 2013. I want to know the primary key that he used to encrypt it. It should be a simple phrase, maybe even a telephone number.

You can tell him that we know it is the key to switching on – activating - a piece of junk DNA in *'theovulum aureus'* so that it concentrates a metal called tantalum instead of gold. Do you understand?"

"Yes."

"Then repeat what I said."

Maruška felt a surge of searing pain in her back as she repeated word for word what had been said.

"But you can surely decrypt anything with your supercomputers."

"That may be, but it takes time – time I do not have. You have six hours. We need that key. No one else is to know it."

"I understand."

"After that, keep Tobin alive for 24 hours while we check the key. Then you can kill Tobin – but only on my orders."

"It will be a pleasure."

"No mistakes this time, Maruška."

"I don't make any."

"Oh, but you do – remember Fiskardo. We should have had that key by now."

The connection dropped and Maruška felt a stab of pain between her shoulder blades. She swore as tears of pain coursed down her cheeks. She would have her revenge.

*

Sicilian Channel

Well Off Course

The winds of the Mediterranean basin are many and varied. The names are exotic but enough to strike fear into the hearts of some. Tramontana, Mistral, Bora, Scirocco, Meltemi, Gregale. They have been cursed by sailors – and others – over millennia, carrying sand, snow, dry air, wet air. A boon to many, fatal to some. They damage crops and kill people. Cars and yachts are named after them.

The fearsome Bora arrives with as little as 20 minutes notice, other winds can be foretold by the way the clouds lie over a mountain range in the evening.

Some blow for weeks, others for hours.

That year had been a bad one for Mistrals. Funnelled down the Rhone Valley, gathering strength *en route*, the Mistral bursts onto the Gulf of Lyon, with winds of as much as 50 or 60 knots in winter when the snow is heavy on the Vosges plateau. It can spread its misery from the northwest as far as Crete, re-gathering strength as it is pulled by low pressure over the Tyrrhenian Sea between Sardinia and Sicily, and raise vicious seas in the shallow Sicilian Channel.

Under Helena's watchful eye in the café at Souda, Steve was checking the five day forecast. Not good, but there were signs of a change in the pressure pattern at the end of the five days. He thought he had found a weather window and hoped that it would stay open long enough for his leg west to Malta. I'm not going to be caught at the arse-end of a Mistral, he thought. He planned to leave Crete early the next morning.

*

The easterly wind had failed after two and a half days at sea. Generally, three day forecasts could be relied on, five days were pretty good, but his weather window had slammed shut. All Steve had needed was a good three day start. Shit happens, he thought. It had been at 03:00, when he went up on deck to take a look around the horizon the AIS alarm had woken him with a target at 8 miles. It was a container ship heading west-north-west at 18 knots – bound for Rotterdam. The wind, a shade north of east, had eased, and there was an oily swell on his starboard quarter, barely lit by the setting moon.

He's had difficulty sleeping – it usually took him a few days to get into the rhythm of being at sea. Helena and the idyllic week before leaving Crete had been on his mind. He'd toyed with the idea of becoming a lotus eater, but knew deep down that it wouldn't work for him. He couldn't see himself surrounded by a gaggle of children, nor could he see himself harvesting olives. Fishing – perhaps he could have done that? He was realistic enough to realise that is was a fantasy best left as just that, without letting it turn into a real live nightmare.

Sensitive to the sounds of Adèle, he heard an unfamiliar tapping noise. He checked down below and realised that the sound was coming through the mast support – a strong steel pipe in the cabin, under the mast, that carried the compression loads of the mast down into the keel. He put the deck lights on and went up. The moon had long set and the Milky Way arched clearly over his head, disappearing behind a bank of cloud to the west. He'd have to watch that. He swept his torch over the mast and rigging – the deck light lit only the foredeck. Cursing, he went forward quickly. One of his starboard lower stays had parted. He'd had the wind on the starboard side since leaving Crete, putting the load on the starboard rigging – he was lucky. The mast was pumping slowly in the swell – a gentle bowing unsupported by the broken stay. The bottlescrew – used to tighten the rigging - had fractured. He didn't have a spare.

After digging through the bosun's locker he used a couple of wire clamps and a short length of stainless wire to fix the problem, but he wouldn't want to trust it in heavy weather any length of time. He sat in the cockpit with a mug of tea and some biscuits. He'd made good progress since leaving Crete – almost 350 miles directly towards Malta, but now the wind had failed. The situation was manageable, but with the wind having fallen the oily swell was now arguing with a cross sea from the northwest. He put his empty mug in the sink and went to the chart table to write up the log.

He cursed when he saw that the barometer had fallen another 3 millibars in the last two hours – there was bad weather on the way, probably a gale or close to one. Just then Adèle rolled awkwardly and he heard the wind as a wave hit her under the starboard bilge with a thump, making her steel structure vibrate along her 36 foot length, and making the rigging rattle. He switched on his tablet computer and again reviewed the 5 day forecast he'd saved at Souda. It was clear that the low pressure over Tunisia must have moved north eastwards towards Italy and deepened. This was not a typical summer pattern and he started to prepare for a blow. It had been a bad summer all round.

The damaged starboard lower mast stay was a problem – it effectively limited his heavy weather options to keeping the wind on the port side – and that could mean he'd end up in southern Italy if the wind did not change. It all depended how hard it would blow, for how long and crucially, from what direction.

He tuned in the short wave radio to Deutsche Wetterdienst and got the RTTY signal. Plain text, reliable German service – it was a wonder they still kept it going after all these years. The forecast was not good. Gale warnings for the surrounding sea areas, with heavy confused seas expected given the last two days of vigorous easterlies and the expected north-westerly gale. Then he checked the automated Italian voice forecast, but couldn't get any reception on the VHF – the range was well over 50 miles from Italian stations.

Even if he didn't have the problem with the rigging, the chart was not encouraging – the waters to leeward were shoal in the southwest corner of the Gulf of Sirte, where the Libyan-Tunisian border met the sea. He'd been there before – way back in 2011 on HMS Manchester. Just then, he heard the wind howl in the rigging and he climbed quickly into the cockpit. Lightning flashed. There were no stars ahead. Then the weather front hit him.

A huge crack of thunder deafened him as the wind climbed to forty knots and the rain started – morning would show red sand in the cockpit, brought originally from the Sahara, sucked up into the atmosphere, transported and then dumped with the rain. The sails had been set for a broad reach on the north-easterly wind, but were now flogging wildly.

Quickly Steve hardened the sheets, working almost by feel alone, the warm rain washing the salt out of his hair and into his eyes. Within three minutes he had furled the genoa, saving the sail and reducing the noise to from banshee to simple cacophony. Then after deep reefing the mainsail, he put Adèle on to a broad port reach with the helm a-lee. After fifteen minutes she was riding comfortably, with the Libyan coast 200 miles astern. He was now 'hove-to' to, hoping to wait whilst the weather passed. Adèle was riding comfortably, with only the occasional sheet of spray across the decks. She was making about half a knot to the north, with more west than north in the wind. That at least was preferable to a seven knot charge towards Libya with a jury-rigged stay.

After a quick check for shipping – the container ship was by now well over the horizon - he went below, realising he had added a couple of bruises as he opened the whisky bottle. He checked the radar and then turned into his bunk. For the rest of the night the sea remained awkward and unpredictable. The wind settled at about 30 knots – just below a gale – gusting 45, and the westerly seas finally killed off the dying seas from the east. What should have been a simple trip from Crete to Malta was now anything but. His thoughts were of Helena as he dozed off.

*

When he woke up after a couple of hours, the dawn was just lightening the eastern sky. The wind had settled in the west and he was gently fore-reaching towards Malta. He had been dreaming of Helena and the almost idyllic last week in Crete spoiled by a very sour ending. He was still stiff from the dream and cursed the fact that she was still in his mind after their goodbyes.

His thoughts turned quickly to Adèle. He could feel that her motion was more regular and the noise of the wind had fallen an octave or two, from a shriek to a low howl. The wind had backed a little to the south and he went to check his repair. It was holding – although it was hardly being tested as the lee rigging usually carried no serious load. With the wind a bit freer he unfurled some of his genoa with the deep reefed main and found he could make three knots in comfort, towards southern Sicily.

As the morning wore on the wind strengthened again – at noon he logged it at 30 knots plus – though gusts were less frequent. He tuned in to the latest forecast and it was apparent that the low pressure over Sardinia had moved east. The wind in the Sicilian Channel was still north-westerly, but he was getting the benefit of a kink in the isobars – freeing the wind, but strengthening it. Still, anywhere was better than Libya – though he hadn't been there since the time of Gaddafi. The last news story he'd heard mentioned the 'third new government' – that was a sure indicator of more problems following on from a long period when the country had two governments – one in Benghazi and one in Tripoli. The country now appeared to be under the control of extreme Islamists.

He checked that chart and noted his progress over the last few hours. The wind had backed slightly and the self-steering gear had faithfully followed it round. He could now lay a course for Malta. After a simple lunch of tinned chicken soup and the last of his fresh bread, his mind turned to other things, and he replayed the week with Helena, cruising the north coats of Crete.

*

After the farewell to Cristos, Helena had joined him aboard late the following morning. She had brought a bottle of wine and some local delicacies which they worked their way through as Steve gave her a rundown on the safety equipment. He was impressed – she knew her way around a boat and asked all the right questions.

"Where do I sleep? I can see you have no double berth!" He saw the twinkle of amusement in her eyes, even though her forehead was wrinkled in a frown.

He pointed to the cabin floor.

"Down there."

"Do you treat all your women the same way?"

"No. You are special – I don't usually sail with female company."

They both laughed.

"I've cleared the single cabin opposite the forward heads. It needed doing anyway."

"That will suit me fine – at least to start with!" - said with a wink and a smile, he had no reply.

"What's your plan then *kapetánios*?"

"Well, we seem to have done lunch already. I would like to get to Souda within a week – that's the only plan. Let's keep today down to a short passage so that you can learn the ropes. Where would you suggest for tonight – you know the water if your father was a fisherman?"

"There is a quiet anchorage off the east of Spinalonga Island. To the west of the island the bay is very crowded, but pleasant." It's about 18 miles from here."

"Quiet sounds good, and about 4 hours is fine for your first trip."

"Hah – you speak as if I have never been on a boat! I will show you all the secret places as we go along the coast."

She smiled, but he missed the possibilities implied as he started working through his checklist. "OK, we'll leave in half an hour. Stow your gear."

"Yes, I will put my bags in my cabin first, if that's what you mean."

Steve smiled at that, and the cruise started.

*

Two days later they were sailing in a cooling light southerly wind, blowing down from the mountains. They were crossing from Dia Island, bypassing Heraklion and bound for an anchorage to the southwest of Stavros Point. Adèle was sailing at about five knots and there was little sea.

The previous day had been overcast and relatively cool, but the sun today was strong and they sat under the sun awning. It was a little after midday and they both had a chilled beer to hand.

Steve watched as Helena rubbed sun lotion into her arms and legs, then her stomach. Then she unhitched her bikini top and started to rub lotion into her breasts as she sat across the cockpit from him.

"I love the sun, don't you? I love the feeling of warmth and freedom, with no clothes to constrain me."

"I have to go up forward and check the forestay."

"Hmm…your forestay looks quite healthy to me."

She could see the blush form on the lighter tanned area under his chin as he realised that his attempt to escape and hide the discomfort in his shorts had rebounded.

"Very funny."

"You said it *Kapetánios*."

They laughed together and clinked their bottles, "*Yiamas.*"

"Here, you can put some on my back and shoulders."

He started to rub very slowly, with one hand steadying himself against the boat's gentle dipping to the swell.

"Your hands are rough – I mean the skin, not the rubbing."

"It's all the sailing, salt water and hauling on lines."

"You should wear gloves."

"No one has complained before."

"I'm not complaining – it feels good, probably exfoliating me."

"What's that – something sexual?"

"No. Never mind, just shut up and carry on, it's lovely."

As he concentrated and looked at the texture of her skin, felt the relaxed cords of her muscles and kneaded her vertebrae gently, he felt her body respond.

"You never told me about your trip to Piraeus. How did it go?"

She talked on quietly and over the next ten minutes she gradually teased out the story of his time on the *Adventurer*. He could feel her body quicken under his hands and explained that it had been a quiet trip, well paid, with no untoward incidents. He kept it vague, but his mind was wandering.

"If you put any more cream on it will be coming out the other side"!

"Oh, sorry – I got carried away."

"That's allowed – just a little. Who's on watch?" she said.

"Damn, I am!"

He checked the horizon and the sea ahead then southwards to Herakalion.

"All clear bar a couple of fishing boats inshore and a ferry leaving Heraklion heading east. I'd better check the chart. Don't go away."

When he came back up to the cockpit five minutes later she was lying on her tummy.

"Now you can put some cream on my lower back, but remember you are on watch."

"Yes, *kapetánios*" he said with a laugh, starting to work the lotion across her lower back then the cheeks of her bottom. He was using both hands now with one hand on each cheek, moving in a gentle circular motion.

"Your hands are very good. You've obviously done this before?"

"Many, many years ago, when I was first married."

"It must be muscle memory then. You can take the bikini bottom off if it helps."

"OK. But there's not much of it. Brazilians would call it dental floss." He was trying to act as if this was quite a normal event - as if he was unfazed by it - but his blood pressure continued to rise. He desperately wanted her.

As he unhitched the flimsy ties at the sides she raised her tummy to allow him to remove the front of the tiny bikini.

He resumed work with his hands, her cheeks parting and closing in rhythm as his hands worked in circles. He was totally lost as she talked quietly, asked him a bit more about events at Fiskardo. He was finding it increasingly difficult to keep his story straight.

She moaned occasionally as her breathing quickened and conversation stopped. Then, he felt her muscles spasm in his hands, once, twice, three times and then she relaxed slowly.

"Thank you so much, sir" she said mock dramatically, "Er, er, I think I am well-oiled no?" her breathing was steadying slowly. "Now the oil is coming out at the front."

"Can I do anything else for you - madam?"

"Not now, maybe later – and it's still 'Ms'. Ask not what you can do for your crew, but what your crew can do for you!"

"Winston Churchill – sort of?"

"Exactly – sort of."

She pushed herself up and turned towards him, her full breasts patterned with the weave of the towel and her nipples still erect. His look was obvious.

"You like them?"

"You could say that."

"I work hard to stay in shape."

"Then all I can say is keep up the good work."

She took his right hand and raised it to her left breast, reaching out and stroking his obvious erection through the shorts with her other hand, looking at him and arching her eyebrows

"Your turn now, *kapetánios*?"

"I didn't ask."

"I'm using initiative, I hope you don't mind."

Adèle lurched as a slightly bigger swell caught her and Steve grasped the support of the sun awning.

"That's it, be sure to hold on tight."

They laughed, and he held on firmly as his shorts started to slide down and she grasped his erection.

He didn't think to ask how a Greek girl from Crete could paraphrase Winston Churchill, but he soon recognised that she really was very capable with her mouth.

*

Steve started from his reverie. The AIS alarm beeped gently, insistently. He cursed Helena, he cursed the weather and he cursed the radar - ship at 8 miles closing from port. The AIS calculated the closest point of approach and although Adèle was the 'stand-on' vessel the ship would not need to alter course. He could just make out the vessel's silhouette when they were at the top of a swell. She would pass astern, just as Helena had, and was now in his past. His mouth hardened into a firm line and he forced his mind back to the present.

He checked the chart display. Malta was about twelve hours away at the present rate of progress. That meant a night approach, which didn't appeal. He had visited Malta years ago on HMS Manchester, but couldn't remember much about it. The chart showed fish farms, some reefs and an easy approach into Valetta. Nothing he couldn't handle, but things were always easier by day. In these times of heavy security, night entry attracted more suspicion and official interference. Arriving from the south at night would almost certainly mean he'd be boarded. Not that he had anything to hide – other than two pistols hidden in a waste oil container.

On deck, the rigging lash up was holding and he could see that the whitecaps were not so frequent – the wind was easing. He decided not to increase sail but to lose a few hours sailing slowly, and then enter Valetta mid-morning.

Four hours later the wind had disappeared completely and all that was left was a swell and an awkward cross sea from the Adriatic. The barometer was climbing and he started the engine, making enough way to fill the mainsail and dampen Adèle's rolling.

*

After the disturbed night he settled in his bunk again and his mind went back to Helena. The few days cruising along the north coast of Crete had been among the most enjoyable days of his life. He had been completely captivated by her – and fooled. She was smart and educated – History at Oxford she had told him when they were anchored in Fodele Bay eating lunch. Far too posh for his usual taste. He would usually steer clear of women like that – and most of them would steer clear of him.

"I did stretch the truth a bit about my parents. My father worked in the British Embassy in Athens when he met my mother – she was a secretary in the Embassy. It was her father – my grandfather who was the fisherman. So, I had a Greek upbringing but my passport is British."

"That explains why you speak English so well."

"Yes, that and my education."

"A clever woman like you must surely have a career?"

"There's no need to be sarcastic. I do freelance work."

"Like working in a *kafeneion*?"

"That job was temporary, just to get a feel for Siteia and its people. I'm a writer, actually. Travel guides, tourist brochures – mainly focused on the history of the islands."

"I'm beginning to wonder what other secrets you have."

"Oh…I have plenty."

"I hope they're all good."

"It depends. Are all your secrets good, then? You seem to have a few."

"I have a few and yes, some are not so good."

"Any you want to tell me about?"

"Not right now. Let's change the subject, stay away from secrets – mine and yours. Here, let me top up your glass. We'll move into the marina after siesta."

"Good. Tonight we eat in Xilouris. It is a taverna on the waterfront, very popular with Greeks. I called Andrei - the padron - earlier and booked. I've eaten there before."

"That sounds just right. I don't want to get too pickled though – it's my last night and I need a clear head for the morning."

"Don't worry, I'll help you with the checkout and with your lines."

"I can manage fine."

"I know you can, but I'd like to see you off. And tonight, after supper I want to say goodbye properly – and you'll be no good to me if you are pickled."

"A man can't argue with that. What time are we eating?"

"As late as possible."

"You are winding me up!"

She smiled and raised her eyebrows in that knowing way that was beginning to make itself a home in his emotions.

"It was a good idea to eat here. That was the best Greek meal I've ever had.

"Out of how many?"

"Oh – about six or seven, not counting your cooking this week, and Cristos's specialities of course. Greek food never appealed to me - neither did their women for that matter. I hate to say it but I've been proven wrong."

"I'm so glad to hear it." Mock relief was clear in her voice. "I said the food would be the best. Andrei is a good friend, and Greeks know how to treat their women properly."

"OK, point taken." He reached for her hand across the table and held it gently, rubbing her knuckles with his thumb.

"Do you know everyone in Crete?"

"Only those who can help me with my work. I also write restaurant reviews for websites. And I get to eat free quite often – but I still write the truth. I'll pick up the bill for tonight. Expenses."

"That's stretching it a bit given that you don't expect to pay. And I thought you'd been on holiday this week with me."

"I'll stretch something else if you're not careful!"

"I can't wait. But you'll have to keep the volume down or you'll frighten the shit out of the couple on the next boat."

"That's the trouble with marinas."

The food had certainly been good, but despite the banter there had been awkwardness between all evening. They had both avoided talking about the future – any future – beyond Steve's plan to take Adèle to Malta.

As they kissed deeply on the dockside the next morning, Steve could not bring himself to ask about her plans. He had his plans and did not want to complicate his future. The trouble was that he could visualise another, with her, one that they could shape together. He looked into her eyes – a blue-green colour not quite matching, with a fleck of gold in the iris of her left eye. He wanted to remember, but he knew that when he was sea he would want to forget. He always seemed to be running away.

"I don't know what to say."

"How about *sto epanidin*? That's Greek for…"

"Don't say it. Maybe goodbye is best."

"Fine, you say it your way and I'll say it mine."

He stepped aboard Adèle and started the engine.

"OK, if you can let go the bow line, I'll take it from there."

"Have a good trip."

The slow throb of big engines brought him back to the present. The false dawn was breaking as a ferry from Tunisia approached, *en route* for Malta. Adèle's engine was running smoothly as he motor-sailed on what was now a calm sea with little swell, until the ferry's wake shook him up. Malta was still a few hours away and after doing his checks and reviewing the weather forecast he watched the sun come up. Yet again his mind drifted to Helena as he pictured that morning at anchor near Stavros point.

They had been swimming and he had climbed back aboard. A few minutes later Helena had come up the boarding ladder, her hair streaming water down over her golden breasts and down her thighs. He had poured some fresh water over her hair and watched her towel off, carefully drying under her breasts and the dark, neatly trimmed hair between her thighs.

As he sat there deep in early morning thoughts, he could almost taste her. He was finding it hard to put her out of his mind.

"What the fuck?"

He jumped up. There was a repetitive warbling sound, like no alarm he had aboard. The engine temperature looked normal, the radar was clear, and there was nothing in sight – the ferry was well past him and Malta was over 20 miles away.

Down in the main cabin he realised that the sound was coming from the chart station. It wasn't so much loud, as piercing. He opened the drawer under the chart table and there he saw a phone under his papers. He'd forgotten all about it, and then he remembered Cassidy, but he'd given that phone to the dosser in Siteia. Or had he? He couldn't really remember.

He picked up the phone and looked at it. Incoming call, number withheld. Touching the green icon he said "I told you before you can fuck right off, whatever your name is."

"So that's how you really feel is it?" It was a woman's voice, a voice he knew but couldn't place.

"Who is this?"

"Forgotten me already?"

"Helena? It can't be, how, er… what, what's going on?"

"I left the phone for you, so we could keep in touch."

"But I'm at sea. And it's not your phone. Is it?"

"Long story for later. It's a custom sat phone. You are 17.6 miles from Valetta, and your track in 010 degrees. Magnetic."

"But…but, I don't understand."

"We need to talk. I am in Malta. Head for the marina in M'Sida, Marsamxett Creek. There is a berth ready for Adèle. I will meet you on the way in. I have to go. See you later."

With that, she cut the line. He could not call back. He swore and then paranoia started to kick in as he started joining up the dots.

Father a diplomat?

First class education?

Custom phone – and was it the one Cassidy had given him and that he had then passed on to the wino – or had he?

Mooring - all arranged.

"Fuck her, no one is using me again."

*

Five hours later he shaped his course to enter Grand Harbour. No way was he going into Marsamxett because Helena said so.

His plan was to go into Grand Harbour Marina, clear the paperwork and then anchor in Bighi Bay. Through the entrance, ahead and to starboard he could see a cruise liner, low in the water, apparently damaged. The buildings ashore seemed to be wrecked. He turned to port into the marina, past the few megayachts moored stern-to off Fort St Angelo. Then he cursed. Loudly.

"What he fuck is going on here?"

On his port side, second berth in, was *Auric Adventurer*.

Then a grey RIB came along his starboard side and then there was a hail 'Coming aboard'. He turned in surprise to see Helena climb onto the deck. At least it looked like Helena, but her hair was blonde.

In the RIB three men in body armour and carrying what looked like H&K 47s – safeties off - watched very carefully.

"Get off my boat."

"Steve, we can do this the easy way or the hard way. Those are anti-terrorist police in the RIB. The *Queen Katherine* has been attacked by terrorists. The port is closed to small vessels. You have permission to enter Marsamxett

– I will accompany you. I'll explain everything as we go. Believe me, you have no choice in this."

With that one of the police stepped nimbly aboard. Steve could see that he was handy and pumped up. He cursed to himself and cut the throttle. As Adèle slowed he turned to port, passing close under the bow of the *Adventurer.*

"Yes I know" said Helena, "there's a lot happening here and we need your help."

"Who's we?"

"Let's just say the good guys, for now."

"Do I have any choice?"

"No, not right now. They mean business."

She waved to the RIB. The helmsman raised his arm and it peeled away.

An hour later they were moored to a buoy off Sliema waterfront in Marsamxett Creek. The RIB collected their watchman and headed out.

Steve poured a whisky.

"Will you join me, though I don't know why I'm being so polite?

"Not right now, I need to keep a clear head."

"You've got a fucking nerve! This had better be good."

"It wasn't supposed to turn out this way. This has nothing to do with you and me."

"Pull the other one."

"You saw the *Queen Katherine*?"

"Yes."

"We estimate about four tons of explosive, in a trawler right under her stern. 300 hundred dead and twelve hundred injured – approximately. We think that the operation was run out of Algeria, though there are links with Tunisia. The trawler came up from Libya, but was Maltese in origin and disappeared three weeks ago, along with her crew."

"Jesus!"

"No, not Jesus. Islamists. All our assets are fully stretched. That's why I suggested pulling you in."

"To go to Algeria?"

"That's one option."

"Forget it. Your eyes – they've changed colour, your hair too. Who the hell are you?"

"Contacts and you know who I am. I have told you the truth."

"Which version?"

"Don't change the subject. Forget me – for now. You saw *Auric Adventurer*?"

"Yes. I saw her. Too many memories."

"Tobin has been kidnapped, two bodyguards murdered."

"I'm not losing sleep over that cunt. If I'd known about it before I got to Piraeus I wouldn't have taken that job. Too much history there. And I'm not apologising for my language – I've learned you're no lady."

"It sounds stilted I know, but what happened between us wasn't planned. I really fell for you, but that's not why I'm here."

"Stilted – is that supposed to be cheesy?"

"Don't waste your sarcasm on me."

"What was the pickup about in Siteia, the satphone – I suppose you know Cassidy too?"

"No comment. Since the immigration crisis started in 2014 and IC – Islamic Caliphate started sending trained bombers across with asylum seekers and refugees, the UK has had assets in place all across the Mediterranean islands. Crete and Malta are strategic. My base was Crete and I just kept an eye on people passing through. It's quite simple, given my family background."

"I'll bet. Nothing is that simple."

"When the ship got bombed a few days ago – it happened just after you left Souda, in fact, we pulled all our assets into Malta to help out."

"Who's we?"

"Let's just say HMG."

"I fucking knew it. I'm not getting involved."

"Maruška Pavkovic is here in Malta."

"Maruška, here in Malta?"

"We think so. It's a coincidence isn't it, what with Tobin going missing?"

"But how do you know about Maruška Pavkovic?"

"Part of my job to know."

"So that's why you questioned me about Fiskardo."

"Not really, I already had the full story – at least as far as Borthwick knew it. You didn't tell me much. Not that I can remember everything about those moments. I got a bit carried away."

"Yes, you're a regular Mata Hari. Suck their cocks and they'll tell you everything.

"No, that's not how it was, at all."

"Come off it. You're in it up to your neck. You even know Dickwick. Christ knows what's going on."

"Borthwick does work for HMG through his company."

"Fucking hell. Is there no one I can trust? Dickwick doesn't know the whole story anyway."

"Maybe you'll tell me one day?"

"No chance."

"Anyway, I don't believe that you didn't know about Borthwick's connections."

"I'm learning not to trust anyone. Especially mates and friends – and tarts,"

Helena didn't react, although his meaning was clear.

"I still make mistakes. No more. You seem to have lost your Greek accent in the last week, and changed your hair and eyes. Very convenient. Who are you really? How did it feel, screwing me for information?"

"That's not the right question, but I'll answer it anyway. I enjoyed it – a lot, and as I told you, I learned nothing new."

"I'm not surprised, I don't know any kinky tricks. Do you do it often?"

"Never before, and what I did with you was what I wanted for me, not HMG. In fact I still want it. I've been dreaming about you, your body, all the scars that tell stories I don't know about." She smiled – a sad, wistful smile, a smile about something lost, something that might have been.

"Check the files, I'm sure HMG have all the stories there."

"For God's sake Steve, I'm not fucking you about. Even if HMG did not want me here, I'd be here. I planned to meet you, spend some time with you and maybe go on to Gib with you."

"So how are you and Cassidy tied up – what's the story with the phone? It all sounds too neat to me. You set me up didn't you."

"Partly yes, I won't lie to you. But I was already thinking about resigning. I'll tell you everything, in due course – that's a promise, Official Secrets Act or not. Right now we need you to find Tobin."

"Can't the locals handle it?"

"They're overwhelmed with the bombing investigation. Malta is only a small country - they are severely stretched and we're not pushing them too hard. Tobin is an item of considerable interest to us. He has information that could compromise the UK. We need to make sure that he stays alive – and on our side. So, we need to keep close to him. It's clear from Fiskardo that somebody either wants him dead or wants the knowledge he has. We think that the Chinese are involved. There is a link to the death of the man you shot on the *Adventurer* at Fiskardo – he was killed in the hospital in Argostoli, before he could talk. He's still a Mr X to us, although we suspect a Stasi background. And a link to China."

"I heard about that from Borthwick. Gas embolism he said."

"Yes. Injection of air. Anyway, the Maltese are not equipped to deal with the likes of China. They still lean on us for support."

"So how do you know Maruška is here?"

"A Greek trawler arrived a week ago. The owner – we'll call him Nicos - is what we call a person of interest – for many years he's had wide involvement moving anything illegal in the Balkans by boat. That included involvement with a Serbian known as Vidovic – Maruška used to work for him – in those days we believe she was known as Andjela Karanovic. That recent movement does not fit the pattern – Nicos usually gets his trawler maintenance done in Greece. He usually stays clear of Malta. Apparently he needed repairs to the trawler. It's in the Bezzina boatyard in a dry dock right now – that's at the top end of Grand Harbour. He's never been hauled in – we and the Greeks just watch him, carefully. That gives us useful intelligence.

This background is just between you and me – I've said far too much already and put my career on the line. I trust you."

"Just now you were packing it in and sailing off with me to Gib!"

"Yes, and I wasn't planning to spend the rest of my life in a high security prison. Or have an accident."

"You're not serious?"

"We're effectively at war. Rules of war, although the British public doesn't see it all. The war with IC is out in the open, but there are other wars. Here:"

She held out her smartphone. The page was an Al Jazeera news announcement dated 3 days previously.

In a video just released, Islamic State has claimed responsibility for the successful attack on the infidel cruise ship 'Queen Katherine' in Malta. A spokesman made the following statement:"

"The jihad mission to blow up the Queen Katherine was planned by us and carried out by our Algerian brothers ICIM ('IC in the Maghreb'). This video shows the fishing boat that was used and her crew of martyrs, together with a recording of the live webcast made during the operation.

Malta has been an infidel bastion since the Great Siege by the Ottoman Caliphate was interrupted in 1565. This attack by ICIM demonstrates IC ability to strike at British and Crusader assets anywhere, and to remind the world that the Crusader infidels have only a temporary hold on Malta.

Defences built by the Knights of St John 500 years ago are useless against the modern weapons used by our martyrs.

This attack is just the start. IC looks forward to the day when Malta is part of the worldwide Islamic Caliphate."

Al Jazeera has taken an editorial decision not to publish the full video at this time.

"The bastards. They broadcast the attack as it happened?"

"Yes, but obviously they did not pre-announce the broadcast. They wanted the recording. It's chilling to watch. Not only that, they had a camera drone and other webcams set up around the harbour. It's totally obscene. You'd think that it would cause disaffection for IC, but no. Too many people buy in to their philosophy.

Putting that aside – if that is at all possible - we are waging high intensity cyberwars with both Russia and China. Right now. These wars involve high value economic data and know-how. The public doesn't see those either. Tobin is tied in to that. The IC is a minor problem compared to those. That's why we need you."

"What's wrong with your lot, the SBS and all that crew?"

"All our specials are here helping the Maltese out. HMG have almost emptied Poole and Hereford. There are at least four separate operations under way."

"And if I wasn't here?"

"Hypothetical. You are here. Tobin has crucial information we need, but first we need to find him."

"What does he know that you need so badly?"

"That I definitely cannot share with you, sorry."

"That says a lot about trust."

"Maybe, but you will probably know in good time. The Chinese want it too. That's part of the problem. Right, now, today. Here's the plan, as far as it goes. Your contact in the Malta police force is Deputy Commissioner Mauro Gauci-Maestre. His number is in your phone – he is expecting to see you this morning, in about half an hour. They will be glad to get this Tobin business off their backs – they are completely overwhelmed by the bombing of the *Queen Katherine*. It's taking all their manpower just to put the bodies together and ID them."

"That's as maybe, but I'm not a bloody detective, and I don't want to be."

"He thinks you are. He's been told you are highly unconventional, part of a special unit. Whatever you need he will get it, weapons included – even a chopper. Any problems, text me and I'll lean on them. Remember, we need Tobin alive."

"He may already be dead."

"We believe otherwise. He has information we need, and the Chinese want him dead, for that reason. But first they need the information – and they would certainly need to validate it.

Maruška is starting to make very delicate overtures – she has a problem, we believe, a serious problem. The Chinese may have a hold on her – a physical hold. The Greeks 'loaned' us the body of Mr X from the hospital in Argostoli and we flew it back to the UK for our own LV autopsy team."

"LV?"

"Slang – Lit-vinenko. After the Russians used polonium 210 to kill the dissident Aleksander Litvinenko in London in 2006, we set up a unique autopsy protocol for 'special cases'. Anyway, our people found an embedded molecular nanochip, with GPS, powered by the body's heat, connected to a nerve bundle in his spinal column. Do as we tell you or you get a kick. Just like a dog. We think that Maruška has a similar chip controlling and tracking her. Our tech people think it's capable of killing a person, given the right command, by disrupting a body's nerve signals. We have no idea how the Chinese managed to plant it – it would have needed a general anaesthetic."

"Shit. A GPS you said – transmitting her position?"

"Yes, the problem is we can't yet lock onto the position relay signal that the chip emits. Our techs are trying to get the chip working. It's extremely small and delicate, and we have to suppose that the Chinese know we have it. The signal would be very weak and possibly encoded. This is highly advanced stuff. We have no idea how they do it. If we could crack it then there's a possibility we could track Maruška. Anyway, I've already said enough to get us both shot. You seem to be very good at getting information out of me. How come you know so much?"

"I need to know as the saying goes. Leave it at that."

"Yes, and I didn't have to fuck you to do it."

"There'll be time enough for that."

"In your dreams."

She smiled and could feel his mood lightening, very slightly. "I have plenty of those."

"So do I, and they are not very pleasant."

"Isn't it a hell of a coincidence that the *Queen Katherine* gets attacked, Tobin gets kidnapped and Maruška is here all at the same time?"

"A very good question – and one reason why you are on the case. You are smart and ask the right questions despite behaving like a dickhead much of the time. As it happens we know of no link and we cannot even come up with a way in which they could be linked. If you have any ideas, please say so."

"None right now."

"Just get Tobin. You'll have to start with the police reports. There's a car available for you, with a driver. Bryan Elliott. He's a Brit who lives here and can handle a small boat. Ex-army, nothing too heavy but helps us out from time to time. He won't ask questions, but work on a very strict need to know basis- you know much too much already. You also have access to a RIB – the traffic situation is a nightmare after the bombing and a boat will be quicker for getting around this area. You have all the security and police passes you could ever need there in your phone. Just swipe it past their readers with your thumb on this button."

She took his right hand and grasped the thumb.

"Put your thumb here, like this…"

The electric tingle was still there between them. They both felt it and their eyes met.

"Ok, ok, I know how to use a finger scanner on a phone, they've been around for years."

They looked at each other, no words spoken, time standing still, memories still fresh.

"Ahoy there Adèle!"

"Ah, here's Bryan with the RIB."

"My watcher - I get it. I'll just tidy myself up then, if it can't wait. Maybe Bryan can take you ashore and come back for me?"

"I'll wait for you."

"You don't trust me? It's not that I can go anywhere, is it?"

"No, but I'll wait in the RIB anyway. One more thing – neither Bryan nor the Malta police know about the Maruška connection. Keep it tight. You're just looking for Tobin."

"Where to guv'nor?"
"Police HQ I guess."
"We'll drop off Ms Williams first and head over to Valetta."

Steve's mouth opened and he looked at Helena. She shook her head barely noticeably.

"We'll do a full briefing later, Steve."

"There's obviously a lot I need to catch up on, things are changing so quickly."

"It's a very fluid situation."

Bryan pointed towards the towering north bastions of Valetta. "Police HQ is just across there. Boat is the quickest way – many roads in Valetta are closed, and it's bad enough there on a good day."

Five minutes later, Steve stepped ashore for the short but hot, steep uphill walk to police HQ.

*

Malta Police HQ was a modernised block with a classical Maltese exterior, and the late morning heat was building despite the high ceilings. There was heavy security but Steve's phone got him through – and he noticed that Bryan had one just the same.

"I'll be in the waiting room – there's aircon there."
"I don't know how long I'll be."
"I'll find some coffee then."

In his corner office away from the sun, the Deputy Commissioner was brusque and obviously pressured. He stood up to offer Steve a damp but firm handshake. Typically Maltese, he was a head shorter than Steve, with dark brown eyes and thinning hair. His midriff betrayed a poor balance between food and exercise. Steve judged him to be about forty years old, and physically unfit.

"Take a seat Inspector."

Steve looked around and then quickly realised that he was the Inspector in question. He sat down, a surprised look still on his face.

"Sorry Sir, I don't usually use my rank. I prefer to be called Steve."

"That is good. Ms. Williams said you were unconventional. Call me Mauro. Here is my card."

While Steve examined the card, Mauro picked up a thin buff file from his ornate mahogany desk which carried a modern holographic display panel and keyboard. "Despite all of today's technology, some of us still think that paper has its uses. It is much easier to keep secure. It's harder to share too, but that is an up to date copy – as of 6 o'clock this morning – of the Charles Tobin incident. My assistant will show you to an office where you can read it. I prefer that it does not leave the building."

"That's suits me Mauro. I'm not really a files man."

"Well, that may be, but you'll have to send me a daily report. Send it to my assistant, Marco."

"I'll do that."

There was a knock at the door, and a uniformed policeman entered.

"Ah, Marco. This is Inspector Baldwin. He is taking over the investigation of the kidnapping of Charles Tobin and the murder of his bodyguards. Give him whatever assistance he needs." He turned to Steve.

"The only assistance we cannot give you is people. Anything else within reason you can have. Now, I have a meeting with the Commissioner. Good luck, and don't forget the daily reports."

Mauro stood up and offered his hand.

Marco led him to a small office on the third floor, south side and hot. The air conditioning was rattling and seemed to be pumping warm air in. Steve put the incident file on the desk and sat down.

"Here is my card. I will organise water and coffee for you. Call me on extension 213 if you need anything. I have been told to take you to the armoury on the way out. If you can make a list of what you may need then I will prepare it, if we have it."

Steve sat down and dropped the two business cards into the bin under the desk. This was definitely not his cup of tea. Marco and Mauro sounded like a TV comedy show from his childhood. And he was now a fucking detective. Twenty four hours ago he had been at sea worrying about his rigging and what the weather would do. Now his world had been turned upside down again. He shook his head in total disbelief. Still, it would be good to finally sort out Maruška. Finally?

He opened the folder and started reading, not noticing an overweight Maltese lady enter with coffee and a glass of water until she spoke. He looked up from the file and thanked her, but was immediately back, immersed at the scene of the kidnapping. The reports were extremely thorough and well written. There was no speculation, just facts and estimated timings, together with witness interviews.

His requirements for equipment from the armoury were minimal but sufficient in case he should run into Maruška. When he paused to drink his coffee he called Marco and told him what he needed. A sports bag was required, to contain lightweight body armour. Eyes were raised at his request for two Sig-Sauer 230s with shoulder holsters and ammunition available from stock, but the Fairbairn-Sykes knife they did not have.

It took him about forty five minutes to read the through the reports a couple of times and make some notes on the pad, and then he called Mauro.

Sicilian Channel

"I'll come and collect the file and then take you to the armoury. I have located the knife you wanted – one is being biked over from the MDF stores at Luqa – that's the Malta Defence Force. It should be here very soon."

*

Finding Maruška

All Steve had to go on was the police report – and his scant knowledge of Maruška's personality.

"Where to guv?"

Bryan looked at him, almost like a spaniel waiting his master's order.

"Were you ever a London cabbie Bryan?"

"As it happens, yeh, for a few years after my unit was cut in one of the defence reviews."

"I'd never have guessed." Bryan's face remained impassive - it was clear that Steve's sarcasm was lost on him.

"Where did you serve?"

"All around – Turkey, Syria, the Baltic and a spell in the Far East."

"What regiment?"

"RMP."

"A monkey?"

"Yes, for my sins, but I prefer the term Redcap if you don't mind, Sir."

"Don't call me 'sir' – I was only joshing you."

Bryan smiled. "Really?"

Steve's face creased in a laugh. "All right, score one to you. So that's how you got to serve in all those places?"

"You'd be surprised what I got up to, but that's for another day."

"OK, fair enough. At least your police experience will come in useful – I haven't got a clue about being a detective. Here."

Steve opened the rucksack and held it out to Bryan.

"I take you can use one of these?"

"Are you serious?"

"Never more."

"Sure. The Glock is ok, though I'm not in practice."

Bryan checked the weapon – expertly.

"Me neither, but it's obvious you know your stuff. They didn't have SIGs. Let's go and look at the kidnap scene – Vittoriosa is it?"

"That's right, one of the three Cities – ancient name Birgu. Dead easy by RIB, less than five minutes out round Fort St. Elmo and then into Grand Harbour. Too far to walk."

"Ok, but we could run?"

"What? In this heat, with a 200 foot uphill climb, and then a ferry across? Sorry Guv, I follow orders, but I have to say that…"

"Keep your knickers on, Bryan, I was only kidding. Maybe I'll go for a run this evening. You can come too."

"Fuck off, Sir."

They laughed.

"You had me worried there, Guv' – not that I couldn't have done it, mind – I'm still in shape."

"I can see that, good for you. The RIB it is then. I need to get a feel for what happened. Reading the file isn't enough - I need to see the location. You can give me your take on it as we go. I've been dumped in at the deep end – I'm no bloody detective!"

"Right'o. Cast off the bow line and I'll tell you what I know."

Bryan backed the RIB away from the MDF dock wall just as the Gozo ferry passed them. He turned slowly then gunned the engine and the RIB climbed up onto the plane and levelled out. They had to raise their voices over the sound of the spray and engine.

"I don't know a lot, just some rumours, bar chat, the newspapers and what Ms. Williams told me. People are more concerned about the bombing and what it will do to tourism, what with Malta being declared an Islamist target."

Over the sound of the engine and thump of the small chop against the hull Bryan started to flesh out the background.

"They snatched him about midnight, as he came out of Del Borgo's. That's a fancy restaurant a short walk from his yacht. He had two minders with him."

A Defence Force picket boat hailed them as they turned to pass under the footbridge into Grand Harbour. After checking their credentials they were waved on and Bryan accelerated away.

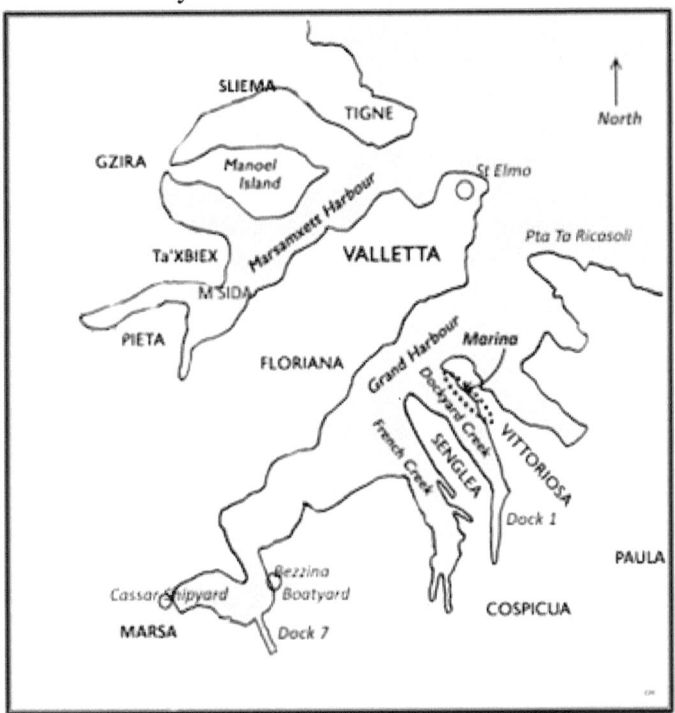

The *Queen Katherine* was a sad sight, surrounded by harbour vessels and tenders, with a large salvage barge alongside her. She was to be raised off the bottom and towed away for scrap. There was also talk about sinking her offshore and marking her as a war grave. Some bodies would never be recovered and the British Prime Minister had said that the attack was an act of war. Of course, the UK would never dignify IC with a formal declaration of war – that would effectively grant them recognition as a state.

Bryan turned to port at Fort St. Angelo and headed south into Grand Harbour Marina, past the *Adventurer*. There were workmen on many of the yachts, starting repairs to the blast and debris damage from the explosion the cruise liner.

Bryan raised his arm and pointed up at an old apartment block on their starboard side. "That's where I live, just there. It used to be the naval captains' quarters back in Nelson's day. The area is called Senglea, another of the Three Cities. The people there don't take to kindly to the English – it can be a bit rough, dockworkers. I like it though, keeps me on my toes."

"So, you could see Tobin's yacht from your balcony."

"Yes, though I wasn't in when it all happened, I was visiting a lady friend, you know what I mean, keeping fit?" He winked and Steve got the drift.

They moved on down into Dock 1 – now used as a marina – and tied up.

"Del Borgo's is just up here."
"Fancy a coffee?"
"At five euros a cup?"
"I'm buying. It's on expenses."

They went down the steps into the cool basement. It was an old building, with ornate stonework and vaulted ceilings, with black forged-iron fittings set in the wall.

"They used to keep their animals here. That's what the Maltese did in the old days."

A waiter approached them. Bryan held out his phone and showed his credentials. He looked at Steve "Cappucino?"

"Fine." Turning to the waiter, Steve spoke. "The men who were murdered the other night – which table did they use?"

The waiter led them to a corner table.

"This one – the guards. That one – the man and then the couple."

"What did he do."

"I have explain already to police."

"I need to hear it from you."

"OK. He eat alone – use phone a lot – we don't like – disturb other customers. Ask him to stop. He very angry, but he stop. Buy drinks for other customers. Then he have brandy and two ladies join him."

Despite his accent, the way he pronounced the 'ladies' carried an implication, a suggestion of something doubtful or unsavoury.

"Did he know them?"

"No, they eat first at that table there. Then they have drink with him and he leaves with guards. Good tip. Women follow soon after."

"How soon?"

"I don't know – other waiter take their payment. Two, three minutes maybe."

"Can you describe them?"

The waiter's description lacked detail and matched the police statement, although jeans and trainers on women seemed out of place in Del Borgo's.

"Did you notice anything strange about the women?"

"No. But then next day I remember I think one from same country as me - I think."

"How do you know?"

"She speak with French accent, but like a Serb who live in Paris."

"A Serb, Paris?"

"Yes, I use live in Paris. Serb area. Not like. Here better."

"How could you tell she was a Serb from Paris?"

"I clear dishes from their table. She mention 'Paris' – like only a Serb say it."

"That's not in your statement."

"I remember later. I help if I can."
"How did the other woman sound?"
"I no hear her speak. Now I get your coffee."
"We've changed our plans. Here."
The waiter palmed the twenty Euro note and Steve turned to Bryan.
"Let's go and take a look in the street."

"According to the file, the police took no notice of the couple of women – they turned here – and the waiter who was locking the door after them, said they went a different way to Tobin, up here."
"Yes, St Dominic Street. Tobin would have headed for the harbour. No one saw the snatch?"
"Apparently not. It happened on the corner, here."
There was little blood left in the cracks between the cobblestones, and the faint chalk marks outlining the positions of the bodies of the guards had all but disappeared.
"Point blank, base of the skull, one each. Cool and professional, and must have been simultaneous or it would not have been so clean."
"Must have been two of them - too much separation for one person assuming there was one each side of Tobin – the body spacing suggests that. Nothing heard?"
Steve was visualising the scene.
"The police say no. How do you think that they kept Tobin quiet and got away – the police don't seem to know?"
"Cosh or gas, probably. Late at night the roads would have been clear, but you'd have to have local knowledge. A Tom-Tom GPS is useless in Malta. It's a warren down here. They'd need a car too. It could be locals though."
"Does it sound like locals to you?"
"No, but they could have hired a driver?"
"Yes, but risky."

"If you ask me guv, this is an outside job – though they could have used immigrants – Malta is full of asylum seekers – and some of them are real bad sorts, even IC sleepers. I reckon they got him down to the harbour and away in a boat."

"Yes, make the police think that it was by road, point us away from the boat. Let's check the quayside nearest here."

"For what?"

"Ideas, Bryan, ideas. You're the detective, so you say."

"Strictly a redcap."

"Land of the blind, mate, land of the blind."

Access to the nearest stretch of quay was through a security gate with keycard access.

"They wouldn't have brought him here – look – it's monitored by CCTV. Let's walk between the access gates to each line of mooring pontoons. You head that way and I'll head up towards the *Adventurer* – when you are done come on up and we'll talk to the crew."

"Anything?"

"Not a sausage, you?"

"I think there may be a small patch of blood on the quayside."

"Show me."

"Good work, Bryan, you've got sharp eyes."

"I've seen enough blood in my time. Let's take a scraping for the lab. It hasn't rained and there's no sign of dog shit – that's everywhere in Malta. Worse than France – and that's saying something."

"Sounds like a good idea - we'll never get any scene of crime people down here today."

"Maybe we should check the CCTV anyway – the cameras might have got some peripheral images."

Steve turned. "I think I'll hand all this over to you. You seem to know what you are doing – I'm no detective."

"Happy to advise, but Ms. Williams obviously had her reasons for pulling you in."

"Yes, and I haven't got a bloody clue what they were."

At the marina office, the manager helped them go through the CCTV camera recordings. The one nearest the suspected blood patch showed three people pass through the edge of the frame – a man and woman were holding up a man who appeared to be drunk. It was a brief shot, no more than two seconds and the time stamp was about right – just after midnight.

Bryan turned to the manager "Don't erase that. Make a copy. What about comings and goings?"

"We have a camera which monitors the approach to the Marina."

"Let's see it before and after the time of that last one we looked at."

They changed camera recordings and rolled back a couple of hours. It had picked up the RIB arriving – unlit – with three people aboard. Despite all the lighting around the dock, the shapes were indistinct. Then just after midnight, an unlit RIB with four people leaving.

"Ok, that's great. Email the video files to me, address on this card. Thanks for your help."

Steve and Bryan were walking back to the RIB. "Good thinking, about the video copy. Your experience is really useful."

"All part of the job, Guv. That's what monkeys are for."

"OK, ok, point taken. I'll say no more."

"You seemed interested in the fact that one of those women seemed to be Serbian. It's unlikely that two women would carry out a kidnapping. Anyway they headed the other way."

"As you said, we gather information. I'm keeping an open mind for now. Right, let's see what the crew have to say. I should tell you that I know some of them. I worked in a security team on the *Adventurer* back in Greece."

"Not that incident in Fiskardo?"

"You're well informed."

"The days are long and I've got plenty of time to watch the news. Besides, I see all the superyachts arrive from my balcony and curiosity gets hold of me. I like to find out a bit about them and their owners. Most of them are owned by companies in the Bahamas or Cayman Islands, controlled by people who are bent – that's 'bent' as in crooked. There's plenty of dirty money here and I don't think Tobin is an exception to that rule."

"You're probably right."

"I'd bet on it."

The day was very hot and the heat was reflecting intensely off the high buildings and forts around the dock. They hailed a crew member and Bill Johnson came down to meet them.

There were some new faces in the *Adventurer's* crew and the old hands were surprised to see Steve. Their mood was sombre and Bill Johnson was having a hard time of it – back in his cabin there was an open whisky bottle. Steve introduced Bryan as a colleague, and left it at that.

The visit did little more that confirm the facts in the file.

"I'm on a security detail helping the Malta Police over the apparent kidnapping of Mr T. Tell me Bill, the new security outfit that came aboard in Argostoli – who are they?"

"Transglobal - I think that they operate out of Rome."

"Rome?"

"Yes, our new security manager hired them after Mr T sent your bunch packing after Fiskardo."

"What happened to Mike Robinson – why the new guy?"

"Mike went on a bender and they found his body in the dock in Argostoli. Another one off the crew list. The new guy is Frank Abadelli. His team are a bit rough and ready, but seem ok – for Italians. Sorry – can I offer you guys something?"

"It's a bit early for Scotch thanks. Water would be fine." Bryan's disappointment was evident as he said "Same for me too."

Bill called the stewardess for iced water.

"Who reported him missing?"

"Frank – Abadelli – he called me about one a.m. after Mr T's close security guys did not call in – there was an hourly routine. We walked up to Del Borgo's and by the time we got there the police were checking the bodies of the guards in the street. We explained who we were and that Mr T was obviously missing."

Bill could add nothing more to the police statements.

"Can you call Mr. Abadelli now to meet us?"

"He's in Rome – at least that's where he said he was going – to his Head Office. He left the day after Mr T disappeared."

"Didn't the police tell him to stay?"

"I don't know. He doesn't report to me."

"What's his phone number?"

"Here, it's on the crew list. You can take that."

"Thanks."

Steve handed the list to Bryan, "Where did you go after Argostoli."

"When the police finally released the *Adventurer,* Mr. T was back in England and sent orders for us to come here to Malta. We came straight across and cleared in. Straightforward trip."

"Anything else?"

"Not really, Mr. T flew in and then insisted we head up the coast for a meeting. We anchored for 24 hours."

"Where?"

"Off Portomaso, a couple of miles up the coast. Mr. T went ashore to the casino one night with Mr. Thompson, then they had a meeting aboard the next day. A couple of

Italians came over. At least they looked Italian, but spoke more like Americans. Brothers I think they were. Not the type of people I would choose to mix with. Heavy. Mr T seemed to know them well."

"Did you get their names?"

"I'm not sure I should say any more. I'm not allowed to disclose any information about the owner and his guests. More than my job is worth."

"What job? Right now you haven't got an employer."

"Fair point, still…"

"I know that Bill, don't forget I signed the same non-disclosure documents too, but much more stringent. Bugger that, we're trying to find Tobin. What do you think he would want?"

"OK, ok. They are known as the Tumino brothers. They had security with them – a couple of heavies, and a lawyer, didn't get his name."

"Anything else?"

"I heard that their father got shot recently – assassinated. They were pretty cut up about it."

"How do you know?"

"Jenny, the stewardess, talking out of turn. She's on a warning."

"Can we speak to her now?"

"She off today. One more thing – the Tumino brothers."

"Yes?"

"I heard that their helicopter crashed on their estate in Sicily. They were killed, along with the pilot, as they returned from their meeting with Tobin."

Steve looked at Bryan. "I'll check into it."

"Yes, there's a lot of bad stuff happening around Tobin and those he deals with. They were probably Mafia anyway."

"What would Tobin want with them?"

"I've no idea and I really don't want to know."

"And what about this Thompson pal of Tobin's?"

"He flew back to England the next day, before the kidnapping. He's worked for Tobin for years. Used to be a British Cabinet Minister."

"Why wasn't he at Del Borgo's with Tobin?"

"He was ill I think – said he'd some bad fish, asked me for some Immodium to stop the shits. I double up as the ship's quack."

"No doctor?"

"No."

"OK. Thanks. What are the immediate plans for the *Adventurer*?"

"We stay here until we get orders from Mr T – wherever he is."

"For how long?"

"No idea."

Steve felt the vibration in his pocket – a text from 'Macdonald'. Urgent.

"Ok, thanks Bill. We have to go."

"Fine, we are certainly not going anywhere."

"Anything else Bryan?"

"We need a sample of Mr Tobin's DNA for elimination purposes."

"Like what?"

"Dirty washing."

"Hair sample?"

"If it's got follicles."

Steve and Bill Johnson looked at Bryan.

"That's hair roots – there's no DNA in hair itself."

Johnson called a steward and he headed off to the Owner's Suite with a plastic bag accompanied by Bryan.

"One more thing. What's the chain of command in Tobin's operation?"

"I don't know. He has several offices and we get paid out of his head office in England."

"Thompson?"

"He works for one of Tobin's other companies. Not the one that runs this ship. So, currently, I have no boss. I'd better start looking for a new job, something a lot quieter."

"Thanks Bill."

"No problem."

They talked a bit more about Tobin. Bill Johnson had no insight to offer. Bryan turned to Steve. "I'm done, got some pubic hair samples – with follicles."

"Are they his?"

"Only one kind in the owner's dirty sheets. They're changed every day and last week's laundry's not been done yet."

"Too much info, Bryan."

"Maybe, but it's important."

"I know. Bill, we've got to move."

"I'll show you to the boarding ramp."

"We'll come back later to catch up with the other crew. Take care, Bill."

"I think I'll take up gardening actually, Steve. The *Adventurer* seems to be jinxed."

*

Steve was scanning the text from Helena as they walked back to the RIB as Bryan spoke.

"For a minute there I thought we had some suspects."

"What?"

"Suspects. Those Italians."

"Yes, I'll mention it to Ellie. She can organize the legwork on that, though it's most likely deskwork."

"Ellie?"

"I mean Ms Williams."

Bryan looked at Steve for a moment too long, suspicion obvious. "Ms Williams. I think I understand. We need to follow all the leads, Steve."

Steve ignored the implication. "I know that, but time is tight. What's your gut feel?"

"We shouldn't work hunches, just follow evidence, but we're on ground zero here. The Italians are dead, but it still smells - a lot."

"Let's work with what we've got here and let the others do the smelling in Italy."

*

Sitrep

Steve was seated in the Jubilee pub on the waterfront at Gzira, with Adèle in sight on her mooring a few hundred yards away. Bryan had left the RIB with Steve and gone home in the car. It was early evening and Helena was due in a few minutes.

His text to Marco was brief.

"Sitrep day 1. Read incident file, visited scene of kidnap. Talked to witnesses. No theory at present."

"Hi."

"Oh hi."

Steve stood and kissed Helena on each cheek.

"That's very Mediterranean of you."

"Well, I'm not sure whether this is business or pleasure."

"Let's make it a bit of both. What are you up to?"

"Just copying you in on my daily report, though I can't find you in the contact list. Who are all these people in the phone?"

"Most of them are just fictional. Here, give me the phone."

She found the entry and passed it back to him.

"You are kidding me?"

"Not at all. Can't be too careful."

"Fine, daily report on its way."

"I'll read it later. Just tell me."

"Nothing much to tell, Ms Williams."

"You can cut that out, don't link me to that name – bad tradecraft. You never know who's listening."

"It may be your trade, but it's not mine."

"Oh, but it is. You accepted the King's shilling."

"That was a long time ago."

"And what about duty to your comrades – i.e. me?"

"Point taken. Does Ms. Williams have a first name?"

She smiled. "Doris."

"That's fancy, Dot."

"Well, what would you like to call me?"

"How about Ellie."

"You got it in one. Keep as close to the truth as you can."

"So you really are Helena?"

Her eyebrows raised and a smile played on her lips. "For now."

"What can I get you?"

"Sparkling water will be fine, thanks."

They chatted about the weather and the half-dressed lobster-coloured English tourists walking past, while the waitress set the water down with another pint of John Smiths for Steve.

"We've got our Rome station looking into Transglobal Security and Abadelli. As for the Tuminos, they are really bad news - an old Sicilian family, tentacles everywhere, including a family branch based in Las Vegas. We're still digging."

"There's some good news too."

"I can't wait."

"You can cut out the sarcasm too, Steve, it's unnecessary and wastes time."

"Sorry, you and your sort have that effect on me. I learned the hard way."

"Put it behind you. Let's find Tobin and then get on with *our* lives. The good news is that our techies are close to solving the nanochip problem. The bad news is that we think the Chinese have cracked our quantum comms chips."

"Meaning?"

"They might be able to decode our mobile phone comms."

"So this all singing, all dancing phone I'm holding has been cracked by the Chinese."

"Potentially. We can update it with a new layer of encryption - but we're not doing that yet – that would give the game away."

"Fucking great."

"Let's talk about the good news – and you can cut out all the swearing – it doesn't add anything! We think that the nanochip in Maruška communicates by uploading a quantum worm to any nearby mobile phone it detects, using NFC.

"Near field communication?"

"So I'm told." She looked at him quizzically and continued.

"That one-off virus carries the location data and worms its way back to the Guoanbu."

"The Guoanbu. I heard of that bunch when I was in Djibouti."

"Oh. Yes, well, we believe that the worm picks up the network path as it goes, so another quantum worm can return down the network pathway. It's almost instantaneous. We've still got a lot to do, but it's amazing technology."

"So you can track her?"

"How do you work that out?"

"It's obvious isn't it? The worm must know where it's going – you would have to check every phone circuit in the world or know where she was to intercept. Unless it goes to a local Chinese embassy and gets uploaded to a satellite. Or you know the destination."

Her eyes widened. "Don't stop, I'm all ears."

"OK. The fact that she is in Malta – you think – narrows the field to about seventeen miles by, what, seven miles, and one Chinese embassy?"

"Shit, shit, shit." Helena knocked the chair over as she stood up. The other customers turned in interest to watch the goings-on. "I need to make a call - back in five minutes – don't go away."

Steve ordered another pint of John Smith's and watched the local news channel. It was continuous coverage of the

Queen Katherine bombing. Five minutes turned to ten, then fifteen, twenty. The news clips were now re-circulating. He was just getting out of his seat when Helena came back in, smiling broadly. Two tourists who had been waiting for a free table turned away in disappointment as he sat down again.

"Mine's a very large gin and tonic, please. Sorry I took so long."

He crossed to the bar and ordered, taking an orange juice for himself.

"You're not joining me?"

"I've had too much already. I had just about given you up. You look happy. Are you celebrating something?"

She punched him on the arm and whispered. "Could be! You clever bastard – you may have cracked this."

She gulped her gin and tonic. "Let's walk and talk, safer that way."

They crossed the road and walked east towards Sliema and Tigne Point.

"We have asked the US to re-task one of their satellites."

"The Yanks are in on this?"

"The *Katherine* is our cover. We're not sharing the nanotech with them, yet. How do you know so much about comms technology when our technical people couldn't work it out?"

"I worked comms in my troop for a time. It's not about knowing the technology, just thinking it through. Your people probably couldn't see the wood from the trees."

"Your file said that you had a high IQ."

"You've read my file?"

"Yes. Another white lie I'm afraid."

"So that was all bollocks about my scars?"

"The stories yes, but what I feel, no."

He shook his head.

"You're pissed off with me?"

"Are you surprised?"

"So, what's the story?"

"This isn't for the files ok?"

"Fair enough, scout's honour."

"In a mad moment a few years ago I realised that I needed to earn a living after the RM. The world was changing, we had the IOT, comms everywhere. I couldn't go on doing odd physical security jobs for the rest of my life and my Marines pension is crap. I saw an ad for a distance learning course – a Masters Degree in Cybersecurity and signed up. I must have been mad. It's very slow going as my maths was way behind, but I can work a bit on it when I'm at sea or in harbour. It's still security, but brain instead of brawn. At least that's the theory. Hopefully it's something I can use wherever I am – if I ever qualify."

"That's not in your file."

"Not everything is – particularly since I left the RM."

They walked and talked, arm in arm in the hot evening, as roller-bladers swerved through the crowd along the promenade. It was busy. Perversely, the bombing had increased tourist demand. Lightning wouldn't strike twice and the holiday videos would be really different.

"Re-tasking a satellite will not guarantee interception - it passes over in low orbit and has to be in the microwave beam. Signal backscatter is weak."

"If you say so, but my people say that we can get to the traffic. Geo-something."

"It's going to take hours to re-task a geostationary satellite, then they have to decode the packets – even if you know which ones they are. They must have got GCHQ to hack in to the mobile networks here. That's the best approach. Decoding is still a problem if they are using quantum encryption."

"They don't tell me much, but sound confident. Hours, they said. So, we have some time to ourselves. Look, here's the Sliema Tower Hotel. Fancy a night ashore – maybe even a bath?" Her raised eyebrows and quizzical smile told him everything.

"Can't – I have the RIB and anyway, I quote "it's not good tradecraft" is it?"

"Got me there. But we could have a secret assignation?"

"Another time, maybe. This hotel looks a bit upmarket for HMG anyway."

"Everything is booked up by the Press and military."

"Enjoy your bath. I need to get back to Adèle. I'm meeting Bryan on the waterfront at 7 am."

"Another time then?"

"That's what I said." They kissed politely, and Steve turned.

"I'll call you as soon as I hear anything."

Steve removed his tee shirt and started a gentle jog back to the RIB, about a mile along the waterfront.

He didn't see Helena in the taxi as she passed, on her way to the British High Commission in Ta' Xbiex, two miles away – she was late for her meeting.

*

It was late at night in the British High Commission in Ta'Xbiex, and Helena was interviewing a receptionist who was not pleased to have been called from her monthly girls' evening in the bar at the Royal Malta Golf Club.

"I've already written down all I know in the report."

"Then tell me again, please Louise – a lot depends on it."

"The security guard checked her ID…"

"I've already interviewed the guard."

"She gave him the letter and then he came in to the desk and gave me the envelope."

"Let's pretend go through the video once again. I want you to give me your impression."

The CCTV clip rolled again on the tablet screen.

"Medium height, smartly dressed – blouse and designer jeans, high heels, auburn hair typically Maltese. Except…" Helena raised her eyebrows and said nothing "…except that her build is not Maltese, not quite. Just an impression.

Then what?"

"I put the envelope in a security case to isolate it. I phoned the staff upstairs and they sent someone down. They took it for scanning immediately – standard biochem and x ray."

"What do you remember about the envelope?"

"Addressed to the High Commissioner by name. Marked URGENT."

The envelope had passed all the scans, was pronounced safe – at least in the sense of explosive/biochem hazard, and had been opened by the High Commissioner late in the evening.

It was printed by hand in block capitals and contained information which was potentially far more hazardous than what the scans could have detected. It simply said:

TOM BROWN
11° 07' N° 42 50' E
I HAVE TOBIN AND THE KEY
BRITISH FLAG TO BE LOWERED HALF MAST BY
3PM TODAY OR INFORMATION GOES TO CHINA
AND TOBIN DIES
AWAIT FURTHER INSTRUCTIONS

Within an hour, the message had passed through the Malta Head of Station to the Middle East desk in Vauxhall Cross.

Tom Brown had been the cover name of an MI6 agent tracking Maruška in Djibouti the previous year. He had worked with Baldwin and his remains had been found at the coordinates quoted in the message.

The message had been immediately escalated to 'C'. Two hours later Ellie Williams was in the safe room at the High Commission with the Head of Station, in a conference call and receiving instructions.

Following the rise of Islamic Caliphate over the period 2014-16, Malta had regained strategic importance, being on the route of economic migrants and asylum seekers travelling by the boatload from North Africa to Europe. In this flow of people was embedded a steady stream of trained Islamist fighters, destined to become sleepers in Europe, awaiting orders to become martyrs.

The UK Government had recognised that Malta had become a key focal point, and had stepped up what had been a one man station (in particular and reportedly, the disgraced Rick Tomlinson) into a modest but efficient MI6 operation.

Elint was still gathered in Cyprus but Malta was increasing in importance as a focus for humint. And now, following the *Queen Katherine* attack, Malta Station was at full stretch.

*

Cape Bon Onwards

Anwar dozed in the afternoon sun. They had rounded Cape Bon well outside Tunisia's 12 mile limit at noon. During the late morning they had seen the hump of Pantellaria to the south and kept well clear.

"Progress is good, I think."

"Yes, for sure" Anwar replied. Are you hungry?"

"I could eat something."

"Then I will get some bread and cheese. We are on autopilot. Just stay here and watch for any fishing boats. There are no ships near us. I will only be a few minutes."

"Yes, Captain." Ben-Zhair smiled. He was feeling good, his seasickness cleared.

He pretended to keep watch – he was no seaman whereas Anwar's father had been a fisherman, simple and true with no political inclinations. So, Anwar knew about boats, but he also knew about politics. He had done well at school and gone to University in Oran. At University he had learned more about the history of Algeria from some of his peers. That had led him, more or less directly, to being on this boat as part of the mission. For now.

*

The swell gradually subsided as they left the Gulf of Tunis astern and the hot afternoon wore on. Anwar had noticed some cloud from the northwest earlier that day, but his father's weather lore had long been forgotten. The easterly swell had died completely as they passed over the north end of Banco Estafette the waters began to deepen into the Western Mediterranean Basin. The sea was from the northwest now, and building, with the wind.

Anwar could no longer doze. Though his weather knowledge was scant, he was uneasy about the prospects ahead. He reduced speed by a few knots to try and make the ride more comfortable – the boat was beginning to pound now. He had come down from the flying bridge and he was glad of the padded seat at the inside steering position.

Just after four pm, ben-Zhair reappeared. He did not look too good – there was a green tinge to his face, and he looked clammy. He held tightly to the grab rail in the deck saloon, trying to adjust to the motion of the boat.

"How long will this continue, Anwar?"

Anwar shrugged. "Only Allah knows – may He be praised" he replied, "but at our present speed we have another 10 hours of this – at least. *Insha'Allah* it will be less."

There was green resignation and frustration in ben-Zhair's expression. He was not enjoying the ride and his patience with the religious aspects were thinning. "Anwar, I am sure that Allah knows we praise Him, when at sea we do not have to follow prayer rituals exactly, and we do not have to praise Him continuously. We have done great work for Him today so I think that He will forgive us some prayers and praises. He is all-seeing, all knowing."

"Of course. I understand. I can reduce speed some more if you would like me to."

"No, no, it is important that we keep to the plan."

"As you wish, but I think it will get worse."

Ben-Zhair cursed under his breath. Then they felt the bang through the deck of the boat. 'Meltemi' slewed to starboard across the sea and an unhealthy banging continued from under the stern.

Anwar swore.

"What is that?"

"I think we hit something. We may be damaged."

Anwar checked the instrument panel and could see that the revolutions on the starboard drive shaft were falling. He shut the starboard engine down.

"I will go and check in the engine room."

Just then there was shrill alarm and a red light came on. The legend beneath it said "Bilge Water Level."

He switched on both engine room bilge pumps on the panel, then after resetting the autopilot and reducing the power on the port engine, he went down through the hatch into the engine room.

By the time he returned, ben-Zhair had been sick into the galley sink. Anwar did not feel too well himself, and the sight of ben-Zhair's half-digested lunch made him gag.

"I think that we have damaged the starboard propeller. We must have hit something. There is some leaking but I have tightened the gland. We are safe for the moment, the pumps can cope. We should make for the nearest harbour."

"Where is that?"

"Bizerte. It is about 25 miles to the South."

"But that is in Tunisia."

"Yes, but Annaba is another almost 100 miles further, and the weather is getting worse. We have the night ahead."

"We are not going to Tunisia as long as we can make progress towards Annaba."

Anwar looked unhappy.

"As you wish - you are the leader. But the coast is dangerous in this weather and there is only really one other harbour – Tabarka. But that too is in Tunisia – just. Even Tabarka is 70 miles – about 150 kilometres."

"As you said, I am the leader of this mission. If the boat is in no immediate danger then we continue towards Annaba. Tabarka remains an option, though that is so close to Algeria as to make no difference."

"It shall be" Anwar said as he turned to the galley, shaking his head. He found a plastic pan in one of the cupboards and handed it to ben-Zhair.

"For you" he said. "I will clean up. You will find some anti-seasickness tablets in the first aid box – there." He pointed to the bulkhead just as the 'Meltemi' hit a big sea and ben-Zhair retched into the pan, just managing to hold on to the grab rail.

Sicilian Channel

Anwar checked the radar and AIS. They were a little south of the main shipping tracks, but he could detect at least eight ships within 20 miles. AIS gave the details of the ships as he moved the AIS cursor around and it passed over each ship's symbol. There was an oil tanker header to Gulfport in the US, two grain carriers, a deep sea tug and all the general cargo ships that make up a typical day on this busy route from the Suez Canal.

The cursor passed over one target which showed the data of a ship called the *Chong Ryon San* with a speed of 17 knots on a heading 270 degrees true, with a mixed cargo, non-hazardous, headed for Annaba in Algeria, and with an ETA three hours later. It fitted into ben-Zhair's greater plan, but even he was unaware of that detail and the coincidence. Anwar would never know its significance.

*

Two hours later ben-Zhair felt better though a little sleepy as a result of the pills. In the heads compartment he struggled against the motion of the boat as he cleaned himself up, but Anwar would have to unblock the toilet later.

He knew that he had made history, but the prospect of even greater glory was tantalisingly close. Then he headed up to the deck saloon. The spray was flying but the wind had shifted and they were now making more than 12 knots under the one engine.

"As you recommend, Anwar, we will divert to Tabarka, but only until the weather forecast improves. You are the captain."

"It's better now, but there may still be worse to come."

The worst of the weather held off and a little over eight hours later they passed inside the ancient Genovese fort at Tabarka. Anwar stopped the boat just inside the marina and prepared the mooring lines. As he belayed the stern line on the cleat ready docking, ben-Zhair cursed his earlier seasickness. He had forgotten to change the vessel's ensign to a Moroccan flag, and the self-adhesive registration numbers for the bow were in his cabin. He had three sets of ships papers, but now he would have to stick with the Maltese version.

Next would be the bureaucracy and the bribes for the officials. He sighed in resignation – Anwar could sort all that out. It would be one of his final tasks.

*

Sicilian Channel

Tobin in Tape

It had been almost twelve hours since Tobin had been taped to the old wooden chair – an ornate Maltese carver. At first he had resisted. He was used to dealing with very tough people and difficult circumstances – even the Mafia - but this was new territory for him.

Maruška's persuasive technique had quickly worn him down – and frightened him. He was sitting in his own mess, but although he didn't have full control of his body his mind was still working, just, and his animal instinct was guiding him.

She had started out ruthlessly after the others had been sent out. She pulled up an old box and sat facing him. He could smell her perfume.

"You are the fucking bitch from the restaurant."

"And Fiskardo too."

The surprise was plain on Tobin's face and he was not normally one for showing his emotions.

"Let me explain the situation to you. You can scream as much as you like – we are well soundproofed in here.

You may think you have a way out or will be rescued, but let me tell you now that in twenty four hours you will be dead. Before then you will answer my questions and I will verify the answers.

But first, a little game. What would you prefer to lose first – a hand, your eyesight or your cock?"

Tobin kept a straight face and imagined himself at one of his games of poker. The stakes were being laid. He didn't yet know what she wanted.

"Whatever your name is, I can make you richer than you can imagine. Do you know the price of gold? How would a hundred kilos of gold in a Swiss bank appeal to you?"

"I'm not interested in money – I have plenty of that, but I have no time to bargain."

She brought her hand from behind her back and swung a hammer down on his right hand, taped to an arm of the chair.

Tobin screamed and barely controlled his bowels. He groaned with pain that was unlike anything he had experienced before, not even in after his fights in the miners' drinking dens in Alaska.

"There goes your first of three. What next? An eye or your cock? Or would you like to taste your testicles? I have done such things to men before now. Believe me, I can do it and will do it. I even enjoy it – a lot, but sadly I don't have much time for enjoyment. With her left hand she blatantly rubbed her crutch and moaned. She waved her hand under his nose. I am not going to sit here in your stink. I smell so much nicer that you do. So it's better for you if you just tell me what I need to know. Then the pain will end. Do you understand?"

She slapped his face to bring him out of his faint.

Tobin nodded through his tears, disgusted at his smell – but still able to think. He focused himself, put himself back at the poker table.

"Tons of gold, more than you can imagine."

"Don't waste my time. Believe me I know what real pain is and I can give you plenty more."

"What do you want to know?"

"Starbucks, Southampton 2013 – did you send an email from there?"

"Hundreds."

"Don't try to be clever. I have no patience." She raised the hammer as another wave of pain went through his shattered hand.

"Any particular day?"

"September 16th, 2013"

"I probably sent several."

"This one was encrypted."

"I encrypted many of my emails."

Sicilian Channel

"This one could not be de-crypted. It was about *Theovulum Aureus*."

Tobin's heart rate stayed the same – it was still about 180 and couldn't go much higher – but he realised what they wanted and that it could keep him alive if he played out his hand very carefully. His logic wrestled with his pain. He looked her in the eyes and just held her stare.

"Give me the primary key. Give me that and you can keep your writing hand until I kill you. Naturally we can verify what you tell us."

"Why haven't you asked the other party what the key is? Several people received this email. Why ask me?"

Maruška looked confused – she obviously didn't know that a primary key was only known to one party and maybe she didn't know that the other recipients were dead. Here was the opening, the blink in his opponent's eyes. Stretch it, raise the bid.

She held the hammer over his left hand. "I ask the questions."

His mind worked against the pain. How long could he hold out physically? How many false keys could he give them? He certainly couldn't shit any more.

"OK. '*Auric Adventurer*' the name of my ship. Each letter has a number in the alphabet. 'A' is number one and so on. Raise each number to the power 4 and express it all as a string of digits. Then add 2177 at the end. Then cube it and add 3 at the end – that's the key."

"Say it again into my phone."
She checked that the recording was OK.

"That had better be the right answer or"

"…or you will kill me".

Tobin's needle worked.

"And I am going to enjoy it."

"Fuck you."

He had 24 hours. Eyes or testicles – it was a terrifying thought but at least he had some time to think.

"Yasmine! Where the fuck are you when I want you?"

Whilst Maruška ranted, he closed his eyes and tried to imagine a place and time when he had been happy. It was a struggle, but it was better than the waves of pain, but even they started to subside. His mind settled on the Swan River in Perth, a sunny Sunday afternoon when he was eleven years old. He focused hard, trying to recapture the smell of the day, the emotions of a child playing.

It was another ten minutes before the others returned.

"Yasmine, bandage his hand to stop the bleeding. Give him water. Strip him and clean him up. I will be out for half an hour. We need to keep him alive for now."

"But Marie, his mess?"

"Clean him up I said."

*

Breakfast with Bryan

"So, you're the policeman. What's the next move then?"

It was just after 7 am. They were seated drinking coffee at a café across from Grand Harbour, opposite the point at which Tobin had been put in a boat, with *Auric Adventurer* just in sight about a quarter of a mile away. To their right, the derrick which had replaced the masts in Nelson's ships was just visible past the old buildings which had once been the shore-quarters for ships officers.

"We gather all the info we can – look at the sources that the Malta police will not have considered now that we know they moved Tobin in a boat. See where it leads us. Can you ask Marco if there are cameras around the harbour and whether they have harbour radar recordings?"

"I don't do bureaucracy."

"OK, I'll deal with it. Give me his number. I'll use your name."

"If we're going to make quick progress we need to start thinking like they do – or did."

"Lead on Sherlock!"

"Well, they used a boat not a car or truck. I think that means he's close to the water, maybe on a bigger boat."

"Which might have taken him to sea."

"Granted, but leaving the harbour by sea would be very difficult with the security clampdown that's in place. I think he could be near the harbour, close to the water."

"Or they could have put him in a car and taken him somewhere else."

"Yes, but there's risk in moving too far. The police are on their toes, checking everything that moves. For now let's work on another boat or a location close to the harbour. If it's a car it would have been early morning if at all – maybe you can get traffic cam data from the harbour authorities?"

"Me?"

"Yes, why not?"

"Weren't you listening? I don't do bureaucracy – a daily report is enough, and I think you'll be doing that from now on. You know police procedures and all that crap. You can deal with Marco. If you have any problems I'll call Mauro or get Ellie on the case."

"OK."

"Now, what about close to the harbour itself?"

"Well, on the north side is the cruise terminal, another marina and bar/restaurant area, secure docking areas and cliffs under St. Elmo Fort – though there is a road. All very public, secure or awkward for a transfer or temporary prison. It's all secured since the attack on the *Queen Katherine*. Then, coming west we have the Ferry terminal – for the Sicily ferries, the old tanker and tug area – with security. They've got the ferry operating out of Pieta – over the other side of Valetta – since the attack. Then, the old power station – being re-developed – and then the Cassar Shipyard tight up in Marsa Creek. That's the area where the North African asylum seekers tend to congregate."

"Secure?"

"Not really, and the dockside is backed by old warehouses."

"OK, let's put that on the list. What next?"

"Well, then you're round into Dock 7 then – fairly open - and then the Bezzina Shipyard. That comes round then to another shipping terminal and then the major docks in French Creek – over the hill behind us. Then we're back here and to the east is Kalkhara Creek – open and public. There's another bay – not much there."

"This shipyard you mentioned – Bezzina was it?"

"Yes."

"Let's check that out too."

"Any particular reason – they will have security there?"

"Just something I heard somewhere."

"OK. By the way, I've been meaning to ask – any idea why they should want to keep Tobin alive?"

"Not really."

"Information? Ransom?"

"Yes, could be either. You're the policeman – you are supposed to be the expert on motives."

"Yes, there's always a list – money, revenge, sex, information. His kind usually have knowledge that's of value to someone. Any information would have to be very valuable to go to this extent of operation. I wouldn't rule out sex or revenge – that would usually mean killing. Money even – a business deal gone wrong – what about those two Italians who visited him with a lawyer and heavies? They're dead now, anyway. Information is my bet, but let's keep open minds. "

"That sounds reasonable - if he is still alive."

"You don't have any theories yourself given your involvement at Fiskardo?"

"No theories then, and none now. We're just under orders to find him – alive. I'll call Ellie and get her to check out those Italians – and that Transglobal outfit too, just to dot the i's and cross the t's."

Bryan was experienced enough to recognise that there was more to this and that Steve was stonewalling.

"Fair enough. The Bezzina dry docks are nearest. I suggest we start there.

"OK. I'll just call Marco and ask for the recordings and logs of harbour radar and any video recordings to be collated for us. Then we'll take a look around the shipyard and Marsa Creek.

Ten minutes later they were approaching the Bezzinas' floating dry docks. There was a trawler in one – Nicos's trawler.

"80 tons I reckon" Steve shouted to Bryan as he started to cut the revs and slow the RIB.

"How do you know?"

"My Dad was a trawlerman – I was brought up on a fishing boat."

Steve felt his phone vibrate.

A text from Macdonald.

"Search area narrowed to Marsa, between Dock 7 and Cassar shipyard. Meet me outside Bank of Valetta, Triq Is Salib Tal Marsa. No action without authority. ASAP."

He read it to Bryan.

"Do you know where that is?"

"Yes, I know the Bank."

"Let's get going."

"OK, we'll take the RIB into Cassar's Shipyard. The Bank is 100 metres from there."

"We don't want to be too obvious."

"There are plenty of ships and tugs there to keep us out of sight from the shore, and even an old submarine. We'll have to show our credentials in the yard."

"OK. ETA?"

"Ten minutes to the Bank."

"Right, let's go."

*

The Search for Maruška

After tying up the RIB and showing their police passes, they emerged through the security gates of the Cassar Shipyard. "Talk to me Bryan, tell me about the area we're in" said Steve.

"To your left is the African market and beyond that the road leads round past some old warehouses and on to Dock 7."

They turned right towards the Bank. There were several groups of African workers standing near the roundabout and talking. "This is where the Maltese pick up casual workers in the morning."

"And the warehouses?"

"Run down, used for carnival floats, car repairs, storage and so on."

"You seem to know it well."

"I once went out with a local woman who was a float designer."

"Could Tobin be in one of those?"

"Maybe. Lots of strangers, people coming and going at all hours, but there are lots of disused industrial buildings around here. Hang on, just thinking – if they moved him by RIB, where would the RIB be now?"

"I wondered about that, but they would have ditched it."

"Yes, even if they'd left it tied up here – and that's not likely – it would have been lifted and sold by now."

As they crossed the road to the Bank, Helena climbed out of a white panel van with tinted windows which was parked about twenty yards away up the slight hill, towards Marsa itself. Apparently they were in the floor tiling business. She opened a side door.

"Bryan, wait outside and keep your eyes open. Low profile."

"Yes Ma'am."

Helena stared at him and thought better of reacting, not sure whether he was being insolent or genuine.

"Get in Steve."

The door closed.

"Anything?"

"No. We came in through the shipyard, but it's definitely the sort of area that I think she would use. Lots of transient people, old warehouses. Anything more on location?"

"No, still working on it."

"Any further contact with Maruška?"

"Nothing yet, but we expect to hear within the hour."

"How?"

"We don't know – she's running the show until we can get ahead."

"What's next then?"

"Waiting."

"That's no good."

"That's all we can do."

"What about a closer look at the warehouses?"

"Too dangerous. We can't take the chance that they'll kill Tobin. We need him."

"Why now, why not before?"

"We were waiting for developments. We now know that China is involved. Trouble is, we've lost control of events."

"You have something Maruška needs – knowledge of how the nanochip works."

"If she has one in her. We don't know that for sure. She may not know herself."

"Yes but then there's no harm in floating it. Either she will know or not."

"And how do you propose we do that? We have no way of communicating with her."

"Don't you have her mobile number?"

Helena looked incredulously at him.

"And how the hell would we have that?"

"What are your people doing? You said they could track the comms with the chip. How did you triangulate on her to this area? Surely they can inject data into the stream when she is online? In fact, you could probably do more than that and send her a text. Jam the satcomms of the Chinese Embassy – you can do that if the US has a bird flying over, with a steerable spotbeam."

"We wouldn't do that. We'd have to tell the Cousins too much about the operation."

"The Cousins?"

"The US, CIA whatever."

"The *Queen Katherine* attack is the best cover possible. Surely it's worth a try? And if GCHQ were really on the ball they could do that *and* take control of the chip – if Maruška has one."

"Jesus. Get out and check Bryan. I need to make a call."

Steve closed the van door.

"Did you get all that?"

"Yes", came the reply over the link to London, from Ogilvy, Head of the Middle East and Africa desk had been listening in. We're on it, although we can't control the chip yet – something about decoding protocols. We could kill her if we get it wrong."

"So, no harm done then?"

"Don't talk to me like that! We do not want to be defenceless against an army of a million Chinese controlled by nanochips - we must have that technology. That means that we want Maruška alive."

"So that you can study her?"

"Exactly. Make sure that she lives. Tobin too."

"No pressure then?"

"Just do your job. And keep Baldwin under control – tight control."

Helena couldn't resist it. "You mean our leading technical brain?"

"Cut the sarcasm. I have a meeting with 'C'. The *Queen Katherine* attack is our priority here. Finding Tobin and Maruška is yours. Get it sorted."

"What about her location?"

"I'll put you through to our mission maven in Cheltenham. Now."

The connection was transferred immediately and Helena spoke to the technical lead in GCHQ as she opened the side door and Steve climbed back in.

"I've got GCHQ here. Talk to them."

"Call me Dave."

"OK Dave, I'm Steve. Any more news on location?"

"She's using parasitic mobile technology – we think the chip locks on to any nearby mobile phone, nabs two or three available channels and hops between them – and between the radio masts - so we can't easily triangulate. The transmission intervals are random and burst-mode so we can't lock on. Also, her smartphone probably does the same. At least we can now track the actual datastream through the Chinese Embassy uplink, but only intermittently when the US has a bird overflying. We're trying to organise drones to give us full time access."

"Can you backtrack the datastream?"

"We're working on that."

"If you know where she is approximately then you only have to monitor a small number of masts."

"Over 200 masts in Malta, five in the area we're interested in. We're working on decoding the datastream. If we can identify the chip's GPS coordinate string then we're halfway there."

"That's all I need."

"Maybe, but my boss needs a whole lot more."

"OK, keep us posted."

"Will do."

Steve turned to Helena. "We have to know when she's online with her own or any other smartphone."

"It all hangs on what she does next. She has to contact us in some way to move forward. So we're waiting on her."

"OK. I'll set up a watch on the warehouses while I'm waiting to hear from Marco about some traffic cam clips."

Sicilian Channel

"Right, we'll meet here again in six hours' time. That's 16.00 ok?"

"Done."

*

Steve and Bryan strolled back towards the Cassar shipyard and in through the security gates.

"Have you got a pair of binos Bryan?"

"Yes, in the RIB if they haven't been lifted."

"Ok let's get them and talk to the management here."

Half an hour later Steve was seated on a box in the filthy bridge of a decrepit patrol boat which was lying between the dockside and an old submarine. The smell was a sickening mix of diesel oil and rat urine, the heat was oppressive in the late morning sun and the outside aluminium skin of the wheelhouse was too hot to touch by hand. Using the binoculars he had a clear view down the line of warehouses which led to Dock 7. The African traders' stalls had few customers in the heat which shimmered off the dusty road. Along the line of warehouses he could make out an old truck, a wrecked trailer and a small car. The licence plates were unreadable at that distance.

"This is a real long shot isn't it, Guv?"

"Maybe. We have good intel that he's in this area and these warehouses tick all the boxes. Until we know more, this is what we go with."

They settled into a routine planning to rotate their watches every two hours. Just after midday Steve walked down to the African market stalls. He was trying to look innocuous amongst a group of very dark Somali and Sudanese when there was a tap on his shoulder. He turned to see a Maltese man who flashed a police badge and asked to see his ID. He pulled out his smartphone for the policeman to check his picture and scan his data for an online check.

"You pick me out amongst all these Africans? Do I look more like an Islamic terrorist than them?"

"Sir, you don't fit in."

Then the policeman sharpened his stance and changed his attitude instantly as he read his phone and saw Steve's authority level. "Your ID is confirmed - it seems you are one of us. Sorry for the trouble, Sir."

Just then, a hire car left the warehouses away through the Dock 7 bypass road. Steve started to run and thought better of it – the car had disappeared.

"Thanks to you we just lost a suspect! Are there any cameras on that road?"

"Sorry Sir, no cameras in Dock 7 as far as I know."

"Are there any monitoring this market area?"

"No Sir, I do the watching."

"Fucking great." Steve turned in disgust and headed back to the shipyard.

When he got back to the patrol boat bridge he was still cursing.

"Did you see the car leave?"

Bryan looked sheepish.

"Yes, but I didn't see the driver."

"But you must have had a good view."

"No, I didn't. The truck was in the line of sight of the driver's door and the car went out the other way. Anyway, you were there."

"Got stopped by the local plod for an ID check. Missed the car."

*

Key Problems

It had been a long, hot day. In the late morning Maruška had been shopping for a change of clothes and some makeup, then on to Ta'Xbiex to deliver a package. She had been changing clothes in the Vivo store toilets in Marsa when a call came through from Wan Chuntao. She stopped in a pharmacy and when she finally got back to the warehouse Tobin was slumped naked in the chair. His rank smell still lingered although he had been cleaned up. It was late afternoon and he was dozing when the she slapped his face. He woke with a start to see Maruška in front of him. She was smartly dressed and could have passed for a wealthy Maltese woman. There was no sign of Yasmine or Mansur.

"Dressed for a party?"

"No, a funeral. Yours. You lied to me. I warned you what would happen."

She pulled out a kitchen knife from her handbag.

"You know what this is?"

"It looks like a toothpick."

"It's a boning knife. I'm not giving you the choice of eyes or balls."

Tobin could not hide his fear as she prepared to start work, The sweat erupted on his brow and ran down into his eyes and beyond. .

"For the last time what is the primary key?"

"I gave it to you."

"It didn't work."

"It does work. It exposes the next level of encryption. For which you need another key."

"You didn't tell me that."

"You didn't fucking ask."

He screamed as the knife went deep into the muscle of his left thigh. Although expertly positioned to miss the major blood vessels, his blood ran. He screamed again as it she twisted the knife.

"How many levels of encryption are there?"

"Two, just two. Jesus Christ."

"What is the other key I need?"

She held out the phone as he spoke, breathing heavily and groaning.

"*Theovulum Aureus*. Each letter position raised to the power 4 as before. Add the string 3479 at the end. Cube it and add 6793 at the end – as a string."

"That's it?"

Tobin looked at her and nodded, then looked down at the knife standing vertically in his thigh.

"Spell out theovulum aureus, letter by letter."

Tobin slowly spelled the words. "Don't include the space as a character."

"You cannot imagine the pain and loss you will feel if there are more problems." She twisted the knife again and he screamed.

"Is there anything else I need to know?"

"No, you have all the encryption keys now. You can decode the junk DNA string."

Maruška held the phone to her mouth.

"Did you get that?"

"Yes" replied Wan Chuntao. "All of it. Keep him alive - for now – until we are sure." The call ended.

After Yasmine and Mansur Abdul-Hadi returned, Maruška gave them further instructions about Tobin's treatment and then left. Against her inclination and base urges she had to keep Tobin alive. It was the first time she had ever given antibiotics to a prisoner.

Outside the warehouse the piles of litter were covered with dust and debris that had been carried across from the explosion three days before. The African market stalls in the corner near the storm drain were buzzing but little business was being done. Even here there had been two people hit by debris from the explosion. Policemen were moving through them checking identity papers. Their hostility to the refugees was plain and the tension was palpable.

One of the other warehouses had its doors open. Two Maltese men were loading a white truck with cardboard boxes and glanced at her with interest as she pulled her sunglasses over her eyes and unlocked the car. She drove the hire car out to the Marsa roundabout while the two Maltese men talked about her clothes and wondered about the screams that they had heard. They laughed – lots of bad stuff happened in the area, and prostitutes were plentiful.

The road through the ancient gate into Valetta was jammed with a police road block as she turned down the hill into Pieta. She followed the road around into M'Sida and pulled into the parallel service road. Looking across the moored boats she could see the British High Commission. The Union Jack had been taken down. So, her message had got through. She adjusted her position as she turned the aircon up in the late afternoon sun and cursed as she noticed Tobin's blood on her jeans. It had dried quickly and was still very obvious.

*

"Was there to be an acknowledgement of her original message?"

"Yes. The Union Jack at the High Commission lowered to half-mast from by 3pm today."

"And did you do that?"

"Yes, five minutes before 3pm. We kept it down for a couple of hours and now we are waiting."

"OK, so it's a line of sight check she needed and she would have had the flagpole in sight at 3pm, maybe some time before. Let's get a map and see where she could have seen it from. Let's get Bryan in on this too – he knows the area. You'll have to brief him in – at least to some extent."

"OK, I know I can't keep him in the dark much longer."

They were in the panel van near the Bank of Valetta, just after 4 pm, and after Bryan climbed in, Helena kept it vague and explained that a trade for Tobin was being floated and that they had established a link with the kidnappers. They studied the Google earth map she projected onto an inside wall of the panel van.

"Well, they couldn't check the flagpole from Valetta – that's now been closed off" Bryan said. "There are not a lot of possibilities, but I'd bet that it was from across M'Sida creek. There." He pointed to the map. There was a service road across the Creek, alongside the main road. "Easy exit – just one way but a few turn offs up into Hamrun or on up Valley Road. Who's 'they' by the way?"

Helena sighed. "I can't tell you that – need to know - but they are led by a woman who's known to us. OK, that service road sounds reasonable. She'd have to travel back to wherever she's got Tobin. If it's the warehouses in Marsa, how many routes are there?"

"We concentrate on the lights at the end of this service road, the Valley Road interchange and the Marsa roundabout near the warehouses."

"Would she chance a stolen car?"

Helena looked at Steve.

"She's a risk taker but not stupid. Bus – possible but no control. Taxi – unlikely, but possible. A rental car is most likely, but she covers her tracks very well."

"Okay, let's go with the percentages."

"That will be easier, all hire car licence plates end with a K or QZ." Helena smiled. "Good work Bryan. I take it that we can get traffic camera recordings?"

Steve sighed. "OK, I'll call Marco and get him on to it. It will take a lot of work – and time. I still haven't heard back on the other data I wanted." Steve turned to Helena. "When are we expecting to hear from her again?"

"No idea."

"How?"

"No idea. We have to assume that the Chinese monitor her mobile phone, so it may well be old style tradecraft – like dropping that flag. I need to head back. You guys stay local and low and don't go near the warehouses."

"Just one thing Ms. Williams."

"Yes?"

"Well, we're putting all our eggs in one basket. We should be casting the net wider, looking for more options, following the evidence."

"You are right Bryan, and what you say would be right in normal circumstances. However, we don't have any real evidence do we, other than a video clip from the Marina? We don't have much time and we don't have a lot of manpower. So what would you suggest we do next?"

"Point taken."

"Fine, but I do expect you to keep working on what we do have."

"Any news on the Italians?"

"A real bad lot, according to London. We suspect a link between the Tumino brothers and Transglobal Security."

"You mean that Tobin's security was being run by the Tuminos?"

"Yes, it looks that way."

*

Bryan had gone to get sandwiches and water when Steve's phone vibrated.

"Yes Mac, what is it?"

"Contact."

"How?"

"eMail to the British High Commission. Codewords valid. Simple but effective. Requesting a secure mail address at our end."

"And where do you respond?"

"Another email address. Very secure – TOR has got nothing on this one. It's completely virtualized. It's not that the mail server is invisible, it just doesn't exist. At all. Our guys can't get at it. If it did we could track it when it's forwarded to her smartphone."

"Put me on to Dave in Cheltenham."

"I can't do that. I don't know a Dave."

"For Christ's sake, the guy I spoke to earlier."

"If you are not in our panel van, comms will have to go through me."

"OK, OK." His exasperation was clear. "Dave or whoever needs to hack the servers in Malta. They have probably got pluckers."

"Pluckers?"

"Yes, software routines which identify specific email addresses in data, pluck them out of the datastream, strip them of all metadata and forward the message to another address. To the outside it looks as if they have been black holed. It's done in the first servers the data hits after leaving the sender."

"But how could she have done this?"

"It would have to be a government-level operation for that kind of know-how – like China."

Helena could see that fitted well into the wider picture which she hadn't shared with Steve.

"Would they keep copies before cleansing the metadata?"

"No, that would defeat its purpose. It has to be completely untraceable."

"How do you know all this stuff?"

"Just wondering, that's all. I've been thinking about the problem to avoid boredom. Ask Dave if it's possible. Also, ask him about his end."

"What do you mean?"

"Well, when you send to her email address, the email is redirected if you are routing through the Malta servers. But it will be too late now. She will send a new email address each time. You need to avoid the Malta servers. You need to use a dedicated link through a satellite and send from London, or anywhere but Malta – or China."

"OK. Where are you right now?"

"Watching the warehouses from the old patrol boat. What's her next step?"

"We've sent the secure email address, so we are waiting too. I'd better call Dave."

"So there really is a Dave?"

"Yes, really. I'll let you know as soon as I have anything new."

"OK. Before you go, we're betting on her being close by. Can't we focus our phone mast monitoring on this immediate area?"

"We've already started."

"Good. Got to go, I can hear Bryan coming."

"Ok, scrub the meeting at 16.00. I'll call you back."

"Wait."

"What?"

"That van of yours – can we do a drive-by of the warehouses?"

"It's already been done."

"Great. We're pretty sure that it's the fourth warehouse along."

"We filmed them during the drive-by. Let's see – the fourth. Yes. Wooden doors. The next one along has a steel roller shutter door, and the one on the other side has wooden doors with steel sheeting nailed on."

"That sounds about right."

*

Evening Heat

"Macdonald?"

"Yes."

"I think we're closing in."

"What do you mean?"

"The licence plate on that blue hire car – I sent Bryan to the hire company and they had her details – not that they will help. The good news is that they did have a security camera in their office. The picture looks like it could be the second woman in team. The description fits the woman at Del Borgo's – more or less. Hired last week for a fortnight. The clerk said that she had an African guy with her – seems he waited outside. They drove off together."

"You're turning into a good detective at last."

"Ha bloody ha. Bryan's the smart guy here. I've asked Mauro for plans of the warehouses. He wasn't pleased to be bothered. His gopher Marco is a waste of time."

"Don't do anything more. Keep that sort of stuff away from the police or they will dive in and screw it up. They don't know what they're up against. That's an order. We're still waiting for that email from her. Nothing moves till that comes through."

"Politics was never my strong point."

"That's pretty obvious, but you are good at some things." She smiled. The video was off on his phone and he couldn't see it, but he heard it in her voice. "I'll run some interference and ask for other plans, scrub your request. We'll get them another way."

"You can interfere with me any time."

"Not on the phone I can't, but it sounds like you're back on track."

"Maybe."

"I'll call when I have an update."

"Likewise."

"By the way, we tagged the rental car with a GPS tracker."

"How? We've been watching and we only saw the drive-by of the panel van."

"Sticky GPS microbug fired from an air pistol as we drove past."

"Clever."

"Yes. Remember that. I've got a team behind me."

"And me at point."

"Too hot for you?"

"Too boring."

"Boring is better than dead. In the meantime, watch and wait – nothing more."

"OK, unless we see some action there."

"Unless nothing! Sit tight and keep me posted."

The line dropped. Steve shook his head and sighed as he raised the binoculars to his eyes.

The truck had gone and he had a clear view of the rental car.

Bryan had been despatched to get a takeaway and some torches while Steve was on watch and fighting to stay awake in the high evening heat and humidity inside the patrol boat. He listened to the rats scratching about and wondered again about the Italian connection.

*

The Tenth Bureau of the Guojia Anquan Bu (Guoanbu – the Ministry of State Security in Wuhan, the capital of Hubei province), the Scientific and Technological Information Bureau, is focused on collecting economic, scientific and technological intelligence for China. Wan Chuntao's early rapid rise through its hierarchy had been slowed by the Gate of Tears operation. She knew Maruška, had personally recruited her, met her in Shanghai and now controlled her, absolutely. She had set new standards in running agents, but still that earlier operational setback rankled.

The attempt to correct matters in Fiskardo had been 'kept off the books'. This operation in Malta was a hangover from that and she desperately needed it to succeed.

She switched on the electronic blackout of her cubicle, opened the Agent Management app and stroked the icon on her screen. The GPS data showed that Maruška's phone was on and she was not moving. Chuntao had learned the hard way not to 'tickle' an agent who was moving – they might be driving a car. A colleague had lost a promising young agent in Toronto that way. She was now working on a farm in Tien Shan.

Wan Chuntao tapped another icon and 4,800 miles away Maruška spluttered as her Coca Cola Lite spilt over her clothes and dribbled out of her mouth, She swore. Mansur and Yasmine stared at her as she grimaced.

"It's nothing. I need a change of clothes and some fresh air. Give me the keys to the car."

*

They were tearing a piece of pizza off the 12" Maltese Special.

"Shit, the car's moving. I didn't see the driver get in."

"Coming this way."

It was dusk and the headlights switched on.

"Can't make out the driver."

"We need a car."

Steve dialled and Helena answered immediately.

"Movement – the car."

"Yes, we just picked it up on the tracker."

"We need a car."

"There's a small Fiat parked outside Cassar's."

"You knew?"

"Be prepared as the Scouts say. We sent it over earlier. Use that. Keys on the front wheel driver's side. Send Bryan. He'll know the drill. Observe only – no clever stuff, ok?

"OK."

"I need you at the warehouse. The percentages are still in our favour."

"I'd be better than Bryan if it is Maruška – she'll eat him for breakfast."

He turned to Bryan. "No offence mate." Bryan shrugged in resignation.

"No. Bryan goes – very carefully. We're wasting time. His phone will track the target – he knows the tech. Tell him to keep well clear."

Helena cut the call.

"Bryan, get going – there's a car outside." Steve added the details as Bryan climbed down the companionway from the bridge.

"Remember, no heroics. We just need a description of the driver."

Five minutes later, Steve's phone rang again.

"Warehouse plans should be in your phone now. Plan an assault – 2 or 3 options. We'll only have a small team."

"How many?"

"Two. You and me."

"That's crazy."

"Fewer people, fewer accidents."

"Give me Bryan and you stay out."

"No way. Bryan's not right for this. Follow orders."

"I got body armour and tools, but we might need gas."

"Whatever let me know."

"I'll look at the options."

"Good."

"Any email yet?"

"Nothing. Dave's team are hacking the Malta phone network servers and doing a code compare. If they have been infected then God knows how many others elsewhere are like that. It will be a few hours before we know for sure. If your idea is right, then we can certainly use this to our advantage."

"Including 'elsewhere' I guess?"

"I couldn't possible comment. Wait, the rental car has pulled into the Pavi supermarket in Marsa – not far away. Bryan is just parking up. Call you back."

*

Steve settled down to watch and wait, and used the time to check the warehouse layout plans which Helena had sent through. He pondered the very limited assault options. The plans were poor quality - little more than sketches and showed that the warehouses were typically flat-roofed, with at least 25 feet of headroom inside. The roofs were concrete or stone laid over steel beams, without skylights, though there was an access door onto the roof. They varied in length from back to front, and the fourth warehouse was about half way along the row.

The assault options were fairly simple – front doors, roof door or both. Steve discounted the idea of going in through the walls from one of the adjoining warehouses – the walls were 12 inch stone blocks – and tunnelling under was out of the question.

He estimated the amount of C4 required for a stone wall and realised that the bang would be much too big. The roof door was the best option. Then his phone rang. Helena.

"Just listen."

Steve listened to Bryan's commentary.

"I'm parked on the second floor of Pavi's car park, about 30 yards away from the target car. Dark corner, poor lighting. Someone approaching from the elevator – seems to be looking around carefully. It's a woman by the walk, about 5' 6" tall, slender, wearing a baseball cap pulled down hard and what looks like a black track suit. Black trainers, with a Nike sports bag. Can't see the face. It's too dark here to use my camera phone without the flash."

"Don't!" It was Helena's voice.

"I'm not daft." Bryan's voice was lower.

"She's stopped. Left hand to chest. Moving again. Seems to be in pain. Opening door, throwing sports bag in. Getting into driver's seat. Not moving, she's sitting in the seat using her phone."

"Just wait, make sure she doesn't see you. I'm going offline."

"Copy that. I'll sit tight and wait."

"Steve, you still there?"

"Yes."

"Listen, we've bugged the car."

Steve heard a woman's voice, speaking in accented English. The audio quality was muffled, but the words were clear enough. His pulse rate increased. It was a voice he recognised.

Then, another woman's voice, accented English, oriental sounding.

The conversation ended.

"Did you get that?"

"Yes, it's Maruška for certain. I don't know the other voice. What the hell was that scream?"

"I think that's her control chip. I'm sending Bryan back. Meet me at the Bank in fifteen minutes."

*

As she came out of the elevator into the car park, Maruška briefly scanned the bays and then walked towards the rental car. The next few hours would be critical. She staggered briefly as the sharp pain hit her, then took a deep breath.

Once the door was closed she took her phone out and hit the key combination for Wan Chuntao.

"The key does not work."

"You heard the interrogation – you have a recording of his voice, of what he said."

"That makes no difference. Go back to him, get what we need. You have one hour. I am losing patience." Wan Chuntao made an adjustment to an intensity setting slider in her screen and Maruška felt a stab of pain worse than she had ever experienced before. She screamed as the searing pulse seemed to reach up her spine to the base of her skull and simultaneously penetrate deep into her heart, as if a red hot poker was being twisted in it. She lost consciousness.

When she came round, she wiped her streaming eyes and checked her watch. It had only been fifteen minutes since she had come into the car park.

Bryan saw her scream and slump into unconsciousness. "Bryan, head straight back".

He switched off the radio, got out of his car and walked slowly towards the rental car. He could feel the bulk of the SIG under his left shoulder, but did not touch it. He was just five yards away when he saw her shake her head and rub her eyes then bang the steering wheel repeatedly. She turned to look at him and started the engine, slamming the car into gear and flooring the throttle as she opened her side window.

Bryan walked on and held his nerve – whoever she was she had no reason to recognise him. He showed little interest as her car squealed past but he had to jump aside to avoid it.

*

There had been no movement since Maruška had returned to the warehouse an hour earlier and Bryan had come back a few minutes later.

"You might have got a look at her face, but it doesn't really help us very much."

"Well, we know it's a woman – and she has some sort of problem."

"Don't they all?"

They both laughed. Boredom – tension – boredom – the pattern was playing havoc with their adrenaline and the laughter was a stress reliever.

"I'm going to stretch my legs – I'll be out an hour or so. Buzz me if anything starts happening."

"Will do."

Steve sauntered out of the gates of the shipyard turning left past the café, crossing the storm channel which drained into Marsa Creek. The market stalls were packing up for the evening as he walked along Xatt Il Mollijet towards the warehouses. There was little traffic as he turned right, up the short hill past the cold storage depot and left onto Garrick. He paused at the corner and switched the smartphone to 'vibrate' only.

He re-checked the plans and confirmed the warehouse layout. There was no rear entrance to the warehouse itself. He carried on walking, then stopped to check a Google earth picture. The gate was there, and he could see an access road round the back of the transport yard. He waited and looked carefully at the entrance. A gate, no barbed wire. The high floodlights from the dock shone over the warehouse block and reflected weakly off the wall alongside him. There was deep shadow to the left.

He stood a couple of paces back from the chain link gate, took a look around and then after a couple of quick strides he jumped, scrambling over. He moved carefully into the shadows and stopped to listen. There was a smell – a very unpleasant smell. Dog shit. He cursed quietly. He must have stepped in it. The hairs at the back of his neck stood up. No wonder there was no barbed wire. Then he heard the dog barking, getting nearer, obviously alerted by the sound of him scaling the gate.

He saw the vague shadow run at him with a low growl – the dog had been trained not to bark. Nice people in the transport business. He swore quietly and in one smooth movement he kneeled, turned his shoulder to the dog to protect his own neck, bracing his left arm and readying his right. The dog hit the Fairbairn-Sykes knife with its chest and collapsed onto Steve. There was a faint whimper, then silence. Steve cursed quietly and rolled from under the dog's corpse.

*

"Thanks for bringing a change of clothes."

"You're welcome, though you shouldn't have gone near that warehouse. You didn't follow orders."

"Prepare the options you said. Do you expect me to go in there – with you – without a recce first? No way. I only took a stroll round the back."

"We're not going in."

"Not going in? You're writing off Tobin then?"

"No. We got the email. She's ready to negotiate."

"There's no time."

"Maybe. Bryan's sighting more or less confirmed that she's got a control chip. But I have my orders – no takeout tonight."

They were sitting in back of the panel van, parked near the shipyard.

"So, what happens next? How can it work? Surely she will need insurance. After all, once you have Tobin then you can knock her off. She's not stupid."

"No, she's not. She wanted money for Tobin – alive, but she could easily sell the key to both sides anyway. There's more though. She said that she wants specialist medical treatment, the sort that only governments can provide. In return she can provide us with details of Chinese wet operations over the last eight years and a system they have to manage agents. She has one implanted and wants it removed. And she wants a guarantee of immunity."

"What a surprise. She's taking a hell of a chance."

"Yes, but she has no choice. The problem is that they could easily kill her if they suspect anything. If she has the same type of nanochip as our Mr X in Argostoli then it's near her C6 vertebra and it's too small for any regular x-ray or MRI machine to spot. This isn't like chipping a dog or a cat. I'm told that it's connected directly into the spinal nerve bundle, but our medical guys can't work out how the connections were made. We only found it by using a new machine – some sort of deep penetration terahertz pulsed laser I think they said – part of the new autopsy protocol. There's only one machine of its kind – in Cambridge."

"So, how will you handle the extraction?"

"Don't know yet – or I'm not being told. We would have to take her back to the UK, but we know that they can track her position. We're beginning to wonder how much control they could exert with this technology – even over a population. Tobin is becoming less of a concern. London are frantic to get hold of her. Any ideas?"

"It depends. Do you really want to control her or just get the technology?"

"Ideally both, though controlling her seems to be a pipe dream right now."

"So, lead her on, get Tobin back, knock her off and ship the body back to London. Let me go in – isn't that what I'm here for?"

"You're a hard nut Steve."

"I learned from the best – your London team. They fucked me over properly in Djibouti."

Helena stared at him briefly and shook her head.

"There has to be an answer, but we only have hours to make the arrangements."

"What about radio isolation – keep her away from any cell phone. Didn't you say that's how they communicate with the chip."

"That's the only angle we've come up with – or you did, in fact, but there may be others. She needs convincing."

"Baffle her with tech talk. My Dad used an old navy saying 'bullshit baffles brains.'"

"Maybe, but the bad news is that our techies still haven't found any problems with the servers. We don't know how it all hangs together technically."

"I'll think about it."

"Do that – you came up trumps last time."

"Don't bet on me this time."

"Don't worry, I'm hedging my bets!"

He punched her gently in the shoulder and they laughed, temporarily releasing the huge tension that had been building.

*

Maruška took out the Chinese cell phone and removed the battery. Then she walked into the plastic-lined 'cell'.

"You obviously don't respond properly to pain."

Tobin groaned.

"I told you everything. You're going to kill me anyway. What's the point in me lying?"

"You're trying to buy time hoping that someone will come to your rescue."

"I'm not. I'm not some kind of agent who has been trained to resist. I need treatment or I will die."

"That is inevitable. I think we will have an audience for this. Mansur, Yasmine! Come and join us."

Tobin watched them. All his life he had always been in control of events around him, but the last twenty four hours had been completely different. Now he was really afraid, terrified of what might happen. He was all in and close to the end of the game. His life. But he knew that as soon as they had the key then he was expendable.

"Mansur, tie his hands behind the chair."

Tobin winced as his hands were cut free from the arms of the chair and wrenched around behind it. His broken hand was swollen and throbbing inside the bloody bandage. The wound in his thigh was painful, but it too had been bandaged.

"Now cut the tape from his ankles, open his legs and re-tape them, one to each leg of the chair."

He was too weak to struggle and had lost all dignity hours before.

Then he kicked out with his good leg, but there was no energy in his muscles and weight behind it.

They laughed.

She put her hand on his forehead.

"Temperature going up. Some infection I think. You see Tobin, I hurt you, then I bandage you and give you antibiotics. Hurt, treatment, hurt. The cycle goes on, but soon you will give up the key or your body will fail you. Which first?"

Tobin shut his eyes and shook his head. Where were the police? Where was Frank Abadelli? Another useless security team. He snapped around as Maruška spoke.

"Yasmine, Mansur - watch and learn how to make a man talk."

She pulled the boning knife out from the back of her tracksuit waistband. She stroked the blade with her thumb, close to his face.

"Do you recognise this? It really does need sharpening since it's last outing.. Still, it will do the job." Then she snapped on a pair of latex gloves.

"A lot of experience has taught me that this is not really a *physically* painful procedure, but *mentally* it leaves huge scars. Most men will do anything to avoid it."

She knelt down in front of Tobin and held his scrotum with her left hand.

Tobin croaked. "Did they convert it to hex?"

"I don't know what they did. It's too late now. Don't make up stories to save your balls."

Tobin gasped, the fear constricting his speech.

"I'm not. The keys I gave you must be in hex."

"Hex. What is hex?"

"Hexadecimal, counting to the base 16."

"Why didn't you tell me that before?"

"I thought they knew cryptographic keys."

"Too little, too late. The key is too short in length anyway. Even I know that. Mansur, hold his shoulders."

Tobin twisted and jerked in the chair, then groaned as she sliced open his scrotum. The pain was more mental than physical as he first struggled then tried to think about happy days as a child, sailing on the Swan River in Perth.

She had done this many times before during the Balkans war when she was a teenager learning her trade. It was all about a man's natural protectiveness of his genes, built into his DNA, to be protected at almost any cost.

"Last chance!"

Tobin shook his head and sweat arced away from it, glistening in the light.

"I've told you everything!"

"It will be worse if you struggle!"

One more cut and the job was done. She held up his left testicle in front of his face, but he had already passed out.

Maruška shook her head in admiration. He was a tough bastard alright.

Yasmine stared on impassively – she had no sympathy having been subjected to tribal genital mutilation as a young girl. Mansur was white despite his Arabic complexion.

"Yasmine, put a compress on him and keep him warm – he will go into shock, we still need him alive. Give him some of that sports drink with glucose and a couple more of these antibiotic pills. He will not bleed much. Mansur, feed this to the dog outside. I have to go out."

Outside the warehouse she climbed into the rental car as Mansur followed closely behind, to be sick in the gutter – and feed the dog.

*

"Movement." It was Bryan's voice over the radio link. "It looks like target 1 as best I can tell. Target 2 also – but he's going back in. Shall I follow?"

"Negative. We'll take this one. Keep watch on the warehouse. Steve, get ready to move."

Steve moved forward into the driver's seat as Helena started the tracker.

They picked up the car at Paola, just as it came off the bypass and passed the prison. Maruška found a space and parked the car, then went into a ChickKing café.

Steve drove on and found a space down a side street.

"Stay put Steve, I need to make a call."

Helena got out and walked back towards the ChickKing. "Dave, use the car tracker coordinates, we believe she's using the phone now, within fifty metres of the car."

Maruška ordered a chicken piri-piri with fries and sat at a corner table at the back. She took out a phone from her sports bag and studied the email in her inbox. The British knew she had back pains and said she had a nanochip in her spine. Was it possible? Could Wan Chuntao have done it? She realised that it was indeed possible and could have been implanted during her trip to China all those years ago.

She cursed as she remembered an evening when she and Chuntao had both got drunk – very drunk – in the training school near Aotougan. Then she wondered - did Wantao really get drunk that night?

Picking at her fries, she realised that she had a simple choice – one side or the other. Or maybe both? The choice was not that simple after all, but one step at a time could work. Or maybe two steps in parallel?

She took a clean, unused cell phone out from her bag and switched it on, then sent the critical text to Helena's cut out number.

Another jolt of pain. She turned on the Chinese cell phone after replacing the battery, not sure whether it had been totally secure to send the SMS on the other phone. She didn't trust the technology at all.

"Yes, Chuntao"

"What's happened?"

"The phone failed as I was about to re-interrogate Tobin."

"It showed no problems here, just that it was switched off."

"I don't care what it fucking showed, it's your fucking technology. I've removed and replaced the battery and it seems to be working now. Tobin said that the key should be in hex."

"We have already tried that. Does he think we are stupid? We have the best hackers and codebreakers in the world."

"Then break the fucking code if you are that clever."

"We have quantum computers which have been working on this for weeks. We have the source code of the encryption software – you obtained it last year for us in Eilat. UltraGoodPrivacy. Remember that?"

"I remember. That nice Jewish researcher." She felt a frisson of excitement at the memory of his death struggle.

"Yes, and we still cannot break it. There are no trapdoors. We have to have the key."

"I can't keep him alive much longer."

"Then try again."

"He needs a few hours to recover. He's in shock right now."

"You have three hours, no more."

"If he lasts that long."

"Three hours. Make no mistake – your own life is now at stake."

The line dropped.

Maruška was breathing hard and wondered how long she herself had. Maybe with a chip in her spine she could just be 'switched off'. She shivered.

*

Change in China

Wan Chuntao was thinking about her recent conversation with Maruška. The time for termination was approaching, but it would not be her decision, it would have to come from higher authority. They had a lot invested in Maruška. Then she read an instant message on her screen - it could only be trouble. She knew that the difficulties getting the information from Tobin would have been noted on her performance record. She logged off her session and closed down her touchscreen. As she left her cubicle she passed her hand over the scanner and the chip embedded in her hand was read.

She did this twice more on her short walk to her manager's office. She knocked and entered. The office was barely two metres square, and there was a man she did not recognise sitting in the spare chair. Her manager Mao Mingli spoke.

"Wan Chuntao, you are being placed on special assignment."

Her pulse quickened but her face betrayed no emotion.

"Please go with this man. Your personal items from your work area will be sent to you. You are not to discuss this with anyone."

She nodded her head deeply.

"I understand."

She stood aside as the stranger got up from the chair and led her out of the office.

As they walked they identified themselves at two body chip scanners, entered an elevator and descended six floors below ground level. At room number S623 they identified themselves to another ID scanner. By now Wan Chuntao was terrified, although externally she appeared to be a picture of inscrutability.

The stranger knocked on the door and they entered. Another desk, another stranger. The man at her side left the room and she was invited to sit down.

"Wan Chuntao. You are being placed on special assignment. I do not know what it is, but you are to report to Building 4, room S27 in 30 minutes. Your ID is being reprogrammed now. It will enable you to move to that building and permit you access."

"Honourable sir, please permit me to know the reasons for being moved."

"Comrade Chuntao, it is not your place to ask such questions, only to serve the People's Republic in whatever way you can do best. However I do know that you are not being punished. You will be escorted. Go now."

The door opened and a security guard entered.

Thirty minutes later Wan Chuntao was seated around a conference table in Building 4, along with two other women and four men. They did not speak. Each had been given numbered tags. Wan Chuntao's said Northern Wind Five. A fifth man entered and stood at the head of table. By his demeanour and dress he was obviously very senior. He started to speak.

"Welcome. You are now members of the 'Northern Wind' project team. This is a highly classified project which only the Chairman of the Party and six other people know about – besides yourselves. I am the head of the project and I am to be known as Northern Wind One.

This project is a matter of the highest priority to our country and you have all been selected for the special skills you bring to the team. Failure cannot be countenanced and success will bring you great professional credit – although you will never be able to talk about it.

A very great threat to our country has been discovered. We must neutralise that threat. You will each be assigned specific tasks. You must complete them with great diligence and speed. This is the only time you will meet with each other and you must not discuss the details of your work except with your direct superiors - either Northern Wind Two or Three. You will each be assigned an office.

If there is anything – and I mean anything – that you require to complete your task then ask your superior. You will not leave this building until this project achieves its objectives. That should not take more than two weeks. This floor of Building 4 is dedicated to this project. Now go to work – you must succeed."

Two men entered the room from a side door. They introduced themselves as Northern Wind Two and Northern Wind Three. Wan Chuntao and two others were taken to individual offices. Wan Chuntao entered room number S623/5 after her ID chip scan. Her few personal possessions were already in place, together with the latest version of the terminal she had used in her previous role. There were tea facilities and a small washroom, together with a small desk, two chairs, a pull-down bunk bed and a large screen display. "It's almost better than home" she thought.

She tried to log on and found that her credential still worked. There was a voicemail from Maruška. She could not access it – it had been tagged as 'Closed'. That could mean anything.

Her inbox was empty bar one message from Northern Wind Three – 'Make tea and wait for me. I will brief you shortly.'

There was a knock and she tried to open the door. It was locked. She scanned her ID tag and the door opened. She bowed slightly as NW3 entered.

He sat down. He was about thirty years old, dressed in a good quality western suit and an open necked shirt. He smiled briefly and then started to speak.

*

Taking Tobin

Time to clean up, she thought. Back in the car, Maruška headed down the hill back to the warehouse, her instincts and antennae on high alert – but not sharp enough to notice her very discreet tail. The recent jolts of pain were wearing her down. It was clear that there was huge pressure to get this information out of Tobin, but she was running out of tricks and he was a really tough bastard. Unusually tough, but he had to keep him alive.

Helena's phone tingled as it downloaded the text from her cut-out number.

"Shit. I think she's close to panic."

"Why?"

"She wants extraction within 2 hours or Tobin dies. It's to look like she's been taken in an assault. No negotiation at all. I must confirm before 9.45 – that's 15 minutes away."

"Helena, before we go any further – I think this stinks. It's too easy. All she has to do is open the door and walk out to us. We're being bounced here. Why does she want it to look like she's been taken in a raid?"

"Good question. Maybe it's just that she wants us to take out her team."

Helena continued composing the response message.

"She can easily do that herself. And I do mean easily. We'd be going in on her timescale, no surprise. It's suicide."

"The problem is that we want that technology even more than we want Tobin."

"Don't commit yet, or better still, tell her no."

"She will kill Tobin."

"So what – he may be dead already. We can go in on our timescale and nab her."

She keyed in 'Please advise next action', tagged it as MOST URGENT, pressed 'SEND' and Maruška's annotated text was forwarded to her controller in Vauxhall Cross then routed immediately to 'C' - Sir William Gore.

They both nodded to the guard as they walked in to the shipyard and headed for Bryan in the derelict patrol boat.

Two hundred metres away, Maruška took out her pistol and screwed on a suppressor from her sports bag. Safety off, one in the chamber.

She reached for the door handle and then gasped as a jolt of pain hit her. She groaned again as she speed dialled Chuntao. The conversation was short and sharp.

"Forget Tobin. We will deal with him. Leave the warehouse immediately. You will plan to go to Tunis as quickly as possible. Check your email within the hour for further instructions. This is of the highest priority. Do you understand?"

"Why?"

"No questions, Maruška, just do it now." The call ended.

Maruška kicked out and banged the steering wheel with her fists.

"Well fuck you! After all this I am going to finish the job."

As she climbed out of the car the dog was lying alongside the door, obviously not hungry but ever hopeful. She kicked the dog viciously. It yelped loudly and ran off. She knocked gently on the door with the correct code and Mansur let her in.

"Wait here, both of you."

Tobin was dozing, but his pulse was still strong. Tough indeed. She checked his temperature with the back of her hand. She looked at his hand and his thigh as he stirred. No infection yet, but it would soon set in. She slapped his face. He looked at her, knowing what was next.

"You are out of time."

Maruška set her cell phone to record. Then she turned and smiled at Tobin as her cold, professional and psychopathic self resurfaced.

"You are a brave man, but you only have one left, right?"

He stared at her in silence.

"You have ten seconds."

She started counting.

"OK" he said. "I'll tell you."

*

"There's no easy way in – she chose it well. So, are you up for it Bryan? There's no time to set up a full-on special services team."

"Just the two of us?"

Steve nodded.

"It's got to be better than drinking myself to death slowly in a dockside bar in Valetta. I was getting bored with the girlfriend anyway."

"When we're in place on the rooftop and give the go-ahead, Helena – sorry Ellie – will create a diversion by ramming the warehouse door with the van…"

" …rear end first" said Helena. She checked with the binoculars. "The doors are still clear."

Steve continued. "We don't have long and we've only got our sidearms and a couple of knives. We don't have anything fancy for the rooftop door. We need to find a jemmy or steel bar."

"Yes, improvise. I'll look around this hulk – there may be a tool box, maybe a bolt cutter and other bits."

"Good thinking. You've got five minutes to see what you can find."

"Or it's a no go?"

"No, we go, however."

"And afterwards?"

"I don't know, we'll have to make it up as we go. Go find some tools."

Bryan nodded then moved quickly with a torch, heading for the engine room.

"This is madness, Steve."

"Ellie, this is reality, and it's tough. But it is your call. We don't have surprise unless we act now. We're probably outgunned and we have to keep two of the five alive."

"Keep her alive. Remember, she said she wants out."

"I'll do my best, but I'm not taking chances with her. We assume that she will not be hostile, but the others will be. Tobin is probably trussed up. If this is for real she will want to protect him – he's her passport."

"Where are we taking him?"

"I've been thinking – last week I went to a meeting at a villa that the High Commission rents. Somewhere down on the Freeport road I think. I don't know if I can find it in the dark. Near a vineyard."

"It's worth a shot. Maybe Bryan knows it."

There was some shuffling and then Bryan was back. "OK, I've got a few tools. Should do the job."

"Great, let's get going."

Helena's phone vibrated. A text. 'No action until advised. Urgent call imminent.'

"It's too fucking late now" she said to herself - Steve and Bryan were already on their way.

They would have to chance using the High Commission villa out near Zeitun. She hoped that it would be empty.

*

Tobin spoke quietly and with rapidly fading strength. "The key is an Australian song called *Waltzing Matilda*. Use the official lyrics written by Marie Cowan – no variation. All lower case, with no spaces or punctuation. Add one full stop at the end. Four verses, four choruses.

Convert it to binary, simple ASCII. That's the key. You'll need the encryption software as well."

"We already have the code for UltraGoodPrivacy."

Tobin's eyes widened and he nodded. He had thought that there was one more delay possible but it had gone.

"A song. That sounds like it could be a long key."

"That's because what it protects is very valuable and that's why I am prepared to offer you a huge sum, more than you can imagine – say $20 million – to let me go."

"You don't seem to value your life very highly. What use will the money be to you when you are dead? Say $50 million and I'll think about. $20 million is a joke. I have more than that in just one fund."

"OK"

She laughed.

"Money means nothing to me – and I have a contract."

"Then break your contract."

"My reputation is important."

"$50 million important?"

"No. It is not about price. This subject is closed."

She picked up the Chinese phone. "I hope you got all of that. I'm sure it's the truth this time." She sent the recording to Chuntao's mailbox and checked the time – 9.55 p.m. - then removed the battery from the phone.

Next she checked her local phone. No response to her ultimatum. She would wait another 15 minutes, no more.

Tobin watched as she drew the pistol from her waistband and cocked it. She looked at Tobin and raised the gun.

"It is too late now, my clients have the key. You can tell me why the key was worth $50 million to you."

"Even more than $50 million. The Chinese? I know exactly why they want it. *Theovulum Plutus*."

"What is this '*theovulum plutus*'?

"Plutus was the Greek god of wealth. I really should have called it *Theovulum Plutonius*, but I couldn't resist the idea of Plutus. It is a bacterium I developed – an *extremophile*. It extracts plutonium from seawater. Extracting gold was easy. Plutonium was more of a challenge."

Tobin watched her eyes widen. Despite his damaged body, he could still read an opponent, but Maruška knew tortured men. She recognized the truth – and the value of the information. It was almost priceless.

"$50 million you said?"

Tobin nodded, hope still alive.

"Make it $100 million."

"Whatever."

She raised the gun. There was nothing to lose.

"Yasmine, Mansur – come in here now."

Tobin closed his eyes. He did not pray.

She turned smoothly and shot Mansur in the centre of his chest. It knocked him off his feet and there was a soft groan. Then he was silent on his back on the floor, his heart stopped and his brain quickly dying.

Tobin opened his eyes. His heart was racing but he was much too weak to exploit the situation.

Maruška turned her gun towards Yasmine.

"Now Yasmine, put your hands on your head."

Yasmine's reaction was slow but compliant.

Maruška watched Yasmine's eyes – they were wide and questioning, her pupils dilated - but she was dangerous and far more capable than Mansur had been. A mistake. She should have shot Yasmine first. Never mind, first come, first served. She stepped towards Yasmine. Mansur's body twitched suddenly and Maruška's eyes glanced towards it.

In that instant the short throwing knife was out from Yasmine's collar and flying as she dodged down to the right, away from Maruška's gun hand and towards Tobin.

Maruška's own movement was a tenth of a second too slow and the flat knife pierced her tracksuit top embedding itself in the fold of muscle in her right armpit, as her gun fired. The soft nosed bullet entered Yasmine's face through the front of her jaw and smashed its way through the bone, on through the soft palate and out through the back of her neck leaving a fist sized hole. It really was a lucky shot, but the more you practice the luckier you get.

Tobin jerked in shock then shook his head to try to remove the bone, flesh and hippocampus which slowly dribbled down through his hair, into his eyes and dripped off his chin. Yasmine was slumped across his knees, shattered head hanging down.

Maruška grimaced and then checked her shoulder, the flat knife protruding.

She left Tobin and went to attend to her shoulder in the temporary living area. A few minutes later she returned.

"A flesh wound as the American films say. Not quite according to my plan, but it's your lucky day."

Maruška wiped her gun and after removing Mansur's from under his body, she wrapped his fingers around her own gun. She drew Yasmine's gun and fired a shot into Mansur's entry wound.

She looked at Tobin and pushed Yasmine's body off his knees.

"It's not a perfect set-up but it will probably fool the Maltese police for a while. They shot each other – you understand?"

Tobin nodded.

She picked up Mansur's gun and checked it, then pulled out a H&K from her sports bag and placed a chair behind Tobin. She sat and whispered in his ear.

"Now we have to get you out to the car."

"I need a doctor."

"No doctor, no ambulance."

"You are fucking joking you crazy bitch. That's not the way to $100 million. You need to keep me alive."

"A crazy bitch maybe, but I never joke. I'm going to undo the tape and get you to the car."

*

Bryan whispered. "Steve, this is madness! We don't have the gear. No night vision, no stun grenades, nothing but knives and sidearms. And we're out of shape."

They were on the roof of the warehouse ready to jemmy the door.

"But we do have surprise, Bryan. You're a volunteer – at least I think you are - and I'm not out of shape! Go home."

"I'm not letting you do this on your own."

"Then get ready – Helena's hitting the front door in 30 seconds."

They heard an engine revving and over the edging wall Steve could see the van stop and then the engine revved again with a squeal of tyres. He jogged back to the door, but neither of them heard the silenced shots in the warehouse below them.

*

Then they clearly heard the shot from Mansur's gun from down below just as Helena dropped the clutch.

"What the fuck?"

Bryan put his weight against the jemmy and the rotten wood gave way easily, with barely a sound.

Then, a loud crash as the van hit the wooden warehouse doors at almost twenty miles an hour and they burst inwards. Steve was first through the roof door and running down the stairs, descending along the rear wall and then at half height along a side wall gallery. There was an illuminated area below which appeared to be enclosed by plastic sheeting.

As he hit the bottom step he heard a voice – Helena's. "Drop your weapons now!"

Then there was a shot and plaster fell from inside the roof and a bullet ricocheted.

He couldn't see Helena but by then he was crouched with a bead on Maruška who was holding her gun by the barrel, above her head. "Drop your weapon. I will not say it again." Helena's voice.

"She's covered" he said.

"I will not resist" said Maruška as she let her gun slip to the floor.

"OK Steve, Bryan, two minutes, check the warehouse carefully." Steve could see the naked Tobin struggling weakly in a chair and two other bodies on the floor. Bryan was moving alongside him now and they carefully checked the bodies, removing the weapons.

"One minute".

Helena motioned to Maruška. "Down on the floor, on your belly."

Steve moved toward Maruška and kneeled down, grasping her arms and pulling then behind her, threading on a plastic cable tie as Maruška spoke.

"She's a tough bitch Steve – are you taking orders from her then? I remember the last time we were this close. Do you want to take me from behind right now? She can watch. I'd like that, but would she – and would you?" She laughed.

"Shut up, you insane bastard." He cinched the cable tie even harder and she moaned. "Ah, that's so good. Give me more."

"Back off, Steve."

He looked across at Helena and she shook her head. "Ignore it." Bryan was cutting the tape off Tobin's arms and legs. He looked at the bandage on Tobin's thigh and his smashed hand in bandages, the blood between his thighs. "Jesus."

Tobin groaned. He could barely speak. "She cut out one of my testicles."

"Fucking hell."

Tobin groaned again, forcing the words out "Take me to my yacht. I have everything you need there and I will call my local doctor. You will be very well rewarded."

"No way – you should be in hospital – and we're not risking that yet,"

"Three minutes" Helena shouted. "Leave their weapons, look for any phones, iPads and laptops. And Bryan, grab that duct tape. Let's move. Now."

Steve pulled Maruška up by her arms but she made no sound as the shoulder joints twisted hard. Helena opened the back of the van and Bryan bundled Tobin in, then Steve dragged his captive in.

A couple of drunks watched in puzzlement from the waterside as Helena gunned the engine and the van doors were pulled shut as it accelerated, heading around the back of Garrick Street and out on to the Marsa bypass. There were no blue lights in sight yet – the police were still fully stretched after the ship bombing. At that same moment – and too late - a black Range Rover with a driver and two Chinese passengers pulled out from a space in front of a Chinese restaurant in Hamrun, headed for the warehouse.

*

At the Villa

Less than twenty minutes later the panel van stopped outside the stone-pillared gates to the villa – really an old farmhouse - between Zabbar and Zeitun. It had been easy to find – Bryan knew the vineyard, which was on the side of the Freeport road.

There were no lights on and the padlocked gate yielded easily to Bryan's jemmy. In its day it had been the centre of a small vineyard, but now the land was owned by the Marsovin wine company. The farmhouse itself had been gentrified and was on long lease to the British High Commission as a Villa. They drove up the track to the main building. It would do for a few hours.

Bryan quickly broke a rear window and unlocked the patio doors. There was no alarm system as far as they could tell – unless it was silent.

Bryan helped Tobin stagger in, limping very awkwardly.

"Put him on that couch there."

Steve dragged Maruška into the kitchen. Kicking her feet from under her he put cable ties around her feet, shackling them together.

"There's no need for that – I am here voluntarily, although I should be going to Tunis."

"Don't kid yourself."

Helena looked across. "What's that about Tunis?"

Maruška looked at Helena and tried to shrug. "That is for negotiation."

Steve tightened the ties a couple of notches. "You are in no position to negotiate."

"You'd better check that first with your lady boss."

Helena's phone vibrated and she left the room as Bryan spoke.

"Steve, what do I do about Tobin? He has a broken hand, a stab wound in the thigh and a missing testicle. He needs a doctor."

"Treat him for shock."

Maruška laughed.

"A pity he didn't get to learn my full repertoire of tricks."

"Like you showed Tom Brown, you mean?"

"Brown? I don't remember – there have been so many men in my life."

"Djibouti."

"Ah yes, I remember now. That was good. He died slowly, crying like a baby. He told me everything. The memory gives me great pleasure when I am alone at night."

"How's the ear?" Steve twisted her left ear, hard.

Her reply was cut off as Steve wrapped the duct tape tightly round her ears, mouth and over her nose. She struggled and tried to kick. He found a kitchen knife and cut two small holes for her nostrils, just as her kicking was starting to slow.

He saw her breathe hard and fast, although there was no fear in her eyes.

Helena returned.

"Bryan, bandage her arm. Steve, in here."

He followed Helena into a salon area where she was looking at her phone. Turning, she looked at him and shook her head. "London. Fan, shit etcetera. It's ok. I'll explain later."

"What the…"

She held up her hand. "It's cool – just. I can't say any more in the present company. A couple of cars are on the way over with the cavalry, plus a doctor for Tobin."

"But she's killed our people – your people, the firm's people."

"I know, but we need her. This goes way, way over Tobin – and it's not the technology." She moved away into the hall and lowered her voice. "Or techies have cracked the Chinese comms and the chip. There's a technical team on a fast jet from Brize Norton right now – with a very senior person. ETA two a.m. Tobin is nothing – we're into a whole new operation – and it seems that she's a key."

"Tunis?"

"We think so – there are links to the *Queen Katherine* bombing, but could be much bigger.

Steve nodded and then it sunk in. "Tunisia? What the hell! No way!"

"I thought you'd planned a visit?"

"No fucking way."

Helena shrugged her shoulders and pursed her lips.

"No time now, but I'll tell you what I can later. Let's get ready for our backup."

There was a call from the kitchen. "Tea anyone?"

"Yes thanks – two and strong."

"I'll make some for Tobin too."

When it came, the tea was flavoured with brandy.

"It's good Bryan."

"Yes, Boss, we all need a pick-me-up. That brandy was a lucky find."

"What do you expect – this is an embassy villa. There's probably coke too if you look hard enough."

"That's enough Steve. Bryan - we're expecting visitors, friendly. How's Tobin?"

"Still got one spare of each, but his hand's pretty badly mangled – he says she used a hammer on him. A knife wound in the thigh. Deep, but expertly done – plenty of pain but no danger of bleeding out."

"Believe me, he was lucky. She puts Dr Mengele in the shade."

"Mengele?"

"Never mind Bryan, long story, World War 2."

Helena went to talk to Tobin just as headlights came up the track from the road.

*

The team of four entered the house in pairs. They were followed by a fifth man. They were in plain black overalls underneath body armour, and carrying H&K MP5s and Browning sidearms. They wore balaclavas.

Helena stood ready, hands visible.

"I'm Dave. I'm in charge here."

"No, you are not" said Helena. "I am."

"On what authority?"

"Black Swan."

"White Egret. Ok, acknowledged."

"Acknowledged."

"Why is everyone called Dave?"

"Don't know Ma'am. That's just what I'm known as."

The two troopers moved smoothly into the other rooms.

"Clear."

"Clear."

The calls came progressively as each room was checked.

"One casualty."

"OK."

Two more armed men appeared from other rooms. They had not come in through the kitchen.

"Steve, Bryan – all clear now."

Steve and Bryan came in through the kitchen door to the surprised looks of the SAS troop. No weapons visible.

"They are my guys."

Another man came in, behind them, weapon raised. Steve shrugged. They were good.

"Set a perimeter."

Four troopers left the kitchen.

"Can't be too careful Ma'am. I have been ordered to secure this site and all personnel. Within that constraint, what are your orders?"

Helena pointed to Maruška. "She is to be held here pending further orders. Extreme caution advised. The casualty needs first aid urgently and then secure medical attention - and I mean secure. He is a British National, captive under the Counter-Terrorism and Security Act 2015, but not hostile. He has been tortured – not by us – by her." She nodded in Maruška's direction.

"She removed one of his testicles."

His face winced under the balaclava. "Ouch. OK Ma'am, there's a chopper *en route* from Bulwark with more backup, though they're only marines. We'll ship him back there – they have a hospital aboard." He touched his throat mike. "Get the doc in here now Jim."

The low sound grew quickly into a soft, low beat and then a red light went on in the paddock at the rear of the villa followed by illumination from the silenced Merlin helicopter as it descended and hovered while two fire teams of Royal Marines dropped and deployed.

There was some headshaking in the SAS troop.

"Now the fucking marines. That's all we need."

"Shut it Shane. We've got to work with these guys."

Then the Merlin touched down and the RM Lieutenant and 'Dave' exchanged professional courtesies. Handshakes were brief and formal - the inter-service rivalry was obvious. After a short pissing contest about authority, Dave pulled rank and gave the orders for deployment – and for responsibility.

Two medics ran in to the villa with a stretcher. The doctor briefed them quickly and within three minutes Tobin was sedated and airborne, headed for HMS Bulwark.

Steve turned to Helena. "What now?"

"We wait. Our Middle East Head of Station is flying out right now with the technical team."

"You'd better put the kettle on then, Bryan."

"And I'd better charge my phone. Steve – where are those phones from the warehouse? They are important."

Fifteen minutes later, Helena's phone pinged and she disappeared into another room.

"So, Steve what's the story with the woman?" Dave said, nodding at Maruška.

"It's enough to say that she's a match for any of your guys – plus. She just offed two of her own team."
"A black widow, eh?"
Steve nodded back.
"I'll brief the lads then."

*

It was almost 2 a.m. The aircon was on and working hard to reduce the oppression of the sultry Malta autumn night and chill the plentiful mosquitoes into inaction. An autumn storm, clouds pregnant with water and alive with lightning, was drifting down from Sicily and its wind was beginning to raise dust around the villa.

Bryan and Steve were in the kitchen drinking tea with the marine lieutenant. In another room, a couple of technicians were re-assembling the phones taken from the warehouse. They were fitting their own GPS trackers and other refinements which would work even when out of range from a phone mast. Batteries were exchanged for the latest high capacity gold nanowire versions. Earlier, they had rigged a small satcomms dish outside the villa, with a high-bandwidth link to GCHQ. Maruška's phones had been hooked up and analysed remotely over the link.

In the dining room, the Head of the Middle East Desk, Alex Ogilvy, sat in one of the ornate dining chairs at a long mahogany table. Helena sat in a chair at the end of the table and Maruška was bound to another, directly opposite Ogilvy. The duct tape had been removed from her mouth and hung from her hair. One of Ogilvy's London team sat at the other end of the table with a tablet computer, He had not been introduced. The door was shut and a marine stood outside, with another outside the window.

Ogilvy's presence was imposing. He had a distinguished field service record, although his height – well over six feet - and red hair did not make him the most inconspicuous of people. He had been the replacement for the traitor Booth, who was now dead. It had been heart failure according to the Times obituary and was technically accurate, though it had not been due to 'natural causes'. The cover-up had been comprehensive and in Langley the CIA remained completely unaware of the reality.

The most versatile agents tended to blend in, but Ogilvy certainly didn't. His hair was now shot through with grey and his heavily lined face betrayed years of stress, though his pale blue eyes were still clear and his look would cut ice. With a firm, square jaw and penetrating gaze, he commanded attention, but the surprise came when he spoke. His voice was gentle and quiet, but backed by the sharpest of intellects.

Despite the comms intercepts, there were still many gaps in Ogilvy's knowledge of the Chinese operation. It always helped to compare stories from different sources and try to fill those gaps. Jacob started the live audio feed to London and the debrief started.

"We can save time if you give us the passwords to your laptop and then you can tell us about Tunis."

"Free my hands first, then we will talk about an arrangement. Then, maybe, I will give you the passwords."

Ogilvy nodded. Helena cocked her gun while Jacob took out a knife and cut the cable ties. He passed her a bottle of water. Helena did not relax her finger.

"Those are the terms – Marie, Andjela, Maruška or whatever your name is tonight. Let me emphasize that we understand how you are being controlled. We can reduce the effects of that with a jammer and possibly with drugs, but you have to agree. Once this operation is over then we will remove the nanochip that you have in your body. You will be free of the Chinese – and us. I assume that you will want to disappear then. Given your record, I think we are being extremely generous with these terms. I could lock you up for the rest of your life - or just end it here, without a problem or any questions."

"You need me, you want the knowledge I have. Anyway, how can I be sure of all this?"

"You can't. That's just it, but in case you doubt that we understand the technology…" Ogilvy turned to his colleague. "Jacob, please." Jacob touched an icon on the tablet. Maruška jerked silently, her lips pressed hard together, then relaxed slowly as the pulse stopped. She started breathing deeply.

"Sorry about that – a bit too strong I think. But I'm sure you'll agree we've nearly got the hang of it. I'm certain we'll get better at it. So, we have deal?"

Maruška nodded. It was a way out.

"I'll take that nod as a 'yes' then. Would you like some tea or coffee?"

"Water."

"Right, this is what happens next."

Within half an hour a technician had checked Maruška's laptop for explosives and for any software self-destruct code. She had provided the passwords and he had sent an image file to GCHQ for analysis. A full system scan had been carried out and some low-level code had been injected.

The technicians had uncovered the link to her cloud storage and email, and hacked the Chinese TOR client software using the satellite link to harness the power of the quantum computers at GCHQ. Ogilvy was finally up to speed on the latest Chinese instructions she had been sent, but still the expected briefing had not yet come through to Maruška.

He had interrogated agents before – both hostile and friendly, with both the softest and hardest techniques – and it was soon plain to him that Maruška did not know why she was being sent to Tunis.

Ogilvy woke Jacob, the lead comms technician. It was almost 4 a.m. and they were all exhausted. Outside, the false dawn was still an hour away and the marines were struggling to maintain vigilance and blood circulation.

At that same moment, two black Range Rovers were passing through the outskirts of Tarxien, one turning left towards Marsascala and the other continuing down to Birżebbuġa to meet two crewmen off a Chinese container ship which was berthed at the Freeport. Time was tight if they were to meet the deadline. Such operations were rarely carried out at short notice, but the orders had come from the highest authority.

"A problem, Jacob, and I need a quick solution. I've just seen the latest intercept. The Chinese are going to change Maruška's phone in Tunis – and they're taking back the old one."

"So, that compromises both the hardware and software I put in there, and also our control link and tracking, Sir?"

"Exactly."

"Well we need to either recover the phone and clean it, or burn it. That's the first step."

"Cleaning it is easy, we have until she gets on the ferry – four hours. Then we've lost our link."

"Ouch."

"Precisely."

"We can put a tracker on her or maybe have it stolen in Tunis?"

"No, that will not work. She is being met at the ferry terminal."

"Ok, then we'll have to doctor the new phone?"

Ogilvy nodded. "Ever been to Tunis?"

"No, but I think I'm going soon."

"Yes, with Bryan – him downstairs - in a 4x4. You'll be on the same ferry as her. I'll arrange some local help as well. Don't worry – she'll fall into line. We know how to push her button. Get some more sleep."

Upstairs, Steve, Bryan and Helena were dozing in a bedroom, Maruška had been re-bound to a chair in another bedroom pending her transport to Zabbar before she joined the ferry. Her doctored phone and laptop sat ready in a plastic carrier bag – a reminder that she was completely under control.

It was a quiet night – the storm had passed to the north - and the threat level was considered low. The marines were patrolling outside but this time was the worst on what was, essentially, sentry duty. With the dawn their body clocks would start to speed up, but none of them had taken uppers, and the adrenaline rush after the flight in from *HMS Bulwark* had now worn off.

Inside the villa, there was a knock at the dining room door. "Come". Ogilvy raised his eyes from the decoded intercept. It was the marine lieutenant.

"Sir, we have orders to return to Bulwark. The helo is on its way."

"What? You're leaving us with no cover?"

"I did query the order, Sir. I was told – in no uncertain terms - that you have a capable team. They certainly look the part to me."

"You're not withdrawing until I say it's OK. I'll get this sorted with London, now."

"Very well Sir. We have about ten minutes,"

Ogilvy called London again, and again without success. The duty officer at Vauxhall Cross said that Sir William would contact him. It was too late for Gore to be at the opera. Where the hell was he? What could be so important?

Fifteen minutes later, Helena and Steve stood across the table from him.

"They had their orders. I couldn't get them changed – 'C' was unavailable."

"Shit."

"Yes Baldwin, exactly. I think that the situation is low-threat, but we'd better be prepared."

Then the lights went out and the French doors burst open.

Steve pushed Helena hard and dropped instinctively, feeling for the Glock 17 in his waistband. Who, where? He slid the action on the pistol. There was little light from outside, just a weak glow from some streetlamps on the road and the vague grey of the false dawn.

Then there was a flat sputter and slight flash, followed by another, then a grunt – a man's grunt, the sound of a body falling to the floor.

Steve eased himself round the end of the table. Under the table he could the vague shape of a body, then heard the sound of feet, moving quickly, a pair of legs across the thin light. He snapped off two shots, the unsuppressed Glock delivering flashes and bangs like the worst of a Malta thunderstorm.

He thought he heard a groan from outside, but his eyes were still recovering from the gunflash.

"OK?"

There was a whispered "OK" from Helena.

Another shadow crossed the open doors and disappeared. Then, there were two shots from the kitchen and the sound of feet on the stairs and going into the bedroom overhead – Maruška's room.

"Stay here. I think Ogilvy's hit."

Steve moved out through the dining room door into the broad hallway, and on towards the stairs. Where was Bryan? Jacob? They had been in the kitchen after the helo had woken them all from their thin sleep.

What of Maruška? What was the purpose, who were the intruders? He moved to the bottom of the stairs. His eyes were readjusting to the low light from the pre-dawn that was brightening by the minute.

Then, a shadow in front of him.

He pushed the pistol against the neck of the man, holding it at arm's length.

"Don't think about."

He felt the body stiffen, the whisper was urgent.

"Steve?"

"Fucking hell Bryan, you'd be dead if it wasn't for that disgusting aftershave!"

The body relaxed. Steve tapped Bryan's arm.

"Status?"

"Jacob's in the kitchen, he's ok I think. I got two off. No hits."

"I think Ogilvy's taken one, condition unknown. I clipped one – legs, so could still be a threat. Outside."

"How many?"

"Four, five?"

There were two shots from outside, unsuppressed.

Helena, Steve realised, and he was torn, torn by the natural protective instinct when a woman was in a fire team. He fought the instinct.

"Up. Maruška's room. You take left."

They eased up the stairs in the semi darkness and turned.

"Clear."

They edged along the landing. The door to Maruška's room was closed. Steve nodded and stood aside as Bryan charged it. It was heavy, it was walnut, it was Maltese – and a chair had been propped against it.

Bryan groaned and bounced back.

Another two shots outside.

"They've gone out through the window – they wouldn't fight their way downstairs."

Steve turned and ran into the next bedroom, over to the window. He threw it open. The light was stronger now, the sky was clear and a fine autumn day was promising itself.

Sicilian Channel

He could see Helena behind a wall and Maruška running with three men across a field, turning into a road. A fourth man was trailing them. Helena was moving and firing, but her aim was well off. Steve realised that she would not want to hit Maruška.

The drop from the window was on to paving slabs – and about ten feet. As Steve rolled aside Bryan landed next to him - both intact. There was blood on the patio next to the French doors and it trailed across the driveway. Steve could see Jacob tending Ogilvy in the dining room.

They sprinted across the driveway and lawn, into the field – to meet Helena on her way back.

"They got away."

"Even the wounded one?"

"Yes, two Range Rovers. It suits us."

"Suits us?"

"Yes, we thought it might pan out this way. The Chinese will have no suspicions about Maruška."

"Is that why the Marines were withdrawn?"

"I honestly don't know, but I do know that Ogilvy was trying to stop it."

"Bloody hell – isn't that just typical!"

"It's just one of those things Steve, just one of those things."

Then, suddenly, the shooting was rapid and continuous Helene and Baldwin dropped as one to the floor, scuttling for the cover of bushes.

"Shotguns. What the fuck? Where? They're all around us."

Bryan was strolling towards them, laughing.

"Get down Bryan for Christ's sake!"

"It's ok, it's just for the birds."

"The birds?"

"Yes, the Maltese love to shoot small songbirds at dawn - with shotguns. There are stone hides all across the fields here." Bryan waved his arms.

As the sun was coming over the horizon, they could make out the hides in the fields beyond the vines. And they could hear the Maltese indulging in their very strange tradition.

Two hours later the call finally came through to Ogilvy from Sir William Gore.

"We've just been attacked and Pavkovic has gone. Why the hell were the marines withdrawn - SIR!"

Sir William ignored the question.

"Casualties?"

"Me. Shot in the thigh, superficial. We found one Chinese dead in the orchard. No ID. Helena got him."

"Unfortunate. You should really be more careful. You've cleaned up?"

"Yes Sir."

"Good. It worked out more or less as planned and Pavkovic retains credibility. Now, I don't have much time for idle chat. This latest intercept - are you sure of our source?"

"Absolutely – but we are reliant on GCHQ. We only have to consider whether it's genuine or not."

"Your view?"

"Solid gold."

"I agree."

Condescending bugger, Ogilvy thought, wincing at the pain in his thigh.

"Her cover is that of a French journalist, Cherif Hatoui?"

"Yes, but she's too smart to be obvious about that."

"Anything you need immediately?"

"The Book of Common Prayer, Sir." He didn't see the rueful smile on Gore's face, but he could hear it in his voice.

"Apart from that, Sir, we need to have heavy firepower close at hand."

"That's taken for granted. I have to call the PM now. He's called a Cobra meeting at ten a.m. our time."

Sicilian Channel

*

Back at the guest house in Zabbar, Maruška was fully expecting awkward questions about her recent location from Wan Chuntao. She had her story ready.

She logged on. The briefing was in her inbox. When the decode was complete, she sat back on the bed, hardly believing the details. Ben-Zhair – 'find him and we will let you retire'. She could see why he was so important, but couldn't believe it.

The passage to Tunis had been arranged, but avoiding the security difficulties of a flight meant two ferry trips.

An hour later she awoke with a start and searing pain. Wan Chuntao. Fuck that woman.

Her smartphone vibrated on the table beside the bed.

"What now?"

"Aren't you going to thank me?"

"For what?"

"For getting you out of that Villa."

"I would have got out myself anyway. The British are fools."

"But they knew about Tobin?"

"Obviously, but I don't know how. They killed two of my team."

"I know, we found the bodies in the warehouse."

"How did they capture you?"

"Gas."

"Gas?"

"Yes, they had gas masks on. Mansur and Yasmine were shot and I held a gun to Tobin's head but passed out. Your people should have got there earlier."

"We had difficulty locating you – there were problems with your signal and gps coordinates."

"I thought that Chinese technology never failed."

"Enough! Now, about your cover. They gave you the documents? You have a new passport and a pass for Agence France Presse?"

"Yes, a journalist, no problem. Can you provide weapons in Tunis?"

"Yes. We'll send a car to meet you. There will be other equipment as well, including a Geiger counter."

"Isn't that for radiation?"

"Yes. There will be a new phone too, as you seem to be having problems with your old one. Give it to the courier. Don't miss your ferry – you have 4 hours to get to the terminal."

The line dropped.

*

London

"Right everyone, please sit and we'll start" said the Prime Minister.

The tension was electric – no one present could ever remember a Cobra meeting being held in the bunker complex below Downing Street.

This was also the first Cobra since the huge reorganisation of the Security Services. There had been a huge power battle in Whitehall following the death of the traitor Booth, and following the ICIM attack on the *Queen Katherine* the result had been inevitable. 'C', the head of MI6, now reported directly to the Prime Minister and not to the Foreign Secretary. It had been a difficult step to take, because it removed a layer of deniability from the prime Minister.

The change had resulted in the resignation of the Foreign Secretary and his replacement by Shami Munchetty. She was seen by many as the best of a weak list of candidates and more change was expected during the next reshuffle in the spring. The Home Secretary had fought hard to retail control of MI5 and had succeeded – just.

"This is a formal meeting of Cobra to update us on progress in the investigation of the atrocious attack on the *Queen Katherine*, but there is one more item we will cover at the end. It may take some time and is the reason that we are in this room. Sir William, if you please."

All eyes turned to Sir William Gore, head of SIS. He had a commanding presence as one might expect, but clearly the stress of recent events was taking its toll. His eyes were heavy and his face pallid and damp with sweat. As he opened his presentation it was clear that he was extremely tired.

"Thank you, Prime Minister. The information we have assembled at present indicates that the planning for the attack on the *Queen Katherine* took place in Algeria. Information from our French colleagues at the DGSE on Quai D'Orsay indicates that the leader of the operation is likely to have been one of three people - Mansour Bouyali, Abdelkhader Maliani or Abu ben-Zhair. We are seeking to confirm this through other channels. We believe that ben-Zhair was in Malta – actually in Grand Harbour – at the time of the attack. There is intelligence to support this, although it is only probable – not definite.

We believe he travelled immediately after the attack by small boat to Tabarka, small harbour in Tunisia. This comes from satellite imagery and Malta radar data – this part of the Mediterranean has seen a lot of migrant trafficking, as you know. From there we know no more but assume that he has travelled back into Algeria where he has strong family, political and business ties. He is an Algerian national and was closely associated with the now defunct GIA terrorist group which morphed – via the Salafists - into the ICIM – Islamic Caliphate in the Maghreb.

We have diverted additional intelligence resources and I am liaising with the Director of Special Services. I have nothing more to add today."

"Thank you, Sir William. That is the latest. I'm afraid we have not time for discussion."

The PM turned to General Mike Rushby GCB, CBE, ADC, the current Chief of the Defence Staff.

"General."

"Prime Minister. We have deployed an additional battalion of the Princess of Wales's Royal Regiment to Malta to assist with clearing up operations in Malta. One squadron of the SAS has been deployed, and a squadron of the SBS is standing by on HMS Bulwark off the Algerian coast. Planning is well underway for a range of tactical options should we need to extract anyone from Algeria. Thank you Prime Minister."

"Thank you, General. Now, we come to the additional item. It is not related to the Malta attack – as far as we know

now. I shall be unable to attend tomorrow's meeting of Cobra. It will be chaired by the Deputy PM."

The Chancellor nodded as the Prime Minister continued "I will be attending what is to be a secret session of the UN Security Council – the 'P5'. It has been called because of information which has come to light about the latest North Korean underground nuclear tests. Sir William, once again, if you will."

There was an audible intake of breath by most of those present and the sense of excitement in the briefing room was even more palpable as eyes once again turned to Sir William.

"Thank you again Prime Minister. This matter now carries the rather unfortunate code name 'Blue Angel' – a random computer selection I might say. We have information both from our own sources and the United States which shows that the radionucleide residues of that North Korean nuclear test have finally percolated through to the atmosphere – and have radioactivity signatures which are typical of a fusion bomb.

So, we must conclude that North Korea has successfully tested a hydrogen bomb.

Add to that the fact that they now have a credible intercontinental ballistic missile capability and we are faced with a nightmare scenario. I'm afraid it gets worse – there is a very strong suspicion that North Korea has shared the technology with Iran, in contravention of the Nuclear Arms Deal which Iran finally signed in January 2016."

Around the table the silence was absolute.

*

On January 6, 2016, North Korea announced a fourth nuclear weapons test, described as a miniaturised hydrogen bomb test.

There was little doubt in the West (or China) that the underground test had taken place at Punggye-ri, but the claim that it was a fusion bomb was belittled. Hydrogen bombs have a much bigger bang than fission bombs (a fission bomb is actually used as the trigger in a fusion bomb – at least in the 'conventional' design).

The explosion was measured as being about 5.1 on the Richter Scale (as used for measuring earthquakes) which is typically produced by a device in the range of 8-10 kilotons (read 8-10 thousand tons of TNT equivalent). A fusion bomb would typically yield 100 kilotons – 15 to 20 larger than the smallest fission bomb.

One area of concern in the West was the claim that this latest device was miniaturised – a key requirement if the weapon is to be used on the tip of a missile. In a double-whammy, North Korea had also successfully tested a submarine-based ballistic missile launch system a month before, in December 2015. Then, in early February 2016, North Korean successfully tested an intercontinental ballistic missile – the Kwangmyongsong - placing a satellite in orbit.

*

On March 7, 2016, CNN reported that North Korea had threatened a pre-emptive nuclear strike. These threats were regular, but gaining credibility.

*

Epilogue

"Steve, this could be the most important thing you have ever done for you country. Look on it as a holiday."

No sooner were the words out her mouth than Helena realised that it was a stupid thing to say, that where Steve was concerned she had become almost incapable of restraint.

"How many times have I heard that before – and got stitched up? Help 'my' country? I've bled for my country too many times for HMG and I've got fuck all to show for it – I can't even wear a campaign medal. I'm tired of being a pawn on some berk's chessboard. This morning was just another example. And why did Ogilvy get shot in the leg with no other casualties on our side? Those guys were wearing night vision gear. It all stinks to high heaven. No way am I going!"

"Keep your voice down Steve."

They were in one of the bedrooms of the villa.

"I don't bloody care who hears me."

"Just hear me out, please. I can't answer all your questions."

"Can't or won't?"

"Can't, but if you will not respect basic security then I'll have you arrested."

"You wouldn't do that."

"You are still subject to the Official Secrets Act. Not only that - you might have difficulty getting your boat out of Malta. The bureaucracy here can be a nightmare."

"Is that a threat?"

"No, just a fact - if they turn their mind to it".

"And why should they do that?"

"Ogilvy might suggest it."

"Ogilvy or you?"

"Does it matter?"

"Yes, it matters a lot."

She shrugged. "Listen Steve, Ogilvy's position is understandable. There's a lot at stake here – a world war could start."

"Pull the other one."

"The *Queen Katherine* bombing was just the beginning. What if I said that a terrorist group had a nuclear bomb?"

"I wouldn't believe you."

"Well, they do – and Maruška is the key."

"Jesus Christ. First you want her dead, then you must have her alive, now she has the key to a terrorist nuclear weapon and you let the Chinese kidnap her."

"Don't exaggerate, she doesn't have a key."

"Exaggerate? Do your bosses really know their arses from the elbows?"

"The situation is erm…fluid… and for what it's worth, I don't think that they do. But then, that's hardly their fault. We'll be following closely – with you or without you. Look at it this way – you and me on Adèle as cover. Tourists. You did tell me you'd like to see the country."

"I don't remember saying that – I never even thought it. Anyway, why not use the SAS or some of your regular secret agents?"

"The SAS are hard men, not intelligence agents. They will be there for us to call on. As to our regulars, we don't have anyone with the right profile who we can insert in time."

"And I'm not an intelligence agent, you bloody know that."

"No, but I do know that you are an all-round star – with the right profile. You proved that. And you speak Arabic and French."

"You can cut out the flattery! I'm done with this bollocks."

"I'm not flattering you. Why are you fighting me all the way on this?"

"Because I'm tired of being stitched up and stretched out, a bit at a time, 'just a little further Steve'. It's the same old story. I'm tired of hearing it."

"Ok. Fair enough. But you do want Maruška. She *is* a part of this operation."

"What? I thought you were shipping back to the UK, in chains. Oh, I forgot – you let the Chinese have her back."

"And she's already on her way to Tunis. We have new intel. As I said, the game has changed."

"That's the problem – to these people it's just a game, and we're in the middle of it, pushed around, dispensable."

Helena ignored the comment, and worked away to reduce Steve's resistance, to penetrate his armour.

"We think we know what Tunis is about. We know a bit about what the Chinese are doing and what they want her to do. As I said downstairs, we're monitoring their comms with her – thanks to you. Mostly it's good for us. We just let her carry out her mission – and watch her of course. Make sure there's no double-dealing. We know that the Chinese have re-tasked a satellite to monitor the Libya-Tunisia-Algeria region.

The thinking is that you and I head for Tabarka in Adèle and moor there. It's lower profile than Tunis and gives us a good cover story. Bryan will take the car ferry over – following Maruška - and meet us over there."

"Is Bryan up to this?"

"What do you think?"

"He's done OK so far. A bit of a plodder."

"That's how he's meant to look on this operation – he's playing a part."

"Nursemaid you mean. And his aftershave is disgusting."

"Monitoring is just a part of his role. He's versatile and his record is very good. Believe me, there's much more than meets the eye. I've known him for a few years and worked with him before. And the aftershave is his own choice – or at least that of his Maltese ladyfriend."

"Anyway, it's not a plan yet, but it's a start." She raised her eyebrows. "Comments?"

"How long have you got?" He was being pulled apart by the tension between duty and his desire to be at sea, away from the duplicity and game-playing, away from people like Ogilvy.

He threw his arms up in resignation. "It sounds ok but I'd need to check on Tabarka. I guess it's a couple of hundred miles, but with this wind we can probably do it in thirty six hours. And we have no idea what Maruška will be up to."

"That's where you are wrong – and that's why we have techies here."

"Why not go straight to Tunis? That would make much more sense – and it's nearer too."

"Because we don't think that's where the action will be. She has been given a name – Abu ben-Zhair. There's credible intel that he was behind the *Queen Katherine* bombing and that he's got an even bigger atrocity planned. We think Maruška's headed ultimately for Algeria – Annaba looks to be the likely destination. Tabarka is only six miles from the Algerian border and less than 80 from Annaba."

"There you go again. Stretch me a bit further, feed me crumbs of information. Algeria – hell, that's a whole new ball game."

"But you've been there too, so you're qualified."

"Only out in the desert - a natural gas plant at In Amenas when there was a terrorist attack. Bloody dodgy place. In and out by helo. Never again. We'd stand out a mile in Algeria – no tourists and police everywhere."

"Maybe it will not come to that."

"She'd be mad go in to Algeria and we'd be mad to follow. I might pull it off, but you? No way."

"Let's take it one step at a time. Is Adèle ready?"

"We just need some fuel, water, food."

"HMG will pick up the tab. And I can promise you a good bonus."

She winked, but he shook his head. "I've heard that before too. I just can't believe it. To think that a few weeks ago I thought you were just a pretty Greek waitress. I must be a real schmuck."

"I am *very* good at my work."

"And I'm just a poor bloody sailor with a soft spot."

*

After some final business at the old marina in the evening, ben-Zhair had taken two taxis out to a tourist hotel to the east of Tabarka. There, he had met one of his Algerian security team and set off in an old Toyota Landcruiser headed for the Algerian border.

The driver congratulated him on the attack in Malta. He knew that the success of the bombing would be a huge morale-booster for the team at Tabessa, although most of them would not live to see the results of their work on the *Sword of Allah* project.

As they bumped along the old track, the sun was setting over the mountains to the west, casting long shadows over the fertile valleys that fed Tunisia and Algeria. Although the border was less than ten miles away, it would be necessary to take a longer route, bypassing the main roads and finally crossing the border well inland before dawn.

He reflected that although the attack on the '*Queen Katherine*' had been a huge coup, it was just the start. The Twin Towers would become nothing more than a footnote to history when he, Abu ben-Zhair, wielded the *Sword of Allah* against the infidels later that year. His great plan was just at the beginning, and the Cause of All Causes campaign would make him one of the greatest figures in the history of Islam when it finally came to fruition in a year or so.

It had been a long time in the planning, but the outcome would surely change the world forever. Islam would reign supreme, with a worldwide caliphate and he, ben-Zhair would be the man of power. *'Insha'Allah'*.

*

On Saturday, April 2nd 2016, Reuters News Agency reported:

"U.S. President Barack Obama urged world leaders on Friday to do more to safeguard vulnerable nuclear facilities to prevent "madmen" from groups like Islamic State from getting their hands on an atomic weapon or a radioactive "dirty bomb."

Speaking at a nuclear security summit in Washington, Obama said the world faced a persistent and evolving threat of nuclear terrorism despite progress in reducing such risks. "We cannot be complacent," he said.

*

The Sword of Allah

The double agent Maruška has gone rogue and is still active as ICIM threatens world order with a new weapon – 'The Sword of Allah'. The hunt for ben-Zhair moves into North Africa as a terrifying prospect begins to unfold for Europe and the United States. Maruška is on the loose again, being used as a bloodhound for both British and Chinese intelligence services.

Sicilian Channel

"The Sword of Allah" is the second book in James Marinero's 'Maghreb Trilogy'

Available Autumn 2016.

References & Further Reading

Achille Lauro Hijacking, 1985:
http://global.britannica.com/event/Achille-Lauro-hijacking

http://www.independent.co.uk/voices/comment/robert-fisk-how-achille-lauro-hijackers-were-seduced-by-high-life-8604519.html

Barack Obama on terrorists and the nuclear weapons threat:
http://www.reuters.com/article/us-nuclear-summit-obama-treaty-idUSKCN0WY52M

Europe exposure to Islamist threat from Libyan chaos:
http://www.gatestoneinstitute.org/7282/libya-chaos

Extracting Metals from Sea Water:

Burk, Maksymilian (1989) Gold, Silver and Uranium from Seas and Oceans, ARDOR Publishing, Los Angeles, CA.

Dworetzky T (1988) Gold bugs: a sulfur-munching bacterium has been recruited to help extract the precious yellow metal from the increasingly stingy Earth, Discover, March 1988, p. 32.

Guoanbu:
http://intellibriefs.blogspot.com/2008/03/chinese-secret-service-from-mao-to.html

Gadaffi's Ukrainian nurse:
http://europe.newsweek.com/my-years-gaddafis-nurse-66577

Hawala Money Transfer System:
https://www.treasury.gov/resource-center/terrorist-illicit-finance/Documents/FinCEN-Hawala-rpt.pdf

Sicilian Channel

Krypton Fluoride Lasers for Nuclear Fusion Implosion:
http://www.ncbi.nlm.nih.gov/pubmed/26560597

Laser Pumped Fusion Research:
http://www.scientificamerican.com/article/high-powered-lasers-deliver-fusion-energy-breakthrough/

http://www.nature.com/nature/journal/v506/n7488/full/nature13008.html

Malta:
Historical Fiction: The Kappillan of Malta by Nicholas Monsarratt (Cassell Military Paperbacks)
Historical Fiction: The Information Officer by Mark Mills (Harper)
History: The Great Siege by Ernle Bradford (OpenRoad Media)

North Korea Hydrogen Bomb Test, 2016:
http://www.bbc.co.uk/news/world-asia-17823706

North Korea Submarine Launched Ballistic Missile test 2015:
http://www.reuters.com/article/us-northkorea-missile-idUSKBN0UK02P20160106

North Korean Ballistic Missile/Satellite Launch 2016:
http://edition.cnn.com/2016/02/08/asia/north-korea-rocket-launch/

North Korea Nuclear Strike Threat:
http://edition.cnn.com/2016/03/06/asia/north-korea-preemptive-nuclear-strike-threat/

Quantum Computing:
https://uwaterloo.ca/institute-for-quantum-computing/quantum-computing-101

http://www.bbc.com/news/business-35886456

Tomlinson, Richard (ex MI6):
https://en.wikipedia.org/wiki/Richard_Tomlinson

Author's Notes

This story has been a long time in the writing. During writing, I spent a several periods in Malta, getting to know the territory, history and people. The story expanded and I started to see it in a wider context as the world and politics evolved – "Events, dear boy, events" as Harold Macmillan once said.

So, this book became another stage in Steve Baldwin's travel on from the Red Sea. As always, much of the technology mentioned actually exists or is just a small extrapolation of existing science – it is not a product of my imagination.

Malta is a fascinating island-country as I have tried to portray, and yes, there is an old patrol boat and a submarine in the Cassar shipyard! If you are inclined to read more around the content of this story then I have provided a references section – these are not referred to within the story as I did not want to interrupt the flow.

The RMS *Queen Katherine* is of course a fictional vessel, and I hope that Cunard will forgive the liberties I have taken. Also, of course, her name is an invention, although Catherine of Aragon was, as the first wife of King Henry VIII, the Queen of England from 1509 until 1533.

My objective has been to entertain and inform and I hope I have achieved that. I really welcome feedback and if you would like to contact me then please feel free to do so, either by email or on Facebook.

Also, if you can find the time I would really appreciate a review of the book, whether on Amazon one of the other platforms. Good or bad, reviews can only help me to improve my storytelling for the benefit of readers.

I have included some of my research pictures in the ebook version, and I hope that readers find that they add to the story. If you don't think so, then please let me know.

Sicilian Channel

Finally, I should like to thank Rosy Jensen for her unstinting encouragement and support, and for all she has taught me about Malta.

James Marinero
Las Palmas, April 2016.
james@jamesmarinero.com
Facebook: facebook.com/james.marinero

About the Author

James Marinero grew up in West Wales and has at various times been a chef, a milkman, maths lecturer and private tutor. He spent over 30 years in IT as a consultant and project manager and ran his own retail computer business for several years.

He has been passionately involved with boats and the sea for over fifty years and is now achieving a lifelong ambition to write novels, spending much of his writing time on his boat which he has sailed extensively in the Atlantic and as far as Brazil.

During his various careers he has worked in the Middle East, Russia, Scandinavia, the US, Kazakhstan and much of Europe. His educational background includes a degree in Physics, a postgraduate degree in Oceanography and an MBA.

His personal interests, career, education and travel background have equipped him well to write adventure and techno-thriller novels.

When he is not on his boat he lives on the Hampshire coast.

Sicilian Channel

www.ingramcontent.com/pod-product-compliance
Ingram Content Group UK Ltd.
Pitfield, Milton Keynes, MK11 3LW, UK
UKHW041414180426
11947UKWH00007B/122